WINGS
OF
FIRE

BOOK ONE
THE DRAGONET PROPHECY

BOOK TWO
THE LOST HEIR

BOOK THREE
THE HIDDEN KINGDOM

BOOK FOUR
THE DARK SECRET

BOOK FIVE
THE BRIGHTEST NIGHT

BOOK SIX
MOON RISING

BOOK SEVEN
WINTER TURNING

BOOK EIGHT
ESCAPING PERIL

BOOK NINE
TALONS OF POWER

BOOK TEN
DARKNESS OF DRAGONS

BOOK ELEVEN
THE LOST CONTINENT

BOOK TWELVE
THE HIVE QUEEN

BOOK THIRTEEN
THE POISON JUNGLE

BOOK FOURTEEN
THE DANGEROUS GIFT

LEGENDS
DARKSTALKER
DRAGONSLAYER

WINGS OF FIRE

LEGENDS: DRAGONSLAYER

by
TUI T. SUTHERLAND

SCHOLASTIC INC.

Text copyright © 2020 by Tui T. Sutherland
Map and border design © 2020 by Mike Schley
Dragon illustrations © 2020 by Joy Ang

This book was originally published in hardcover by Scholastic Press in 2020.

ISBN 978-1-338-21461-1

10 9 8 7 6 5 4 3 2 1   21 22 23 24 25

Printed in the U.S.A. 40
This edition first printing 2021

Book design by Phil Falco

For Kari,
who would totally ride a dragon
(and who saved this book!)

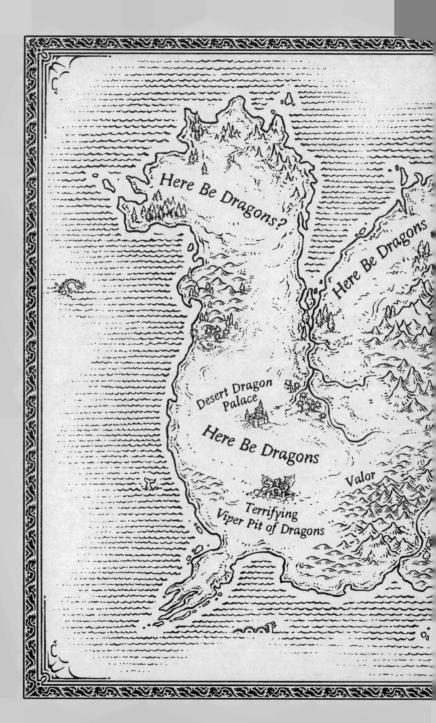

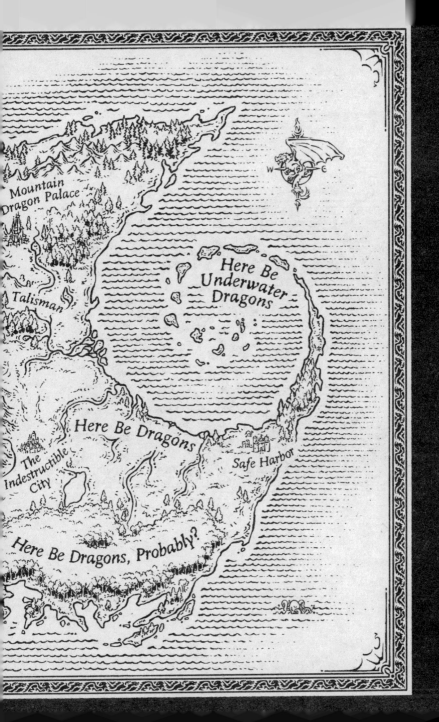

A WINGWATCHER'S GUIDE TO

DRAGONS

Here Be Dragons?

Be Dragons

Dragons

Valor

Terrifying
Viper Pit of Dragons

NIGHT DRAGONS

Description: Purplish-black scales and scattered silver scales on the underside of their wings, like a night sky full of stars; forked black tongues

Abilities: Can breathe fire, disappear into dark shadows

Habitat: Unknown

Watch Out For: These rarely seen dragons could be mutations of other types, or a nearly extinct species; probably not very important

─ DESERT DRAGONS ─

Description: Pale gold or white scales the color of desert sand; forked black tongues

Abilities: Can survive a long time without water, poison prey with the tips of their tails like scorpions, bury themselves for camouflage in the desert sand, breathe fire

Habitat: The vast desert west of the forest

Watch Out For: Their venomous barbed tails, their teeth, claws, fire

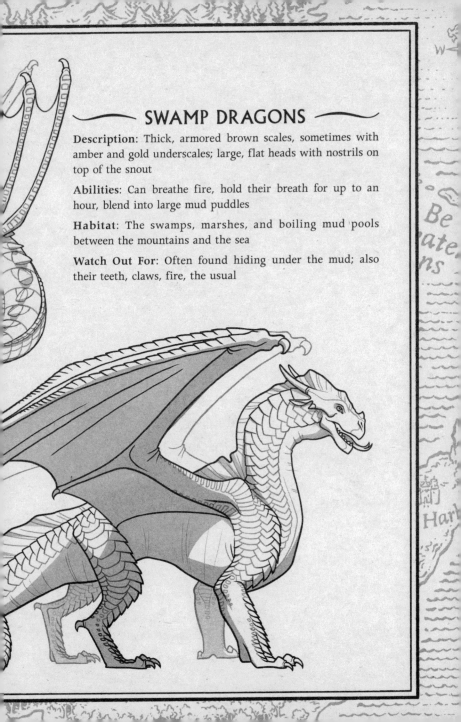

~ SWAMP DRAGONS ~

Description: Thick, armored brown scales, sometimes with amber and gold underscales; large, flat heads with nostrils on top of the snout

Abilities: Can breathe fire, hold their breath for up to an hour, blend into large mud puddles

Habitat: The swamps, marshes, and boiling mud pools between the mountains and the sea

Watch Out For: Often found hiding under the mud; also their teeth, claws, fire, the usual

MOUNTAIN DRAGONS

Description: Red-gold or orange scales, enormous wings

Abilities: Powerful fighters and fliers; can breathe fire

Habitat: The central mountain range

Watch Out For: The way they swoop out of nowhere at top speed; also their teeth, claws, fire

— SEA DRAGONS —

Description: Blue or green or aquamarine scales; webs between their claws; gills on their necks; glow-in-the-dark stripes on their tails/snouts/underbellies

Abilities: Can breathe underwater, create huge waves with one splash of their powerful tails

Habitat: The ocean, but possibly also large lakes and rivers

Watch Out For: Swimming in any large body of water; also, of course, their teeth and claws (but on the plus side, no fire!)

ICE DRAGONS

Description: Silvery scales like the moon or pale blue like ice; ridged claws to grip the ice, forked blue tongues; tails narrow to a whip-thin end

Abilities: Can withstand subzero temperatures and bright light; exhale a deadly freezing frostbreath

Habitat: The icy arctic region of the upper northwest peninsula, we think

Watch Out For: Their breath, which can freeze a human solid; also their teeth and claws

━ RAINFOREST DRAGONS ━

Description: Scales that can shift colors, usually bright like birds of paradise; prehensile tails

Abilities: Can camouflage their scales to blend into their surroundings; rumor has it they can also shoot venom from their fangs

Habitat: The mysterious impenetrable rainforest, east of the mountains

Watch Out For: We have no idea! No recorded survivor encounters, so they're probably the deadliest and stealthiest of all dragons

The events of this book take place
during roughly the same time period as
Wings of Fire: Books One through Five.

~ PROLOGUE ~

It is nearly impossible to steal from a dragon.

Everyone knew that.

Nearly impossible and decidedly stupid, especially when that dragon lives in a giant fortress with a hundred other dragons and you are the size of their average midmorning snack.

But if they did it — if they succeeded — they would be legends. Wealthy legends, with more gold than anyone they knew had ever seen before.

That was Heath's grand vision anyway. Stone couldn't imagine himself as a rich person. But he couldn't stop his little brother and sister once they had an idea in their heads. The best way — the only way — to protect them was to come along, too.

And so now he was here, doing the nearly impossible and decidedly stupid thing.

The dragons' palace loomed out of the sand like a dark mountain.

Three crescent moons overhead curled like ice dragon claws against the night sky, casting barely a glimmer of light on the dunes below.

In the shadows of the castle walls, Stone and Heath crouched in the sand, side by side. Small, wingless, without talons or scales. Teeth scarcely worth mentioning.

We're a perfect dragon's dinner, Stone thought nervously, *just sitting at their front door, like we're asking to be eaten. No other creatures in Pyrrhia walk right up to the dragons like humans do. They must think we're the dumbest prey on the planet.*

Maybe we are, if we really think we can steal their treasure and get away with it.

"What's taking her so long?" he whispered. "We shouldn't have let her go back in." He hefted a bag of gold in his hands. "This is more than enough for the three of us for the rest of our lives."

His brother gave him a scornful look and reached into the other bag. Stone heard the soft metallic sound of gold nuggets running through Heath's fingers. "She wanted to go back for more," Heath murmured. "She said there was rooms and rooms of it. All this sand dragon treasure — *ours*, Stone. We'll be kings."

"Being as wealthy as dragons won't make us as powerful as dragons," Stone pointed out.

"We'll see," Heath said, turning his gaze back to the window above them. The narrow slit was made to be too small for an enemy dragon to slip through — but it was an easy squeeze for a sixteen-year-old human girl like their sister, Rose.

"I think I hear her," Stone whispered.

A pair of small hands appeared at the bottom of the window, and a moment later Rose pulled herself up to straddle the ledge. In the shadows, she could have been anyone, except that no one else had a halo of dark curls quite like hers . . . and no one else would climb into a dragon's lair — twice — as she just had.

Rose dropped a rope down to her brothers, and they both grabbed it, helping her heave the sacks of treasure up from the floor inside. After a few moments, she signaled for them to move out of the way. *Clink! Thud!* went the bags as they hit the sand. With a hiss, the rope slithered down beside them.

Stone squinted up at Rose's silhouette as she inched down the stone wall, finding cracks and dents where she could fit her feet to climb. This whole plan had been Heath's idea, of course; Heath was obsessed with the dragons of the desert beyond their forest. Rose, the youngest, had run the greatest risk, slipping into the dragon palace and finding the treasure room in the middle of the night.

Stone's job was transport. As the oldest and biggest of the three siblings, he could carry all four of the sacks himself, at least until they reached the horses that were waiting a few dunes away — the horses he had stolen from their father's stable two nights ago.

Well, if he gets mad, I'll be able to pay him three times what they're worth, Stone thought with bitter pride. Rose had almost reached the ground. Maybe they really were going to get away with this.

"Stone," Heath whispered. "Stop breathing so loudly."

"I'm not breathing loudly," Stone objected. "I'm barely breathing at all."

Heath turned to him with an impatient scowl, and then suddenly his whole face went blank.

Stone knew that look. He'd seen that look when Heath's carelessness lit the smithy on fire and nearly set the whole village ablaze. He'd seen it when their father had caught Heath stealing food meant for the Wingwatchers. It was pure terror, and Stone knew instantly, with a plunging cold fear in his chest, what that meant.

He whirled around and saw the dragon looming behind him.

She was taller than the trees around their village, with wings that blotted out all three moons. Obsidian-black eyes glinted in a narrow, snakelike face. Sand hissed between her claws as she flexed them, and Stone could see the dark, dangerous barb of her tail raised behind her like a scorpion's, poised to strike. He'd seen — from afar — what that venom could do to a full-sized dragon. He didn't want to imagine what it could do to a human, or how painful that kind of death would be.

The dragon growled, low and long, with a lot of hissing and guttural sounds. She glared at the stolen treasure and, even more menacingly, at Rose, who'd reached the ground and now stood with her back pressed to the castle wall.

"She's going to kill us," Stone breathed. He had a spear strapped to his back, but the five seconds it took him to reach for it would be all the time the dragon needed to stab him through the heart with her tail.

"Heath," Rose whispered. "There's a sword in the bag nearest to you."

"Don't!" Stone wanted to turn and grab his brother, but he didn't dare move. "Don't antagonize her."

"Right, good idea," Heath murmured. "Except it's a bit late for that, idiot. Not sure if you've noticed, but we're in the middle of stealing her treasure."

Her treasure? Stone finally noticed the black band of onyx, embedded with diamonds, that circled the dragon's head. This was the queen herself.

So. There was no escape. Death, then, already. He was only twenty; he'd expected to do a bit more with his life before a dragon inevitably killed him. *Why did I let Heath talk us into this?*

Abruptly, Heath lunged for the sack beside him. The dragon let out a shriek of rage and stabbed her tail forward, but Stone just managed to dive and roll out of the way. He saw moonlight ricochet off steel as Heath swung the sword up and clumsily jabbed the dragon's underbelly with it. The weapon clanged against her scales. Heath nearly lost his grip, staggering sideways.

Stone leaped to his feet and drew his spear. He ran full tilt at the queen, trying to remember what the Wingwatchers at school had taught them about dragon weaknesses. The only thing he could remember was someone saying, *They don't have any.*

The dragon's tail whipped toward him, lightning fast. He ducked and her tail struck the spear, sending shock waves rippling down his arms. The sand slipped away from his feet and he fell.

"Stone!" Rose cried, darting forward. She grabbed one of the sacks of treasure and swung it in a full arc around her body, hurling it at the dragon's head.

The heavy bag collided with the queen's skull with a loud *crack*. The desert dragon stumbled back, shook her head, and lunged forward with a roar.

"No!" Stone yelled, trying to stand, trying to bring the spear around, trying to fight the sand that dragged him down — too slow, too slow.

A burst of flames shot from the dragon's mouth. Her wings flared, flinging sand into Stone's face. He floundered forward blindly. *Not Rose. Not Rose.*

Heath let out a shout of rage somewhere to his left. There was another clash of sword against scales. Following the sound, Stone aimed for the blurry winged shadow and stabbed his spear upward.

It connected, lodged in place, and was ripped out of his hands.

The dragon roared, but now the roar had pain in it as well as fury.

In the dark, through sand-stung eyes, Stone saw the dragon collapse heavily to the sand with a thud that shook the ground. He heard Heath's footsteps sprint past.

Stone covered his head and cowered as the dragon thrashed and howled.

Heath appeared suddenly at his elbow, tugging him up to his feet. "We did it! We killed a dragon!" His arms and chest were spattered with dragon blood, and he was carrying something grotesque and dripping in one hand. He'd abandoned the sword, which Stone could see still sticking out of the end of the severed tail. "Let's get out of here before that noise wakes any more of them." He shoved a sack of treasure into Stone's hands.

"Rose," Stone said.

Heath flinched away from him. Stone realized that his brother's clothing was charred, and dark burns rippled along his arm on one side. "She's gone, Stone." Heath picked up another one of the bags of treasure, shoved the object in his hand into it, and fled into the darkness.

Stone took a step after him, then stopped. *I can't go home like this. If I return to Father carrying bags of treasure instead of my sister's body . . .* He turned and looked up at the dark walls.

Wings were boiling over the top of the palace like a million bats pouring from a cave. The sand dragons were coming, called by the dying roars of their queen.

And when they catch us . . .

Stone's courage failed him. Still clutching the dragon's treasure, he turned and ran.

Here Be Dragons?

Here Be Dragons

Desert Dragon Palace

Here Be Dragons

Valor

Terrifying Viper Pit of Dragons

PART ONE

CHAPTER 1

WREN

One morning shortly after Wren turned seven years old, her parents wrestled her into her best blue wool dress, pinned her down to oil her curly hair, and took her up the mountain to be eaten by a dragon.

They didn't tell her that was the plan, of course. They didn't say "guess what's going to happen to YOU today" or "bad news about that tree-climbing expedition you had planned for tomorrow." They didn't say much beyond "stop wiggling!" and "don't you DARE bite me!"

If they had *told* her she was off to be a dragon's breakfast, she might have pointed out that the dragon *certainly* wouldn't care what her hair looked like, so there was no need to spend the last minutes of her life *torturing her*.

But instead she thought she was trapped on another boring walk with the dragonmancers for an Edifying Lecture About Dragon Behavior, and so all she wondered, as they marched through the woods, was why her parents were holding her hands so tightly, and why none of the other village children had been dragged along.

She was too young to remember the apprentice who'd been sacrificed five years earlier, especially since it was forbidden to talk about the gifts the village gave the dragons. And despite what the dragonmancers thought, Wren hadn't fully understood what she'd read in the books she stole from them.

Wren did notice the strange sideways looks from the other villagers, but it did not occur to her that those were "good thing it's HER getting fed to a dragon and not ME" kinds of looks. She thought they were the usual "there goes Wren, the girl with a dragon's temper" faces she always got. She liked making a horrible face back so she could see them blanch and turn away quickly.

But really, she should have been more suspicious. She should have realized her parents were being too quiet. It's just, one never really *expects* to be fed to dragons.

And then suddenly one dragonmancer stopped and raised his hands, and then all the villagers stopped and stared at Wren. The other two dragonmancers produced ropes from their robes and grabbed her.

The tall, thin one said something like, "Hear us, oh mighty wings of flame," in her snooty voice, and the short one with bumps all over his face said, "We offer you this gift, that you may spare the rest of your lowly worshippers." Then the leader, the smug one who always ate all the goat cheese at village celebrations, started to say, "Thank you for the lives of those —"

But Wren didn't let him finish. She recognized the words

they were chanting. She'd read them in one of the books she'd "borrowed" from the head dragonmancer's study. This was the Gift for the Dragons ceremony, it was real after all, AND THIS TIME SHE WAS THE GIFT.

After a lot of wrestling and screaming and fighting, they finally managed to tie her up, but they didn't get to say all their stupid blessing words. One dragonmancer staggered away with his nose bleeding; another clutched her scratched-up arm; the third was hobbling as they hurried off. Wren shouted every bad word she knew at them as the villagers scurried away, avoiding her eyes. Her parents didn't even look back once.

They left her on a giant stone slab overlooking the river, where the sky was wide open and the dragons would be able to see her easily.

The idea, of course, was that the seven-year-old would sit there politely and wait to be eaten, like a good little human sacrifice.

But that was obviously not going to happen. Although she was quite little, Wren was never polite and rarely good. And Wren was very much *not* on board with the plan where she got eaten and all the smug-faced meanies in her village did not. That was the ULTIMATE definition of unfair. Wren was a younger sister, so she knew all about fair and unfair, and getting eaten by dragons while jerks like Camellia stayed inside, probably playing with *Wren's* dolls, WAS ABSOLUTELY ONE HUNDRED PERCENT NOT FAIR.

Wren had one brother who'd agree with her, she was

pretty sure, but her uncle had taken Leaf hunting this morning. *To get him out of the way*, she realized now. Not that an eight-year-old could have stopped the village's plan either, but at least he could have been SUPER MAD. He would have yelled at Mom and Dad. He would have been full of RAGE AND VENGEANCE FOREVER and made their lives miserable for all time and they would have TOTALLY DESERVED IT.

But instead, she knew they'd tell him there was a sad accident while he was gone and little Wren got chomp-chomped by a dragon, too bad. And he'd be sad, but then he'd get over it, and everyone would LA-DI-DA off into their peaceful Wren-less futures.

Moons above, Wren thought furiously as she wriggled her hands free from the ropes. *They'll probably tell him it was MY fault! That I was DISOBEDIENT AGAIN and THAT'S why I got gobbled! They're going to make me into a story they tell other kids to make them behave!*

Now she was REALLY MAD.

She yanked off the rope around her ankles and jumped to her feet. What she wanted to do most was run after the villagers and dragonmancers and yell at them some more. She wanted them to know they were unfair stupid stupidheads and that she absolutely refused to get eaten by a dragon and she didn't even care if a dragon came and ate everybody else because they were all MEAN.

Wren took two steps into the forest and stopped herself.

If I run after them, they'll just tie me up again, but tighter.

They wouldn't listen to her. They never did. The more she

yelled and screamed, the less they listened. This was a fact she had noticed, but it only made her want to scream louder.

Screaming right now would probably summon a dragon, though. Or the dragonmancers, with their cold fingers and scowling faces. Of those two options, Wren might prefer the dragon.

She slid down the muddy bank and crouched beside the river, trailing her hands in the ice-cold water. Droplets flew up around her wrists, catching in the sunlight like diamonds tossed into the air.

It isn't fair, she thought, yanking a weed up from between the river pebbles. *Why did they pick ME? Out of everyone in the village? Why did the dragons send a vision saying they wanted to eat ME?*

"I bet they didn't!" Wren cried. "I bet the dragons don't even care!" She plucked a rock from the riverbed and threw it at a bush on the opposite bank. "They'd eat anyone they found all tied up! If they *could* choose, they'd pick someone bigger and yummier than me. Like Camellia! She would make a much better sacrifice to the dragons! Why didn't they pick *her*?"

Everyone was always saying how SWEET Wren's next-oldest sister was. *She'd be so oily and sugary the dragons could choke on her.*

But the dragonmancers loved Camellia and the way she listened to them with her eyes wide and her fake "this is *so* fascinating" face on.

Wren stared into the rippling water.

"The dragonmancers would never choose Camellia," she said out loud. "They chose me, because they don't like me. And Mother and Father let them."

Of course the dragonmancers chose the loud seven-year-old who kicked Master Trout in the shins when he scolded her. The girl who stole their books and read all their secrets, even if she only half understood them. They'd be happy to get rid of her.

And maybe Mother and Father were, too.

Nobody tried to stop them at all. Not one stupid person in the whole village.

She knew her parents were terrified of dragons and did everything the dragonmancers said all the time. But she still would have thought they might say, "Could you double-check that vision one more time? Are you sure it's *our* daughter the dragons want?"

Wren rubbed her eyes angrily.

Stop crying. So people are terrible and can't be trusted. That shouldn't be such a big surprise, Wren. They've never stood up for you before. Nobody cares about you and so you shouldn't care about them either.

Well, I think I shall NOT get eaten, she thought. *That will SHOW THEM. I don't need a village! Or parents! Or any of them! I'm smarter than all of them and smarter than the dragons, too! I don't have to be someone's breakfast if I decide not to be. So there!*

But that meant she couldn't go home. She could never go back to Talisman now that the dragonmancers had told everyone her destiny was to be dragon food and her parents had said, "Sure, that sounds right, fine by us."

She stood up, shaking the freezing droplets off her hand, and a flicker of motion caught her eye on the opposite riverbank.

Instantly she crouched, her heart bursting into a gallop and screaming "DRAGON!" even as her mind registered that the animal, whatever it was, couldn't be much bigger than a rabbit.

She took a deep breath.

It's something little. Maybe my *breakfast.*

She kept her eye on the spot where she'd seen it, but the movement had stopped. Cautiously, she slipped into the cold river and splashed across. The other side was rockier, covered in glassy black stones and small tangles of little leafless shrubs.

The thing she'd seen was caught in one of those nets of branches that leaned out over the river. She crept toward it slowly.

A rabbit would be great. Breathe, Wren. Don't panic. It's certainly not a dragon.

It was a dragon.

Or at least, it was a very small, pathetic, skinny miniature of a dragon. Its scales were the palest orange she'd ever seen, like a sunset painted on wool and then left under a waterfall or out in the sunlight for too long. She'd never seen a dragon so pale before — all the ones in the mountains were bright reds or oranges, and the ones that came up from the swamps were shades of mud brown.

Its eyes were closed and it hung limply in the tangled bare branches, its wings drooping toward the river.

Probably dead, Wren thought, and was surprised to feel a twinge of pity. For a DRAGON. What was THAT about. Feeling sorry for something that would probably eat her if it were still alive!

Then again, it wouldn't be able to fit much of her in that tiny mouth. It would take it days to nibble off her pinkie finger.

She snorted, and the baby dragon distinctly flinched.

It *was* alive!

"Hey," she said fiercely. "Dragon baby! Are you faking being dead? So that I'll come up close and poke you and then you can eat my finger?"

The little creature's eyes fluttered slowly open. It glanced around, spotted Wren, and let out a squeak of alarm.

She realized that it was shivering. She wasn't sure if that was from the cold water or because it was scared of her.

A dragon scared of me! I bet that's never happened to any of those stuffy mean old dragonmancers.

Wait. This dragon can't possibly be cold. It's a sky dragon; they all have fire inside them. It could burn up that bush in a second and fly away if it wanted to.

"This IS a trick, isn't it?" she said. "You want me to go, 'aw, poor baby,' and try to set you free, and then you'll set me on fire and eat me! I see what you're up to, little weird dragon!"

The dragon tried to twist itself one way, and then another,

but it was too snarled in the branches to wiggle free. It let out another pitiful squeak, its minuscule claws opening and closing on the air. It sounded like the kitten Wren's brother had once found in the woods, which their parents wouldn't let them keep because they wouldn't be able to keep it quiet if there were dragons hunting overhead. "That kitten will be the death of us all!" was how they'd put it, in typical over-dramatic grown-up fashion.

"Squeak," the little dragon said pathetically. "Sqrble. Eeeek."

"Stop being cute and tragic," Wren said, crossing her arms. "I'm not falling for it."

The baby dragon sighed, closed its eyes, and stopped wiggling. Its wings drooped and its head flopped sideways. It looked like it had given up and was planning on lying there in the bush until it starved to death.

"Oh, fire butts," Wren said crossly. "All right, fine, but if you eat even *one* of my fingers I am *throwing you in the river* and I won't feel bad about it." She clambered out across the stones, feeling the cold water eddy around her bare feet. The branches kept stabbing her as she tried to reach through them, so she started breaking them off and tossing them aside until she'd cleared a path to the little dragon.

It opened its eyes again and blinked at her in either hope or alarm; she wasn't entirely sure. Its face was more expressive than a lizard's, but still not at all human.

"What am I *doing*," Wren muttered. But she reached through the sharp web of sticks and carefully untangled the little dragon's wings, tail, and claws until it slipped free and tumbled into her hands.

She jumped back, holding it at arm's length. It was still trembling, sending little shudders through her whole body, and now she could feel that it actually was very cold. She'd obviously never touched a dragon before, but she would have guessed that they'd be warm or even burning hot, given the fire inside them.

This one was so different, though. Its eyes were pale, watery blue, like a frosted-over puddle. It nudged her thumb with its snout and tried to bury its head between her fingers.

Cautiously, she brought it closer to her. It immediately latched tiny claws in the weave of her dress and stuck its nose under her chin, shivering tragically.

"Why are you all alone?" Wren asked it. "And why are you so cold?" She ran one hand gently along its side, and it leaned into her palm with a whimper. She'd always thought dragons would feel kind of scaly and slimy like fish, but blisteringly hot. Instead the dragonet's skin was more like a lizard's, smooth and cool and a little pebbly, especially the softer scales under its chin and wings. Wren touched one of the wings softly with two fingers and the dragon unfolded it to rest in the palm of her hand.

She was pretty sure this dragon wouldn't eat her. It looked as if it wanted a mommy more than a meal, or at least something warm to curl up against.

Do dragons take care of their babies? Does it have a mommy somewhere nearby? Wren realized she had no idea. She'd been told to avoid mother bears with their cubs, and not to take baby birds out of their nests, but the only thing she really knew about dragons was to hide if you heard one coming.

"Well, if you do have a mommy somewhere, she wasn't taking very good care of you," Wren said. She patted the little dragon's head. "Don't feel too bad. Mine is very, very terrible, too." She felt a stab of deep, lonely sadness trying to sneak into her heart, but she shoved it back down under her anger.

A roar suddenly split the sky overhead, and Wren ducked into a crouch. The dragonet clutched her in a panic, trying to burrow into her armpit.

"Calm down!" Wren barked, although her heart was pounding like an avalanche. Now she could hear wingbeats coming closer — and she was still out in the open, here beside the river.

She wrapped her arms around the baby dragon and bolted toward the trees. Dark green leaves enveloped them as she tumbled into the first large bush she saw and pressed herself against the trunk.

Through the cracks between the fan-shaped leaves, she saw a rust-colored dragon soar overhead. Its yellow eyes glittered as it swung its head back and forth, studying the ground. The air crackled with heat and tiny flames curled from its nose.

It's hunting, Wren thought, her heart going even faster.

This is the dragon who would be snapping me up right now if I hadn't gotten out of those ropes.

She squinted through the leaves and noticed a mark on the dragon's face — an odd burn on its cheek that was smoking as though it was brand-new.

"ROAR!" the dragon in the sky bellowed. "ROOOOOOOOOOOOOOOAR!"

It sounded almost human, although that was a bonkers thing to say about a dragon's roar. But there was something about it that reminded Wren of her mom calling her name whenever Wren had a tantrum and went to hide in the trees. This dragon's roar was like that; it sounded mad and frantic and worried at the same time.

Yeah, right, Wren thought. *As if dragons can have that many complicated feelings! A roar is just a roar. It probably means "WHERE'S MY DINNER HUNGRY NOW" and that's it.*

She wondered if dragons cared about their babies, or if they ever threw them out to die. Maybe they were actually better parents than humans. Maybe they fought to protect their kids.

If my mom came back and called for me right now . . . would I go to her? Would I let her take me home, if she said they'd made a mistake?

No, Wren decided. *Because they could change their minds again tomorrow. Now I know they could throw me away anytime for no reason. So they can never, never have me back.*

The baby dragon in her arms squeaked the tiniest squeak

and wrapped its tail around her arm. Its face was completely hidden in the folds of her dress and it was shivering again.

"Shhh," Wren whispered. "It won't hurt you, but it'll definitely eat me if it finds us."

Another roar shook the leaves, and the baby dragon squeaked again, small and tragic.

"Unless . . ." Wren thought for a moment. "Do you know that dragon?" she whispered. "Is it the one that threw you in the river?"

She knew the baby dragon couldn't possibly understand her, but something about the way it trembled made her think the answer was yes.

Was that its mother? Did she get rid of the baby — and then change her mind? Or is she making sure it's really dead?

Whoever it was, the baby was clearly scared of it.

At least someone is looking for you, Wren thought, hugging the little dragon closer. *But I won't let them take you and hurt you again.*

The red dragon swooped around in another circle, glaring at the river, and then kept flying, following the river south and east toward the sea.

Wren let out a breath and nudged the baby dragon's head up to look at her.

"It's gone," she said. "I won't let it find you. We're safe." She glanced out at the vast, dangerous sky and the unfriendly wilderness that stretched all around them. "Well . . . kind of sort of safe. As safe as a seven-year-old and a baby dragon can be all alone in the mountains anyway."

The tiny creature blinked its large, trusting eyes. Its trembling abruptly stopped, and it put one small paw on her hand. As if it was saying, *Yes. I am safe now; safe with you.*

Wren smiled at it. This was still a pretty terrible plan, saving a baby dragon who would probably eat her just as soon as it was big enough. But she suddenly didn't care. She had a feeling someone had decided to toss aside this baby dragon, exactly the way her parents and her whole stupid village had thrown her away.

People are awful and untrustworthy and mean, so I'm going to make friends with a dragon instead. My dragon is way better than any person I know, so there.

"We don't need anybody else, right, little dragon?" Wren said, stroking one of its tiny ears. "If they don't want us, we don't care. We can look after each other, can't we?"

The dragon squeaked again. Even though it couldn't understand her, it was still a better listener than literally everyone in her village.

"I'm Wren," she said. "Do you have a name? It's probably something like Rawrgllorf, isn't it?"

"Squeak," said the dragon.

"Well, I can't call you Squeak," she said. "When you're big enough to eat me, I'm pretty sure you won't like that name very much." She ran her fingers lightly over his smooth scales, the color of the palest sunset over the mountains. "I think you're a mountain dragon, even though your color is a little wrong. How about Sky? I kind of like the name Sky."

The baby dragon poked its snout into the center of the

palm of her hand and made a little snortling sound. Wren giggled.

"I think that was a yes. Hello, Sky. When you grow up, will you burn down my village for me? Especially the dragon-mancers' houses. That'll show them. I'm going to grow up on my own just fine and then come back and be like, *ha! I did NOT get eaten by dragons and now my pet dragon is going to eat YOU, take THAT!*"

Wren lifted Sky to her shoulder, where he curled around her neck, closed his eyes, and fell into a peaceful sleep.

She had no more family, no village, no people to take care of her. She knew she could never trust a human again.

But she didn't need any of those things. She had a dragon of her own, and she was going to be better than fine. Together, she and Sky were going to be amazing.

CHAPTER 2

LEAF

One could say that Leaf did not like dragons, but it would be more accurate to say he hated them with a fiery burning passion.

He'd disliked them from the moment he was told, "No, you cannot play outside today; the dragons are restless." His entire life was all about rules for avoiding dragons, placating dragons, hiding from dragons, not annoying dragons. He couldn't go anywhere or do anything without a dozen warnings about the dragons, and if he was ever a minute late getting home or played too long with his friends after school, his parents would think he'd been eaten and lose their minds.

It was *stressful* and it was frustrating, and he couldn't even argue that they were overreacting because people from the village of Talisman did get eaten sometimes.

But he didn't want to live like a scared rabbit forever. He didn't want to become one of the grown-ups who were always yelling at kids for being too loud or hiding all wrong. He didn't want to spend his whole life just trying not to be dragon food.

"Follow the rules," his mother said. "The rules will keep you safe. Do exactly what you're told. Listen to the dragon-mancers. Never ever ever ever be disobedient."

"Disobedient children get eaten," his father would agree. "We're always in danger, do you understand? It's a danger-ous world. Dragons *everywhere*. It's a miracle we've even lived this long. We'll probably all get burned up in our beds tomorrow."

This would always make Leaf's little sister roll her eyes and whisper, "Well, how are we supposed to avoid *that* by following the rules? Is there a rule about sleeping in less flammable pajamas?"

Wren didn't even try to follow all the rules. Leaf would run straight home from school, and then turn around to dis-cover that his sister had been distracted along the way by an extra-adorable chipmunk, or she'd heard a weird noise in the woods and gone to investigate ("You don't go *toward* the weird noises!" their father would shout), or she'd thought of a new question for the dragonmancers and gone to bother them. ("The impertinence!" their mother would say through gritted teeth. "You don't ask *questions*. No one *speaks* to the dragonmancers without permission, least of all nosy little girls!")

Leaf thought it was amazing. He wished he were as brave as Wren was — or rather, he wished he could even think of the disobedient things that seemed to come very naturally to her.

His other four sisters, all of them older, had no trouble

following the rules and staying out of the dragonmancers' way. It was only the little one who gave his father heartburn and made his mother so furious.

"I'm not sure what's worse, the dragons or the dragonmancers," Wren would say. "At least the dragons aren't bossing us around EVERY SINGLE MINUTE OF EVERY SINGLE DAY."

But the summer Leaf turned eight, he discovered the answer. The dragons were worse. The dragons were the very worst creatures in the entire world.

His uncle had taken Leaf hunting, which was a rare treat, even if they had to hide under bushes every few steps because everything sounded like approaching wingbeats. He returned late that night, tired and itching from the grass and wood bits all over his skin, and his parents informed him that his little sister was gone.

"Gone?" Leaf echoed, puzzled. "She ran away again?" Once she'd disappeared for an entire day, then reappeared the next morning with a grin on her face and twigs in her hair. Saying she just wanted to see what it would be like to live on her own in the forest with no rules. She'd lost all three of her toys for a month because of that, and Leaf had secretly carved her a little wooden snail to replace them.

"No, dear," his mother said, looking more tense than he'd ever seen her, which was saying something. "She wandered off and got eaten by dragons."

Leaf felt like he was in a story, but the wrong story, one

he'd stumbled into by accident, where very dramatic sad things were happening to someone, but of course that couldn't be him.

"She wouldn't," he said. "You're wrong. Dragons wouldn't dare eat Wren."

His father let out a shaky laugh. "That is what she would say," he said. "But as I'm always telling you, death could swoop down at any moment. We should all be more scared. She should have been more scared," he finished mournfully.

"It was really her own fault," Leaf's mother pointed out. "You know how disobedient she was. She brought this on herself." She had her hands wrapped tightly together, as if she was pressing her feelings flat and thin between them.

"But you won't get in that kind of trouble," Leaf's father said, patting Leaf's shoulder anxiously. "You'll keep being a good boy and following the rules, and you'll be quite safe, won't you? You won't end up like her. *You* understand why we need to be terrified all the time."

Leaf looked around the room, blinking. Wren's toy snail was still perched on the windowsill. ("Keeping watch for dragons?" he'd asked. "No, planning his amazing escape!" she'd answered.) But her favorite doll was now in a basket with Camellia's other toys. That was the thing that made it real. Wren would NEVER stand for that if she were here.

What was he feeling? Was he terrified, as his father said he should be?

"I'm not," Leaf said, shoving his father's hand away. "I'm

not scared, I'm . . . I think I'm *mad*. Why aren't *you* mad?"

"At your sister?" his father said. "Well, I suppose I'm a little —"

"No!" Leaf shouted. "At the DRAGONS WHO ATE HER!"

"Voices down," his mother said sternly. "No yelling, not ever. You know it's forbidden."

"Do you want dragons to find us and eat us, too?" his father demanded.

"Maybe I want them to try!" Leaf said. "So I can punch them in the face!"

"It doesn't do any good to be mad at the dragons," his mother said in her "only grown-ups know anything" voice. "They're just wild animals, catching prey like any other creature. We don't get mad at bears or sharks or raccoons, after all."

"Because raccoons don't swoop out of the sky and burn up entire villages!" Leaf cried. "If sharks could fly and breathe fire, I think we could get mad at them sometimes, too! Plus also, we don't have bearmancers and sharkmancers and raccoonmancers; we only have *dragonmancers*, and isn't that because dragons are supposed to be all smart and mystical and magic? I mean, what are the dragonmancers even FOR if they can't keep our village safe?"

His parents exchanged a weird look.

"Maybe if your sister had *listened* to the dragonmancers instead of *annoying* them all the time —" his mother started, then stopped herself with visible effort.

"They do keep us safe," his dad said hurriedly. "That's how any of us have survived this long. Most of us are still here, aren't we? That's thanks to our three dragonmancers."

"We should be grateful," his mother added. "And obedient. And respectful. Very respectful. Don't disrespect them, Leaf. They do such important work."

"But they failed!" Leaf cried. "They were supposed to protect us and they didn't! They're stupid liars!" He was crying now, and he didn't care how loud he was or whether the entire village and all the dragons on the mountain could hear him.

"Stop that!" His mother grabbed his arm and crouched beside him, glancing into the corners of their hut as though the dragonmancers might have buried little ears in the walls. "Never *never* speak that way of the dragonmancers."

"If you study hard and listen to your elders, maybe *you'll* be a dragonmancer one day," his father said. "Then you'll know even more about how to stay safe."

"I don't want to *study* dragons," Leaf protested. "I want to stab them with swords and shoot them with arrows and kill as many of them as I can."

His parents both winced. "That's ridiculous," said his mother. "And unnecessarily violent."

"And will absolutely get you eaten," said his father, running his hands through his thin hair so it stuck up like it couldn't believe what Leaf was saying either.

"No human has ever killed a dragon," his mother pointed

out. "It's not possible. You might as well walk into their cave and offer to be their lunch."

"It is too possible," Leaf's oldest sister suddenly offered from her hammock in the loft overhead. Leaf hadn't even realized she was up there, listening to them.

"Stay out of this, Rowan," their mother warned. "You've had a long day and you're only barely in our good graces right now."

Rowan rolled out of the hammock and crouched to gaze down at them. Her voice was innocent but defiant at the same time. "I think Leaf should know about the Dragonslayer, that's all."

Leaf's skin tingled all over just hearing the word. *Dragonslayer*. A slayer of dragons. That was the exact thing he wanted to be. Someone who protected good people from terrible monsters, not by chanting mumbo-jumbo and talking about visions, but by *doing something*.

"The Dragonslayer is just a myth," their father said. "Rowan, please, don't cause any more trouble."

"He's not a myth. My friend Grove says it's all true," Rowan insisted. "Grove's family used to live in the Indestructible City and they had wandering travelers come through all the time and some of them had even *met* the Dragonslayer."

"A real dragonslayer? Someone who's still alive? Who is it?" Leaf asked.

"Rowan, do not put ideas in your brother's head," their mother warned.

"It's not an *idea*, it's a fact," Rowan said. She sat down and swung her legs over the edge of the loft. Her hair was partly squashed from lying in the hammock, but her dark brown eyes were intense and hypnotic. Leaf would always remember this moment and the look on his sister's face as he heard about the Dragonslayer for the first time.

"The Dragonslayer was only a young man, but he was determined to fight to free his people, and so he rode far out into the desert one night," she said in a low storyteller voice. "He crept right inside the lair of the sand dragon queen, and he fought a great battle with her, and the blood sprayed and the scales flew, until finally he cut off her head and stole all her treasure and rode back home, triumphant."

"Really?" Leaf breathed.

"No, not really," his mother snapped. "Utter nonsense, like we said."

"He brought the venomous tail of the dragon queen back with him as proof," Rowan said, still using her eerie voice. "The treasure made him the wealthiest man in the entire world. Rich, powerful, dangerous: the slayer of dragons, the hero of men!"

"Yes!" Leaf cried, caught up in the story. "And he saved everybody!"

"Stop mesmerizing your brother!" their mother yelled. She threw a dish towel at Rowan, breaking the spell. "If the Dragonslayer *were* real, the dragons would have caught him and eaten him by now to get their treasure back."

"And you're leaving out the part about the partner he left behind," Father added. "Doesn't sound so heroic when you think about *that*, does it?"

"AHA!" Leaf shouted. "So you know this story! It IS true!"

Mother gave Father an exasperated look. "*No*," she said. "That's *in the myth*. It's a *fairy tale* that only *brainless* families tell their children."

"I'm going to be a dragonslayer, too," Leaf said stoutly. "I'm going to be a hero of men and kill dragons to save people just like him." He seized a stick of firewood and brandished it around the house, jabbing at the furniture.

"No!" his mother said firmly. "Slaying dragons is absolutely against the rules! The dragonmancers forbid it and I forbid it, too!"

"Rowan, what have you *done*?" Leaf's father said piteously.

"Serves you right and you know why!" Rowan called as she climbed back into her hammock.

"Don't you want to be a dragonmancer?" Father pleaded, intercepting Leaf and trying to take the stick away. Leaf ducked under his arm and darted across the room. "Wise and respected and extremely knowledgeable about dragons . . . from a distance?"

"There's no *need* to fight dragons," Mother agreed. "We can appease them and keep them away from us if we just follow the dragonmancers' rules."

"No! Their horrible rules didn't save Wren!" Leaf declared. "It's not fair that dragons get to eat people we love and we can't do anything about it!"

He clambered to the top of the tallest stool and stabbed his pretend sword toward the ceiling. "I *won't* be scared of them! I swear on this sword, one day every little sister in the world will be safe. Because I shall be the next and greatest dragonslayer of them all!"

CHAPTER 3

IVY

"Mommy? Is Daddy famous? All the people at the party tonight were acting like he's maybe famous."

"Yes, he's very famous, dear. Probably the most famous person in the world."

"Because he's the boss of everyone? Or because he did a Dragonstare a long long long time ago?"

"Drago*slayer*, Ivy. Yes. Well, partly because he's the lord of the town, but mostly because he's the only dragonslayer alive today. And it wasn't *that* long ago."

"I thought Uncle Stone dragonstared, too."

"*Slayer*, Ivy. No, Uncle Stone didn't slay the dragon. He was just there when it happened."

"What does slay mean?"

". . . It means Daddy poked the dragon very hard until it fell over and didn't get up again."

"Mommy. I know about hunting. You mean like the way you poke squirrels and rabbits with arrows to get us dinner."

"Ye-es, sort of. But he didn't eat the dragon afterward."

"Why not?"

"Humans don't eat dragons, silly bean. Also, he kind of had to run away in a hurry from the other dragons."

"Other dragons! Why didn't Daddy slayer them, too?"

"There were quite a lot of them, Ivy. And dragons are very big."

"I want to see a dragon."

"No, you don't. We're safe down here, far away from all the dragons. Your father keeps us all safe."

"Why was Uncle Stone yelling at Daddy about running away from the dragons? Did he want Daddy to slayer all of them?"

". . . No, your uncle just . . . gets sad sometimes, and then he thinks about that night and gets upset."

"Why upset?"

"I'll tell you when you're older, Ivy."

". . . Mommy?"

"Ivy, go to sleep."

"Were the other dragons mad at Daddy? I think maybe slayering a dragon is not very nice. I bet that dragon did not like getting poked until it fell over and couldn't get up again."

"It's an animal, Ivy. It doesn't have feelings. And your father is a hero. Now shhhh."

"Mommy. Mommy. Mommy, you know how Daffodil has a pet rabbit? Do you think I could have a pet dragon?"

"NO, Ivy."

Ivy was born in the hidden city of Valor, years after the dragons burned their village to cinders and tried to hunt them all into extinction. She spent her childhood in the cramped tunnels that the survivors and Dragonslayer followers had hollowed out of the earth — the only place where the dragons couldn't find them.

Of course, in her dad's version of the epic tale, the decimated village and vengeful dragons rarely came up. Instead he talked about the obsidian-tipped sword he'd found and how he drove it into the dragon's eye. He described the yellow dragon's fierce roar and the fire that scorched the sand around them as they fought, and he rolled up one sleeve to show the burn scars that covered half his body. Sometimes, if the Dragonslayer's fans gave him enough to drink, he'd talk about the treasure — the gold, the glittering gems, the weight of the lazulite dragon in his hands. His eyes would blur as he described the treasure, the one thing in his life he'd ever truly loved.

But his favorite part of the story, the part he never skipped, was boasting about cutting off the poisonous tip of the dragon's tail. He'd bring people over to see it day or night, even long after bedtime, even people who'd already seen it a thousand times. It sat preserved in a glass box in the family's living room and gave Ivy nightmares.

The other girls in Ivy's class refused to sleep over at Ivy's after Violet said, "What if one day it comes to life?" and then Daffodil said, "Or a WHOLE OTHER DRAGON grows out of it? Like how lizards can grow back from their tails!" and Violet said, "Or WHAT IF one of us accidentally sleepwalks into it and gets all POISONED?" and all the other girls went, "OOOOOO."

Ivy thought these were quite reasonable fears. It really was the creepiest room decoration ever. It had a dark crust of blood along one edge and a barb gleaming with venom that curled like a scorpion's stinger. She didn't understand why anyone would want to look at it even once, let alone keep it in a fancy box on a tapestry-covered pedestal, where one's daughter would have to see it every day.

Sleeping over at the other girls' caves instead was more than all right with her. She was always invited. Everyone wanted to be friends with the Dragonslayer's daughter. She was practically a princess of the underground city.

But even the lord's daughter was never allowed outside. She rarely saw the sun, and she had to imagine the wind.

Her bedtime story was the same every night:

"Once upon a time, a mighty hero went forth into the desert and slayed the sand dragon queen." Ivy's mother would stare dreamily at the flame of the oil lamp as she spoke, stroking Ivy's hair. "He battled bravely into the night until she lay dead on the sand, and then he galloped home with the greatest treasure the world has ever seen."

"Where is the treasure now?" Ivy asked when she was four, and again when she was five, and even more often when she was six. "Can I see it?"

"Shhh," her mother would whisper. "No one can see it. It's in a secret place."

"But he's my dad," Ivy pointed out. "Daffodil says it's weird that he has a big shiny treasure but I never get to see it. Daffodil says maybe it doesn't exist at all or maybe he lost it or something. Daffodil says I should hold my breath until you let me see it, but I practiced and it gave me a super big headache so I'mma not do that."

"Daffodil has so many helpful thoughts," her mother observed.

"Have *you* seen the treasure, Mommy?"

"Of course I have," she'd say, but there was a flicker in her placid expression that made Ivy wonder.

Mother always saw Father as a hero, even when he was snoring loudly in his hammock or complaining about the smell in their cave mansion, which turned out to be coming from a pair of his wool socks that he'd stuffed under the rug and forgotten about. Mother repeated everything he said to anyone who would listen, even when she had to know some of it wasn't true.

At around the age of six, Ivy started noticing all the things that weren't true. That was confusing enough, but what was even stranger was how nobody else seemed to notice or care.

Like when her father told the citizens of Valor that he was going to expand the cave tunnels so there would be many safe and well-built ways to get to the underground lake. And then a year later, he pointed to the one tunnel that had always been there — the one Mother and a team of other moms had dug out on their own years ago — and told everyone he had shored it up and made it safer and bigger and better, and everyone said that was amazing and he was amazing and named it Dragonslayer Way, even though it was exactly the same as before.

Didn't everyone see it was exactly the same as before? Didn't they remember the women who'd worked so hard on it? Ivy was still only little, but *she* remembered carrying dirt in baskets when she was four years old, back and forth and back and forth in a line of children. She remembered her mother talking about how much safer it would be for everyone when they could get water without leaving the tunnels. She remembered her father rolling his eyes and scoffing at the silliness of the plan.

But now he said it was *his* plan, and it was named after him, and everyone nodded and cheered — even Mother?

It made Ivy wonder a little bit whether her brain was working all right. She wanted to ask questions, but questions always made her parents frustrated and grumpy with her, and her teachers only said things like "that's not in the curriculum, Ivy" or "you'll understand when you're older" or "why don't you sit quietly and do another math work-slate, dear."

When she was seven, she had a sweet teacher named Miss Laurel, and she thought maybe she'd try again. She waited until recess, when the children were all sent to run to the underground lake and come back with a bucket of water, and then she approached the teacher shyly.

"Miss Laurel? Can I ask you a question?"

"Of course, Ivy." Miss Laurel was sitting on the floor, trying to sew a tattered book's pages back together. She gave Ivy a smile that looked tired in the torchlight and patted the ground beside her.

"D-did you hear my dad's speech last night?" Ivy sat down and picked up a scrap of paper that had fluttered out of the book.

"In the great hall? Yes, everybody did. It was a mandatory gathering. Do you know what *mandatory* means?"

"That everybody has to go except kids. But Mother brought me anyway."

"Oh." Miss Laurel's forehead wrinkled. "Oh dear." She took Ivy's hand and squeezed it between hers. "Did it scare you, sweetheart?"

Ivy thought about the flickering torches, the shouting crowd, the boy in the torn green uniform standing hunched beside her dad with his hands tied in front of him. Should it have been scary? Mother always brought her to banishments. Ivy usually fell asleep on her shoulder, wishing they could have had a normal bedtime instead.

This time she'd stayed awake and listened, though. This time she sort of knew the boy in trouble. He was one of the nice Wingwatchers who brought peaches to the school after outdoor patrols. Daffodil said he had cute hair and she was going to marry him one day.

"I guess it was mostly confusing?" Ivy said. "I didn't understand what Daddy was saying."

"He was saying that Pine was a danger to the

community," Miss Laurel said gently. "Pine went to the old village and scavenged in the ruins. If any dragons had been watching, he could have led them right back to us."

Ivy took a deep breath. "But . . . Daddy goes to the old village all the time," she said in a rush.

Miss Laurel's face did something strange, like all her expressions were falling off of it at once, so it looked like a mask for a moment.

"I'm sure that's not the case," she said finally.

"He does!" Ivy said. "He brings things back. Spoons and horseshoes and a little ball for me and other stuff."

Miss Laurel patted her head. "Aren't you lucky to have such a brave father to take care of you."

"But, Miss Laurel, why can my dad go there whenever he wants, but Pine went there once and now he's banished from Valor forever?"

"Perhaps you've misunderstood where he goes, dear. Anyway, he's the Dragonslayer and lord of Valor. They're *his* laws. So he can't possibly break them."

"That doesn't seem fair," Ivy said. "And he *told* the Wingwatchers to go looking for iron. Aren't the ruins a smart place to look?"

"But the law —"

"*I* think Daddy made up the law *after* Pine went there," Ivy said firmly.

Miss Laurel stood up and dusted off the book she'd been working on. "That's silly, Ivy. You'll learn more about how laws and lords work when you're older. Now you'd better hurry if you want to have time to play after you get your bucket of water."

Ivy sighed. Miss Laurel was just like the other grown-ups, after all.

She ducked through the classroom door into the tunnel outside and made it about three steps before she was suddenly seized and dragged into a different classroom.

"Hey!" she yelped.

"Shhhhh." Daffodil covered Ivy's mouth with her hands. As always, her long dark hair was tied into pigtails with bright yellow scraps of fabric, which matched her bee-pollen-yellow tunic. Ivy had once heard her mother say that Daffodil's mother dressed her like that so everyone would remember the sunny flower her daughter was named after, and then hopefully forget Daffodil's actual "dreadfully strong personality."

Ivy realized that Violet was in the otherwise empty classroom as well, sitting on one of the tables carved from the rock and blinking owlishly.

Violet and Daffodil were the loudest girls in her year and best friends — whenever they weren't absolutely furious with each other. Daffodil practically vibrated with energy when she had to sit still, and Violet made up all the best pretend games.

Ivy's mother often said "those two are not my favorite children," but there were only so many kids Ivy's age in the underground city, so Mother couldn't exactly stop her from playing with them.

"We heard you talking to Miss Laurel," Daffodil said in a stage whisper that could have been heard on the far side of Valor.

"*You* heard her," Violet said. "You made *me* go get all our water buckets." She waved one hand at three buckets of water lined up beside her.

"Wow," Ivy said. "Did you carry all of those at the same time?"

"Yes," Violet said matter-of-factly. "I'm really strong. One day I'm going to get super tall and lift the roof off the whole city and then we won't be underground anymore and it'll be very shiny and smell nice and everyone will say *thank you, Violet, you're so great* and *I* will say, *you are so welcome, what else can I lift?*"

"No, they'll say *thank you, DAFFODIL*, because *I* was the one who even told you to do that in the first place," Daffodil said, putting her hands on her hips.

"No!" Violet argued. "I thought of it myself! You did not!"

"It was my idea!" Daffodil said. "I said you could lift off the roof! I said it yesterday!"

"But *I* thought of it the night *before* that, I just hadn't SAID anything about it yet!"

Ivy could see that this was nosediving into one of Daffodil and Violet's epic fights, which turned the whole classroom into a war zone at least once a week. She edged toward the door. "I should maybe . . ."

"Look, you're scaring her away!" Daffodil said, pouncing on Ivy and dragging her back into the classroom.

"I think YOU'RE scaring her away!" Violet objected.

"IVY," Daffodil said, heroically ignoring Violet, which Ivy knew from experience was quite nearly impossible. "You were asking Miss Laurel questions about Pine."

"Yes," Ivy admitted. She tried to remember whether Daffodil had been at the banishment. She didn't think so; the bright yellow would have been hard to miss.

"Is he really gone?" Daffodil said. "Never ever to return?"

"I think so?" Ivy said.

"But WHYYYYY?" Daffodil wailed, throwing herself to the ground. She flopped onto her back with one arm dramatically over her face. "My life is RUINED!"

"Did your dad say he had to go let himself get eaten by dragons?" Violet asked.

"No!" Ivy said. "He just said Pine had to leave and never come back."

"Hmmm," Violet said. "So, like, almost the same thing."

"VIOLET, YOU ARE SO MEAN!" Daffodil shouted. "HOW DARE YOU SAY MY BOYFRIEND WILL GET EATEN BY DRAGONS!!!"

"He's not your *boy*friend," Violet said. "He is very old. Like *seventeen* maybe even."

"But he could have been! When I grow up! If he wasn't BANISHED FOREVER!"

"What did he do?" Violet asked Ivy.

"Yeah," Daffodil said, sitting up abruptly. "You told Miss Laurel your dad does the same thing all the time."

"Well . . . I thought so," Ivy said. "But Miss Laurel said I must have misunderstood."

"That is *such* a grown-up thing to say," Violet said, rolling her eyes.

"Did you guys know that there's a law saying nobody's allowed to go to the old village?" Ivy asked.

"What? No, there isn't," Violet said.

"What old village?" Daffodil asked.

"The one the dragons burned down!" Violet said impatiently. "Where everybody used to live!"

"I KNEW THAT," Daffodil barked. "I meant WHAT do you *mean*, the old village, like, what law. It was a good question, shut up!"

"Saying shut up is not nice at all," Violet said, turning up her nose. "That's bullying. You're bullying me."

"No, YOU —" Daffodil started, and Ivy hurriedly intervened.

"I never heard of a law like that before," she said.

"Me neither," said Violet. "My dads work on laws and orders with your dad, and I know they've been to the old village. They brought me a half-burned doll and said maybe I could fix it to make it pretty but that sounded boring, so instead I pretend she's a furious ghost who haunts the ruins waiting to get her REVENGE on the dragons!"

"YES!" Daffodil cried, running to the wall and bouncing off it and running back and slicing the air with an imaginary sword. "Fight me, dragons!"

"But that's all Pine did," Ivy said. She WOULD get through this conversation, no matter how easily distracted the other two were, and even if they didn't remember it for more than a day. She'd never tried telling other kids about the weird things that didn't line up in the world. Maybe they'd say something a grown-up had never said.

"Pine did what?" Violet asked.

"Fight a dragon?" Daffodil chimed in.

"No, no — he went to the old village. That's why he got banished. Because there's a law that says you can't."

They stared at her for a long moment, the quietest Ivy had ever seen them. She waited for Daffodil to poke Violet in the stomach and run away giggling, or for Violet to explain why Ivy was wrong.

"That's not right," Violet said finally. "There's no law like that. Which means someone made up an unfair reason to get rid of Pine. That's grown-up lying, which is worse than kid lying. I don't like that."

"Me neither," Daffodil agreed. "LIIIIIIIIIIIIIIIIIIIIIIES," she added in a dramatic stage whisper, peering through her fingers.

Ivy shivered, half in awe and half in terror. Nobody *ever* said the Dragonslayer was lying. She realized she'd been kind of waiting for someone to say it out loud, so that she wouldn't have to, but now that someone had, it felt stabby and bad in her insides. That was her father they were talking about.

"Maybe I'm wrong, though," Ivy said. "Maybe it's a new law."

"I will find out," Violet said. "I am excellent at thing-finding-out."

"But won't you get in trouble?" Ivy asked anxiously. "My parents yell at me when I try to find things out."

"Then I will yell BACK," said Daffodil. "That is what *I* am excellent at."

"I think we should invite her to join the secret club," Violet said to Daffodil.

Daffodil threw up her hands. "What?! You can't say that in *front* of her! That is so rude! What if I said no?"

"You can't say no," Violet said inexorably. "She already knows about it."

"She doesn't know what it's *called*," Daffodil said, crossing her arms.

"So *are* you going to say no?" Violet asked.

"No! I'm saying yes! But it's not fair because *I* was thinking we should invite her except *I* was going to wait until she left the cave to ask you like a NOT RUDE PERSON!"

"Um . . . should I leave the cave?" Ivy asked. She was already in most of the "secret clubs" formed by the other seven-year-olds. It was actually surprising that she hadn't even heard of Violet and Daffodil's. Maybe it was a very new club. But she guessed it would probably break up like all the others, probably faster because of how Violet and Daffodil fought all the time.

Also, she wanted to go sit by herself for a moment to think about lies and why her dad would tell lies, if that was what they were, and why all the other grown-ups let him, when kids like Daffodil and Forest got in huge trouble for their lies all the time.

"Nope, you're in. Welcome to the club," Violet said, reaching out her hand, which Daffodil knocked aside as she shouted, "WELCOME TO THE CLUB," over her. Ivy didn't know whose hand to shake first without getting in trouble, so she used both her hands and shook theirs at the same time.

"It is a club about knowing things," Violet said solemnly. "It is a club about secrets, so you have to promise to keep them, even when certain people are being very loud about everything." She glared at Daffodil.

"We're the only people in it, but it is not a club *about* excluding people," Daffodil said, apparently missing Violet's veiled jab. "Except Daisy because she is VERY VERY annoying and I hate her." Daisy was Daffodil's older sister, age nine, and, as far as Ivy could tell, a perfectly pleasant, quiet person.

"Don't say *hate*," Violet said. "That is a mean word."

"Fine," said Daffodil. "I LOATHE her."

"What is the club called?" Ivy asked, trying to head off another argument.

"We are the Truth Seekers," Violet said. Maybe it was the hushed, somber voice she said it in, or maybe it was just the exact words Ivy wanted to hear at that moment, but something about it felt right and good and much more important than the other secret clubs.

I hope it doesn't fall apart too quickly, she thought. She'd never *wanted* a secret club to last before. She usually just went along with whatever the others were playing.

"We will find out the truth about Pine," Daffodil said, matching Violet's solemn tone. "We will find out the truth about *everything*."

Everything, Ivy thought as the other two touched their hands to their foreheads and then to hers, and then to each other's, and then made her do the same to them. *Truth that other people don't know.*

Why Pine was really banished. Why her dad told lies to the people of Valor.

And if he was lying about one thing, what else had he lied about? The treasure had to be real; her dad was a lord now. And the severed dragon tail was definitely real. But had he left anything out? Were there lies buried in his story about the dragons — in *everything* he said about dragons?

On the way home from school that day, Ivy borrowed a Wingwatcher's Dragon Guide from the library, and that night she studied the drawings as if she'd never seen them before.

Mud dragons. Sand dragons. *Ice* dragons. Each of them were painted with little tiny scales the color of gems. Sapphire blue, tangerine orange, diamond white. And their faces . . . their faces looked so intelligent.

Maybe Daddy didn't have to slay that dragon, Ivy thought. This was a forbidden thought. The Dragonslayer was a hero. That was the story of Valor in one sentence.

She traced one finger along the shimmering wings of the

rainforest dragon. In the drawings, it had the kindest face, which was a silly thing to say about animals that would eat you in a heartbeat . . . but it still felt true to Ivy.

Maybe some of the Dragonslayer story is a lie, too, she thought, feeling the danger of even thinking the words to herself.

I wonder how the dragons would tell it, if they could tell their own stories.

CHAPTER 4

WREN

Wren would never say there was something wrong with her baby dragon — he was a million percent perfect and she'd bite anyone who said he wasn't, if there was anyone around to try it.

But she had to admit he was kind of a weird little guy.

For one thing, he *loved* animals, in a sort of adorably obsessive way. His favorite was snails. Anytime he spotted one, he would throw himself to the ground nearby and stare at it with wide eyes, watching the little antennae slowly blorb in and out. He could watch snails inch around under the grass for an entire morning if Wren didn't make him get up and keep moving with her.

In fact, *snail* was the first word she learned in Dragon. He said it so often that she finally tried saying it back to him, which he found delightfully hilarious.

As they walked, he'd sit on her shoulder and point and chatter at every bird as though each one was the newest, shiniest, most amazing thing he'd ever seen. He freaked out with joy when ladybugs landed on him, and he moped for days when squirrels ran away at the sight of him.

It also made him a completely useless hunting partner. The first time Wren brought Sky a rabbit that she'd managed to bring down with a slingshot, he gently stroked its fur for a moment, and then he burst into tears.

Tears! She hadn't even know dragons could cry, much less over food!

"Baby Sky," she said as he blubbered into her skirt, "you very silly dragon. You *must* have eaten meat before. I thought dragons *only* ate meat."

He clambered up her lap and onto her shoulder, still boo-hoo-hooing, and buried his cold nose in her hair. Another tear dropped off his snout and slid down her neck.

"Did they give it to you already cooked?" she asked. "Is that why this is weird, because you can tell it used to be a rabbit?"

"Urrrblroarf," the dragon snuffled.

"Well, if you won't eat it, I will," she said. "But you have to eat something." She emptied her pockets of the nuts and berries she'd scavenged while hunting. Sky leaped off her shoulder and pounced on them, gobbling all the fruit first.

"Such a strange small dragon," she said, tugging on his ears affectionately. He made a noise somewhere between a purr and a growl. "On the plus side, if you won't eat a rabbit, then I *think* you probably also won't eat me? What do you think? Are my fingers safe?"

"Mrrrowr," he agreed, or disagreed, or burped; she wasn't quite sure what any of his noises meant yet.

She'd kind of been hoping he could roast the rabbit for her and save her some work, but Sky showed no sign of setting anything on fire. He never had smoke rising from his nostrils the way the dragons flying overhead did. He never sneezed out bursts of flame (although he did sneeze quite a lot for a while after his time in the river). He never even breathed heat, not even on the coldest nights when they both really needed it.

And still it took Wren over a year to figure it out. For a long time she thought he just didn't want to, or that maybe he was sick from the cold river and needed to get better before his fire came back. And then for a while she guessed that baby dragons must hatch without fire and grow the ability to make it later.

But eventually something happened that made her realize that Sky was different from other dragons.

They had been slowly working their way south that whole first year together, intending to get far away from Wren's village and the mountain dragons' palace. Sky was a slow traveler (partly due to all the snail-watching stops), but Wren was in no particular hurry once they were outside her village's usual hunting area.

Wren was hoping the winters would be easier if they came down from the mountains, but when they followed the river toward the sea, they found themselves in a vast marshy swampland where there were literally dragons HIDING IN THE MUD everywhere. After three close encounters with teeth surging up out of the swamp, Wren and Sky retreated back to the mountain foothills in a hurry.

Wren kind of remembered the map she'd found in the dragonmancers' books, although it was sketchy and mostly unhelpful, and every empty space on it had been labeled HERE BE DRAGONS, which made her want to yell, "Oh REALLY, why, THANK you, Mr. Obvious Mapmaker."

From that map she knew there was a desert west of the mountains, but she didn't really know what that meant. She'd never seen a desert or met anyone who had. But Sky seemed to think it was worth a try, so they crossed the mountains through a pass during the warmest part of the year. From what she could tell of the seasons, Wren thought she might have turned eight by now. She didn't know how fast dragonets grew, but Sky was probably a year old, at least.

The pass channeled them up and up a winding canyon for days on end, finally ejecting them onto an outlook with a view of the far western horizon.

Deserts, it turned out, were big and wide and flat and terrifying, if you asked Wren. Sand, sand, sand, as far as the eye could see, and almost nothing else.

"Hmph," Wren said, crossing her arms and glaring at it.

"Hmph," Sky agreed. He'd started imitating several of her noises, especially her grumpy ones, which was extremely cute. But she didn't want him to lose his own language, because she wanted to learn it, too. Imagine being the only person in the world who spoke Dragon! Besides, her mouth seemed to work better with dragon sounds than his did with human ones.

"Look! Yuck!" she said in Dragon, pointing at the endless desert. That was the closest she could get to saying, "There's no way we can live out there! What a dreadful place! There's absolutely nowhere to hide from the sand dragons, and we'd probably boil to death on the first day!"

"Yuck," Sky agreed, lashing his tail furiously. "Too big! Too hot!" And then he added a few more unintelligible dragon growls.

Wren looked north — mountains curving away into the distance — and south, where she saw a waterfall pouring out of one of the cliffs. But there were no clues about which way was safest, no signs saying EXCELLENT HOME FOR WANDERING GIRL AND DRAGON HERE.

She sighed. The one thing she missed about living in a village was having things to read. She didn't miss a single one of the stupid awful treacherous people (*maybe Leaf . . . don't think about Leaf*), but she missed stories she could bury herself in, or piles of new facts about something she didn't know. The village school had only had a few books, and she'd zipped through them all before she turned six. That's why she'd stolen the ones from the dragonmancers, because she'd been so desperate to read something new.

But at least new books came to Talisman now and then, sold by wandering tradesfolk, or sometimes someone would write a new one. Out here in the wilderness, she hadn't seen a book in *forever*, and she missed reading so much, it felt like half her soul was curled in a corner, waiting to be brought back to life.

Plus, it would be ever so useful to have a new book with a MAP in it to consult right about now. She knew the Indestructible City was farther south and east, between the next big river and the swamps, but the dragonmancers' map was all question marks and tree doodles and "here be dragons" beyond that.

"Maybe we could go to the Indestructible City and steal a map," she said to Sky in her own language, which she was starting to call Human in her head. "I don't want to talk to anyone. But if we could get in and out without being noticed . . ." *I could steal something to read, too!* On the other hand, the Indestructible City was the most well-fortified human settlement in the world. So, maybe not the *best* place to try to rob.

"Rrrrrbllrrp?" Sky said, which she thought meant something like "What these words mean?"

She hopped off the boulder and found a stick she could use to scrawl in the dirt. Carefully she drew the vague shape of the continent, with a little palace up near the top (she was pretty sure that's where Sky had come from) and a small dot for her own village, plus rivers and mountains and the big desert to the west. She circled the whole thing and tapped it. "Map. Map? Map in Dragon?"

He nodded wisely and made a sound, which she imitated until she could remember it. She hoped this was the right word for *map* and that it didn't mean *drawing* or *scribble* or *you're such a weird little human, Wren*. Sometimes she wasn't entirely sure Sky even knew the words she was asking about. He was so tiny when she found him; he might have been thrown away by his parents before he learned about maps.

But he always acted very confident about whatever word he was teaching her, so she went along with it. At least he seemed to understand her — and she couldn't exactly stroll up to another dragon and check.

"Need map," she said in Dragon.

Sky shrugged and gave her a toothy grin. "Happy us," he answered.

She grinned back. "Yes, happy us." In Human she added, "But it would be useful to know where we can go without being eaten, or to find a safe place where we could live. Don't get me wrong — I love strange places because they're far away from my family and those rat-faced dragonmancers. But every strange place could be hiding a danger we don't even know about, and I want to keep you safe."

"Safe," Sky repeated in Dragon, nodding sagely.

"Well," Wren said, regarding her sketchy map. "I guess we can at least try heading toward the Indestructible City. If it looks too alarming, we can go right past it."

That night, as they made their way over a large rocky plateau, Sky nudged Wren and pointed to their left. A faint orange light was coming from behind one of the boulders.

Wren dropped to the ground, making herself as small as she could. Sky did the same beside her.

They listened for a long, still moment, waiting to see if the light moved. It didn't, but Wren thought she heard distant growls. She glanced at Sky and saw his ears pricked toward the sound.

"We run away," she whispered in Dragon.

He shook his head. "Want to see."

He almost never argued with her, especially about which direction to go or how fast. So she nodded and followed him as they crawled quietly toward the light.

It turned out to be coming from a hole in the rocks, along with a thin wisp of smoke. There must be a cave underneath them, Wren realized, and someone down there had built a fire.

Sky wriggled to the edge and peeked over, blinking as smoke wafted into his face. Wren stretched out on her stomach next to him.

There were dragons down below.

Could be worse, Wren thought, propping her chin on her hands. *Could be humans.*

She counted four small dragons galloping around the cave, chirping and rawring and wrestling one another. Another was curled on an outcropping, holding something in his claws. Something that rustled and rolled like paper, which he had his snout buried in with a riveted expression.

Is he reading *that?* Wren thought with surprise. *Dragons can read?*

Sky was probably too little to have learned to read Dragon before she found him. She wondered if she could teach him to read her language.

Hang on, she thought. *All of those dragons are different colors*. She squinted. The firelight and the fuzz of smoke made it difficult to tell at first, but she was pretty sure she could see five different sets of scales — yellow, blue, green, black, and brown. The only one that was familiar was the brown, which matched the mahogany scales they'd seen on some of the swamp dragons.

None of them were red or orange, like the dragons Wren was used to seeing. In the last year, she'd occasionally seen a few white ones flying overhead, and some that were a pale yellowish white, but neither of those were down there either.

Are there really that many different kinds of dragon?

And how can they all be together without killing each other?

She'd thought the red dragons and the brown dragons were enemies. She'd assumed all the dragons fought with any others who looked different from them.

But maybe they're actually friends. The baby dragons in the cave all looked happy enough to be together — even the black one, who kept making remarks in a scolding tone from his perch on the wall. *Maybe dragons are better at getting along with each other than people are.*

This fit nicely with her current Theory of the World, which was that dragons were better than people in every way, full stop.

She glanced at Sky and saw the saddest look she'd ever

seen on a baby dragon. It made her want to cuddle him and surround him with bunnies and snails.

"What's wrong?" she whispered in Dragon.

He pointed to the biggest baby dragon, the brown one. It was playing with the others, but every now and then it would stop to go back to the fire and breathe a few more flames on it, making sure it stayed alight.

The little yellow dragon bounded up beside him and did the same, adding her tiny flames to his. The brown dragon nudged her side and accidentally knocked her over, then looked comically alarmed when she bounced up and jumped on him.

Immediately the blue dragonet ran over and leaped on top of both of them, and they rolled for a while, yipping and roaring. A year ago, Wren would have thought those were roars of fury and that they might tear each other apart. But now she recognized the sounds Sky made sometimes. The little dragons were laughing.

Wren didn't know the word in Dragon for *lonely*. She didn't know how to ask whether Sky wished he had dragon friends like that instead of her. She did know she didn't like the feeling she had at that thought, as though something had bitten a large chunk out of her heart.

"You want to go there?" she asked awkwardly, pointing down into the cave. She didn't know how to get him there; the hole for the smoke was too small even for a tiny dragon to fit through. But she'd help him search for another way in, if that was what he wanted. There must be an entrance to the cave somewhere nearby . . . and if Sky needed dragon friends, she'd help him find some, no matter how long it took.

He gave her a puzzled expression. "Me there?"

"Need dragons?" she tried. "Happy yum friends?" *Yum* was obviously not the right word for this question, but it was the closest she could think of to *something you love and want and are excited about.*

Sky wrinkled his snout and made a little snort-chortling sound. "Eat dragons no thank you," he said.

She tried one more time. "Happy us," she said. "More happy you them?"

To her surprise, tears suddenly appeared in his eyes. He leaned his long neck over and buried his face in her hair at the curve of her shoulder. "No no no," he mumbled. "More more more happy you me us all the days."

Wren's heart swelled. She slung one arm around his neck and hugged him closer. "Are you sure?" she whispered in her own language. "You want to stay with me instead of joining other dragons like you?"

However much of that he understood, he nodded fiercely.

"Happy me," she whispered in Dragon.

A louder growling came from below them, and a full-grown red dragon suddenly swept into the cave. She knocked the wrestling dragonets to the side and roared something at them as they scurried back against the walls. Wren saw the little emerald dragon sidle into a nook where she'd be out of the red dragon's line of sight.

Sky gasped, a faint breath of air against Wren's cheek. He wiggled closer and stared at the red dragon.

Wren wouldn't have recognized her, except that Sky started trembling like a leaf, exactly the way he'd trembled the first day she held him, and she'd never forget that.

The red dragon in the sky, searching the river . . .

Could this be the same one? Wren waited until she turned her head — and yes, there was the burn scar she'd seen before, dark against the red scales.

"Who is that?" she whispered to Sky. The closest she could come in Dragon was, "What called this?"

He mumbled something back that she didn't understand, but she didn't need words to see that he was still scared of the red dragon.

"Let's go," she said, crawling back from the hole. She stood up and lifted Sky into her arms, although he was getting too big and heavy for that. "You're safe with me. Safe us."

Sky snuggled into her arms and took a deep breath, in and out. "Safe us."

Wren kept walking for the rest of the night, long after Sky fell asleep on her shoulder, putting as much distance as she could between them and the mysterious cave of multicolored dragons. Whatever they were doing down there, and how all those different kinds of dragons had ended up together, she didn't need to know. It had nothing to do with her.

All Sky needed was her, and all she needed was Sky.

As the golden line of the sunrise appeared over the ridge to the east, Wren remembered the little dragons breathing flames on the fire. Those dragons had been a lot smaller than Sky. But they'd had no trouble breathing fire.

It's not a dragon thing, she realized. *It's a Sky thing.*

He doesn't have any fire. He's supposed to, but for some reason, he doesn't.

He wasn't sad about not having dragon friends — he was sad that he can't breathe flames like that.

I bet that's why the red dragon threw him away. The mountain tribe didn't want a baby dragon with no fire. She was probably searching the river to make sure he'd really drowned.

Poor little Sky.

"I'd love you with or without fire," she whispered to his snoring snout. "You're perfect just the way you are. Even if you are weirdly obsessed with snails."

His eyes popped open and he blinked at her.

"Snails?" he chirped hopefully.

CHAPTER 5

LEAF

Leaf would not have guessed that his second-favorite sister would turn out to be Rowan. She was the oldest, and she usually ignored her five — now four — little siblings as though they were ants running about underfoot. She much preferred to be off with her friend Grove, hunting or fishing and talking about whatever teenagers talked about.

But one day when he was nine, after he'd asked her to tell him the Dragonslayer story for the four hundredth time, he came out of school and found her leaning against the school-house wall, holding a thick book.

"Rowan," the teacher said, eyeing the book suspiciously. "That's an unusual accessory for you."

Or for anyone in our family, Leaf thought sadly, *except Wren*.

"I'm going to help Leaf study," Rowan said, with an air of innocence that struck Leaf as far more ominous than anything else. The teacher didn't seem to notice, though. "Mother and Father think he could be chosen to be a dragonmancer's apprentice. So naturally I want to help prepare him."

Behind the teacher's back, Leaf raised his eyebrows at her, but she kept her gaze on the teacher and didn't crack.

"Hmmm. I'm not sure *your* level of scholarship would be any use to him," the teacher said snippily. "But if your parents are fine with it, I don't suppose I care." She turned and regarded Leaf for a moment. "Of course . . . if you *are* chosen to be a dragonmancer, dear boy, I hope you'll remember your *real* teacher fondly."

She swept away down the path, leaving Rowan and Leaf alone. Rowan burst into giggles as soon as she was out of earshot.

"Old toad," she said. "Bet you she'll be a lot nicer to you from now on, just in case you do end up a dragonmancer."

"Thanks," Leaf said, slightly awed by the sight of a grown-up being expertly manipulated by a sixteen-year-old. "Are you really here to help me study?"

"Yes," she said, "but not this boring stuff." She dropped the book in her bag and beckoned him around to the back of the schoolhouse and then into the woods, weaving through the trees until the village buildings were out of sight. In a small clearing, she tossed her bag at the foot of a tree and scrambled into its upper branches. A moment later, two wooden swords fell with a clatter onto the grass.

"Oh!" Leaf said, wide-eyed. "What? Really?"

Rowan swung down out of the tree and put her fists on her hips, grinning. "Well, if you're really going to slay a dragon one day, you'll *probably* need to practice a little first."

"You're going to teach me to fight?" he cried.

"I'm going to train you to be a great warrior," she said, "but *only* if you promise not to tell Mother and Father. As far as they know, we're studying for the dragonmancer exams."

"But then . . . won't I have to *take* the dragonmancer exams?"

A sly look flitted across Rowan's face. "Well, sure, but you won't actually pass them, don't worry. Hardly anyone does. They've had only six apprentices in the last ten years, remember? And I'm not sure they're learning anything besides how to fetch and carry and make goat cheese. The ones who've survived, that is."

Leaf picked up one of the wooden swords and slashed it through the air. "But *I'm* going to learn to be a great warrior. Hah! Hiyah!"

"Rule number one," Rowan said, eyeing him skeptically. "Don't shout like a maniac and warn the dragon you're about to attack. I mean, seriously."

From then on, they went into the forest and trained every day after school. It was hard work, nowhere near as fun as following Wren around and listening to her notice things and complain about the village. But it made Leaf feel like he was *doing* something, or at least, *getting ready* to do something — something Wren would be proud of him for, if she were still here.

And it helped him discover that Rowan was way more interesting than he'd expected.

For one thing, she knew a *lot* about dragons.

"We think there are six or seven different kinds," she said one day, parrying his thrust.

"What?" he said, stumbling back. "There's more than one kind? I thought they were all the same."

"Leaf, seriously. Haven't you noticed the difference between the swamp dragons and the mountain dragons? Their faces are different, their scales are different — Grove says even their dens and castles are different, according to what he learned in the Indestructible City."

"You said six or seven — what else is there besides the swamp kind and the mountain kind?"

"There are desert dragons, like the one the Dragonslayer killed. Arctic dragons, apparently, who live in the ice and snow. And ocean dragons who live under the sea, we're pretty sure."

He shuddered. He'd only seen the ocean from a distance, from the top of a mountain — but he did *not* like the idea of dragons lurking underwater. The same hungry threat coming from above and below at once was too creepy to think about.

"And maybe one or two more," Rowan went on, spinning into another attack so he had to dodge away. "Grove swears he once saw a totally black dragon, but I've never heard anyone else mention them. Plus there are parts of the continent where no one's ever been, so there could be other dragons there."

"I wonder if any of them are easier to fight than the others," Leaf said. "But we're closest to the mountain dragons, right? The red and orange ones. Those are the ones I have to slay to protect the village — the ones who ate Wren." He jabbed his wooden sword toward Rowan, and she easily knocked it away into the bushes.

He harrumphed and went to retrieve it. When he came back, Rowan handed him a blueberry the size of his fist; she had one for herself as well.

Leaf sat on the grass, holding the berry in his hands and remembering blueberry expeditions with his little sister. She'd make him laugh with imitations of the stuffy dragon-mancers, and he'd challenge her to tree-climbing races so he could win, and then she'd get furiously angry and throw all her blueberries at him and scream, and then he'd fake apologize, and then she'd get even more furious, and then ten minutes later they'd be swimming in the lake and laughing again, and then the next day, after he'd forgotten all about the fight, he'd climb into his bed and discover she'd filled it with squashed blueberries.

He sighed. "I miss Wren."

Rowan gave him an odd, searching look. "Do you think you would hate dragons so much if they hadn't taken her?" she asked. "I mean . . . like if it turned out it was someone else's fault?"

"How could it be?" Leaf asked. He thought for a moment. "You mean, like if someone pushed her off a cliff, and then the dragons found her and ate her?"

"Yes," Rowan said carefully. "Something like that."

"Then no," said Leaf. "I would hate that person instead.

But I think I'd still have to slay the dragons to make sure it didn't happen to anyone else. Right?" He traced one finger along the flat of his sword. "Don't tell anyone, but I a little bit hate the dragonmancers for not seeing the dragon coming that day. They're *always* telling us to hide in the shelters, or when to avoid the forest, or that we need to spend an entire day gathering some particular fruit as tribute for the dragons. All they *do* is have visions about the dragons. But on the most important day, when it's the most important person . . ." He trailed off, swiping at his eyes.

Rowan nudged his shoulder with her knee. He knew that was the closest she ever came to physical affection or sympathy. It helped the tiniest bit.

"But Mom and Dad say it's not their fault," Leaf said. "I guess they told everyone to avoid the river that morning, and Wren went anyway." Disobeying the dragonmancers did sound like something Wren would do, but standing still out in the open long enough for a dragon to spot her and catch her . . . that didn't sound much like his little sister at all. She never stopped moving. She was quick and clever, and he would have thought she could roar dragons out of the sky with her own fury.

Furious — that's what he needed to be. There wasn't time for sad. He needed to train, to become strong and powerful, and then he needed to go slay the dragons who'd done this.

He finished his blueberry and jumped to his feet. "Let's go again."

Rowan came at him and he ducked under her arm. She

spun and whacked his shoulder with the flat of her wooden blade.

"Good move, but too slow," she said. "Try again."

They whirled and jabbed for a while in silence. Leaf's arms ached and he was pretty sure he'd have bruises all over his back tomorrow. But he refused to complain or ask for a break. Every bruise made him stronger, more ready to stand between the dragons and the children of Talisman.

Rowan whipped his sword out of his grip again, and this time he had to climb a tree to retrieve it. She turned in a slow circle, studying the clearing and the forest as if to make sure there was no one else nearby.

"Do you ever wonder whether the dragonmancers are hiding something?" she asked as he swung himself back down.

"Wren thought they were," he said. "She once said they were just grumpy old folks ordering everyone around."

"I think that might be what Grove thinks, too," Rowan said, glancing out at the trees again. "He keeps hinting at it, but because he's smarter than Wren, he won't say it directly."

"He's not smarter than Wren!" Leaf objected. "I mean. He's OLDER than Wren. So he KNOWS more things. But that's not the same."

A flash of pity crossed Rowan's face, and Leaf knew why. He couldn't stop talking about Wren in the present tense, even seasons after losing her.

"You know what, you *should* become a dragonmancer apprentice, if they'll take you," she said.

"No way!" Leaf said. "I want to keep learning how to stab

dragons, not be locked up in a hut with some musty paper and even mustier old people teaching me how to bow and scrape."

"But that's not all you'd learn," Rowan said. "You could find out all their secrets!"

"I don't *want* to be a dragonmancer," Leaf protested.

"You wouldn't have to be," she said. "Get in there, put your head down and pretend, and learn everything they know — like what happened to most of their apprentices, and how do their visions work, and why have they forbidden anyone to go try to steal treasure? And then tell me everything, and we'll use their knowledge to go kill all the dragons!"

"YES!" Leaf cried. "Wait, no. This is a trick. How much studying are we talking about? Like, *years* stuck inside with those grouches? Aaaaaargh. Can't you do it?"

"I tried, actually," Rowan said, looking down and whacking the nearest bush with her sword. "Last year. They said I failed the tests. But I have a theory it's not about the test scores — it's about who they trust."

"Why wouldn't they trust you?" Leaf asked.

Rowan made a weird, wry, inscrutable smile face. "Maybe I already know a little too much," she said. "Anyway, they seem to like you. I bet you could do it."

"Yyyyyyyyyyyyyyyyyyyyyuck," Leaf said firmly. "No, THANK you."

Rowan suddenly tensed. Leaf froze in place. They both tilted their heads, listening.

The warning bell was ringing.

Which meant dragons were coming.

"Quick," Rowan shouted, grabbing his hand and running toward the village. Leaf realized they were still clutching their swords; there was no time to hide them. He knew his child-sized wooden sword would be less than useless against a dragon, but somehow the weight of it in his hand made him feel a little safer.

They pelted through the forest, branches whipping at their faces. The bell pealed on and on desperately. The bell towers were built a ways up the mountain, deliberately far so the sound wouldn't draw the dragons to their village. Leaf imagined the apprentice out there pulling on the rope, knowing he or she had to stay with the bell instead of racing to a shelter like everyone else.

He didn't think it was much of a mystery why the dragonmancers' apprentices rarely survived very long.

No, Rowan, he definitely did *not* want to be one of them.

He wondered if this one had been sent to the bells because of a vision, or whether actual dragons had been spotted. Despite his conversation with Rowan, despite his frequent doubts, he still wasn't quite willing to risk his life testing the theory that the dragonmancers were lying.

They burst out of the forest behind the schoolhouse and saw someone running up the road toward them. At first glance, Leaf guessed it must be one of his parents — but as the figure came closer, he realized it was Grove.

That's weird, he thought. *Grove came looking for us . . . well, for Rowan . . . but Mom and Dad didn't.*

They must be in the closest shelter to home. They had three other kids to protect, after all. They must trust Rowan and Leaf to get to safety on their own.

But it still wasn't the greatest feeling.

"Grove!" Rowan cried. Leaf never saw her face light up that way for anyone else.

"Oh, thank the moons," Grove called, looking enormously relieved. "I wasn't sure you'd hear the bell out there." He paused by the schoolhouse, trying to catch his breath.

Rowan tugged open the trapdoor that led to the schoolhouse shelter. That was where all the kids had to go whenever the alarm rang during the school day. Leaf had done it often enough just in the last year that he knew how many steps led down to the hollow below and exactly where the candles were, even in the dark.

He wished they could hide in the schoolhouse instead. It was supposedly camouflaged from the air — hidden by trees and roofed with leafy branches — but there was still a fair chance a dragon would set it on fire one day.

Leaf was about to follow Rowan and Grove into the shelter when he heard a sound from inside the schoolhouse.

"Leaf!" Rowan called. "Come on, hurry!"

"Wait —" he said. "I'll be right there." He tossed her his sword and darted up the back steps into the school.

Someone was huddled under one of the desks, crying.

Someone small, with thin shoulders. Too small to be Wren, and Wren never cried, but still, for a moment, Leaf felt his heart try to reach out and catch her.

He crouched beside the desk and recognized the child. It was Butterfly, the teacher's youngest son — Leaf thought he was about four years old.

"Hey," Leaf said softly. "Don't be scared."

"Don't be SCARED?!" Butterfly yelped, raising a tear-streaked face to glare at Leaf. "Dragons are coming to EAT ME!"

"Pffft," Leaf scoffed. "You're too scrawny. They wouldn't like you. I bet you taste like chicken feet."

"No, I don't!" Butterfly looked outraged now. "Mommy says I'd be the most delicious thing they ever eated! They want to eat me so much they fly here looking for me all the time!"

Who would SAY that to a four-year-old? Leaf wondered, and then remembered that his parents said stuff like that all the time.

"That is completely stupid," Leaf said. "Is there one super-delicious rabbit in the woods that we're all looking for when we go hunting?"

"Um." Butterfly blinked a few times. "I don't know! Is there?"

"No! We catch whatever rabbits we can, silly. Same with dragons. They eat whatever they can get. They're not hunting for *you* especially."

"Mmmmmmmaybe . . ." Butterfly said skeptically. "But they *are* scary."

"I guess," Leaf said, waving one hand. "You don't have to be *super* scared of them, though. Be smart scared instead."

"Smart scared?"

"Like, it's a good idea to hide from them, especially when you're little. But is this the best, smartest hiding spot?"

"I don't know." Butterfly rubbed his grubby face. "I came looking for Mommy."

"No, it isn't. The best hiding place is in a shelter, with a big strong warrior like me guarding the door."

Butterfly laughed. "You're not that big and strong."

"Bigger than you," Leaf said. "I bet I could carry you on my back all the way outside."

"Outside?" Butterfly said warily.

"AND down into the shelter," Leaf said. "WHILE singing about dragons."

"I like songs," Butterfly said, scrambling to his feet. Leaf turned around and let the four-year-old climb onto his back. He was heavy, but Leaf managed to stand up and head for the door.

"*Oh, dragons are totally stupid! And dragons are totally bad!*" he sang off the top of his head. Butterfly giggled.

"*The way they keep eating our . . . goats . . . it makes me so terribly mad!*"

"You have a very bad voice," Butterfly said, snuggling his face into Leaf's neck.

"*Whenever I see a dragon, I want to shout, 'Go away!' But since I'm polite, and never start fights, I just hide for the rest of the day!*"

His ridiculous song had gotten them across the school-yard to the shelter steps. The warning bell was still clanging ferociously in the distance, and the treetops were stirring as if the wind — or dragon wings — were rising.

Rowan was standing a few steps down, waiting for them. She lifted Butterfly off Leaf's back and carried him into the shelter. Leaf glanced around for a moment, making sure no one else was coming. Then he closed the trapdoor, and Grove lit one candle, and they were safe in the semi-dark.

Hopefully safe. More or less safe. Leaf had heard of other shelters caving in, or of fires set close by that smoked out the people hiding so they were caught. But those stories were few and far between — and this was a good shelter, sturdily built by the whole village to protect the schoolchildren, stocked with pallets to sleep on and barrels of water in case they were trapped down there for long.

It was also quite large, too big for just the four of them. He swung his sword in the open space, then stopped quickly, glancing at Grove.

"He knows what we're doing," Rowan said. "Don't worry. He thinks it's great."

"Yeah. The world needs more dragonslayers," Grove said with his charming grin. "Wish I didn't have to work so I could join you." He sat at the bottom of the stairs, leaning against the dirt wall, his long legs stretched out in front of him. Butterfly promptly sat down in his lap and curled up, as though no one could possibly mind his dazzling four-year-old presence on their knees. Grove chuckled and patted Butterfly on the back.

Leaf understood why Rowan liked Grove. Grove was different, and that's what she'd always wanted. He even looked a bit different from the other village boys; his eyes were narrower, his hair was a long, shaggy dark mop instead of close-cut, and his clothes were dyed dangerous colors like orange. Mostly, though, he carried himself like someone who'd Seen the World and Knew Things.

Grove was the only person near their age who had traveled beyond their village. He and his father had arrived in Talisman two years earlier, looking for a place to settle after their own village, farther south, had been burned to the ground by dragons. That fire was how Grove had gotten the burn scars on his hands and face. Whatever other family they'd lost, neither of them ever talked about it.

That much Leaf knew from Rowan's stories. But she usually never let her little brother or sisters get anywhere near Grove. Apparently they were "embarrassing," although Leaf had no idea what she could possibly mean by that.

"Hey, Grove, have you really been to the Indestructible City?" he asked. Rowan sighed theatrically and slid down the wall to sit beside Grove. Butterfly stuck out his feet to rest them on her.

"Of course I have," Grove said. "It's massive. And it's never been burned. We figured for sure it'd be the safest place to live."

"Isn't it?" Leaf asked. "Why didn't you stay?"

Grove thought for a moment, tilting his head toward Rowan. "It's . . . hard to get in, and then . . . it's not as safe as it sounds. I mean, it's safe from dragons, but . . ." He trailed off.

"But what?" Leaf pressed. "What else is there? Bears? Wildcats? Do they have a spider problem?" Wren had really hated spiders.

"No," Grove said, looking amused. "More of a human problem."

Leaf swished his sword, practicing his footwork. "Really? Do people attack them?"

"No, that would be impossible. More like . . ." Grove glanced at Rowan. "I mean, it's the people *inside* the city that are the problem."

"Don't give the children nightmares," Rowan said with a yawn.

"I'm not children! I won't get nightmares! And Butterfly is practically asleep already. Tell me!" Leaf yelped.

Grove glanced at Rowan again, and she shrugged.

"All right," Grove said slowly. "Do you know anything about the Invincible Lord?" Leaf shook his head. "He runs the Indestructible City right now. His family always has, but this lord is different from the ones who came before. He has all these ideas about who is useful and who isn't, and what he can use everyone for. He has plans to expand beyond the city, risky plans, and he'll do anything to make them happen. To him, everyone's expendable."

"I heard he wanted to hire the Dragonslayer," Rowan interjected.

"Really?" Leaf thought about that — the power of the Indestructible City combined with the might of the Dragonslayer. They could take on the dragons together! Maybe they could save the whole world!

"The rumor says he's been trying to get the Dragonslayer to come to the city for years," Grove agreed. "But I think 'hire' might be the gentlest way of putting it."

"What?" Leaf glanced from Grove's face to Rowan's, but he didn't understand the expressions they were making.

Grove shrugged. "I wouldn't trust him if *I* were the Dragonslayer. Besides, kid, the IC has a *lot* of rules. Everyone's mad strict and scary. Not my kind of place. So when my dad heard about the legendary 'magically protected' village of the dragonmancers, he decided that would be better for us."

"Doesn't everyone have dragonmancers?" Leaf asked, and at the same time Rowan snorted, "You came *looking* for dragonmancers?"

"Most places don't," Grove answered Leaf. "My village didn't; the Indestructible City doesn't. Talisman is special. Apparently."

"I'd choose a stone city with dragon-fighting catapults over a mountain scrap heap guarded by three old lunatics any day," Rowan scoffed.

"Not this stone city," Grove said. "You wouldn't like it there either." He tipped up her chin. "We'll make our own. We'll steal a castle from the dragons and live there."

"Ooooo," Leaf breathed.

"I wanna castle," Butterfly mumbled sleepily.

"A dragon-sized castle would be extremely stupid for us," Rowan said with a laugh. "At least until we learn how to fly or quadruple our height."

"I'll help you steal it!" Leaf said. "Any day! I'll be ready to fight dragons soon, right, Rowan?"

"Maybe if you spend more time practicing and less time making up songs for grubby children," Rowan said, gingerly lifting Butterfly's feet off her lap.

Grove laughed, and Rowan stood up to continue their swordfighting lesson in the flickering candlelight.

They might have been joking, but Leaf wasn't.

One day, kids like Butterfly wouldn't have to be terrified all the time. One day, Leaf wouldn't be hiding in a musty shelter while the dragons soared overhead.

One day, the dragons would be hiding from *him*.

CHAPTER 6

IVY

Ivy heard her mother coming and slid her papers under the book she was pretending to read. She didn't think she would get in *trouble*, exactly, for drawing dragons all the time, but she knew her parents didn't love it. "Why can't you spend your time on something more useful?" and "What a waste of paper" were two of the comments she'd gotten so far when she'd tried to share her drawings with them.

Mother poked her head around the door. "Those girls are here again," she said disapprovingly. "But I can tell them you're studying."

"No, no! I'm all done with my homework," Ivy said truthfully. "Please let them stay."

Her mother sighed and went back out to their front room, where Ivy could now hear Violet and Daffodil arguing with each other. The Truth Seekers club had lasted, against all the odds, over a year now. Despite all their fighting, Violet and Daffodil were fiercely loyal — to each other, to the idea of their secret club, and, it turned out, to Ivy as well.

Daffodil tumbled into the room first, flinging herself into Ivy's hammock so it swung back and forth. Her yellow ribbons were crooked, and she looked like she'd just been running from one end of Valor to the other, although she kind of always looked like that.

"Oh my stars, hi," Daffodil burst out. "I have been so busy today, you can't even imagine. The Wingwatchers are having a big meeting tonight and I was trying to figure out how to sneak in but it's almost impossible except I think maybe I found a secret tunnel into the cavern that I *might* be able to fit through if I cover myself in butter and hold my breath and don't eat anything for the rest of the day."

"Do you have any snacks?" Violet asked innocently, coming through the doorway.

"I have carrot slices and nectarines," Ivy said. She slid the bowl over as Violet folded herself neatly onto the floor beside her.

"Aaaargh, you're both so mean!" Daffodil said, lunging out of the hammock to grab a piece of nectarine.

"You can't sneak into that meeting anyway," Violet pointed out. "That tunnel is way too small, and even if you fit through it, they'll definitely notice you huffing and puffing and smelling like butter. Plus the meeting is after bedtime, and your parents are way strict about bedtime."

"And Daisy would probably tell on me if I snuck out," Daffodil grumbled, narrowing her eyes.

"Besides," Ivy added, "if you spy on a Wingwatchers

meeting, they might not let you become a Wingwatcher one day, and that would be super sad."

Violet raised her eyebrows. "Wait. Do you want to be a Wingwatcher?"

Ivy glanced down at the curling tail on the drawing poking out from under her book. "Maybe," she said. "I mean . . . they know so much about dragons."

Violet leaned over and slid the drawing out so she could look at it. "Whoa, cool," she said. She held it up for Daffodil to see.

"You're getting so good at those!" Daffodil cried. "Which kind is that?"

"The sea dragon," Ivy said. "I think the face looks a bit too horsey. The wings are always fun to draw, but the legs are SO hard."

Violet picked up the book to squint at the real drawing, then back at Ivy's. "Well," she said loyally, "maybe yours is what they really look like. It's not like anyone around here has ever studied one up close, so how would we know? I like yours better."

"Me too!" Daffodil said quickly.

"You didn't even look at the book drawing," Violet pointed out. "You're just saying that because I said that."

"No!" Daffodil objected. "I'm saying that because I like Ivy and I know everything she does is the most awesome, so there!"

Violet rolled her eyes. "Well, *I'm* saying it because I *mean* it."

"Hopefully I'll see one someday," Ivy interjected hurriedly. "And then I'll know what they really look like and be able to draw them even better."

"You are literally the only person I know who *wants* to see a dragon," Violet said.

"That's not true!" Daffodil said. "I want to see a dragon!"

"But, like, you only want to see one so that you can tell everyone you saw it. You're looking for another crazy Daffodil adventure story. Ivy wants to see one because she's actually really interested in them."

"It doesn't matter, though," Ivy said. "We can't start Wingwatcher training until we're twelve at the earliest." Four more years until she'd be allowed to train, then another year after that before her first possible mission outside. She had to wait five *years* to see a dragon, even though she lived in a world full of them.

"Well," Violet said, glancing at Daffodil. "How about a Truth Seeker mission instead?"

Daffodil flailed her way out of the hammock and peeked out the door. "Coast is clear," she whispered, staying where she was to keep watch for eavesdroppers — or, more specifically, Ivy's mom.

Violet tugged a scroll out of her satchel and unrolled a drawing that turned out to be a scribbly map. Ivy lay down on her stomach next to her and studied it. She'd seen maps kind of like this in the Wingwatcher's Guide, but this one had a few details she didn't remember seeing before.

"Did you take this from school?" Ivy asked, tracing one

of the rivers with her finger. Their year didn't study geography yet, but the older kids did.

"I snuck in and copied it from the teacher's scroll," Violet said. "That's why it's a little wobbly. So how long do you think it would take to get from here to here?" She jabbed her finger at one section of the mountains and then another section farther north.

"Um," Ivy said, scrunching up her forehead. "All morning?"

"Ivy!" Violet said, giggling. "Way longer than that! Days and days and days!"

"Oh," Ivy said with a shrug. "What's that little drawing up there near the top of the mountains?"

"That's the mountain dragons' palace," Violet said. "I mean, that's what this mapmaker thinks it looks like anyway."

Ivy's heart went *thump* and *skip* and started fluttering weirdly in her chest. "They have a palace?" she said. "In the mountains?"

"Of course they do," Violet said. "Like the one the sand dragons have in the desert that your dad snuck into."

Ivy couldn't quite explain the feeling she was having, of wanting to see something *so badly* and knowing she'd never ever be allowed to. What did a dragon palace look like? Was it beautiful? Did it have rooms for different things — an eating hall, a throne room, a *library*? How could dragons be vicious wild animals, the way her dad described them, but also have castles where they lived together and queens who ruled over them? How did a wild animal obey a queen or build a castle?

She wished she could ask her father about the palace in the desert, but his dragonslaying story was always the same: lots of gory killing, very vague on the details around it. He never talked about sneaking inside or how he carried out the treasure or what any of the dragon stuff looked like.

Maybe Uncle Stone would tell me . . . if I could get him to talk about that night at all.

Ivy's uncle had never married, and although he was supposedly as rich as the Dragonslayer, he was never seen spending his treasure. He lived alone in the smallest cave in the underground city. Sometimes he came over for dinner and spent the entire evening staring glumly into his soup. Ivy found him a little unsettling and way too quiet, except every once in a while when he yelled at her dad and was way too loud.

"So . . . you know how your dad was away for a few days?" Violet asked, studying Ivy's face.

Ivy nodded. Her mother had fluttered around the caves in a state of nervous disarray the entire time he was gone. It had been rather exhausting. "He took my favorite horse," she said. "I was worried he wouldn't bring her back."

"Do you know where he went?" Daffodil asked from the door.

Ivy thought for a moment, but she couldn't remember being told. "I thought it was a regular gathering expedition," she said. Although, come to think of it, there had been a lot of noise around him coming back this time. A few more men shouting "Heath the Hero!" or "Hurrah for the Dragonslayer!" — their voices echoing through the tunnels and filling up the great hall.

"He says he went to this palace," Violet said, tapping the little drawing of a castle way up north in the mountains. "He was gone for three days, and when he came back, he told everyone he rode up to the gates of the mountain dragons' palace and shouted at them to come out and fight, but none of them would because they're scared of him."

"Why would he do that?" Ivy said incredulously. "Last time he only fought one dragon — what if a whole bunch had come out to fight him? He would have been eaten up SO FAST."

"*I* want to know how the dragons knew who he was," Daffodil demanded. "I mean, did all those dragons actually think, 'Oh no! It's the Dragonslayer! Everybody hide!'? *Seriously*? Because how? Did the sand dragons describe him to the mountain dragons? Or draw them a picture? Aren't we totally miniature to them? Can they even tell us apart?"

"Those are great questions," Ivy said. Her dad had always acted as if, of course, everyone in the universe knew who he was, so she'd kind of assumed that included all the dragons. But really, did the dragons have any idea what he looked like?

Did they ever think about "the Dragonslayer" at all?

"Thank you," Daffodil said, looking delighted.

"No, they're not," Violet said. "Those questions are missing the whole point."

"Oh yeah, well, YOU'RE MISSING A WHOLE BRAIN," Daffodil shouted.

"Why, Violet? What's the real question?" Ivy asked quickly.

"Just look at this map!" Violet said. "He was gone *three days*. How could he possibly have gone all the way to this palace *and back* in just three days?"

Ivy stared at the map. She only sort of understood it — she knew the little triangles were mountains and the wiggly lines were rivers. She didn't quite know how far it really was to the top of the map; she only sort of knew where Valor was on it: somewhere in the wooded foothills at the southern part of the mountain range.

But she heard the urgency in Violet's voice and she felt a weird shivering in the universe. Was this another Dragonslayer lie? If it was such a big, obvious one, wouldn't lots of people have noticed it? Or if they had noticed it, why didn't they care?

"Is there any way?" she asked, putting her little finger on the palace and stretching her thumb toward Valor. "Maybe there was something magic in the treasure that makes him go really fast?"

Daffodil laughed. "Your dad *never* goes fast."

That was true. The Dragonslayer tended to dawdle, to stop and chat to anyone he saw, to sit down and eat whatever extra food was lying around.

"But maybe he did it somehow," Ivy said. "Or else where did he go for all that time?"

"THAT is an ACTUAL great question," Violet pounced. "We should find that out!"

"We totally should!" Daffodil agreed.

"Wait —" Ivy started.

"But how can we figure it out?" Daffodil asked, looking at Violet. "What do we do?"

"We follow him!" Violet said, her voice dropping to a thrilling whisper.

"Yessssss!" Daffodil agreed in a matching whisper.

"Oh, dear, oh no," Ivy said. "Following my dad? *Outside*? We definitely aren't allowed to do that."

"We aren't *allowed* to read my dads' law scrolls or steal books from the library either," Violet said, glancing pointedly at the *Wingwatcher's Guide* on Ivy's floor. "But we've done those things anyway. For truth! For justice!"

"So we can know more stuff than other people!" Daffodil cried, raising one of her fists in the air.

"No," Violet said, frowning. "This is not about beating other people at knowing stuff, Daffodil."

"Um, it totally is," Daffodil said. "You love being the person who knows the most things. I saw your face when you won the spelling contest!"

"I didn't *steal* that book," Ivy interjected, "by the way. I'll give it back. I'm just not . . . finished with it yet."

"Anyway, I have a plan, so everyone shush," Violet said.

And that was how, ten days later, Ivy found herself sneaking behind her father as he left the caves again.

She was technically supposed to tell Violet and Daffodil;

her instructions were to run and get them so they could all follow him together. But there wasn't time for that. He left the cave so suddenly, and Ivy was pretty sure the important part was following him. More important than getting the others. She thought. She hoped they wouldn't be mad about this. She'd have to remember every detail to tell them, to make up for going without them.

Heath sauntered through the tunnels, whistling. He didn't head toward their small stable of horses, so he couldn't be planning a long trip — and he hadn't made a glorious announcement to a gathered throng of worshippers before leaving either, so this wasn't one of his Dragonslayer Quests. He'd told Mother he was "going outside," and she'd simply told him to be careful — but he'd also taken a shoulder bag hidden under his shirt, and he avoided walking past Uncle Stone's door, so he was definitely Up To Something.

Ivy was good at not being noticed, and her father was exceptionally good at not noticing things, especially things he thought were unimportant, like little girls. She stayed several paces behind him, pressing herself against the wall whenever he stopped to chat with one of his followers.

She ran into a problem at the tunnel exit, though. Her father chose one of the exits with a ladder up to the sky, where a Wingwatcher stood guard at the bottom.

Ivy crouched behind a bench carved out of the rock. Her heart was pounding. She'd never been this close to this exit before — certainly never without permission. It smelled different here. She didn't think she was imagining that.

"Hello, Holly!" Heath boomed cheerfully as he approached the bottom of the ladder.

"It's Foxglove, sir," the Wingwatcher said. Ivy didn't know her very well, although Foxglove had left school only a couple of years ago to train with the Wingwatchers. Her hair was shaved into a close dark fuzz over her head and her forest-green uniform was neat and unwrinkled.

Most interestingly, Foxglove's expression was hard to read. It wasn't the usual adoring gaze Ivy's father got all over Valor. She looked calm, focused . . . unimpressed. Ivy smushed her face around, trying to imitate her. Violet and Daffodil would be so startled if Ivy could make a cool "I don't care" expression like that.

"Any dragon sightings today?" Heath asked, ignoring the name correction.

"No, sir."

"Too bad, too bad." He cracked his knuckles. "Can't wait to meet another dragon with the pointy end of this guy." He patted the sword at his waist with a grin.

Foxglove raised her eyebrows but said nothing.

"Well, I'll be back soon," Heath said. He put one hand on the ladder.

"Sir," Foxglove said. "I am required to ask what your purpose on the outside is. By your own decree, sir."

Heath frowned at her. "You are required to ask *other people*. I am THE DRAGONSLAYER and the lord of all of Valor."

"It was my understanding that the laws apply to everyone, sir," Foxglove said evenly.

Ivy held her breath. She knew that expression on her father's face; this moment on the edge right before he exploded with anger.

But instead he shifted from a glare to a smug grin as oily as Ivy's hands after the olive harvest came in.

"Very good, Holly," he said, wagging one finger at her. "I like to see my people following my laws. Where would we be without them, am I right?"

"It's Foxglove, sir," she said again.

"I am going outside to assess the status of the orchards," he said grandly. "Check up on the fruit harvesters. Lord business. Don't you worry about it."

Foxglove gave another slight nod, stepping back so he could climb up the ladder. He went without saying a word of farewell.

Ivy rubbed her temples, thinking. How could she get past Foxglove? No self-respecting Wingwatcher would ever let an eight-year-old climb outside on her own. Unless maybe she asked really nicely? Ivy was a big fan of asking nicely; she found that this nearly always worked, at least with grown-ups.

Foxglove was a teenager, though. That was a mysterious in-between kind of person who might do absolutely anything. They were *inexplicable*, Violet would often say wisely.

But she had to try, or her father would be too far out of sight in a minute.

Ivy jumped up from behind the bench and ran over to Foxglove. A wonderful moment of surprise flashed across the Wingwatcher's face before she went back to her very cool "nothing here is interesting" expression.

"I have to catch up with my dad!" Ivy said breathlessly. "Please let me go after him? I promised I'd give him something before he left and then I forgot and he'll be so mad if I don't give it to him! I promise I'll come right back." She smiled her "I love you the best of all my teachers" smile, which also usually worked.

"No way, kid," Foxglove said, not unkindly. "I can't let you out there alone."

"I won't be alone! I'll catch up to my dad. I'm really quick, I promise."

"What do you have to give him?" Foxglove asked.

"Um." Ivy panicked. She reached into her pockets, fumbling to see whether she had anything at all. "Just a . . . this . . . super important . . . um . . . potato." She held it out, utterly betrayed by pockets that were usually full of interesting rocks and scraps of nonsense. But two days ago, Mother had taken her pants to wash them and must have emptied out everything, so all she had was the potato she'd dug up in gardening class that morning.

Foxglove slowly raised one incredibly elegant eyebrow at her.

"It's really important," Ivy said. "This potato could change everything. I can't tell you anything else. It's top secret potato business."

"I see," said Foxglove. "Let me guess. We're going to take down the dragons with potatoes."

"Oh," Ivy said, startled. She had never thought of "taking down" dragons before, even though her dad was the Dragonslayer. She kind of thought of that as Dad's thing, but not something she'd ever want to do. "M-maybe we can use the potatoes to make friends with them instead."

Now there was a definite shift in Foxglove's face. Maybe something even a little bit like a smile.

"Have you ever been outside?" Foxglove asked. Ivy shook her head, and Foxglove crouched beside her. "Are you good at keeping secrets?"

Ivy thought about that for a moment. "Yes from Mother and Father," she said finally. "No from Violet."

"Hmmm," said Foxglove. "Is Violet good at keeping secrets?"

"The BEST," said Ivy. "It's VERY ANNOYING."

Foxglove laughed. She glanced around at the empty tunnels, then up at the sky-scented hole above them. "What if we just go . . . see what he's doing? Together? And if he looks busy, we won't even bother him."

"Yes," Ivy breathed, her eyes wide. "That would be *perfect*."

"All right. Let's go," Foxglove said, pointing up. She lifted Ivy onto the ladder, then climbed up right behind her, her strong arms ready to catch Ivy if she slipped, although of course she didn't because she was good at climbing.

Ivy crawled out of the hillside into an indescribably vast forest of trees, all of them something like eighty times her size (she guessed). The air smelled like apples and grass and it kept flying into her face and up her nose instead of staying still like the air in the underground city. It was also noisy; the whole outside was whooshy and sh-sh-shhhhmmy and crickle-crackly and a little buzzy, too, and SUPER BRIGHT, like, WHY WAS THERE SO MUCH LIGHT EVERYWHERE. Ivy sat down in the dirt and closed her eyes for a moment, listening to the whooshing and feeling the light try to burn off her face while the air tried to blow it out. It was a lot; there was a LOT HAPPENING.

"Foxglove, what are you doing?" said a young male voice nearby.

"Just taking Ivy to find her dad," Foxglove said, in one of those grown-up voices that was secretly saying something else. Ivy cracked an eye open and squinted up at her. The other Wingwatcher had his arms crossed, looking down at Ivy, but he didn't look mad. He had a "planning something" face that looked a lot like Violet's.

Hey, Ivy realized. *Foxglove knows my name! A very cool teenager knows my name!*

"But we might not find him," Foxglove said significantly. "So if he comes back without seeing us, no need to mention this."

"Right," said the other Wingwatcher. "I was looking for dragons in that direction anyway." He pointed at a spot of blue sky beyond the trees.

Blue sky! Ivy thought. She'd seen it through holes in the

ceilings of a few caves, but it was so much bigger and bluer out here. *Try to remember it better than that. Daffodil isn't going to settle for "bigger and bluer."*

"Ready to walk?" Foxglove asked Ivy. Ivy scrambled to her feet and took Foxglove's hand. They edged down the sloping hill, between towering craggy trees on a carpet of pine needles.

At the bottom of the hill, Ivy started seeing more and more fruit trees — apple and pear and peach, with berry bushes tangled between them. She slowed to match Foxglove's cautious, quiet pace, and then stopped completely when Foxglove froze and squeezed her hand.

Up ahead, Heath was sauntering through the trees, holding a half-eaten apple nearly the size of his head in his hand. He glanced right and left as he went, on higher alert than he had been in the caves.

Foxglove tugged Ivy behind a tree. "Where is he going?" she whispered.

"I don't know," Ivy answered. He'd had a bag, but he wasn't using it to carry apples. What else could he be going to get? "He just said 'outside.'"

The Wingwatcher peeked around the tree at him. "The old village is in that direction," she whispered.

"But — the law," Ivy said. "I mean, didn't Pine . . . he can't . . ." She trailed off, surprised by the suddenly grim expression on Foxglove's face. Foxglove was staring after Heath, looking very much like maybe he was her least favorite person.

"That's right, Ivy," she said. "He *can't* go there. At least, if the law is fair and applies to everyone." Foxglove's fingers twitched on the hilt of her dagger.

"So he probably isn't," Ivy said. "Maybe he's going to get pears for Mother. He'll be back soon, right?"

Foxglove looked down at her, and the frown slowly cleared from her forehead. She opened her mouth, maybe to say something reassuring, but she was interrupted by an unearthly sound from the sky.

It was like an avalanche, or a thousand giant tigers roaring at once, or thunder in a hurricane the size of the continent, or like something else enormous and terrifying that Ivy had never heard before. It gave her instant goose bumps and made her want to curl up like a hedgehog somewhere safe, preferably with Violet and Daffodil and a bunch of pointy swords.

Foxglove hissed an unfamiliar word ("that was CURSING," Violet informed her with a scandalized expression when Ivy asked about it later) and grabbed Ivy. Before the sound had finished echoing off the mountains, Foxglove had thrown Ivy halfway up the trunk of the nearest evergreen and was scrambling up behind her.

Move, legs, Ivy thought frantically. She forced herself to reach up and grab another branch, sticky with sap, and haul herself higher. A few moments later, she was about halfway up the tree when she felt Foxglove's hand on her ankle.

"Stop there," Foxglove whispered. "Stay completely still."

Ivy didn't have to be told twice. She clung to the trunk, tucking her legs in and imagining herself as a knot in the bark.

Small, brown, indistinguishable. Definitely inedible. She was glad she was wearing her old gray tunic and pants instead of the new dark purple ones her mother had made for her.

The dragon roared again, and now she heard a new sound — this one coming from below her. She squinted down without moving a muscle and saw her father racing through the trees. His eyes were wild and he'd dropped his apple. Ivy had never seen him move so fast. He ran as though the dragon were right behind him, breathing fire on his heels. She could hear his heavy, panicked breaths as he tore past.

But the dragon wasn't down there. It was up in the sky. Ivy could hear the wingbeats.

She couldn't resist. Carefully, slowly, she inched her head up and back until she could see the blue expanse beyond the thicket of branches.

A flash of black scales soared overhead — wings tilting, flickering tail, breath of flame on the air.

A dragon, a dragon, a dragon.

It swooped around again. This time she caught a glimpse of its face — not horsey at all, but perfect, long and elegant, with the most intelligent eyes. And the scales were more than black; they caught the sunlight in shimmers of dark purple and blue and green, and small diamond-white scales flashed under its wings.

The dragon roared once more, and then it lashed its tail and swept away west, toward the desert.

Another long moment passed before Ivy realized she'd been holding her breath, and she slowly let it out.

"Wow," she whispered.

She wanted to stay in the tree longer, remembering the dragon — maybe waiting to see if it came back — but before long she felt Foxglove tug gently on her ankle.

They descended quietly, and Foxglove reached up to help Ivy down from the last branch, which was way higher than Ivy would have been able to reach on her own.

"I guess that was your first Wingwatcher lesson, kid," Foxglove said. "If you hear a dragon, *hide*. Do *not* run. Dragons are *much* faster than you, but they won't usually bother with prey if it's in a sharp, sticky tree like this one, and if the branches are thick enough and you're motionless enough, it hopefully won't even see you." She glanced in the direction Heath had been running. "Only a coward or an idiot would run from a dragon."

Ivy was nearly startled out of her dragon daze. Was Foxglove talking about her father? The Dragonslayer wasn't a *coward*. That wasn't even *possible*.

He had been running awfully fast, though.

"You're so lucky," Foxglove said. "The black ones are the rarest. I can't believe you got to see one on your first time out! What did you think? Were you beyond scared?"

Ivy smiled at her. "It was the most amazing thing I've ever seen," she said. "I *loved* it."

"Loved it!" Foxglove echoed. "The dragon? Or the exciting-terrifying running-and-hiding part?"

"The dragon," Ivy said promptly. "I loved the dragon."

Foxglove raised her eyebrows again. "Well, I haven't

heard that before," she said. "I thought I was the only one who secretly thinks dragons are kind of great."

"You do?" Ivy breathed. "Do you get to see dragons every day?"

"Not *every* day, but that's basically our job," Foxglove said with a grin. "Watching the skies so everyone is safe. Studying the dragons so we can understand them as much as possible. We lost a lot of books and a few of the older watchers when the village burned, but we're trying to bring back everything we knew."

"I want to be a Wingwatcher *so much*," Ivy said passionately.

"I'll put in a good word for you," Foxglove said. "That is, if I'm not banished before then. Come on, let's get you home. We didn't learn much today, did we?"

Ivy disagreed, although she didn't say so out loud. She'd learned to hide, not run, from dragons. She'd learned that dragons were even more amazing than she'd thought. She'd learned that her dad acted like a cat with its tail on fire when he heard one. And she'd met Foxglove, a Wingwatcher who understood her.

They started back toward Valor, but Ivy kept tripping over tree roots because she couldn't keep her eyes off the sky. She wished the dragon would come back. Or that another one would fly overhead.

Foxglove stopped her near the entrance and went ahead to make sure Heath wasn't around to catch them going back in. Ivy took a deep breath, trying to fill her lungs with all the outside air they could hold.

"I don't want to go back underground," she said when Foxglove returned. "I want to see more dragons. I want to stay out here. Why can't I be a Wingwatcher now?"

"I don't think the old folks are quite ready for eight-year-old guardians yet," Foxglove said, crouching to meet Ivy's eyes. "But tell you what, come back whenever Squirrel and I are on duty, and I'll give you a little early training, if you don't tell anyone but Violet."

"Really?" Ivy breathed.

"Really, Ivy Who Loves Dragons," Foxglove said. "Just promise me you'll never ever ever go outside without a Wingwatcher."

"I promise," Ivy said.

She went home, covered five small scrolls (which were supposed to be for math homework) with sketches of the dragon in flight, and fell asleep to dreams of wings and scales.

CHAPTER 7

WREN

Not far from the Indestructible City, Wren and Sky found a sheltered valley that was full of hiding spots and hard enough to get to that Wren was pretty sure they'd be safe there for a while.

Or, more specifically, that Sky would be safe hiding there while she went into the city.

"No!" Sky yelped when she explained this plan. "No leaving me!" He threw himself across her lap and looked as pitiful as a small dragon with lots of sharp teeth could look.

"I don't want to! But it's very dangerous for you," she insisted in Dragon. "No dragons there." She didn't know much about any villages besides her own, but she was quite sure none of them would be pleased about a girl strolling in with a man-eating predator by her side. They wouldn't give her a chance to explain that he was a cuddly vegetarian — especially in the Indestructible City, the one place in the world that fought back against the dragons.

"More dangerous alone!" he cried. "Sad Sky, very very very sad Sky." He snuffled tragically.

"I won't be gone long," she said in her own language, hoping he'd understand. "Trust me, I don't *want* to talk to people or have anything to do with people. But I don't have scales to protect me, and I need something new to wear." The blue dress had been big on her that day, a year and a half ago, but now it was painfully tight, short in the arms, and ragged along the hems. She knew a lot about finding food and shelter in the forest, starting fires, and hiding from dragons, but she didn't know anything about making new clothes, especially without a flock of sheep handy. "Also a map if I can find one, and maybe something to read."

His answer was garbled by his sniffles, but from the words she caught, she guessed he'd asked, "What if you don't come back?"

"I'll always find my way back to you," she said as fiercely as she could, which was pretty fierce given how much of the Dragon language was growling and rawring. "No matter what happens to either of us. And look, while I'm gone, you can learn to fly." She zoomed her hand over the meadow flowers, scattering dandelion seeds into the air.

It worried her a little that Sky couldn't fly yet. Not having fire was one thing, but he certainly had wings, and she had no idea how to teach him to use them. That seemed like a dragon parent's job that she couldn't fill.

For a while he'd flapped his wings occasionally, especially when he saw birds overhead and got excited. But once he'd realized that Wren couldn't fly, he'd stopped even trying. He seemed perfectly happy to walk beside her — or, if he could charm her into it, what he really preferred was for her to carry him. But that was now impossible, as much as Wren loved him. He seemed to be growing markedly bigger every time they fell asleep; by the time they reached the valley, his shoulders were level with Wren's waist and his wingspan was wider than her outstretched arms.

Sky grumbled and muttered and stomped around the valley for two days, but finally Wren convinced him that he could not follow her to the Indestructible City. It had apparently never occurred to him that most dragons ate humans, and most humans therefore found dragons terrifying. Apparently he'd thought Wren always hid from adult dragons in the sky because they might be looking for *him*, not because they'd find Wren a delicious snack. He was thoroughly outraged by the idea of someone snacking on his Wren.

"I would BITE them!" he cried. "I would ROAR at them!"

"I know you would," Wren said, scratching behind his ears. "Just like I would bite and roar at any human who tried to hurt you. But me against the entire Indestructible City is a fight that wouldn't go well."

"Fiiiiiiiiiiiiiiiiiiiiiiiiiiiiiiiiiiiiiiiiiiiiiiiiiiiiiiiiiiiiiiiiiine," Sky grumbled, sounding so much like a dragon version of Wren's older sisters that she burst out giggling, which offended him even more.

The next morning she made sure Sky knew where all the best hiding places in the valley were and then hugged him good-bye. She climbed through the hidden passage and started down the mountain.

Through the trees, she caught glimpses of the river glittering down below — a different river than the one she'd found Sky in. Leaves whisked around her bare feet, and she discovered that the birds sang at full volume when Wren wasn't accompanied by a dragon.

It was awfully strange to be without Sky. Wren hadn't been away from him for more than a few moments since the day she'd found him. Right away she missed his humming, his weight leaning against her hip, his little yelps of glee when he spotted an animal.

She wished she could make it to the city, get inside, get what she needed, and get back to the valley in one day. But she had a feeling it was all going to be more complicated than she hoped. Could a nine-(ten?)-year-old girl in a ragged dress just walk right into the Indestructible City?

Is this a terrible idea?

People can't be trusted. What if they try to feed me to the dragons again?

Maybe only my village is full of awful people.

Or maybe this place is worse.

She frowned, tugging at one of her sleeves. *I'll just look at it first. I don't have to go in if it looks dangerous.*

Wren had heard that the Indestructible City was built halfway up a cliff overlooking the forest, but she was still startled when she reached the end of the trees and saw it, towering far overhead as though it were a city on one of the moons.

She hadn't known that the cliff would be so high or so steep. She hadn't realized how hard it would be to get to the city — or how impossible to sneak inside.

At first glance, the only way to enter the city was by climbing an endlessly long set of stairs that had been chipped out of the cliff face, cutting back and forth on a path into the sky, and now worn smooth and alarmingly slippery by thousands of feet going up and down. There was no railing; nothing to hold on to, and nothing to keep someone from tripping and plummeting off the cliff to their doom.

Soldiers guarded the bottom of the stairs and the gate at the top, as far as she could see. A few people were climbing the stairs, but far more were gathered around the foot of the cliff, within sight of the soldiers. Wren could see wagons and tents and rugs spread on the ground; she saw families asleep in huddled piles, far back in the line, and she saw others stirring pots over campfires. Some of the travelers looked as though they'd been there quite a while . . . as though they'd made camp, and were prepared to wait as long as necessary for a shot at the stairs and the safety of the city.

She climbed a tree and watched from the forest for a while to see if there were any other ways into the Indestructible City. There was a waterfall plunging from the top of the cliff, not far from the city walls. Wren could see a contraption set up along the outermost wall to gather water from it.

Hanging from a set of pulleys next to the waterwheel was

a large platform with tall woven sides. Wren studied it for half the morning before it finally moved, creaking slowly all the way to the bottom of the cliff. There, a trio of hunters wearing animal pelts loaded the platform with a live goat and a pile of deer carcasses. *Oh*, Wren realized. *It's for things that would be too heavy or unwieldy to carry up the stairs.*

As she watched, a group of travelers approached the hunters and started talking to them. She couldn't hear what they were saying, but there was a lot of hand-waving and pointing. Finally the travelers handed over a basket — Wren guessed it contained food or herbs, but what were they paying for?

Then one of the travelers came forward supporting a hunched, limping elderly man with a long white beard. She helped him climb over the side into the platform basket with the goat and the dead deer, and he settled himself awkwardly on the bottom.

That looks like an uncomfortable ride, Wren thought as the platform jolted into the air. *But better for the old man than the steps, I guess.* The platform banged against the sides of the cliff as it was hauled up, and she imagined being surrounded by the smell of the carcasses. She would have thrown up over the edge onto the heads of the hunters, she was pretty sure.

But that was the only other way into the city apart from the steps, and it was clearly guarded and policed by people who would demand payment for anyone to use it. That wasn't going to work for her. She would have to climb the steps along with everybody else if she wanted to get inside.

Did she want to get inside?

Those were also the only ways *out* of the city, other than leaping off the cliff, which meant a quick escape wouldn't be possible if she needed it. Wren did not like that at all.

Also, small point, but the people stuck on the steps, inching slowly toward the city, were sitting ducks for any hungry dragons flying by. Wren wondered how many of them got eaten every day. Surely the dragons must know about this easy one-stop snack parade.

She swung her legs for a moment, thinking. She *really* needed something new to wear — she'd torn a new hole in her dress just by reaching up to the tree branches. But was it worth the risk of talking to people . . . and maybe getting stuck in the Indestructible City?

She studied the line of people waiting to climb the steps. Near the front was a group that seemed to include a few families and several children; they had half their goods packed up as though they were hoping to be allowed in today. Maybe she could sneak in as one of them and avoid any questions.

Wren jumped down from the tree and wandered casually toward the base of the cliff. No one paid her very much attention as she wove through the encampment; most people were nervously watching the sky or trading stories of close escapes and clever hiding spots.

She reached the big family group as they got to the foot of the steps, where two men stood with slates and frowns and stiff shoulders. Both men were wearing leather armor covered in sharp, thornlike spikes. That would make them difficult for a dragon to pick up, Wren supposed, but it looked uncomfortable and hot, especially for climbing up and down the cliff. *Plus they look like a couple of grouchy porcupines*, she thought. She wished Sky could see them.

"Intent?" one of the men snapped.

"We're looking to settle here, if we can," said a tall woman with a baby on her hip. "Our village was destroyed."

"We've been waiting in this line for three weeks," a man behind her added.

"No room for refugees at the moment," the soldier said brusquely. "New lord's orders."

"Isn't there a quest?" the tall woman asked. "We heard there was a way to earn a place in the city."

"Not for *all* of you," he said, raising an eyebrow at two little boys who kept pushing each other, despite their father hissing at them. "The Invincible Lord will generously admit one family, consisting of no more than six people, *if* they bring the Dragonslayer to him."

A dragonslayer? Wren wondered. *Like . . . a person . . . who slays dragons?* She felt indignant on Sky's behalf. *That jerk! I hope someone eats him.*

"What does the new lord want with the Dragonslayer?" another woman in the group asked.

"An alliance, of course," said the first porcupine soldier. Wren didn't like the gleam in his eyes. "If the Dragonslayer worked for the Invincible Lord, they could save us from the dragons forever. They could build new Indestructible Cities. We could take back our world."

"That's what the Invincible Lord says," interjected the

second porcupine soldier. "He says this world should be for people, not dragons."

Wren snorted to herself.

"We sent one of our villagers to seek the Dragonslayer, to ask for his help," said the tall woman with the baby. "But our village burned before the Dragonslayer arrived. What if he's dead? Or what if he won't come here?"

The first soldier shrugged, rattling his spikes. "Sounds like a problem you'll have to solve. That's why it's called a quest, isn't it?"

"Or you can keep waiting and see if the lord changes his mind," the other offered with a grunt.

They don't care whether these people live or die, Wren thought scornfully. *They wouldn't lift a finger if dragons swooped out of the sky to eat them right now. This is just another place where powerful people step on everyone below them. The Indestructible City is no better than Talisman.*

She slipped quietly behind one of the bigger men in the traveling party and started to sidle away.

"May we enter to trade, at least?" the tall woman asked. "We have been traveling for so long, and some of our children need medicine." Her baby made a sad, restless sound and she pulled it closer to her, wrapping one big hand around its little head.

Wren wondered whether the woman would trade that baby for a safe place to live — or if a bunch of dragon-mancers told her to.

"You may have a pass to visit the market for a day,"

said the porcupine soldier in a bored voice, "if you leave your children down here with us." He pointed behind him to a fenced-off area up against the cliff. Inside, three children huddled together silently. The oldest looked younger than Wren.

The other soldier smiled an unfriendly smile. "That way we know you'll come back," he said.

The woman took a step away from them, wrapping her other arm around her baby, and the two bickering boys fell silent, staring up at their father's anxious face.

"Orphans must be stamped and turned over to the city," the first soldier went on. "We'll find a place for them."

"You mean forever?" asked the tall woman. "You keep the orphans?"

"Invincible Lord's orders," said the second soldier with a nod that rattled the spikes on his helmet. "They're safer with us, after all."

Nope, Wren thought. *Nope nope nooooooooooooooooooo thank you, nope.* She ducked under someone's arm and wove quickly back through the group, who were all muttering and whispering about the new lord's rules.

She wanted to run all the way back to Sky immediately, but she didn't want to attract the guards' attention. She doubted they'd want to chase her in all that armor, but it would still be safer to put a lot of distance between them before she made a break for the forest.

Toward the end of the line, she nearly ran headlong into a pile of orange fur, which turned out to be a positively enormous cat in the arms of a boy.

"Wings above," Wren yelped in surprise. She remembered the kitten she'd wanted from years ago. Would it have grown as big as this creature?

The cat hissed lazily, as if it couldn't really be bothered to scare her away. Its face was flat and gorgeously grumpy and its fur was long and silky. It was seriously nearly as big as Sky was.

"Don't touch my cat," the boy said, narrowing his eyes.

"I definitely won't!" Wren said. "Why WOULD I? I like my face *not* clawed off."

"She doesn't scratch," he said. "But I do. If anyone touches her." He was a hair shorter than Wren, with bushy eyebrows and a moon-shaped face and one silver earring shaped like a dragon, which was entirely too excellent for a person this obnoxious.

"I'm not going to touch your stupid tiger," Wren said. "But when it grows up and eats you, don't be surprised. You deserve it."

"Did you growl at us?" he asked. "When you nearly ran into my cat?"

Oops. Had she said *wings above* in Dragon? "I wasn't growling *at* you," she said. "It was more of a general growl at everything, probably, if I did."

"Why are you going to the back of the line?" he asked. "Are you running away from your parents?" He considered that for a moment. "If you are, I should tell."

"Don't you dare," Wren said fiercely. "I know eight different ways to kill you before you take your next breath."

He regarded her skeptically. "You do not. You're tiny."

"You're tinier than I am!"

"Nuh-uh. Besides, I have a cat."

Yeah, well, I *have a dragon,* Wren heroically managed not to say, with very impressive self-control, if she thought so herself.

"And I have guards to protect me," the boy said, as if that fact was extremely boring, but something he had to live with. "So where are you going?"

Guards? Wren wondered. *Why?* He did look much more pampered and much less desperate than everyone around them.

"I have decided not to go to the Indestructible City today," she said, lifting her chin. "Not that it's any of your business. Good-bye."

He did not move out of her way. The cat blinked thoughtfully at her.

"You look silly," said the boy. "That dress is too small for you."

"Well, that cat is too big for you, and so is your stupid face," Wren said. She wondered where his parents were, and why they let him have a cat that size, and whether he was planning to try to carry it all the way up the steps to the Indestructible City.

"Oh," he said. "You're funny. Are you one of the new clowns for the manor? Is that why you're dressed like that?"

"Why are you bothering me?" Wren demanded. "I don't like people. I don't want to talk to you."

"I don't like people either," he said. "Only cats. No, wait. Only this cat. Her name is Dragon."

"You are so weird," Wren said. "It is WEIRD to name an animal after a totally different animal!"

"Is it?" he said indifferently. "Dragon doesn't care. I'm Undauntable. What's your name?"

"None of your business," Wren answered. "Wait, what? You're what?"

"Undauntable," he said. "That's my name."

"That's even worse than Dragon for a cat," she said. "You made that up. Undauntable? That's like putting a sign on your head that says 'Go ahead and try to daunt me!' Do your parents hate you?"

He scowled with enormous ferocity. "NO. They think I am PERFECT."

"Then they should have called you Perfect," Wren said. "If they were so determined to give you a terrible name."

"It's NOT terrible," he shouted. "I AM Undauntable! What's your so-great name, then?"

"Still none of your business," Wren said. "I have places to be, good-bye."

He shoved the cat in her way so she had to stop again.

"Will you tell me your name if I get you a new dress?" he demanded.

"Definitely not," Wren said. "I don't want a new dress and I don't want anything to do with you."

She turned to go another way and discovered a new,

gigantic porcupine solder bristling with spikes, standing just behind her.

This was a rather alarming discovery.

"That's my bodyguard," said Undauntable. "So you *probably* shouldn't kill me any of your eight ways."

"You're from the city," Wren realized. She should have guessed from the earring and the clean, shiny look of his clothes — what she could see of them beyond the cat (which she was NOT going to call Dragon. It could be Cat, if it had to be anything). And maybe his silly name was also a clue. Maybe all the kids in the Indestructible City had absurd pompous names, like the Invincible Lord. "What are you doing down here?"

"I got bored, and so did Dragon," he answered. "New people at least have a chance of being interesting."

Easily bored, rich, and powerful usually means dangerous. Wren narrowed her eyes at him, wondering what the safest way out of this conversation was.

"Bodyguard," Undauntable said. "Find me someone in this line who has a dress to trade in this girl's size."

"Do NOT do that," Wren said. "I don't want a dress; I want a tunic and pants, and I will get them myself." She hadn't thought of trading with someone in the line. That would be much easier than going up to the city, although it might also draw more attention to her than she would like.

"With what?" Undauntable said, sizing her up. "You don't have anything to trade."

Wren slipped her hands in her pockets and felt a small,

cool shape. "I have this," she said, pulling it out. It was one of Sky's baby scales that had molted off him recently. In the palm of her hand, it looked like a small, pale orange jewel.

Undauntable gasped, and even his bodyguard's eyes widened. "Is that a dragon scale?" Undauntable demanded. "I've never seen one that color before."

"Like I said, none of your business." Wren pocketed the scale again and turned to saunter back up the line.

"Wait," Undauntable said. "I want it. Please let me have it. I'll give you way more than anyone else here for it."

"You don't have anything I want," Wren said loftily.

Undauntable hefted the cat over his shoulder and seized a pouch off the bodyguard's belt. "Here," he said, pouring round silver pieces into his palm. "You can have all of these."

"What good are little bits of silver to me?" Wren asked. "I can't eat them or wear them or read them."

"What?" Undauntable said. "How backward is your village? You don't use coins?"

Wren didn't think her parents had used "coins" in Talisman, but she wasn't sure. "I just don't want them," she said.

"Yes, you do," Undauntable said impatiently.

They argued a bit more, until finally he walked her up and down the line and showed her how everyone would accept the silver coins in exchange for the things she really wanted. It was kind of a weird phenomenon. No one in Wren's village had ever traded like this, with bits of shiny metal instead of useful things, as far as she could remember.

But the travelers were eager to take them, so they must be useful in other places.

The dragonmancers had all the shiny metal, she suddenly remembered. She'd seen lots of it in Master Trout's secret cabinets when she stole the books, but she hadn't thought it was very interesting. *Maybe this is like the "treasure" the books talked about. All those pages of notes on which dragonmancer had what stuff.* She'd skimmed that part; it was beyond boring to read about how two gold rings equaled one ruby equaled whatever whatever, with lots of notes on dividing it fairly into four exactly equal parts. *Yawn.*

With Undauntable's help, Wren ended up with dark green pants — too long, but she could roll them up and then unroll them as she got taller — a moss-green tunic, fawn-brown boots that felt weird after a year of bare feet, and a soft wool cloak dyed the gray of a stormy sky. She also got a map of the continent, two loaves of cranberry nut bread, a canteen on a strap for carrying water in, five books she'd never read before, and, in the end, Undauntable's silver dragon earring, because she couldn't think of anything else she needed and he insisted she needed more to repay the price of the scale.

"All right, you can have it," she said, dropping the little scale into his hand.

"Where did you find it?" he asked. He breathed on it and rubbed it shiny, then held it up to the light. "I bet this came from a baby dragon," he said shrewdly. "If we could track it down, I could have a whole chest plate made of these."

Wren shuddered. She did not like the image that popped

into her head of Undauntable hunting down Sky, searching for more scales.

"I found it in the swamps," she said, pointing northeast — the opposite direction from where Sky was hidden. Undauntable did not look like a guy who'd enjoy wading through swamps. "If I find another one . . . I could bring it back to you."

"Yes!" he said delightedly. "Do that! Don't sell it to anyone else!"

"All right," she said. "I'll come back and look for you in a year. Maybe a little sooner if I finish these books and need something else to read."

"A year?" he said, dismayed. "That's so long!"

"I think you'll survive," she said, rolling her new possessions up in her cloak.

"I know *I* will," he said. "*I* am the prince of the Indestructible City. But you will almost certainly be dead in a year."

"Thaaaaaaaaat's cheerful," she said, trying not to let on that she was startled by this news. A prince! No wonder he was so weird. Wait, did that mean the Invincible Lord was his father? *I bet that's a fun family to be part of . . . although I guess they can't actually be worse than mine.* "You'll just have to wait and see."

"I don't like waiting," he called after her, stamping his foot as she walked away. "This is extremely aggravating!"

"Saddest story ever told," she called back with a wave.

Wren couldn't go directly to the forest and her valley, not

with Undauntable's eyes following her. She headed south instead, following the river until the Indestructible City and its porcupine soldiers and all its alarming people were out of sight.

And then she swam to the other side, veered back toward the trees, and ran all the way home to her dragon.

CHAPTER 8

LEAF

It was funny — or perhaps terrible — how you could spend your entire life training for one purpose, only to have everyone around you suddenly decide you were destined for something else.

Of course, Leaf's parents had been hoping that "dragonmancer" would be Leaf's destiny from probably the day he was born. But Leaf had never wanted that, never hoped for it, never even thought about it. He'd barely paid attention during the dragonmancer exams. He'd only taken them to keep up the pretense that Rowan had been studying with him all these years.

He thought sometimes that it was odd how nobody had guessed. Didn't anyone wonder how he'd gone from a scrawny ten-year-old to the strongest, fastest person in the village? Did anyone think it was strange that someone who supposedly had his nose in his books all day could also walk on his hands, scale any cliff face, swim upriver against the current, and lift boulders twice his size?

But none of that mattered. He'd spent all that time and

worked so hard to become someone who could slay the dragons that had killed Wren, and then all at once he was someone else: age fourteen, stuck with an official dragonmancer's apprentice invitation, parents who were over the moons with joy, and an older sister who was entirely too amused about the whole thing.

Saying no was not an option. Even Grove wanted him to do it; he said, "Whatever the dragonmancers are hiding, this is our chance to find it." Rowan's group of friends who were obsessed with fighting dragons all thought this was a fantastic development.

But they weren't the ones who had to milk the goats, chip the candle wax off the floors, and sprint into the hills about once every three days to ring the warning bells. They weren't the ones sleeping on a thin straw pallet in a cramped room with another apprentice, who spent all his time either snoring or talking about the last two apprentices and how gruesomely they'd been eaten.

Leaf had been assigned to the leader of the dragonmancers, Master Trout, who seemed nearly as displeased about having a new apprentice as Leaf was to be there, even though it had been Trout's idea in the first place.

That's because he hates everything, Wren's voice whispered in Leaf's mind. *He was supposed to be born as a tarantula and instead he came out more or less human, so now he has to talk to people instead of biting them and that means he's always frustrated and hungry.*

The worst part about being around Master Trout all the

time was that Leaf couldn't stop remembering all the jokes Wren had made about him: the way his receding chin made him look like a smug turtle; the way he spoke with maddening slowness, as though nobody else could possibly keep up with his brain; the way he would be casually cruel to small children or people begging for help, and then he'd chuckle quietly to himself for the rest of the day, thinking he was the only one who'd noticed.

Leaf wondered what Wren would think of how he now scurried around doing Trout's bidding day and night. The dragonmancer never stopped talking, but Leaf couldn't tune him out, because Trout would switch from a boring lecture to imperious orders midsentence, in the same disdainful tone of voice, and if Leaf missed an instruction, he'd lose a meal, or he'd be sent to the alarm bell three days in a row.

He wished Wren were there to puncture the gloating bubble around Master Trout's head. She would have pointed out how small and mean the dragonmancer was, the icy pebble where his heart should be, and she could have made him laugh about it, instead of feeling smothered by it all the time. Leaf could imagine Wren setting him free, but he couldn't figure out how to do it himself.

Maybe that was why he started having conversations with her in his head.

Do you think I should run away? he thought at night when the snoring kept him awake. *Maybe I can go be a dragon-slayer right now.*

You absolutely should do that, said the Wren in his mind.

Running straight into dragon fire sounds way more fun than this boring place.

Where would I go, though? he asked. *To the mountain dragon palace? By myself? And after I kill a dragon there, then what?*

First you should go to the Indestructible City, she said. *Ask them to send you on a quest! Then when you come back covered in the blood of dragons, they'll probably give you gold and a house and ooh, maybe a PARADE, and then you can demand that they build a statue of me for everyone to remember me and weep for me forever.*

The Indestructible City is way in the opposite direction from the dragon palace, he said. *Maybe I could find a village closer to here. A place where everyone is living in terror, and then I could free them from the dragon that hunts them.*

One tiny problem, Wren pointed out. *You're fourteen. When you offer to slay a dragon, the villagers will one hundred percent laugh at you.*

They will not! OK, they might. But I know I'm ready.

Eh, said imaginary Wren. *Your left-handed swordfighting needs work. I bet you could kill a dragon with the smell of your armpits, though.*

Thanks, Wren. These pep talks are so helpful. Go away and let me sleep.

He dreamed of fighting dragons every night.

The only thing getting him through the apprenticeship, apart from his imaginary sister, was his free day once a week, when he would go into the forest to train with Rowan and her friends. Rowan and Grove had gathered a few more people their age who believed the dragons could be fought and the world could be different.

One was Cranberry, Rowan's best friend. Her hair was twisted into lots of tiny braids, with the tips dyed dark red to match her name, and she had the most perfect teeth Leaf had ever seen. She had been part of a traveling entertainment troupe before they'd been attacked by dragons and she'd been separated from them. She'd turned up in Talisman when Leaf was twelve, and she was still hoping the rest of her troupe would find her there. In the meanwhile, she'd taught Leaf all her acrobatic moves; together they'd practice cartwheels and handsprings and backflips.

There was also a pair of brothers, Mushroom and Thyme, who were clearly there because everyone liked Thyme and so they were stuck with Mushroom. Thyme was short and charming and didn't take training seriously, but he loved talking about what the dragon palace must be like and all the many kinds of treasure they would find there.

His twin brother was more square-jawed, a little taller, a lot gloomier, and tended to complain whenever he was tired, or it was raining, or when his brother did something better than he did, which was often. Leaf had seen him glaring at Thyme behind his back more than once, especially whenever Thyme had Cranberry's full attention.

But Leaf didn't really care about all their drama, or the treasure they spent so much time talking about. They made him laugh and helped him train, but most important, they kept him focused on his goal. He was going to be a dragon-slayer. Together they would find the dragons and start getting rid of them. Even if Thyme or Mushroom or Cranberry were only doing this for treasure, the result would be a safer village and a safer world.

"Have you found anything in old Trout's house yet?" Grove asked him one day, after Leaf had been an apprentice for half a year. "Any secrets?"

He asked casually, with a grin, as though this was a joke. But there was a layer of intensity under his smile. Two days earlier, the dragonmancers had had a vision that Grove's father had expanded his small farm too far, enough to attract the dragons' attention. They'd ordered him to cut down his sunflowers, pull up half his vegetables, and give all of that plus two goats to "the village," which, according to Grove, meant it would all be going into the dragonmancers' pockets.

Grove had argued with Master Trout at the village meeting, in front of everyone. He'd asked to at least have a vote on how the food would be redistributed; there were families who actually needed it. But Master Trout refused to call a vote; he pointed out that he was the one in charge, and Grove was an outsider who should sit down and listen to his elders.

None of the other landholders had stood up for Grove or his father. They all avoided his eyes and stayed out of their way, afraid of attracting the dragonmancers' wrath.

So Leaf knew there was more to Grove's question than usual.

"He locks his study and we're not allowed in," Leaf said. "Sometimes he brings out a book and gives us a lecture on dragon kings or how much they eat, and then he takes it back inside and locks the door again." He tossed his knife high into the air and caught it neatly as it spun back down. "If there are any secrets, they must be in there. But I doubt we'll find anything like you're hoping for, Grove. I can't see Trout leaving himself notes like: 'Excellent lie about the visions today! More sunflowers for us, mwa ha ha!'"

"Maybe not," Grove said, stealing the knife out of the air as Leaf threw it again. "But there must be *something* we can use, or why would he lock it?"

"It's not all lies," Cranberry said from her perch in a nearby tree. "I've been keeping track: their visions about dragons flying overhead are right more than half the time. I want to know the secret to *that*."

"Lucky guesses," Grove said dismissively. Leaf snagged the knife out of his grasp again, but Grove was so worked up he didn't even notice. "Dragons are always flying overhead; there's nothing amazing about predicting that. I think everything they say is a lie, and we need some kind of proof. You'll have to break into the study next time he's out, Leaf."

"It's too dangerous to ask Leaf to do that," Rowan chimed in. "He practically belongs to Master Trout right now. The dragonmancers could do all kinds of terrible things to him if they catch him spying on them." She gave Grove a significant look that didn't mean anything to Leaf.

"You're right. I'll do it," Grove said. "Just tell me the next time he'll be gone for a while, and I'll find a way in."

The opportunity came six days later, when Master Trout went to a vision session with the other two dragonmancers and Leaf's fellow apprentice had the day off, so Leaf was alone in the house. Grove crawled through the garden and ducked past the goats, and Leaf let him in the back door.

"His study is up here," Leaf said, leading the way upstairs. His heart was pounding, but more with excitement than fear. If Master Trout returned and caught them . . . Leaf guessed he would probably be banished from the village, but at least he wouldn't have to be an apprentice anymore.

Grove tinkered with the lock for a while — a long while, long enough to tip Leaf a bit toward nervous. But finally something clicked in the mechanism and the door swung open.

"His secret lair," Grove whispered, and Leaf thought of tarantulas again. "You don't have to come in," Grove added. "Go for a walk, make sure someone sees you. Give yourself an alibi."

Leaf shook his head. "I want to see what he's hiding, too."

The room was dark and shadowy; the only window was covered with a thick curtain, and all the lamps were out. It smelled like cinnamon-dusted mold, one sharp, pleasant scent scattered over a deeper, wetter, more rotten odor. A movement on the desk made Leaf's heart leap out of his chest, until he realized it was a small cage with a coiled snake inside.

"Creepy," Grove said, pointing to the snake. He strode over to the desk and studied the papers on it for a moment without touching them.

Leaf headed toward the bookshelves instead. They lined two walls, but were only about a quarter full of books. The rest of the shelf space was taken up by weird oversized artifacts, most of them gleaming with gems. A diamond-studded hourglass as tall as Leaf was. A loop of metal that he thought at first might be a belt, but with a ruby embedded in it like a ring. A copper cup that Leaf could have climbed into, etched with flames.

"These are dragons' things," Leaf realized. There had been a rumor a few years ago that someone found a dragon-sized silver spoon in the woods, but the dragonmancers had spirited it away and hushed up the story. *They must collect any objects dropped or lost by the dragons. Or at least, Trout does.*

There's so much here, though. Have the dragons really just casually dropped all this treasure? He supposed the dragonmancers had been here since the founding of the village, thirty or forty years ago. Maybe over that much time, it was possible.

But it made him wonder what was in the large, triple-padlocked safe behind the desk.

He took a step back from a heavy gold paperweight shaped like an eye and felt something in the wooden floor below his bare feet. When he crouched to look closer, he discovered a deep scratch arcing out from the bookshelf. As if the shelf had been dragged back and forth several times. Leaf hooked his fingers in the shelf, and it slid easily forward along the groove.

An enormous piece of paper was nailed to the wall behind the bookshelf, taller than Leaf. The edges were crinkled as though they wanted to roll in, and the drawing on it was part map, part blueprint.

"Grove?" Leaf whispered. "What am I looking at?"

Grove came to stand beside him and they stared at it for a long time.

"I *think*," Grove said finally, "it looks like . . . a palace."

"A dragon's palace," Leaf agreed. "In the mountains. This is the home of the mountain dragon queen, isn't it?" *That's where I need to go. That's where Wren's killer is.*

But . . . why does Master Trout have this?

The blueprint was covered in little notes and details — *good spot for climbing* and *heavily patrolled* and *frequently set on fire; do not go this way.* Some of them were in a language with letters Leaf didn't recognize, but many of them were legible, and some of those were in Master Trout's own handwriting. Leaf knew it well by now.

"Has Trout *been* to the *dragon's palace*?" Leaf wondered. "How would he know any of this?"

"And where did he get this drawing in the first place?" Grove asked. "Did he draw it himself?"

"No," Leaf said. "He can't even draw a straight line. His sketch for the garden plot was a mess." He reached up and gently ran one finger over the strange symbols that were inked over every room.

"Did . . . dragons draw this?" Grove said in a hushed voice. "Is that dragon language?"

"That's not possible," Leaf whispered back. "Dragons don't have a written language, do they?" And surely they couldn't make art or detailed blueprints like this. He glanced sideways at the flames carved into the giant copper cup. That was a kind of art, he supposed. And now that he looked closer, there were little etchings around the rim that matched some of the symbols on the map.

He felt a strange creeping unease crawl along his skin. He'd always thought of slaying dragons as akin to wiping out a plague of deadly insects, or fighting a bloodthirsty shark. If they could draw maps and write, that made them something else again. Not human, but not as mindlessly animal as he'd thought either.

Hey, Wren interrupted his train of thought, *if they're so smart and literate and talented, maybe they should know better than to eat equally smart, literate, talented seven-year-olds!*

"I think that's it," Grove said. "This is the dragons' map of their own palace. Trout must have stolen it from the dragons — a long time ago, judging from how many notes he's added since then."

Leaf couldn't believe it. He couldn't imagine Master Trout sneaking into a dragon's palace, or escaping uneaten, or even walking as far as the palace in the first place.

"Maybe he sent someone else." Leaf traced the yellowing edges of the map. "That seems more like him. This looks so old — maybe he sent an apprentice a long time ago, before we were even born."

"Maybe that's why Talisman is here in the first place," Grove said thoughtfully. "I've always thought it was weird that someone built a village this close to the mountain dragons. Maybe it started as a treasure smugglers' den, and then the smugglers got old and became dragonmancers instead. Different kind of thieves, but still stealing."

"Do you think that's their big secret?" Leaf asked Grove. "That they used to steal dragon treasure?"

Grove rubbed his head. "I feel like there must be something else. Something bigger."

Leaf stared at the spires of the dragon palace, trying to picture Trout and Crow and Gorge as young treasure smugglers. Or as young anything, ever.

If Grove's theory was right, that made it even more hypocritical that the dragonmancers had forbidden anyone to go to the mountain palace.

Now that sounds like Trout, Wren grumbled in his head. *Stealing treasure for himself, then stopping anyone else from getting any.*

Well, I'm going, Leaf told her, *no matter what they do to stop me.*

"We need this," Leaf said, tapping the map. "This is exactly what we need."

"But we can't take something this enormous," Grove said. "Can you copy it?"

"If I had a year, maybe," Leaf said.

"Start now, then," Grove said. He grabbed a piece of paper from one of the messy piles on the floor; on one side, Master Trout had written the first few lines of a lecture and then crossed them out. The other side was blank. Grove shoved it and a charcoal pencil into Leaf's hands.

"But . . . all these details," Leaf said helplessly. Where should he begin? What was important, and what could he leave out? It was too much. He couldn't do this alone.

"Just do the best you can," Grove said. "I'll show you how to pick the lock and you can come in and work on it any chance you get."

"I wish Wren were here," Leaf admitted. He looked down at the floor. He hadn't said those words out loud in years.

Me too, said the Wren in his head. *I'd be great at copying this map, uncovering Trout's secrets, and figuring out how to break into a dragon palace.*

"Imagine that she is," Grove said, touching Leaf's shoulder. "Think of what her advice would be, and imagine her watching you. She'd be excited about this, wouldn't she? I remember she was always either mad or excited about something."

That's true, Wren whispered. *Stealing something this incredible from those jerkface dragonmancers? You clearly have to. Do it for me.*

Leaf sat down and started to draw.

CHAPTER 9

IVY

"This is it!" Ivy danced around Violet's room, throwing her arms wide. "This is the day we finally become Wingwatchers! I can't believe it!"

"*I* can't believe you talked us into this," Violet said from her hammock. She turned a page of her book. "I'm supposed to be on the law council track."

"Boring!" Daffodil shouted. She grabbed Ivy's hands and spun her around. "We're going to see dragons and watch dragons and ride dragons!"

"Seeing and watching are the same thing," Violet observed. "And you are definitely not going to *ride* any dragons, you lunatic."

Ivy had imagined this day for so long, but she had never thought it would all really happen — that she'd still be best friends with Violet and Daffodil when they were thirteen, that they'd be speaking to one another, that they'd all be starting Wingwatcher training together.

"Let's go now," she suggested. "Let's be early!"

"That will be so novel for Daffodil," Violet said. "I'm not sure her heart could take it."

"I was early for school once last year," Daffodil said proudly. Her face darkened. "Because Daisy *tricked* me about what time it really was. That only worked once, though. I never let her fool me again!"

Now that they were thirteen, Daffodil had switched to a ponytail, and she usually managed to "lose" the yellow ribbon her mother put in, most often before lunch. Out of the three of them, she was probably the most excited about the Wingwatcher uniform, since it meant she could finally wear a dark color.

Violet was the tallest and got the best grades, except when their teachers marked her down for asking too many questions or arguing about details. She'd cut her hair to chin length and she'd convinced Ivy to draw matching dragon wings on the backs of all their hands. Everyone thought they represented their new Wingwatcher status, but they were secretly symbols of the Truth Seekers.

Ivy had thought about cutting her hair, too, but she knew her mother would be upset if she did. Mother was already not convinced that being a Wingwatcher was a good idea, so Ivy didn't want to give her anything else to fuss about.

The Wingwatcher welcome ceremony was in one of the bigger caves, not far from the exit where Ivy had been sneaking out with Foxglove for the last five years. Two Wingwatchers were already there when they arrived: Squirrel and the commander, Brook.

Most Wingwatchers started training at age thirteen, guarding the exits at age fifteen, running missions outside at age sixteen, and then, if they survived, usually retired back to another job inside the caves sometime between ages twenty-two and twenty-five. Brook was one of the few who'd stayed on; she was somewhere in her forties, won every strength competition the village ever had, and apparently loved recruiting new Wingwatchers more than anything else in the world.

"My babies!" she yelled enthusiastically as Ivy, Violet, and Daffodil came in. "So ready to learn! You're my favorites!" She galloped over and shook all their hands, beaming.

"What about me?" Forest asked, coming in behind them with an injured expression.

"You are my favorite *son*," Brook clarified. "These three are my favorite *recruits*."

Forest looked skeptical about that distinction, perhaps because he was Brook's only son. Ivy would not have guessed, five years ago, that he'd ever want to be a Wingwatcher like his mother. She still didn't think he could make it through an entire silent patrol without pretending to fart, laughing his head off, falling out of a tree, or accidentally setting something on fire. Violet was entirely certain that he'd only been allowed to join because of Brook, although, as she said, "They also took Daffodil, so maybe they just have very low standards." Which had prompted Daffodil to steal all of Violet's writing utensils for a week, a very Violet-specific form of torture.

"Ivy," Brook said. "Any word from your uncle Stone?"

Ivy shook her head. Her uncle had left Valor abruptly a year earlier and hadn't been seen since. His cave was still reserved for him, in the hope that he would return.

"Sorry to hear that." The commander shook her head. "He never quite recovered from what happened in the desert."

"What do you mean? What happened?" Violet asked sharply, but Brook was distracted by the arrival of more guests and bounded away without answering.

"Hmmmmmmmm," Daffodil said, giving Violet a one-eyebrow-raised look.

"Indeed," Violet said. "Secrets are afoot. Ivy, do you know what she meant?"

Ivy shook her head, but she had a vague memory of asking her mother why Uncle Stone was always so sad, and getting the impression that there was a reason she was too young to know about.

The cave gradually filled with current Wingwatchers, the other three recruits, and their families. Daffodil's sister Daisy waved at Ivy from across the food table, but Daffodil dragged Ivy away before she could go say hi. Violet's dads both stopped by to hug each of them, still looking vaguely confused about why Violet was doing this at all.

Finally Foxglove came over, beaming, to greet Ivy and her friends.

"I brought you something," Ivy said to her shyly, handing her a folded note. Inside was Ivy's best ever drawing of a dragon in flight — a black one, like the one they'd seen together that first day, with its glorious wings filling the page. In the corner she'd written *Thank you for everything*.

"Aw," Foxglove said with a grin, studying the drawing. "I didn't have to say anything to get you in, you know. Brook wanted you as soon as she saw the first drawing in your portfolio. We haven't had a recruit with artistic talent in years." She winked at Ivy, tucking the drawing into her pocket. "Maybe it's time for an updated Wingwatcher's Guide."

"YES! Can I write the words?" Violet interjected. "I have so many suggestions!"

"So do I!" Daffodil chimed in.

Violet eyed her disapprovingly. "I have *good* suggestions. *And* a passing grade in writing, unlike some people."

"I PASSED," Daffodil objected. "I DID pass. Passing on the second try is STILL PASSING. I am a GREAT writer, Violet Know-It-All Face!"

"Ivy, who's a better writer?" Violet demanded.

"Eep!" Ivy said. "I'm definitely not answering that!"

"Because it's me," Violet said pityingly to Daffodil, "and she doesn't want you to have a huge temper tantrum about it."

"Because it's ME," Daffodil said furiously, "and she knows YOU will act all WOUNDED and OFFENDED for a YEAR if she tells you so!"

"Nobody's writing a new guide yet," Ivy interrupted, trying to sound as soothing as possible. "We have lots of research to do before there's enough information for that."

"Research," Violet sighed happily. Daffodil wrinkled her nose.

"Which will require expeditions," Ivy said to her. "Up into the mountains! Maybe out to the desert!"

"Ooooooooo," Daffodil said with shining eyes.

"I like your wings," Foxglove said, pointing to the back of Violet's hand.

"Yeah, they're awesome. Ivy drew them," Violet said. "Are you planning to retire soon, Foxglove?"

The Wingwatcher looked startled. She'd met Ivy's friends before, and even taken them outside a few times, but she hadn't spent a lot of time in the line of fire of Violet's blunt questions.

"No, I don't think so," she said. She glanced around the cave. "Most of us are . . . planning to stay on for a while."

"I noticed that," Violet said. "I noticed that no one from Pine's year has retired, even though you all could by now, if you wanted to."

Foxglove tilted her head at Violet with a thoughtful expression. After a moment, she said, "Most people don't talk about Pine very much anymore."

"Because they're usually talking about whoever the latest banishment was instead," Violet said. "But I bet you guys still talk about him. Him, and the other three Wingwatchers who've been banished since then."

"It's not actually safe to talk about them too much," Foxglove observed, taking a step back from Violet but still studying her curiously. "If you have thoughts about them, perhaps you could share them with me later, in a . . . quieter setting. Oh, look, Squirrel needs my help with the strawberries. Excuse me." She dove back into the crowd and hurried away.

"You are as subtle as a grizzly bear," Daffodil hissed.

"We're all Wingwatchers now, aren't we?" Violet said with a dazzling smile. "I'm just *interested* in what the older Wingwatchers think about, and talk about, and also hypothetically possibly whether there's a secret Wingwatcher conspiracy afoot."

"What?" Ivy said, startled.

"I've told you there's no way," Daffodil whispered, "and that it's really rude to talk about in front of Ivy!"

"Hey," Ivy objected. "Are you serious? You guys are keeping a secret from *me*?"

"I didn't want to," Violet said. "Daffodil made me."

"And just this once you're terrible at it?" Daffodil threw up her hands.

"She should know," Violet said in a low voice. "She might hear something, now that we'll be around them all the time."

"Know what?" Ivy asked. "What kind of conspiracy? What's your evidence?"

"I suspect someone is planning a revolution," Violet whispered, in a voice nearly as dramatic as Daffodil's. "Most likely from within the Wingwatchers. They're not happy about how Valor is run. I've seen all kinds of clues."

"You *have*?" Ivy's mind was reeling.

"That's the real reason Violet agreed to be a Wingwatcher,"

Daffodil said, folding her arms. "Because she couldn't stand it if there was a conspiracy and she missed it."

"Oh," Ivy said. "I thought it was because we were all excited about dragons."

Violet put one arm around Ivy and glared at Daffodil. "It is also because we are all excited to do this together," she said. "Daffodil, stop ruining Ivy's big day."

"You're the one ruining it!" Daffodil whispered furiously. "Investigating nonexistent conspiracies to overthrow Ivy's dad!"

"Oh my goodness," Ivy said, everything hitting her at once. It couldn't be true. Could it?

The Wingwatchers were amazing and could do no wrong. She'd follow Commander Brook and Foxglove to all three moons and back again.

But if they were really plotting revolution . . . that meant taking down the government of Valor . . . and the government meant Ivy's father, who happened to be swaggering into the cave at that very moment.

"Hello, Wingwatchers!" he boomed. "What an exciting day! Recruits, line up for inspection!"

Ivy stood between Violet and Daffodil (her usual spot — it kept them from elbowing each other, arguing, or pulling each other's hair), with Forest on the other side of Daffodil and Moth on the other side of Violet. She tried to shake off what her friends had said. Violet always saw secrets and conspiracies everywhere. She was right most of the time, but sometimes she was wrong. This had to be one of those times.

The Dragonslayer paced slowly down the line, wearing his Very Serious expression, which he put on for most formal occasions where people would be watching.

"What's this?" he said, stopping in front of Ivy. "How did you Wingwatchers get your talons on the smartest girl in Valor? Young lady, I hope you don't have any plans to run right at the dragons like your brave old man."

"No, sir," Ivy said, but she couldn't stop herself from smiling back at him. He was joking, and it wasn't the most accurate joke — Ivy was far from the smartest girl in Valor (that would be Violet) — but it always felt something like sunlight when her father paid attention to her.

"I'll come poke them for you if you need me to," he said, patting his sword with one hand and clapping her on the shoulder with the other.

"We generally avoid poking them, sir," Commander Brook said, polite but with a hint of judgment underneath. Heath squinted at her.

"Well, good," he said after a moment. "Leave that to the Dragonslayer, eh?" He chuckled. "Just take care of my little girl out there!"

"Dad," Ivy said, embarrassed. Now this was *too* much attention. She didn't want to be treated any differently than the other Wingwatchers. She wondered if she was imagining the looks the older Wingwatchers were giving one another — as though her father were a wasp's nest hanging over their heads. As though they were deciding right then whether they could trust her or not.

"The Wingwatchers are some of the most important people in Valor!" Heath declared, standing back to survey them all. "We have always needed brave young people like you to watch the skies for our greatest enemies. You protect us all. You are our first line of warning and defense. As long as we have Wingwatchers, the dragons will never find us. Of course, if they do, I'll slay them and save us all. But what you do is very important, too. Thank you for volunteering! Let's raise a toast to your sharp eyes and your courage!"

Ivy lifted the glass of apple cider someone handed her. She couldn't help remembering the day she'd seen her father race through the forest, fleeing in panic from the sound of a dragon. *Courage* wasn't the first thing that came to mind anymore when she thought about the Dragonslayer.

What if . . . he shouldn't *be the lord of Valor anymore?*

It gave her chills inside and out to even think those words.

At the end of the ceremony and the toasting and the eating and the mingling, as people were starting to leave, Foxglove found Ivy again and gave her a hug.

"You did it," she said. "That tiny little miscreant I met five years ago has finally become a real Wingwatcher."

"Well, I still have to go through training," Ivy said.

"Pshaw." Foxglove waved her hand in the air. "You already know more than any of your teachers. Which reminds me, don't listen to a word Chipmunk says; he made sure all his outdoor missions were at night and hardly even saw one dragon."

"When do we get to start watching for dragons?" Ivy

asked. "Tomorrow? Can we do a skygazing mission tomorrow?" Skygazing could mean going outside and climbing a tree, or it could mean going to one of the spots in Valor with a view of the sky; either way, Ivy would be happy to stare into the blue all day, waiting for a dragon.

With Foxglove, so far she'd seen ten sand dragons, nine mountain dragons, two mud dragons, and one that was such a weird purplish color that they'd both decided the sun must have been in their eyes. They hadn't seen a black dragon again since the first day, but Ivy loved all of them.

Is Foxglove part of the conspiracy? she suddenly thought. The world went sharp and then blurry around her. *Is that the only reason she's been so nice to me all this time? Because she's using me to spy on my dad?* That first day outside, when they'd followed Heath together, suddenly took on a very different light.

That can't be it. She does like me for who I am. I know she does.

Ivy wished she could go back to the beginning of the day, when all she was thinking about was how soon they could see another dragon.

"We'll see, Ivy Who Loves Dragons," Foxglove said with a smile. She hesitated, then crouched beside Ivy. "Listen, don't let the commander know how you feel about the dragons, all right? She lost a lot of people when the village burned."

"Oh," Ivy said, feeling guilty. "Of course, I'll be careful. I'm sorry. I didn't know." She hadn't even thought about the fact that Brook was old enough to have lived in the old village. That meant she'd known Heath before he was the Dragonslayer.

Ivy glanced across the cave at the Wingwatcher commander, who was trapped in a corner listening to Ivy's father as he declaimed about something.

Brook was very good at keeping her face expressionless, but Ivy was very good at figuring out when people were angry, or about to get angry. She could see the grip Brook had on her cup of cider, and the little lines of tension around her eyes.

How did she really feel about the Dragonslayer?

If Violet was right, and someone in the Wingwatchers was planning a revolution, did Brook know about it?

Could it be Brook herself?

I'm a Wingwatcher now, Ivy thought. *Brook is my commander.*

But Dad is . . . my dad. He made mistakes and lied a lot, but he still loved her, in his way, and Mother loved him, and Ivy loved him, too, the side of him that was her father.

If Violet and Daffodil found proof of a secret conspiracy, what was Ivy going to do?

Will I have to choose between my friends, my dream, and the dragons . . . or my family?

PART TWO

CHAPTER 10

WREN

After seven years living on her own with a dragon, Wren figured she probably knew more about the geography of the world than any other human in it. She'd finally given up on the useless maps most people had and was working on her own. It was beautiful, if she did say so herself, and intricately detailed. It certainly helped to have a dragon's eyes overhead, describing the coastline and spotting landmarks for her.

The summer after she met Undauntable, she and Sky had traveled all the way to the north edge of the mountains, circling far around Talisman and the palace of the mountain dragons. They'd gone to the farthest point of the peninsula and discovered hidden villages there where people lived in relative safety, at least compared to the villages directly below the dragons' wings.

Wren wasn't interested in human villages, though, except as places where she could trade her old books for new ones. She didn't trust people, especially the ones who made clucking noises and asked where her parents were and invited her to their houses for a meal. She never stayed near human settlements longer than a night, and she never went inside their buildings for any reason.

Once they'd reached the top of the continent, she and Sky had turned south and gone down the coast, looking out to the great bay and the distant islands. Sky liked to gallop along the beach and then gallop back, shaking sand off his wings all over her. He loved hermit crabs nearly as much as snails, and then he met his first baby turtle and nearly fainted with joy.

"Is this all because you wish you had your own shell you could hide inside?" Wren asked. They'd developed a sort of hybrid Human-Dragon language between them, shifting back and forth between the two, depending on which words they knew of each.

"SO CUTE," Sky warbled, near tears. He lay down beside the turtle and rested his head on his front claws. "I looooooooooooooooooooooooooove it. Wren! Look at its little head. Look at its little feet! It is the sweetest, best little animal in the whole history of the universe."

"Don't let the snails hear you say that," Wren teased. "They might get jealous."

They'd camped on that beach for days so Sky could make sure the baby turtle made it to the ocean and survived and had a wonderful life ahead of it. Wren kindly decided not to tell him she was pretty sure the ocean dragons ate turtles. Hopefully they'd miss this particular one.

They saw the blue and green dragons often, soaring out

over the water or diving into the waves. Twice Wren saw a sea dragon swoop down and then fly up again with an actual shark thrashing in its talons. She stayed a little closer to the tree line after that. The dragons of the sea didn't seem all that interested in hunting for land animals, but she was quite ready to hide if they suddenly changed their minds.

The river delta and the swamps after it were tricky to navigate, plus potentially full of dragons hiding under the mud, so Wren suggested going back into the mountains. But then Sky had a wonderful idea.

"You could RIDE on me!" he announced. "And I could FLY over the swamps!"

Wren studied him dubiously. They had wandered into a cluster of mangrove trees and not being able to see what was in the water around her feet had made her nervous, so she was sitting up on one of the branches, deciding what to do next. Sky was perched on a tree beside her. He was still very small compared to all the other dragons they saw, but he was more than twice Wren's size by this point, and the tree was drooping unhappily underneath him.

"That would be great," Wren said, "but I'm not sure you're big enough yet."

She was politely avoiding saying, "And also you're a rather dreadful flier." Sky had enormous enthusiasm, very little sense of direction, and a habit of getting distracted by seagulls, forgetting to flap, and suddenly plummeting out of the sky. Wren thought he was very likely to accidentally fly her into a tree.

"Climb on!" Sky offered hopefully. "Let's try!" He edged a bit closer, wobbling as the branch bowed lower.

"Well . . . all right," said Wren. She had kind of been dreaming of this moment since Sky first managed to jump off a boulder and go up instead of down. After all, who would have a dragon for a best friend and never fly with him?

She scrambled onto Sky carefully, settling her legs right above his wings and wrapping her arms around his neck.

"This is weird," she said. "This used to be the other way around."

"Hang on!" he yelped happily, and leaped into the sky.

Five minutes later, they crashed into the ocean. Wren floundered back onto the beach, laughing.

"I'm sorry!" Sky yelped, splashing after her. "I'm sorry! Let's try again!"

"We will," Wren said, "when you're a little bigger." She waded over to him and hugged him fiercely. "That was amazing."

So they went back into the mountains, but the next year Sky was a lot bigger and they were able to fly over the entire swamplands and see the peninsula and islands on the far end of the continent. They also saw another human city out there, as big as the Indestructible City, and just as likely to shoot flaming things at dragons, it turned out, so they flew away without investigating any further.

Later on they followed the Indestructible City's river to the southern coast and flew east, along the edge of the rain-forest, with Wren making notes on her map about the peninsulas and islands down there. They were both curious about the rainforest, but it made a lot of strange noises and looked very dense and hard to fly in, so in the end they colored that whole section of the map dark green, labeled it HERE BE TREES, and left it at that.

Sky practiced until he was a brilliant flier, according to Wren, and he was always very careful when he was carrying her. The only part of the continent they hadn't really explored was the desert and the arctic tundra above it. Every time they looked at the desert, Wren got nervous. She didn't like the idea of being so exposed, of having nowhere to hide from other dragons, or from other people.

Whenever Wren ran out of things to read or needed new clothes, they'd go back to their hidden valley and Sky would wait while she ventured down to the Indestructible City. There, Wren would climb a tree and watch the line at the cliff, for days if necessary — it was never more than two — until Prince Undauntable showed up. Then she would go down, give him another dragon scale, and get everything she needed.

Once, when Wren thought she was around twelve, Undauntable asked her to come into the city to visit his manor.

"It's *really* big," he said proudly.

"Mrow," Cat agreed. Even though Undauntable had grown to be slightly taller than Wren (a fact she disliked), the cat was still much too big for him and he still carried it everywhere. And Wren still refused to call it Dragon.

"You'll be very impressed," he added. He swept his hair back in what he probably thought was a dramatic fashion. He'd grown it long, trimmed his eyebrows, and was wearing one of Sky's scales embedded in a big silver ring. His robes were pale orange, perhaps to match.

"Meh," Wren said with a shrug. She picked up another book. They'd found a family in line who had at least ten books she'd never seen before; she couldn't carry them all, but she was having a hard time choosing between them. "A house is a house. Just a bunch of walls."

"These are BIG walls," he said crossly. "It's way bigger than your house!"

"So?" said Wren. "Your city has far too many walls for me. I have a feeling if I went up there, I'd never be able to get back down." She thought, *And then Sky would try to come rescue me, and they'd shoot at him.*

"That's silly," said the prince. "But you won't want to leave anyway, once you see how big and amazing it is."

"Oh?" said Wren. "And would I get to be adopted by a big, fancy family so I could have my own walls? And maybe a collar so everyone knows I belong to them?"

"You could bring your own family," he said, in the voice he used when he thought he was being sly and gathering information. "How many would that be? I could tell Dad to find a place for you. Wouldn't they be so pleased? Everyone wants to live here and hardly anyone can, but he'd listen to me. Ooh, you could live next door to me! I don't like our neighbors anyway; I don't mind kicking them out."

"I do not want to live in the Indestructible City," Wren said firmly.

"But then you could see *me* all the time," he wheedled.

She arched an eyebrow at him. "What makes you think either of us would like that?"

"The — because — I'm the — everyone wants to be friends with me!" he blurted.

"If I lived next door to you," Wren pointed out, "I wouldn't be able to bring you the dragon scales you love. Just think about that, as you look around at all your hundreds of friends: *I could have one more friend who barely tolerates me, or I could have the most unique dragon scales in the city.* Then you'll feel better."

"You don't understand anything," he grumbled.

"I'll take these five," Wren said to the woman with the books. "You buy the other five," she said to Undauntable, "and bring them to me next time I come back."

"What — just carry them up and down from the city every day in case you show up?" he demanded indignantly.

"Don't pretend like you ever walk those steps," Wren said with a laugh. "You have your own fancy basket these days. I saw it." A person basket had been added next to the cargo platform in the last few years. She wondered how many people used it besides the prince — and she wondered whether he came down often, looking for her when she wasn't here.

She put her new books in the knapsack she'd just bought as well, pretending not to pay attention, but she was pleased to note Undauntable buying the other books behind her and handing them to his bodyguard.

"So when will you be back?" he asked, following her as she strolled to the end of the line.

"I don't know," she said, like she always said. "But we'll both survive until then."

"You'd better," he said. Wren started toward the river and was enormously surprised when he grabbed her hand. She looked at him and he immediately let go.

"I was just going to say," he said quickly, "that I'm very mad you won't come see my house. But — but I hope you come back soon because you are not boring. Don't stay away a whole year again this time."

"Was it a whole year?" Wren asked. "Huh. Well, we'll see." He looked sort of wounded, so she added, "You are reasonably interesting yourself, I guess. Probably the second most interesting friend I have." That seemed to cheer him up, so she did not add that she only had two friends, and that he just barely squeaked into the category at all.

This backfired a little, however, when two years later he asked her to marry him.

CHAPTER 11

LEAF

Leaf spread the blueprint on the table and Cranberry leaned over it with a gasp of awe.

"You did it," Grove said. "Leaf! This is amazing."

"You're crazy brave, kid," said Thyme.

It had taken him months of stolen moments to copy the blueprint, carefully penciling in every detail he could while his heart pounded and every noise sounded like Master Trout returning.

"This is really the mountain dragons' palace?" Mushroom said skeptically. "How do we know? What the heck is this?" He pointed to a smudge in the top left corner. "And over here . . . 'prison'? That doesn't look like a prison. It looks like a bunch of columns."

"I just copied it," Leaf said. "We'll have to trust that who-ever made it — and all the people who added notes to it — knew what they were doing."

Mushroom snorted, but everyone else nodded.

"This changes everything, Leaf," Rowan said. "It was risky, but it means our plan might actually work now."

He smiled up at her. Even though he was a tall fifteen-year-old, she was still taller than him. "I did it for Wren," he said.

Sadness and something else flickered in her expression, and she looked away quickly.

"I don't know," Mushroom grumbled. "If this is even remotely correct, it means our plan is more stupid than it was before. Look at all the levels! Where do they even keep their treasure?"

"According to the notes, most of it is here," Leaf said, pointing to a pair of rooms near the center of the palace. "But we don't know how old this map is, or whether the dragons have moved it by now."

"Great." Mushroom rolled his eyes. "So we're going to sneak into a palace full of dragons based on a kid's scribbled copy of an ancient, unreliable drawing that might be a total fantasy."

"Heck, yeah, I'll do it," Thyme volunteered. "*I'm* not scared." He winked cheekily at his brother, which even Leaf could guess was a bad idea.

Mushroom scowled and stalked out of the room, muttering to himself.

"Thank you, Leaf," Grove said, putting one hand on Leaf's shoulder. "Go back to the dragonmancers. We'll study this and decide what to do."

Two days later, Rowan appeared at the gate of Master Trout's garden in the middle of the day. This never happened, and

Leaf had also never seen her face do what it was doing, which was something like trying not to freak out and something like falling apart and something like she was about to stab someone, all at the same time.

"Um," he said, glancing down the row of beans at the other apprentice, who was out of earshot (he hoped), working on the flower beds near the house. "Hi?"

"Leaf," Rowan whispered, clutching the gate posts and crouching down to talk through the slats. "We have a problem."

Leaf deliberately spilled his basket of beans next to the fence and knelt to pick them up. "What's wrong?" he whispered back. Master Trout was inside the house, but could be spying on them through one of the dusty curtains.

Rowan rubbed her fingers together nervously. "The map," she said. "The blueprint, whatever. It's gone."

Now Leaf knocked over his basket for real. "What?" he cried. "What do you mean? Did you tear it? Can't we fix it?"

"No, it's really gone," she said. "I mean vanished. Like . . . stolen."

"By who?" Leaf's body felt chilled, like icy fish scales were trailing over his skin. "The dragonmancers? Did they find out what I did?"

Rowan shook her head. "It was well hidden. It had to be one of us." She hesitated. "And the only one missing . . . is Mushroom."

"Missing?" Leaf echoed. Something bad was happening, but he didn't understand it. Why would Mushroom steal the map they were all going to use together? Where was he?

"We think he's gone to the dragons' palace on his own," she said. "So he can use the map to steal the treasure for himself."

"*Mushroom?*" Leaf said. "But he'll *definitely* mess it up! Especially by himself!"

"I know!" Rowan said.

"What do we do?" Leaf asked. "How far away is the dragon palace? Does he have a big head start? Can we catch up to him?"

"Catch up to who?" a nasal voice interrupted them.

Rowan winced, then looked over her shoulder as Leaf slowly got to his feet. The other two dragonmancers had snuck up on them and were now standing on the path behind Leaf's sister.

The female dragonmancer, Crow, was tall and gaunt, with brittle hair in a gray toadstool-like shape around her head and wrinkles of disapproval permanently scored around her mouth. She always spoke as though she was the only person in the room whose opinion mattered. She also had a habit of repeating the last thing she'd said again more loudly, as if to stick it firmly in people's minds.

The other one was Gorge, a man with a lizard's faee, terrible skin, and slick hair who couldn't muster a natural smile to save his life. His perpetual expression was sly, insecure, and malevolently gleeful at the same time, as though he knew full well that everyone he met wanted to punch him but couldn't because of his power.

"Yes, children," he said. "Who were you talking about?"

"No one," Leaf answered at the same time as Rowan said, "A friend."

"He went hunting," Rowan added quickly. "Alone, and he's kind of clumsy, so we're just worried about him. No big deal."

"It is a terrible, terrible idea to lie to a dragonmancer," Crow said. "TERRIBLE. I'm sure *you* will not make that mistake, apprentice." She turned a sharp eye on Leaf. "And while you frantically decide how much to tell me, I will generously mention that we heard you say *dragons' palace*, so please, don't leave that part out. Do NOT leave it out."

Leaf knew that she was giving them a chance, and a second lie would have bad consequences. But he didn't know how much they'd heard. Did they know about the map? He had to risk some of the truth . . . but maybe not all of it.

"We think our friend Mushroom has gone to the dragons' palace," he admitted hesitantly. "He — he's always talking about stealing treasure and we think m-maybe he's gone to try."

"Even though we've forbidden it?" Gorge demanded. "What a doomed idiot."

Crow's eyebrows sank down and together and she sucked in air between her teeth. "This could be a disaster," she hissed.

"I know," Rowan said. "He'll probably get eaten —"

"Much worse than that," Crow interrupted. "If the dragons catch him, they could decide to punish the entire village for his crime. We could all be on fire by this time tomorrow! ON FIRE!"

"Perhaps," Gorge said slyly, "someone could do something about this."

"We can stop him," Rowan said. "We'll leave now and catch him before he gets to the palace."

Leaf wondered what she was thinking behind that determined, helpful face. What would they really do if and when they caught Mushroom and got the map back? He had a feeling Rowan, Grove, and Thyme would still want to sneak into the palace. But was Crow right about what would happen to the village? *Not if I kill the dragons first*, his heart whispered.

"It's been a long time since you or I had any new dragon treasure," Gorge said in his slithering voice, sliding his hands together. "So many useless, weak apprentices. So prone to getting eaten before they can achieve their goals."

Treasure smuggler, Wren whispered scornfully in Leaf's head. *That's what they really want. More treasure, more power. They don't care about the village.*

Did they once send apprentices to steal treasure? Leaf wondered back. *Is that why no apprentice has lived long enough to join the ranks of the dragonmancers?*

"That's truuuuue," Crow said slowly. "It would be very enriching for everyone if certain parties returned with dragon treasure and shared it with the correct people. But if the expedition were unsuccessful . . . that would be such a shame. Such a shame."

"Indeed," said Gorge. "If our intrepid explorers snuck off to the dragon palace but did *not* return with treasure . . ."

"I imagine the dragons would require a sacrifice," Crow said. "A big, big sacrifice."

"Wait," said Leaf. "So you *do* want us to steal treasure? Even though you forbade it?"

Hypocrisy from a dragonmancer? Wren muttered. *I'm shocked. SHOCKED.*

"Shhh," said Crow. "Your friend set this in motion. This is all his fault. These are the consequences. I only see one happy ending here."

"We can catch Mushroom if you give us a chance," Rowan said quickly. "Before he even gets to the palace."

"No, no, no," said Gorge. "If you're going all that way, *someone* should go into the palace, steal *something*, and bring it back to us. Otherwise, I'm afraid something terrible will happen."

"Indeed. They want a stranger this time," Crow said in an eerie voice. Her eyes were unfocused, as though another story was unfolding in a mirror of the world between her and Leaf and Rowan. "Yes. They want an outsider who brought danger to the village. Someone with too many questions. I sense this person draws the dragons' wrath . . . their WRATH."

She's talking about Grove, Leaf realized. *But surely she doesn't mean . . she can't mean what it sounds like.*

"What do you mean by a sacrifice?" Leaf asked. "Some of his goats?"

"Has it been that long since our last one?" Crow murmured, reaching a skeletal finger to trail down Leaf's cheek. He squelched his shudder and held himself rigidly still. "I remember it like it was yesterday . . . I know *you* remember, don't you, dear?" she said to Rowan.

"We can stop Mushroom," Rowan said, talking over her last words. "And we can bring you treasure. Let us go after him and we'll make it happen."

"Hmmm," Gorge said. "I think we need our sacrifice standing by, just in case." He beckoned to Leaf's fellow apprentice, who had been watching from the flower beds while trying very hard to look as though he hadn't noticed the other dragonmancers. Tadpole approached nervously, glancing between the four of them.

"Go find young Grove for me," Gorge said. "Take him to the dragonmancers' council hut and make sure he stays there to wait for us. Bring a few men from the village guard if you think you'll need help. We'll be there soon."

"Yes, sir," Tadpole said, bowing a few hundred times before hurrying away.

"You don't have to do this!" Rowan said desperately.

"We *didn't* have to," Crow corrected her. "But thanks to young Mushroom's greed, now we do. Grove will stay with us. All you have to do is follow your friend and return with some treasure, and everyone will be so happy. Ever ever so happy."

Rowan looked as though she'd been snared in a spiderweb as Crow and Gorge turned to walk away.

"We have to go now," Rowan said to Leaf, glancing up and down the quiet path. "Do you need anything from in there?" She nodded at the house.

Leaf wished he could run in, grab the map off the wall, and escape, but he might as well wish for a flying carpet to the dragons' palace. "Nothing," he said, swinging himself over the fence. "Give me a sword and I'm ready."

He was not planning on coming back to Trout's house. Whatever happened at the palace, whether he killed ten dragons or only one, he wasn't going to come moseying back to the drudgery of being a dragonmancer's apprentice afterward. His life as a dragonslayer was about to begin.

They took the long way through the woods to avoid any townspeople. When they arrived at the schoolhouse, Cranberry and Thyme were standing outside it, looking confused.

"Rowan!" Cranberry said as they ran up to her. "A group of villagers just came and took Grove away — we don't know why. Wait, you do — what's happened?" she added, seeing the look on Rowan's face.

"Crow and Gorge found out that Mushroom is on his way to steal treasure," Rowan said. "We have to follow him and come back with treasure for them, or they're going to sacrifice Grove."

The horror and enormity of that exploded in Leaf's head. He'd been trying so hard to convince himself that he'd misunderstood, that none of this could be happening, that Crow and Gorge had been talking about stealing more of Grove's goats instead.

"Do you really think *that's* what she meant?" Leaf cried. "No one would let them do that! We don't sacrifice *people* to the dragons!"

"Of course we don't," Cranberry said, but Rowan looked physically sick, like she really believed the dragonmancers were capable of such a thing.

"All I know for sure is they took Grove," she said. "And I know he isn't safe until we get back here and pay them off."

"Then let's go," Leaf said. Whatever the dragonmancers meant, whether Rowan was right or not, they still had to catch Mushroom and get the map back. "Cranberry, I need a sword."

Cranberry led the way to their secret stash of weapons and handed him a sheathed sword, which he buckled around his back. Two more daggers went into his boots, and then he was off and sprinting through the forest ahead of everyone else.

He knew they would follow him, even though he was ten years younger than they all were. One upside of putting himself in danger to copy the map was that now it was kind of etched in his brain. He didn't like the idea of relying on his memory, but he was pretty sure it was all there: every careful line and each tiny note, painstakingly redrawn. He also knew that the dragon palace was north of the village, near the source of the river, so following the river would make logical sense. But he wasn't sure whether Mushroom would think of it. Doing the smart, logical thing was clearly not Mushroom's strong suit.

They traveled north all the rest of that day and half the night, only stopping because Thyme finally fell over and said he couldn't go any farther without some sleep. Leaf offered to take the first watch and spent most of it climbing to the highest spots around them, looking for any sign of a campfire that might be Mushroom. But there was nothing. No sign of him anywhere.

The same was true on the second day, and the third. They climbed along the ridges of the mountains, keeping the river in sight, with the peaks slashing sharply in the sky above them like dragon claws. Dragons the color of flames flew overhead day and night, bursting through the clouds or swooping suddenly over the next peak and sending them all diving for cover.

They found remains of campfires and once a discarded fishing net, but none of them looked new enough to be Mushroom's. He was nowhere to be found.

On the fourth morning, they came out of a long stretch of trees onto a section of boulders, and there it was at last: the palace of the mountain dragons.

Leaf had been full of wild energy for most of the trip, running on adrenaline and destiny. But as they all squashed themselves into the shadow of a boulder and lay down to stare out at the palace, for the first time he felt a glimmer of fear.

It was *so enormous*. He'd kind of known that from the scale of the blueprint, but he hadn't really absorbed it before. The palace looked like it had swept down from the sky and eaten most of the mountain. Towers seemed to grow out of the gray-black rocks; every ledge was an entrance to the caves and halls carved out of the mountainside. Even from their vantage point, they could feel the crackling heat and smell the trails of smoke that hung in the air like clouds.

And something that wasn't in the blueprint: The palace was swarming with dragons.

Leaf had never imagined there were so many dragons in the world. From his vantage point, he was pretty sure he could see more dragons than there were people in all of Talisman. This was more than a village; this was a city of dragons.

Dragons crawled over the mountain, building new parts of the palace or repairing collapsed towers. Dragons flew from ledge to ledge; dragons soared in from afar to drop bodies of other dragons in the smoking ravine along one side of the palace. Dragons sat on the highest points of the castle walls, spreading their wings to sun themselves.

How could there be *so many dragons* in one place?

Despite all his strength and skill, Leaf felt as small as an ant. An ant who dreamed of killing a whole city of dragons.

He spotted the prison that had been in the blueprint — the tall columns set off to the side, around some kind of arena. He could see more dragon wings glittering from the top of each column, and a sort of web between them all. He wasn't quite sure how a prison like that could hold dragons — but that was one of those mysteries he was perfectly happy to leave unsolved.

"Yeesh," Thyme whispered beside him.

"I know," Cranberry whispered from Leaf's other side. "Like, couldn't you be a little more impressive, dragons?"

Rowan snorted a nervous laugh. "Do you remember the ways in?" she asked Leaf.

Leaf took a deep breath, calling the blueprint back into his mind. There weren't a lot of entrances at ground level, since dragons usually arrived from the sky. They would have to climb half the mountain — with dragons flying all around them — to get to the lowest entry point, which was where a trash chute let out from the palace above. The note beside it had said, *Not an ideal option*.

It might be easier (and less smelly) to go in through the prison arena, which had a low entrance . . . but was also in full view of all the dragon prisoners and any passing guards.

He studied the palace, mapping it onto the blueprint in his mind. If the prison was there and those two towers were there, then the trash chute hole should be . . .

Leaf reached over Cranberry and grabbed Rowan's arm. "Look!" he whispered frantically.

She raised herself onto her elbows and cupped her hands around her eyes.

Not far below the hole, a small shape was making his way up the side of the mountain. His gray clothing blended in with the rocks and smoke, and he was inching upward at a snail's pace, creeping from shadow to shadow. Leaf wasn't sure if that was Mushroom being cautious, or Mushroom being slow and tired.

"Oh *no*," Thyme whispered.

"He must have stolen the map a whole day before we noticed," Cranberry said. "He had more of a head start than we thought."

"What do we do now?" Leaf asked. "It's too late to stop him, isn't it?"

Rowan didn't answer. They watched in silence as the figure climbed higher and higher, and then finally, with agonizing slowness, pulled himself into the trash chute and vanished into the dark interior of the palace.

"I guess now we wait and see," Rowan said finally. "Either he'll come out alive or he won't."

"And if he does," Thyme said, "he might need our help to get away safely."

Leaf didn't say it, but he knew everyone must be thinking the same thing: There was no way a human could walk into that palace and come out alive. The map might help him, but the odds were far in the dragons' favor.

That didn't mean Leaf wouldn't try. He wished he had the map, but he was going into that dragon palace, one way or another. This was something he had to do.

He would take at least one dragon life for Wren's, even if it meant certain death.

— CHAPTER 12 —

IVY

"All you have to do is watch the sky," Foxglove said for the eightieth time. "Stay right here and don't move. If you see a dragon, remember everything about it, and tell us later, when we come back for you. Do NOT leave this tree on your own."

"Oh my goodness, we know!" Daffodil said, laughing. "We'll stay put."

"We promise," Ivy added. She wound one arm around the branch above her.

"Violet?" Foxglove asked sternly.

"I promise, too!" Violet rolled her eyes and shoved herself up to a higher limb.

"If you three misbehave, Commander Brook will never let any fourteen-year-olds outside alone ever again," Foxglove said. "Think of your responsibility to future annoying teenagers."

"It's all we ever think of," Daffodil said sweetly.

"We'll be right here when you get back," Ivy said.

Foxglove made a *hm* sound and swung down out of the tree. Squirrel and two others were waiting for her on the ground, ready to escort a fruit-gathering party. The Wingwatchers would keep an eye out for dragons, help everyone hide if it was necessary, and bring them home safely.

That's what Wingwatchers do, Ivy thought, watching them leave. *They're protectors and researchers. They're not secret revolutionaries. They're not, no matter what Violet thinks.* She hadn't seen any signs of a secret conspiracy during their first year of official training — but then again, she had to be the last Wingwatcher anyone would trust with information like that.

Ivy, Violet, and Daffodil were only skygazing today. This was their third time officially skygazing outside, but the first time they were being left alone to do it. Ivy had practiced a lot with Foxglove, but most of the adult Wingwatchers didn't know that, so she had to pretend it was all new and exciting to her.

Then again, she wasn't really pretending. It *was* still pretty exciting. She could forget all her underground city worries when she watched for dragons.

Violet had seen a sand dragon once, on a secret trip outside with Ivy and Foxglove, but Daffodil still hadn't seen any, and she was infinitely outraged about that.

Ivy rested her back against the trunk and stared up into the blue sky.

"So," Violet said as soon as the Wingwatchers and fruit gatherers were out of sight, "I haven't had ANY luck with either secret. Have you?"

"No, I haven't," said Daffodil. "Although I kind of forgot we were supposed to be working on that."

Violet sighed expressively. "Ivy?"

"I asked my mother again about Uncle Stone," Ivy said. "But she said I'm still too young to hear about it."

"By all the dragons," Violet said. "How bad is this secret if *fourteen* is too young to know it?!"

"I don't think it's because she's fourteen," Daffodil offered. "I think it's because she's Ivy, and her mom never wants her to know anything."

Ivy couldn't argue with that. There were lots of things she only knew because Violet and Daffodil had explained them to her.

"I haven't even tried finding anything about the, um, the other secret," Ivy said. "I figure obviously no one will talk to *me* about it." *And maybe I don't really want them to*.

"No one should talk to anyone about it!" Daffodil said. "It's way too dangerous!"

"Hey, you're the one whose life was RUINED when Pine was banished," Violet pointed out. "I'm basically doing this for you."

"You know nothing about love, Violet!" Daffodil cried. "And you are not doing this for me at all; you're doing it because you're nosy and can't stand it when other people know things that you don't."

"Only when they're important!" Violet said. "I thought you'd be all about starting a revolution. Causing chaos is literally your favorite thing."

"I don't have a problem with chaos. Or revolution! I have a problem with one of my best friends acting like an idiot. You can't be sure all the Wingwatchers are part of this imaginary secret revolution. If you say the wrong thing to the wrong person, they could turn *you* in for treason, and then you'll be banished, and then it'll suddenly be a lot quieter and less stressful around here, so actually, never mind, you keep being you."

Ivy laughed. Out here, with the wind blowing in her hair and the leaves rustling around them and dragons somewhere in the sky, even her friends bickering over dangerous conspiracies felt joyful.

It was still weird to see Daffodil without a speck of yellow on her anywhere — weird, also, to see Violet running through the woods and jumping over fallen trees instead of reading a book. But weird in a good way. Ivy was so, so happy to be outside, in the amazing sunlit world, with them.

Even though they were talking about a revolution against her dad, today it just . . . didn't seem *real*. It was hard to believe that people could be so mad at each other when there was all this sky and millions of trees and towers of beautiful gold-lined clouds overhead.

And in those clouds . . .

"Hey," she whispered. "Do you guys see that?"

It was so far up that she wasn't even sure it was a dragon, except that there wasn't anything else it could be. Birds didn't reflect the sunlight in little flashes; no bird was that big or the color of diamonds, not at the same time.

Daffodil inhaled sharply and clambered onto the branch right next to Ivy so she could rest her head on Ivy's shoulder and look in the same direction.

"Daffodil!" Violet whispered sternly. "You're not supposed to MOVE when you're skygazing!"

"Violet!" Daffodil whispered back in the same tone. "You're not supposed to BE ANNOYING when you're skygazing!"

Violet snorted and cupped her hands around her eyes to stare at the distant shape.

"You really aren't supposed to move," Ivy whispered softly in Daffodil's ear.

"Shhh," Daffodil whispered back. She squeezed Ivy's hand. "My first dragon!"

Ivy more than understood what she was feeling. She still felt it, a little thrill all the way along her skin, every time she saw one.

The dragon circled, swooping lower and lower. It was flying in an odd, loopy way, jerking sideways, then flapping back, then jerking sideways again. It kept shaking its whole body like a wet dog trying to get dry.

"Huh," Daffodil whispered. "I thought they'd be a little more graceful."

"I think there's something wrong with this one," Ivy whispered back.

"Quit having conversations without me," Violet hissed from her higher branch.

"Shhhh," Daffodil said to her with a supercilious face.

As it came closer, Ivy started to feel a new shiver of exhilaration. She was pretty sure this was a kind of dragon she'd never seen before.

It had scales as purely white as the snow on distant mountains, glimmering like cut glass. Its face was narrow, and the spikes along its back were long and sharp. More deadly-looking spikes bristled like needles from the end of its tail.

"By the stars," Ivy breathed, remembering the drawings in the guide. "I think that's an ice dragon."

"It's so shiny," Daffodil whispered.

"Why is it flying so weird?" Violet asked. "Is it coming to land?"

The ice dragon shook itself again and then dove toward the forest, plummeting like a comet out of the sky. Daffodil clutched Ivy's arm and Ivy held tight to the branch above her, trying to keep as still as she could. The Wingwatcher's Guide said ice dragons had sharper eyesight than most other kinds. Even if this dragon was injured, it could probably still snatch them out of the tree and eat them if it saw them.

The dragon crashed into the trees about half a mile away, smashing through the branches and disappearing from sight.

"Oh my goodness," Daffodil whispered.

"Should we go see if it's all right?" Violet asked.

"Violet!" Ivy said. "Foxglove specifically said to stay right here. I'm pretty sure 'don't go charging up to a wounded dragon' was implied!"

"But think of how well you could draw it if you got really close to it," Violet wheedled.

"I'm with Violet," Daffodil said. "Let's go look at it."

"How is it that when you two finally agree on something, it's the WORST thing?" Ivy demanded. "No. We promised Foxglove. I want to see it up close, too, but we can't disobey her! They'll make us stay inside for the next two years! Maybe longer!"

She was saved from the rest of this argument by the sound of footsteps running through the trees. They all froze, listening, until they saw Squirrel appear below the tree.

"Oh, good," he said when he saw them. "We saw a dragon land nearby and Foxglove sent me to check on you."

"Check on us?" Violet asked. "Or make sure we stayed put?"

"Both," he said with a grin.

"We weren't going anywhere!" Daffodil said innocently.

"We wouldn't dream of it," Violet agreed.

"Ivy wanted to, but we told her no," Daffodil added. Ivy swatted her, and she dissolved in giggles.

"I'll just stay here and keep you company," Squirrel said. "Not because we don't trust you, but because we remember being young Wingwatchers, too."

Violet sighed.

"We think it might be wounded," Ivy said to Squirrel. "It was flying all weird and landed in a really awkward way."

"Foxglove is going to — carefully — scout out the situation," Squirrel said. "She'll let us know what she finds."

"Wait. Do you hear that?" Violet asked, leaning forward on her branch.

They all fell silent for a moment.

Thrashing — and panting — coming from the direction where the dragon had landed. It wasn't loud enough to be a dragon, surely. But something was heading in their direction.

Squirrel silently reached up and swung himself into the tree. He crouched right below Ivy, and they all stared toward the sounds.

Something shoved through the bushes, breaking a few branches and shaking the leaves. Something staggered into the clear space below them, breathing heavily. Something paused, maybe fell or collapsed, flattening the grass.

But they couldn't see it. They could see the vegetation moving around it; there was a clear outline of something heavy lying below them now. They could still hear it, gasping for breath. It *sounded* like a human.

So why couldn't they see it?

Daffodil quietly worked a pine cone off the branch next to her. Before Ivy realized what she was up to, Daffodil leaned forward and dropped the pine cone squarely into the center of the flattened grass.

The something let out a yelp — a very human yelp — and then there were some scrambling-around noises.

"Oh, thank the moons," said an extremely human voice. "Wingwatchers." The shape seemed to collapse into the grass again.

"Halt there," Squirrel said sternly. "Who are you?"

"Can't you —" There was a pause. "*Oh.* Oh, right."

Ivy's uncle Stone suddenly appeared below them. He looked bedraggled, windblown, bruised, and thinner than before, but it was unmistakably him.

Daffodil let out a squeak of surprise.

"Uncle Stone!" Ivy said. She scrambled down to the branch next to Squirrel. "Permission to get down, sir?"

"I — I guess this is an unusual case," Squirrel said. "Sure."

Ivy jumped down to the ground and smiled up at her uncle. Not as far up as the last time she'd seen him . . . was it nearly two years ago?

He stared back at her as if she were a ghost.

"Are you all right?" Ivy asked.

He pressed his fingers into his eyes for a moment, as if rubbing out an old image, and then blinked at her again. "You're my niece," he said. "Ivy." His voice was rusty, as though he hadn't used it much in a while.

"Of course I am," she said. "Where have you been?"

"And how did you do that?" Violet demanded from above. "Appear from thin air like that?"

Stone squinted up. "How many Wingwatchers do you have in that tree?"

"You should get up there, too," Ivy said, reaching for his hand. "We just saw a dragon land not too far away."

"Oh, yes," he said. "I was . . . well, riding it isn't exactly the right description."

"What?" Daffodil shrieked.

"Shhh!" Squirrel glared at her. "Keep it down!"

"Riding a dragon?" Ivy echoed, awestruck.

"I needed to get back here," he said. "It seemed like the fastest way?" He gestured ruefully to his torn clothes and the trickles of blood coming from his knees, arms, and face. "Probably should have chosen a less spiky dragon."

"So . . . it was helping you?" Ivy asked.

Uncle Stone frowned at her. "Of course not. It didn't know I was on board — or rather, it knew that *something* was on top of it, but it didn't know what."

"How is that possible?" Violet asked.

"You could steer it, even though it didn't know you were there?" Ivy asked.

"Well," he said. "Not very well. I think it was coming this way anyhow."

"Invisibility!" Violet shouted suddenly.

"SHHHHHHH!" Squirrel tried again.

"You can make yourself invisible! That's it, isn't it?" Violet said. She was leaning over so far she was nearly falling out of the tree.

Stone sighed. "Don't tell anyone, please." He opened his fist to reveal a long, thin, coiled chain made of a silvery-black metal. "It was in the sand queen's treasure. Heath let me have it because he didn't know what it could do." He shook it out and looped one end over his neck, vanishing the moment it touched him.

"Oh my stars," Daffodil breathed. "Actual. Magic."

Stone reappeared, lifting the chain off his neck. He collected the coils into a tangle in his fist, then stuffed it in one of his pockets. "That's how I survived out there," he said.

"Where?" Violet demanded. "Where did you go, and why?"

Stone looked down at Ivy with the sad eyes she remembered from every family dinner. "I had a dream that Rose was still alive, and so I went looking for her, but the desert nearly killed me, and then I ended up in a dragon city, which took me forever to escape, and the whole expedition was a disaster, and I don't know what I was thinking. She's been dead for almost twenty years. There's no way she could have survived even a day out there among the dragons, on her own."

Ivy met Violet's eyes, then Daffodil's. They all looked back at Stone.

"Um," said Ivy. "Who's Rose?"

CHAPTER 13

WREN

Wren was fourteen and she did not have time for Undauntable's nonsense.

She probably should have guessed something was up when she found him examining a jewelry trader's wares and he looked so very pleased to see her.

"Wren!" he cried. She had finally told him her name on their third meeting, figuring there wasn't anything too terrible he could do with it. "I have a great idea!"

"Good for you," Wren said. "I can't stay long today." She'd promised Sky she would be back before nightfall. He'd recently decided he could sing — which was slightly factually inaccurate — and wanted to make up a song for her. "Here's another scale. I need —"

"Stop stop stop," Undauntable said. "Listen. I know you have a stash of these and you're just bringing me one at a time. I also know you don't have a family, because you never buy anything for anyone else, and you're afraid to go into the city, which means you're probably an orphan."

Wren put her hands on her hips and glared at him. "You

seem to think you know a lot of things that aren't your business."

"But you don't have to worry anymore!" he said. "Because of my great idea. You should marry me."

Wren blinked at him, then looked over her shoulder to see if anyone was standing behind her. Undauntable's porcupine bodyguard was there, a little closer than she would have liked. She guessed Undauntable wasn't proposing to him.

"No," Wren said to Undauntable. "To be clear: never."

"What?" he said, his face clouding over.

"I *do* have a family," Wren said. *My family happens to be a dragon; you don't get to know that.* "And I am not remotely interested in getting married or living in a city. For someone who wants to marry me, you don't seem to know me very well."

Undauntable threw his hands in the air. "Because you always LEAVE," he complained. "If I marry you, you'll have to stay. I'll buy you lots of things. You can bring your whole stash of dragon scales so we can be super rich together. And you'll get to be princess of the city! It's a dream come true!"

"Undauntable, I'm only going to say this once, and I really mean this," Wren said. "Yuck."

"But *whyyyyyyyyyyyy*?" he demanded.

"Because I don't want lots of things, I hate cities and people, and I only want to be friends with you," Wren said. *Friends-ish*, she amended in her head. *The kind who have polite interactions once a year and that's it.*

"My life is so unfair," Undauntable said, sitting down on

the ground. Cat curled up in his lap and stared balefully at Wren. "Everything is terrible."

"It is not actually my responsibility to fix your life by giving you everything you want," Wren pointed out. "I'm not a rare dragon scale to add to your collection. I am a person. You are not entitled to have me along with everything else."

"Every time I see you, you make me mad," he said. "But then I'm *so bored* until you come back."

"Undauntable!" Wren said. "That is definitely a problem you need to solve yourself!"

"Ugh," he grumbled, burying his face in Cat's fur.

"You should try reading," Wren suggested. "It's much more fun than getting married."

Undauntable looked up at her to see if she was teasing him, but she actually wasn't. She thought it was a perfectly fine idea, and he must have access to loads of books.

He narrowed his eyes and glanced at his bodyguard in a way that Wren didn't like. Undauntable was spoiled and grumpy and demanding, and he always complained about her leaving, but he'd never done anything to stop her before.

"Have you noticed any new books out here today?" she asked, trying to change the subject. It seemed like there were fewer encampments in the line than usual. She wondered where everyone was. Not in the city, she guessed.

"What if you promise to marry me *someday*?" he asked.

Wren tucked the scale back in her pocket. "Start with a

dictionary," she told him. "Look up the word *never*. And stop acting like people are just more things you can buy."

She marched away down the line of travelers toward the river, feeling very betrayed. Why did her *one* human friendish person have to turn out to be terrible, just like all the others?

She'd gotten about ten steps away from Undauntable when someone in the line screamed and pointed at the sky.

Wren whirled around and saw a dragon hurtling toward the unprotected people gathered at the base of the cliff. Everyone on the ground started screaming and running, while the ones already on the steps froze and cowered into the cliffside.

It was a sand dragon, enormous and gleaming in the morning sun. Its teeth were bared in a delighted grin and its venomous tail was raised behind it like a promise of death to come.

Above her, Wren saw something happening, up in the Indestructible City. There was movement along the top of the cliff, like weapons rolling out. She stepped back to see it better, and then Undauntable's bodyguard slammed into her, knocking her to the ground.

"Hey, ow!" she yelled, kicking him hard in the stomach. He grunted and rolled away, and she scrambled to her feet. Overhead, the dragon swooped by and circled to come from another direction.

"Just trying to . . . get you to safety," the bodyguard

groaned, and Wren realized that this one was a woman. She hadn't been able to tell with the helmet on. "Prince's orders."

Wren looked around. She'd been so interested in the city's defenses, she'd forgotten about Undauntable. "Where is he?" she asked. "Isn't he the one you should keep safe?"

The bodyguard pointed to a crevice in the side of the cliff, not far from the base of the stairs. Undauntable was standing just inside the narrow gap, beckoning to her. His face was scared, but not as frantic as some of the people around him. He lived in a city that fought back, while most of these people had probably lost friends and entire villages to dragons.

Wren jumped up and ran toward him. He reached out his hand, but as she got close, she scooped up a toddler who was standing still in the chaos, sobbing. Undauntable looked extremely bewildered when she shoved the toddler into his arms.

She turned around and grabbed another kid as he ran by. He looked younger than Wren had been when Talisman abandoned her. She pushed him into the crevice with Undauntable and the toddler.

"Wait —" Undauntable said, but Wren had spotted another little girl, trapped by the fence at the bottom of the stairs. She was shaking the gate and crying. Wren ran to her, lifted her over the fence, and carried her to Undauntable's hiding spot.

"This is a lot of —" Undauntable protested. The crevice wasn't very big, and he was now squashed into the back of it, with three crying children around him.

"Room for one more, I think," Wren said, and darted away. "Yes, YOU!" he shouted.

She found one more kid who seemed to be by himself and brought him back. The dragon was flying back and forth over the city now, dodging whatever they were shooting at him and laughing.

"This is too many sticky children!" Undauntable shouted as she squeezed the last one inside. "And not enough you!"

"I'll be fine," Wren said. She tilted her head to look up at the sand dragon. "That dragon doesn't even seem hungry. He's acting like he's here entirely to annoy your citizens."

He was, in fact, roaring something like, "HA HA, PUNY SCAVENGERS! YOU CAN NEVER HIT ME! I AM THE GREATEST WARRIOR IN THE ENTIRE ARMY OF SAND! HA HA HA!"

"So weird," Wren said, putting her hands on her hips. "Like, just a total lunatic."

"This is the fifth time that same dragon has come to attack the city in the last few months," Undauntable said. He tried to squeeze past the children toward her, but they clung to him when he moved and he had to give up. "We thought we'd scared them all into leaving us mostly alone. But this one comes back over and over. It might not be hungry now, although I can't see how you could possibly know that, but it has grabbed at least three people from down here so far."

"HA HA HA!" the dragon bellowed again. "JUST YOU WAIT, YOU COCKROACHES! THE QUEEN KNOWS YOU

MUST HAVE HER TREASURE! ONE DAY SOON I WILL RETURN WITH MY GLORIOUS ARMY AND DESTROY YOU!"

Ah. So that wasn't great.

Maybe if it was Talisman, Wren would be fine with a dragon burning it down. If anyone asked, she'd usually pick dragons over humans any day. But this was a whole city, full of people who might be awful, but who hadn't specifically left her to be eaten by dragons, plus also lots of children, and Wren had to admit she didn't want the dragons to destroy it.

The dragon wheeled away and flew off toward the desert, still HA-HA-HA-ing as he went.

"He's not attacking," Wren said to Undauntable after the dragon was out of sight. "He's scouting out your defenses, so a bigger group of them can attack later." She gingerly patted one of the children on the head. "It's safe to go outside again now."

"That can't be right," Undauntable said as the children scampered away. He emerged from the crevice, looking dusty and wrinkled and disgruntled. Two locks had escaped his slick hair and hung over his forehead. "Dragons can't plan ahead. They're driven by impulse and hunger. They don't spend months preparing for an attack or work together."

"That is so ridiculous I can't even look at you," Wren said. "There are entire dragon armies! They're all having a war with one another. Of *course* they plan and strategize and work together."

Undauntable brushed dirt off his robes, squinting at her. "How on earth could you know any of that?"

She was definitely not going to tell him she spoke Dragon, or anything else that might lead back to Sky.

"I pay attention," she said. "Something the prince of a city should probably do. Just tell your dad he needs to prepare for a massive attack, probably soon."

She remembered she was mad at him and turned to go.

"I'll tell him," Undauntable yelled after her. "Hey, Wren, I'm sorry! I really am! Will you come back soon?"

"Don't know!" she called without looking back.

She couldn't wait to get to Sky — away from people who wanted things from her, away from dragons and humans trying to hurt each other. Away from a city bristling with weapons that left kids in danger because they were outsiders.

Sky was hopping from one foot to another with excitement when she reached the valley. It was long after sunset, and Wren was too tired to light a fire, but she could see his delighted face by the light of the three moons.

"Guess what I found?" he burst out. "I mean, I *think*. I was flying up *really* high and I think I saw something great but I didn't want to go look without you. Can we go look?"

"Right now?" Wren asked.

"It's a thing to see in the dark," he said, "and then to investigate in the daylight. Come on, you can fall asleep on top of me if you're THAT tired."

"How did you get so bossy?" Wren asked affectionately, stepping onto his outstretched talons. He lifted her to her favorite spot, settled in the shoulder curve between his wing and neck, holding on to one of his back spines.

They lifted into the sky and banked northwest, to her surprise. That direction would soon take them out of the mountains and into the desert. Sky flew higher and higher, and farther than she'd expected.

"You came all this way by yourself?" she called, and he ducked his head toward her.

"Why not?" he called back. "You went off by yourself, too!"

But I am sensible, and you are not, she thought. *I can protect myself, and you are my adorable helpless baby dragon*. She knew that was *slightly* absurd of her now that he was three times her height, but he didn't have fire and he had no idea how to fight if a bad dragon came along — or people looking to steal his scales, for that matter.

I guess at least people aren't a threat up this high, she admitted to herself.

"I saw a dragon who seemed dangerous today," she said. "A really big sand dragon. You should watch out for him."

"All right," Sky said carelessly. "Look! There it is!" He pointed, his wings shivering with excitement.

It was a clear night, with the moons bright in a cloudless sky. In the distance, far ahead and below them, Wren saw a cluster of lights on the ground.

"What's that?" she asked.

"I think it's a city!" he said. "Can we get closer?"

"Carefully," she agreed.

They flew onward, deeper into the desert than they'd ever been before. Wren saw the long, dark serpentine shape of a river cutting through the sand. The lights were scattered around the river, closer and closer together as the river approached the sea.

"Wow," she said softly. "Sky, I think you're right. It looks like a big city . . . a dragon city."

"Isn't that amazing?" he said, pausing to hover for a moment. "Wren, can we please sleep nearby and visit it in the morning?"

"*Visit* it? That doesn't sound safe," Wren pointed out. "At all."

"You go to your human city," he pleaded. "Can't I please visit a dragon city?"

Wren felt a stab of her old anxiety, that one day Sky would decide he'd rather be with other dragons instead of her. That one day he would leave her for something better.

But she couldn't say no, when he was so sweet and never asked for anything. If he did want to go be with other dragons one day, she couldn't be selfish about it.

Besides, this didn't mean he was leaving her now. It meant he was curious. That was fine. Wasn't it?

"Let's find a safe place to rest for the night," Wren said, "and in the morning, we'll take a closer look at the dragon city."

CHAPTER 14

LEAF

A roar of fury split the sky and shook the rocks, startling Leaf awake. He sat up quickly and banged his head on the ledge he'd been sleeping under.

Next to him, the others emerged from their camouflage coverings of branches and leaves, blinking.

"That sounded a lot closer than all the other dragon sounds," Cranberry said nervously.

They'd had trouble sleeping this close to the palace, with roars and growls and wingbeats filling the night, especially after lying still all day. At one point in the late afternoon, Leaf had crept back into the forest to walk off his nerves. He'd run through his tumbling training, then climbed the tallest tree he could find. From the top, he could see east all the way to the hazy blue line of the ocean.

Looking south, toward Talisman, he thought he saw a shape arrowing through the clouds — an enormous dragon with scales as black as night. He wondered if the distance was playing tricks with his eyes, or if that was really one of the rare black dragons Grove claimed he'd seen once, too.

Now it was midmorning, and he'd finally gotten about an hour of fitful sleep before the dragon roar woke him. He crawled partway out from under the ledge, rubbing his head and squinting toward the palace.

It looked busier than it had the day before. Dragons were boiling up out of the depths of the palace, pouring into the sky like a swarm of bees. They divided into formations and shot away, some of them north, some east, some west. The rest gathered in a hovering red-orange cloud, staring south.

An orange dragon wreathed in coils of smoke suddenly shot past overhead, flattening the hair on Leaf's head with the wind of its passing. Its roar sounded like the one that had woken them. It soared up to the waiting dragons and roared something at them.

Leaf scrambled back under the ledge. "They seem angry," he whispered. "Maybe Mushroom succeeded."

"I'm afraid so," Rowan said. She pointed to a ridge below them, edged with trees on one side and a steep dirt slope on the other. A human was scrambling through the trees as fast as he could, carrying a sword in one hand and a sack in the other.

"Mushroom!" Thyme shouted. He rolled out from under the ledge and sprinted across the boulders, staying low. "Mushroom!" he called again.

"That seems like maybe a terrible idea," Cranberry said to Rowan.

"Too late now," Rowan said, drawing her sword.

The three of them ran after Thyme. Leaf kept one eye on

the sky, where the orange dragon was still roaring at the others. It looked like it was either giving orders or yelling at everyone for doing something wrong. But as long as their focus was on that dragon, they might not notice the prey darting around below.

Mushroom saw his brother a few yards before their paths converged. He skidded to a stop, his eyes wide and his breath coming in gasps.

"Mushroom!" Thyme cried. "I can't believe you're alive! You idiot! I was so worried!"

"Stay back!" Mushroom shouted, slashing his sword through the air. Thyme stopped abruptly, nearly skidding down the slope, and Leaf almost crashed into him.

"It's all right," Cranberry called. "Mushroom, we can get you back to the village safely. We're here to help."

"Here to steal my treasure, more like," Mushroom snarled. "It's mine! You can't have it!"

"We don't want your treasure!" Thyme said.

"Yes, we do!" Rowan interrupted. "Crow and Gorge found out what you're doing. If we don't take the treasure back to them, they're going to feed Grove to the dragons. We need it to save him."

"Ha!" Mushroom snorted. "There was plenty of gold in that palace. Go get your own!" He glanced back over his shoulder.

The dragons in the sky were starting to scatter in a search formation.

"Please, Mushroom," Cranberry pleaded. "Come with us. We don't have to give the dragonmancers all of it — they'll never know what you keep. We'll protect you and you can help us save Grove."

"I don't care about him!" Mushroom shouted. "You've all laughed at me for years! Well, now *I'm* the one with the power! I'm going to own my own village soon, wait and see! Everyone will do everything for me, like they do for the dragonmancers!"

"How can that be more important than saving Grove's life?" Rowan yelled.

"Mushroom!" Thyme shrieked. "Look out!"

He leaped toward his brother as a crimson dragon suddenly plummeted out of the sky toward them.

In a whirl of motion, Mushroom jumped back, grabbed a piece of treasure out of his bag, and flung it at Thyme.

The treasure, whatever it was, was gold and flat and circular and covered in tiny mirrors. It flashed through the air like a tiny sun — like a beacon announcing, "Here I am! Here I am! Help, I'm being stolen! Look at me, everyone, I'm pilfered property! I'm SO SHINY AND BEAUTIFUL AND HELPLESS!"

It thumped into Thyme's chest and he caught it with a startled expression.

At the same moment, Mushroom dove down the slope and shot away through the ravine, leaving nothing but a cloud of dust behind to defend his brother.

Leaf didn't have time to get angry. The crimson dragon slammed into the ground beside Thyme, drawn by the shining gold and mirrors. It hissed furiously and knocked Thyme over with one of its front feet.

This was the moment. The dragon was right there, right in front of Leaf, all scales and smoke and flame and claws and wings as big as a dragonmancer's house and teeth out of nightmares beyond Leaf's worst fears.

It threw its head back and roared, and the dragons in the sky roared in response.

Leaf glanced sideways and saw that Rowan was frozen, too, her gaze locked on the towering serpentine figure.

Do it. Now. Before the other dragons come.

He thought of Wren. He thought of her sticking out her tongue and shouting, "You can't catch me, I'm the fastest in the world!"

He drove his feet into the earth and sprang forward, brandishing his sword as he ran. He whirled it around his head, aimed for where he was sure the dragon's heart should be, and plunged the blade into the creature's hide.

Except it didn't go in.

His sword bounced right off the dragon's scales and sent him flying backward. He landed in a heap beside Thyme, who had dropped the gold disk and was cradling one arm.

Leaf lay there for a moment with the wind knocked out of him, struggling to take a breath.

If we can't stab them with our swords, how am I supposed to kill one? What have I been training for all this time if nothing I've learned will help?

Rowan and Cranberry appeared, their backs to Leaf; they raised their swords and stood over him and Thyme. He could see their hands shaking, but Rowan yelled, "Leave us alone! We're not the ones who stole your treasure!"

Thump. Thump. Thump.

The earth trembled as dragons landed heavily all around them. Leaf forced himself to his feet and lifted his sword again.

The orange dragon was one of them; he saw now that she was wearing a kind of crown and chain mail, which made him think she must be the queen. She snatched up the gold disk and roared something, first at the humans, and then at the other dragons. A few of them looked at one another and shrugged (actually shrugged! Leaf had never imagined dragons doing something so familiar-looking). Then one pointed at the ravine where Mushroom had disappeared.

The queen snapped her tail at Leaf and his friends and barked an order; then she launched herself into the air and shot after Mushroom.

"She wants the rest of her treasure," Cranberry guessed.

"She's going to kill him," Thyme said in a hollow voice.

"Good," Rowan spat. "I hope she bites his head off."

"He threw you to them to save his skin," Cranberry said. "His own brother."

"I know," Thyme said. "I — I can't believe it."

One of the dragons strode over to them. Leaf did a forward tuck and roll under the dragon's feet and stabbed it in the side — or at least, whacked it very hard with the sharp end of his sword, which once again could not penetrate the scales. The dragon looked down at him with a very human frown of displeasure, plucked the sword right out of his hand, and wrapped his other giant talons around Leaf.

Rowan screamed, but Leaf couldn't call to her; he couldn't even move. The huge claws had him trapped, his arms pinned at his sides. His lungs were squeezed and burning. He felt himself lifted into the air. He caught a glimpse of the ground falling sickeningly away, and the treetops flashing past, and the palace up ahead, and other dragons seizing Rowan, Cranberry, and Thyme far below.

They caught us. Just like that. I couldn't kill a single dragon, and Mushroom betrayed us twice over, and we didn't even have a chance to try sneaking into the palace, and all that work on the map was for nothing, and now the dragons are taking us away to eat us, and I failed to protect anyone.

Then the lack of oxygen caught up with him, and he slipped into darkness.

CHAPTER 15

IVY

Ivy couldn't remember being inside Uncle Stone's cave before. It was small, with almost no furniture, and cobwebs everywhere.

She sat gingerly on the least dusty bench. Violet sat down next to her, but Daffodil was wandering around the cave, inspecting the very few things that could be lifted and inspected.

They'd seen the ice dragon fly away again. Squirrel had escorted them back to the nearest entrance to Valor, then gone to find Foxglove. Ivy had expected her uncle to seek out the Dragonslayer right away, but he'd brought them here instead.

"I'd offer you tea," Stone said, running one hand through his hair. "But I don't seem to have any supplies left."

"You have been gone awhile," Ivy said. "Mother came and took all the food so it wouldn't go to waste."

"Right," he said with a vague nod. "Right." He gave Daffodil a disgruntled look as she pried open the lid of a jar and peeked inside.

"So," Violet said. "Rose?"

"Right," he said again. Stone stepped over to a shelf high on the wall, lifted down a book, and took a worn-thin piece of paper out of it. "Rose was our sister."

"Sister?" Ivy echoed. "I have an aunt?" He handed her the paper and she studied the teenage face sketched on it: dark, laughing eyes, a mischievous grin, wild hair.

"She looks like you," Violet observed, nudging Ivy. "Except she looks like she's about to get into trouble, and you never look like that."

Across the room, Daffodil laughed. "That's true. Your 'about to get into trouble' face is more of an 'oh no, what are Violet and Daffodil dragging me into now' face."

"Rose drew that herself," Stone said. "That's exactly how she looked, especially whenever she and Heath came up with mad schemes."

"So she was an artist like you, too," Violet said to Ivy.

"But . . . she's dead now?" Ivy asked. "What happened?"

"She came with us to the desert queen's palace." Stone sat down heavily on his straw pallet, sending up a billow of dust from the blankets. "She's the one who climbed in to steal the treasure. She wasn't much older than you are now. Brave, and clever, and always doing stupid things, usually because Heath teased her or promised her something."

"Oh no," Ivy said. She'd always thought she was really lucky that no one she knew had ever been eaten by a dragon. Lucky, and living underground, of course. She knew, abstractly, that she must have had family in the old village — grandparents who didn't make it, maybe — but her parents never talked about them. They avoided any mention of the dragon attack.

But the Rose smiling in this sketch felt real. And lost, long before Ivy was even born.

"I didn't see what happened to her," Stone said, wiping his eyes. "Heath said he did, but he didn't give me any details. We were too busy running and hiding. But that's why I thought — when I had that dream, I thought maybe he was wrong. Maybe she survived somehow. I'm such an idiot, chasing a dream of a dead girl into a dragon city." He shook his head and fell silent.

"Where's the rest of your treasure?" Daffodil asked.

"DAFFODIL," Violet said. "Can't you see a MOMENT is happening?"

"There was a pause in the conversation!" Daffodil argued. "Maybe I'm lightening the mood!"

"I didn't take any," Stone said. "I couldn't bear the sight of it after what happened to Rose. I kept the chain, but I let Heath take the rest. So poke around all you want."

"All right," Daffodil said cheerfully, opening another box.

"Wow," Violet said. She glanced at Ivy with a "did you know your dad took *all* the treasure?" look.

Ivy had not known that. She'd assumed Stone must have something, because the night he left, her father had searched Stone's cave from top to bottom, then come home and shouted at her mother because he hadn't found anything. Ivy had been lying in bed, listening, thinking, *leave her alone, it's not*

HER fault and *why do you care where his treasure is; don't you have enough of your own?* He must have been looking for the chain, the one thing he didn't already have. Knowing he had everything else made that memory seem even worse.

She didn't mention any of that, though. She didn't talk to anyone about her father's temper, not even Violet and Daffodil. She could sometimes calm him down when he was really mad, or help him and Mother make peace again after their fights. Or when that didn't work, she was also really good at staying out of his way.

"I can't believe no one ever told me about Aunt Rose," she said instead. "All the times I've heard the Dragonslayer story — but everyone leaves her out."

"That is messed up," Violet said.

"Doesn't quite fit the heroic happy ending, does it?" Stone frowned down at his hands. "I bet you don't hear much about the scorched villages or the dragons' vengeance either."

"The what?" all three of them asked at once.

"My brother destroyed the world," Stone said. He stood up, took the magic chain out of his pocket, and started flipping it absentmindedly through his fingers. "And I helped him do it."

"The world's not destroyed," Daffodil said, looking at him like he'd lost his mind. "I mean, we were just out there. There are mountains and trees and rivers —"

"Not that we get to see them very often," Violet said.

"And there are animals and people and underground villages and —"

"Underground villages!" Stone scoffed. "People living like scared rabbits because it's not safe outside anymore. The dragons are still angry with us, even twenty years later. They are still destroying any humans they can find to punish us for what Heath did."

Ivy felt like the room was spinning. Violet put one hand on her shoulder.

"Hey now," Violet said. "That can't be all the Dragonslayer's fault. Dragons have been eating people and burning places forever. That's literally what a dragon is."

"No, not like this," Stone said. "I remember how it was, and when I start to forget, I read the old stories, the ones they won't give you in school anymore. People used to live aboveground, in ordinary towns, all over this continent. Occasionally someone would get eaten, but the dragons rarely burned whole villages. Not until we stole their treasure, killed their queen, and gave them something to be really vengeful about."

"But . . . everyone thinks the Dragonslayer is a hero," Daffodil said.

"Everyone here, sure," Stone said. "You can't live in Valor unless you do."

That's true. In Valor, home of the mighty Dragonslayer, any criticism of Dad — any questioning of the heroic story — will get you banished. Sent away from all safety, tossed out into the world.

Ivy thought of all the banishments she'd seen over the years, the odd lies and flimsy reasons she'd noticed for why those people had been kicked out. Was it really because they'd questioned the story? Was it because they mentioned Rose, or talked about a time before humans lived underground?

Were they sent away to be eaten because her father needed to protect his image?

She leaned forward, wrapping her arms around her stomach. Daffodil came over to sit next to her, and she felt both her friends put their arms over her back, like an invisible shield around her.

"My dad's a liar," she said quietly to them. "He let his sister die. And all the people he's banished, and who knows how many hundreds of people in all those villages the dragons destroyed. That's all because of him."

"But not because of you," Violet said, shaking her a little. "You're still our wonderful Ivy. Don't blame yourself for what he did."

"Yeah, we love you anyway," Daffodil said. "So what if your dad is the worst? My sister is totally evil, and I'm still awesome."

Ivy let out a half laugh, half sob at the idea that harmless Daisy could be compared to Heath on any sort of evil scale.

"Plus, remember he didn't do it on purpose," Violet said. "He didn't even mean to kill a dragon. Right?" She looked at Stone for confirmation and he nodded. "They just went to steal treasure, like people have been trying to do for centuries. It's a basic fact of human-dragon existence — they have treasure, idiots try to steal it. It was a weird fluke that this one time this one idiot managed to kill a dragon who happened to be important. Right?" She looked toward Stone again, but he had accidentally flipped the chain around his wrists and disappeared. He appeared again a moment later, gazing at the wall.

But then that idiot went on to rule a whole town, Ivy thought, *and he did it with lies and punishments that were probably as bad as executions. Even if killing the dragon was an accident, you can't say that about anything he's done since.*

"We can deal with this, Ivy," Violet said. "Together. We're here for you."

"Maybe we can fix it!" Daffodil said suddenly.

Ivy could feel the daggers Violet was shooting from her eyes even with her head down. "Fix what?" Violet said.

"The dragons being mad!" Daffodil jumped up and lifted the chain out of Stone's hands so deftly that his fingers kept moving for a moment, catching up to the fact that the chain was gone. He gave her his most disgruntled look yet.

"How do we fix *dragons* being *mad*?" Violet asked, her voice dripping with scorn. "Send them a politely worded apology letter?"

"That would be great if we spoke *Dragon*," Daffodil scoffed right back. "But we speak at least one language the same: We all love treasure." She held the chain over her head with a flourish like a banner.

"Aha," Violet said. "So we'll spell out 'Sorry about killing your queen' in gold coins?"

"Shut UP and let me finish explaining!" Daffodil cried. "*What if* we give the dragons back the treasure Heath stole?"

There was an awed silence for a moment.

"Yes," Ivy said. She stood up and pointed at Daffodil. "*Yes*. We can do that! It won't save the people who are gone, but it'll show the dragons we're sorry. And then maybe they'll stop attacking everyone!"

"No," Violet said. "No, no, no. You've both lost your minds. Just think about the logistics for one second! Do we walk up to the sand palace with a sack of coins and wave it at the guards? Here's some treasure — may or may not look familiar — with three extra-delicious snacks on the side! At what point in this fantastic transaction do we escape with our lives?"

"Doesn't matter!" said Daffodil.

"Um, matters a little bit!" Violet yelped.

"We'll figure that out," Ivy said. "First we have to get the treasure."

"That's where your plan falls apart," Stone said gloomily.

"One of *many* places where your 'plan' falls apart," Violet muttered.

"Heath will never give up his treasure," Stone said. "Not in a million years, not to save a single soul, or a thousand souls. He loves it more than anything in the world."

Daffodil and Violet both glanced at Ivy, but she'd always known that, and nothing else could hurt her right now. She was Ivy and she had spent her whole life making peace between angry people. So what if one side of this fight happened to be giant man-eating lizards?

"Then we won't ask him," she said. "We'll find his stolen treasure ourselves and then . . . we'll steal it back."

CHAPTER 16

WREN

The inhabitants of the Indestructible City, according to Undauntable, thought they lived in the most superior, most advanced, most impressive location in the entire world.

Wren really wished she could show them this dragon city and see the looks on their faces.

She resettled on her branch and shaded her eyes from the sun. She had been relieved to find at least a few trees here, this close to the river and the coast, although she wished there were more of them. These would do all right for hiding in, but if she and Sky needed to escape in a hurry, there was a whole lot of wide-open desert they'd have to cross in pretty much every direction.

Except west, because directly west of her tree was the gigantic dragon city. Dragons were already bustling through the streets, although the sun was barely up. There were lots of buildings, more than one market square, bridges over the river, dragons washing things in the water, fruit trees in pots in the courtyards. Some of the walls were painted with scale patterns, crimson red and pale butter yellow overlapping.

Others bore images of dragons in regal, commanding poses and an interesting variety of colors.

In their travels, Wren and Sky had seen palaces surrounded by dragon communities — the swamp palace, from a distance, and the mountain palace, from an even farther distance. They'd seen clusters of oddly shaped mud structures that they thought were swamp dragon villages, too. But they'd never seen anything quite the size of this place.

The strangest part was that the inhabitants were not all sand dragons, as Wren had expected. She had sort of been counting on using that an excuse — "Oh, sorry, Sky dear; only sand dragons can safely go in there." But red and orange scales clearly flashed between the pale yellow ones, and there was a fair number of brown dragons as well. Whatever had brought the three types of dragons together in one city, they seemed to be coexisting peacefully.

That still doesn't mean it's safe for Sky, though. Something about this place reminded Wren very much of the Indestructible City, and that made her nervous.

"What do you think?" Sky called from the ground. She shushed him and clambered down. He was sitting among the roots, beaming at a snail who was noodling peacefully along his tail.

"It's . . . very busy," Wren said. How could her sweet, easily distracted dragon not get trampled in a fast-paced place like that?

"Isn't it exciting?" he said, his eyes shining. "Maybe they

have dragon books! I don't know how to read Dragon. But maybe we could figure it out together!"

See, here was someone who really did know her. That idea was the first suggestion that actually made Wren curious about the dragon city.

"I'm just worried, Sky," Wren said, resting her hands on his talons. "We don't know what those dragons are like. You're a mountain dragon, but you still look really different from all of them." His beautiful, perfect pale orange scales were unlike any other dragon's in the world, as far as she knew. "And you don't have fire to protect yourself." *You don't have anything to protect yourself*, she thought. *Except me, and I can't go with you.*

"Aren't you different from all the other humans?" Sky asked.

"Yes," Wren said, "maybe not so obviously — but that's why I don't go all the way into the Indestructible City. I don't trust them. I'm really, really careful."

"I can be really, really careful!" Sky said brightly. "I promise!"

"You won't forget and speak Human?" Wren said. "Promise you'll fly out of there right away if anyone looks at you weird?"

He touched his snout to her forehead gently. "I'll just walk around and look at things," he said. "I won't talk to anybody. Maybe they have wonderful desert animals for sale!"

Wren laughed. "Please don't come back with a pet camel,"

she said. "And don't make friends with any scorpions! Also snakes; snakes are bad, try to remember that."

"Camels bad, Wren wants a pet cobra," Sky recited, then jumped back with a laugh as she swatted him.

"Don't talk to anyone if you don't have to," she said. "But if they talk to you, act normal. I don't know what that means for a dragon, but probably avoid the topic of snails. Definitely don't let anyone know you don't eat meat. I'm pretty sure that's weird."

"Really?" Sky said. "But hasn't everyone SEEN bunnies?"

"Exactly, don't say things like that," Wren suggested. "Don't volunteer any information, but if they ask, you can say you come from that mountain dragon outpost we saw way up north. Maybe your mom is a soldier there or something. Don't say you're from the mountain palace, in case they're from there, too, or they might ask too many questions."

"Wren, I'm sure no one will even talk to me," Sky said. He squared his shoulders and made a fierce expression. "Because my face strikes terror in the hearts of dragons everywhere!"

Wren giggled. "Not exactly," she said. "You have the most lovely face."

"No, *you* have the most lovely face," he said. "You're the cutest, best pet any dragon could ever have."

"QUIT THAT," Wren said, whacking him again. This was a recent recurring joke that Sky found completely hilarious. "You know perfectly well you're *my* pet."

He lowered one of his front feet gently to touch her head. "Hmmm," he said. "Not by the power of cuteness. You're the cutest one here, ergo, you are my pet."

"Well, then I will probably run off and leave you for another owner if you're not back by midday," Wren said. "So keep that in mind."

"I will!" he said, nudging her head with his snout again. He gently slid one claw under the snail and moved it to the safety of a nearby bush. "Thank you! Be good, Wren! Hide well! I'll be back soon!"

Wren's heart pounded as he skipped away down the hill toward the city. Did other dragons skip, or was Sky the only one? What if he had all sorts of other obviously human habits that would make the normal dragons suspicious of him?

She scrambled back up the tree and found the highest spot with a view of the city. From there, she could see Sky sauntering happily past a dragon farmstead — was that tangerine dragon glaring at him over a field of vegetables? — and then over the river to one of the smaller market squares.

Sky wandered along between the stalls, gazing at the piles of carpets, the pottery, the different weirdly shaped cactus plants. She should have warned him to act less impressed. He must be staring at everything with his wide-eyed "who knew something like this could exist!" face. He looked very small next to all the full-grown dragons around him.

Wren watched him until he turned a corner and disappeared from view, and then she stared at the spot where he'd been until the sun was well over the mountains.

He'll be fine.

He's a dragon in a dragon city.

It's not like anyone's going to eat him.

He's probably having a lovely time.

She wondered whether Sky felt this way each time she went to the Indestructible City. She hoped not; this was terrible.

She made herself climb down to eat something, but before long she was back in her perch. If only she had a new book to read, at least. Stupid Undauntable, ruining everything. This absolutely horrible panicked feeling she was having, like spiders running under her skin; this was *his* fault. If she only had a book she'd be perfectly relaxed right now.

It made her feel a little better to have someone to blame.

Sky will be back soon, and he'll tell me all his adventures, and then I'll feel silly.

The sun rose higher and higher. And then it began to slide quietly away to the west.

Midday had come and gone. Sky wasn't back.

He got distracted by something. Some amazing animal or cool dragon invention we've never seen before.

Or he forgot to look at the sun. He'll come running out soon and apologize for worrying me.

The sun slipped farther and farther away. The sky turned orange and pink and gold, then slowly purple, and then the sun was gone. In the city, dragons lit torches and went on their merry way, packing up their wares or chatting on balconies, strolling along the river or getting their little dragons off to bed. An ordinary dragon day, coming to an end.

It was dark now. Sky could be fluffy-headed, but he would notice the difference between midday and full night.

He would be back by now, unless he couldn't be.

Something has happened to him.

Wren wiped the tears from her eyes and rubbed her face as hard as she could.

He doesn't have fire. He only has me.

All right, fine, dragon city. I'm coming for my friend.

CHAPTER 17

LEAF

Leaf woke up because something was licking his neck.

It was not big enough to be a dragon tongue (he thought, he hoped, he desperately prayed), but it wasn't a small adorable kitten tongue either. And it had the breath of something that had eaten all the garbage in the world.

He pulled away and opened his eyes, and the goat standing over him gave him a calculating stare. It looked pretty sure that it could pin him down and eat his hair if it wanted to.

"Ha, look at that! All four of you alive!" said a voice nearby. "Wow, you've showed up at the right time. She must be planning a feast if she's saving all of us for later."

Leaf blinked, looking around wildly. He was in a room with no windows or doors; the only exit was a giant trapdoor in the grated ceiling. It felt more like a pit or a box than a room, really, but gigantic — a box for dragons to keep things in. Snacks, to be specific. A snack box for dragons, full of live prey for later munching. The air was hot and smoky and smelled awful, like a neglected farm, which made sense given the number of animals milling around.

Not just animals — people, too.

We're not the only people trapped in here, Leaf noted as Rowan crouched beside him. There was a big bearded man leaning against the wall, watching him, and another figure lying on the floor with his arms over his head, whimpering. A third guy had draped himself over one of the cows and was asleep — or maybe unconscious — as the cow wandered slowly from side to side and sniffed the stone floor disapprovingly. Perhaps it was safer to sleep like that instead of on the floor where the cow could walk right over you.

Cows. Goats. Very large chickens. Two foxes, a beaver, several miserable squirrels. Also an alarmed deer and an actual bobcat, who was crouched in the corner snarling. Leaf wondered if it was feeling outnumbered by all the prey, or if it had any idea it was now in the category of prey itself.

As are you, imaginary Wren reminded him.

"Glad you're OK, little brother," Rowan said to him gruffly. She shoved his shoulder. "I know your plan is to kill dragons, but I didn't think I'd trained you to run straight at any dragon you see, you big dope."

"Did you see what happened?" Leaf demanded.

"The part where we got caught by dragons who are going to eat us soon?" Rowan asked. "Yeah, I did notice that."

"No, with my sword!" Leaf said. "I stabbed that dragon twice and my sword bounced right off! It doesn't penetrate their scales!"

Rowan frowned. "Well, that's . . . terrible."

"So what did the Dragonslayer do differently?" Leaf

asked. "How did he manage to kill one? You never said swords wouldn't work on them! That wasn't in the story!"

"He *did* use a sword," Rowan said. "I'm, like, eighty-five percent sure that's what I heard anyway. I don't know what he did to make it work, though."

"Magic sword?" Cranberry guessed from over by the wall. She was sitting next to Thyme, who had his arms wrapped around his legs and was staring vacantly at the bobcat. "Or maybe it was dragon-made, and their own swords are strong enough to stab each other?"

"Arrrrgh," Leaf groaned, dropping his head into his hands. All that training, and he still knew nothing? He was finally inside the dragons' lair, and yet he was further away from protecting his village than he'd ever been.

"Doesn't matter anyway," said the bearded man, and Leaf realized that was the voice he'd heard before. "They took your swords. You might get one back if you're chosen for the arena, but you still don't stand a chance."

"The arena?" Cranberry asked. She shoved away a cow that was snuffling at her boots.

"This dragon queen likes to watch fights," he said. "Mostly between dragons, but sometimes she sends humans out there, too."

"How do you know?" Leaf asked.

"Yeah, if you've been here long enough to figure that out, why aren't *you* dead?" Rowan crossed her arms and arched an eyebrow at him.

He chuckled unpleasantly. "I've been here five days. On

day two, they split up the humans — three for the kitchen, three for the arena, far as we could tell. We haven't seen the first three since, and I'm the only one that survived the arena."

"By fighting a dragon?" Leaf asked.

"Ha! No, by lying down and playing dead until they dragged me out again," he said with a snort. "Not a great trick, though. The other guy who tried it got trampled in the action and wound up actually dead."

"Well, you're good at horror stories, I'll give you that," Rowan said.

"Name's Cardinal," he offered. "But don't get attached."

"You can get attached to us," Cranberry said defiantly. "We're not going to die."

Cardinal shrugged as if it wasn't worth proving her wrong, since the world was about to do that pretty fast.

"Can we climb up there?" Rowan asked Cranberry, pointing at the grate overhead. "Or throw you up there?"

Leaf and Cranberry could toss each other pretty high, but the trapdoor was as far away as three dragons stacked on top of one another. They tried anyway, and they tried putting Cranberry on Rowan's shoulders and Leaf on the very top, and they tried vaulting off cows, despite the cows' objections, but nothing got them anywhere close.

Dragons kept stomping by overhead, rattling the bars of the grate as they walked over it. A long time after Leaf woke up, a dragon stopped to throw some food down through the trapdoor, but the mad scramble to get to it looked almost as deadly as the dragons themselves, so Leaf stayed against the wall and waited it out.

Another long time later, a tangerine-colored dragon opened the trapdoor and swooped down, dropping a bleating sheep and another deer into the muddle of animals before swooping out again.

"How did the dragons catch you?" Leaf asked Cardinal. "You're not from Talisman, and I thought there wasn't another human village anywhere near the palace."

"Lots of folks wander without villages after theirs were burned," Cardinal pointed out. "And the dragons can go a lot farther afield than your town — I met one person in here who lived in a village far down the coast. And then, of course, there are the idiots who show up here trying to steal treasure."

Rowan and Cranberry exchanged a guilty look.

"Yeah, I thought so," Cardinal said with a snort. He nodded at the man who slept on cows, who had turned out to be a very morbid, morose fellow named Arbutus. "That was our plan, too. I bet the dragons think it's real funny how we just walk up and ask to be eaten."

"I'm not here for treasure," Leaf said fiercely. "I'm here to slay a dragon."

Cardinal laughed. "Well, that's even stupider," he said. "But I guess if you end up in the arena, you'll get a chance to try. Should be great entertainment."

A chance to try. A chance. That was what Leaf needed.

"If I did win in the arena," Leaf asked, "would they let us go?"

Cardinal squinted at him. "No. They would eat you. They're *drag-ons*," he said slowly. "You can't reason with them or bargain with them. They're giant mindless hungry monsters."

That's what Leaf had thought, but he was having trouble fitting together "mindless monster" with arena sports, elaborate castles, carefully drawn blueprints, and feast planning.

He could easily believe, however, that the dragons would never let them go. They'd thrown all the humans in with their other prey. No matter how much they played with them first, eventually the dragons were planning to eat them all.

He was *not* going to die without taking down a dragon first.

That's right, imaginary Wren said cheerfully. *I must be AVENGED! With VIOLENCE!*

But how? he asked her. *Where are they vulnerable?*

In their stupid FACES, she guessed. Imaginary Wren still often talked like the seven-year-old he remembered.

She might be right, though, he thought. *The mouth, perhaps. The eyes. Maybe their wings.*

That made sense, but it only made the task more daunting. Dragon faces weren't exactly at an easily stabbable level.

Leaf brooded about the challenge for days. Far above the trapdoor and the grate, they could see a window and the clear blue sky beyond, as it turned to night and back again. Leaf wished he had spent more time climbing to high places to watch the sunrise with Wren — it had been one of her favorite things to do, but he'd usually preferred to sleep through it.

Dragons came periodically to remove or add more prey and to throw food at them. They didn't seem entirely clear on what all the different kinds of animals might eat, so there was a lot of raw fish and bundles of grass.

On the fourth day, the dragons took the guy who'd been whimpering when Leaf woke up, which was a little bit of a relief because he'd had screaming nightmares every time he'd fallen asleep. He'd refused to speak to anyone, so they didn't know his name or where he'd come from or why he was there. Cardinal couldn't guess whether he'd gone to the arena or the kitchen.

What if Cranberry threw me *at a dragon?* Leaf wondered. Would that get him high enough to stab it in the eye? But he'd probably be in the arena alone. He presented the problem to the others.

"Could you climb up a dragon's leg to get to its head?" Cranberry asked.

"It would have to be either asleep or not very aggressive," Rowan pointed out.

"I'm not climbing any dragons," Thyme said. "I'm running in the opposite direction as fast as I can."

"They like that," Cardinal interjected. "It's much more fun for them to chase their prey."

"You don't know that," Rowan snapped. "You're thinking of cats."

He shrugged, unfazed. "Probably true of dragons, too, though."

"Are we sure we can't talk to them?" Thyme asked. "Maybe charm them into letting us go?"

That made Cardinal laugh for a *very* long time.

Finally, on the fifth night, the dragons came.

The sky through the distant window was lined with a sunset-red glow turning to purple dusk above. It had been a busy day overhead, full of dragons darting back and forth, roaring, crashing pots and pans, more roaring, the sound of things falling, and the smell of meat burning. Leaf wasn't sure what was happening, but all the dragons in earshot seemed to be having a meltdown about it.

Three dragons threw open the trapdoor and descended into the pit. Leaf scrambled to his feet and tried to look fierce and interesting enough for the arena. *Pick me! I'll give you a memorable fight! Hand me a sword and point me at a dragon!*

The biggest of the three dragons was crimson red, the color of fresh blood, with a slash across her face that had taken out one of her eyes. A thin gold chain was wound around her horns and neck, which made Leaf guess that she was one of the dragons in charge, at least of the kitchens or food supply or something. She snarled at the other two, jabbing her claw at the panicking mob of animals below.

One of the others, a burnt-orange dragon with a few missing claws, swooped down and seized a sheep, carrying it straight out the trapdoor. The last dragon, darker red with yellow eyes, grabbed one of the deer and flew away with it.

Was that it? Leaf wondered. *Just dinner for the queen?*

Then the dragons came back for a goat and the beaver, then again for a fox and the yowling bobcat. They came back again and again, until almost all the animals were gone.

"Told you," Cardinal said, slouching against the wall. "Saving us for a feast. Maybe it's her birthday." He snickered.

"Yeah, right," said his partner glumly. "Dragons who know their own birthdays. Ha." Arbutus was long and angular and wore his dark hair in a waist-length ponytail. He didn't talk very much; he seemed resigned to their fate as dragon food. Because he spent so much time sleeping on top of cows, he smelled even worse than any of the other humans.

"Maybe she has guests," Rowan said. "I saw a dragon fly by the window earlier who was a different color than the others."

"Sort of a pale yellow," Thyme said. "I saw it, too."

"Could be a sand dragon," Rowan said to Leaf.

Like the one the Dragonslayer killed. I wonder if they're easier to stab.

Oooo, let's find out! Wren suggested with great enthusiasm. *Let's try stabbing ALL the dragons and then make a CHART of which ones are the squishiest and which ones go "CLANG OUCH GROWL" and then eat you.*

Leaf glanced up at the one-eyed red dragon who was still hovering overhead. He was pretty sure they'd been picking out dinner — prey for the feast, as Cardinal had guessed. It seemed unlikely that the dragons were planning to watch a fox and a bobcat fight each other in the arena in the dark. So maybe they weren't taking anyone for the arena today. And with only six humans left, maybe they weren't taking any of them for the feast either. Maybe they'd all get to be in the arena tomorrow.

The carrier dragons returned. The one in charge barked something at them and pointed at Thyme. Before anyone could move, the orange dragon soared down, scooped him up, and flew away, as businesslike as it had been with the sheep.

"THYME!" Cranberry shouted. "No! Thyme! Hey, give him back! GIVE HIM BACK!"

Leaf was so stunned he couldn't even call after his friend. He stared at the spot where Thyme had been a minute ago.

He can't be gone.

Thyme can't end up as a side dish at a dragon buffet. I came here to save people — not to lose more.

The next growl from above didn't break through his daze. It wasn't until Rowan shrieked his name and Leaf felt claws closing around him that he realized the one-eyed dragon had spoken again.

Choosing one more human for the feast.

Choosing him.

CHAPTER 18

IVY

The main problem with finding the treasure Ivy's father had stolen from the dragons was that apparently nobody had seen even a fraction of it in Ivy's lifetime.

They figured this out slowly. Violet approached each of the merchants in Valor and asked, as casually as Violet could (not very), whether the Dragonslayer usually paid in gold, or precious jewels, or what.

Each of them chuckled, or looked nervous, or waved her away, but the general gist of their answers seemed to be: "The Dragonslayer doesn't have to pay for every item like a lowly villager! He's the lord of Valor! He has as much money as a dragon queen! We know *his* credit is good, ha ha!"

"So, wait," Violet would say, "when did he last pay you?"

And then there would be mumbling, and more nervous looks, and soon she'd be shooed out of the shop without much more information.

There did seem to be an informal system of favors in place, Violet pointed out. If, for instance, the Dragonslayer decided on a tailor whose clothes he liked, he'd spread the word, and soon that would be the most popular tailor in Valor. Or if one candlemaker made a special Dragonslayer scent, she was likely to find herself upgraded to one of the biggest caves in the marketplace.

"As far as I can tell, he pays with power and influence instead of with money," Violet explained.

"Huh," Ivy said. "So . . . where is his money? What does he do with it, if he's not using it to buy things?"

"Maybe he piles it up in a cave and rolls in it," Daffodil suggested. "Not that that's what *I* would do with a giant mountain of gold coins or anything."

Ivy had been hoping to catch a glimpse of the gold the next time her father had to buy something big, but apparently nothing was too big for the Dragonslayer to buy on credit from one of his worshippers.

While Violet interrogated merchants, Daffodil was sent to talk to her grandmother, the oldest inhabitant of Valor.

That did not go well.

"She wanted to know where my yellow ribbons were," Daffodil reported with indignation. "She said my uniform is boring and does nothing for my complexion and she told me to sit still, like, eight hundred thousand times and why was I even interested in the dragon attacks and of course she hasn't seen the Dragonslayer's treasure, how rude do I think she is, except of course when he first rode back from the desert and announced his heroic deeds in the town square."

"That!" Violet asked. "Did you ask more about that?"

"I TRIED," Daffodil said. "She said it was very exciting,

bells ringing and everyone admiring the tail barb and cheering. And then WHOOSH and BOOM and ROAR and CRASH and everything was on fire, and Aunt Petal managed to get Grandma into the escape tunnels, and by the way have I heard about how Aunt Petal was the very best of Grandma's children and no one else will ever measure up?"

"She did not say that," Ivy objected.

"She absolutely did," Daffodil said. "With Mother sitting right there! I swear, Aunt Petal sounds as dreadful as Daisy sometimes. Anyway, then I couldn't get Grandma back to the treasure no matter what I tried, plus it was getting very boring, so I left."

"Well," Violet said sarcastically. "Good effort."

"Thank you," Daffodil said, ignoring her.

Ivy's mission, of course, was to search the Dragonslayer's home. She was often left alone, so finding a time to do it wasn't difficult. She started with her parents' room, then her dad's office, then the dining cave where he hosted council meetings and parties. She reached into every nook and cranny and ledge and crack in every wall of the caves. She ran her hands along every fiber of their hammocks, looking for hidden lumps; she riffled through each book on the shelves. She took everything out of the cabinets and looked for secret compartments.

It was really odd and uncomfortable, trying to find her dad's secrets this way. It felt like she'd been colored over with a drawing of a different Ivy — a braver but sneakier Ivy, with a different father, who couldn't be trusted in any way. She could remember the harmless, charming dad she used to think she had, but now she could only see the shadows around him, the ghosts he ignored, the smile that said he didn't care or think he'd done anything wrong.

Her heart pounded as she searched. If he caught her, what would she say? How would she calm him down? Would she be able to lie, or was he such a master liar that he'd see right through her?

She waited for the times when she knew they'd be gone for a while, and then she looked *everywhere*. They owned a lot of elegant carvings and small jewelry and gold leaf–painted vases, but those had all been made by human hands. There wasn't a speck of dragon treasure to be found.

"That is bonkers," Daffodil said from her perch in Violet's hammock. They were meeting in Violet's cave again, because Daffodil had recently had a new nightmare about the dragon tail barb — possibly prompted by the story of the dragon attack on the old village — and didn't want to go anywhere near it. Violet also didn't trust Ivy's mother, and at this point Ivy wasn't sure she did either. Violet's dads were always at meetings or trials or arbitrations, so this seemed like the safest place to talk without being overheard.

"Heath must be really good at hiding things if you really couldn't find anything," Violet agreed.

"Or it's not in our cave at all," Ivy said. "Maybe he was worried someone would try to steal it from him, so he keeps it somewhere else."

"But where would it be *more* safe?" Daffodil asked.

"Everywhere else in Valor is public space — I'd think it would be harder to protect anywhere outside his own cave."

They were all quiet for a moment. Violet was lying flat on the floor in her thinking position. Ivy was at Violet's desk, trying to draw the ice dragon they'd seen. All the spikes made it extra hard, but that helped her mind focus instead of rattling around in circles. Was there anywhere else her dad went and nobody else did?

"Oh!" she cried, dropping her quill. "Of course! Where is my brain? You guys! The old village!"

Violet sat up and Daffodil nearly fell out of the hammock.

"That's probably why he made that law that no one else can go there!" Ivy rushed on. "Maybe Pine got too close to wherever he's hidden it. Oh, oh, and that time I saw Dad leaving with a bag hidden under his shirt — maybe he was going to get some of the treasure. I bet that's it! The treasure is hidden in the old village!"

"That's brilliant," Violet said, grinning. "You're brilliant, Ivy."

"I'm really not," Ivy said. "I should have thought of that way sooner."

"So let's go get it!" Daffodil said. "Let's go right now!"

"We can't." Ivy buried her hands in her hair. "I mean — we *can't*. First of all, we don't know where the village is. Secondly, there's no way we'll be allowed to leave Valor on our own — even our Wingwatcher friends don't think we're ready for that. And most of all, it's so forbidden. I don't think Dad would banish me, but he might banish you two, and

I — that would — it would be the worst thing to ever happen."

She couldn't imagine life without Violet and Daffodil. She couldn't imagine watching them get banished, knowing it was her fault, and she couldn't imagine ever forgiving her father if he did that.

"I can solve all those problems," Violet said. "Foxglove will take us there, and Squirrel will make sure no one catches us."

"Violet!" Ivy threw a ball of paper at her. "Then Foxglove and Squirrel could be banished, too!"

"Well, that's my five favorite people," Violet said, "so if we're all banished together, that's fine by me."

"Ooh, let's get Forest banished, too, then," Daffodil said.

"Daffodil, GROSS," Violet said. "No. I forbid you to have a crush on FOREST of ALL PEOPLE."

"I don't!" Daffodil yelped. "I just think he's funny!"

"You are wrong," Violet said. "He is horrifying."

"He's not horrifying," Ivy said, passing Daffodil a bowl of pumpkin seeds to stop her from leaping out of the hammock and strangling Violet. "His humor is a little juvenile, sure, but it's OK for Daffodil to think it's funny. Most importantly, no one is getting banished, because no one else is going to the old village. I'll go by myself."

"Terrible plan," Daffodil said.

"Absolutely not," Violet said at the same time.

Ivy tried to convince them, but she didn't stand much of a chance when the two of them joined forces. Still, she thought the argument was ongoing until three days later, when Foxglove summoned them for another skygazing mission, and then they got outside and found Squirrel waiting with a knapsack and a grin.

"Uh-oh." Ivy shot a look at her friends. "You didn't —"

"Of course we did," Daffodil said cheerfully. "They would LOVE to help."

"That's a *slight* exaggeration," said Foxglove. "There was a *tiny* amount of blackmail involved." She arched one eyebrow at Violet, who did not look even the slightest bit guilty.

The sky was overcast, full of billowing gray clouds, and the wind whipped through the trees with more strength than Ivy was used to. Far off to the north, a misty skein of rainfall connected the sky and mountain peaks.

If there were dragons in those clouds, would we see them? Ivy wondered. *Would we hear their wingbeats over this wind?*

"What did you do?" Ivy asked Violet.

"I told them we needed a guide to the old village," Violet said serenely, "and if they helped us, I would stop trying to decipher the secret Wingwatcher code I know they've been using."

"This does not mean there *is* a secret Wingwatcher code," Foxglove said sternly. "But less of Violet poking around in other people's business would be great." She strode off down the hill, and Ivy had no choice but to chase after her. The wind tossed her hair in her face and all around, and she thought how hard it would be to fly in weather like this.

"This is too dangerous," she said breathlessly to Foxglove. "I don't want anyone to get banished."

"Neither do I," said Foxglove. "But I think Violet is right that your father is hiding something in the old village, and with you along, we might finally be able to find it."

"With me — finally?" Ivy said. "Wait, you mean you've looked before?"

Foxglove smiled. "Trust me. This is not the first time I've been to the old village. And this won't be the time I get caught."

Daffodil bounded down the slope past them, leaping from rock to rock like a mountain goat who'd just escaped from trolls. Violet was following them, more slowly, talking to Squirrel as they walked. Ivy glanced back and saw three more Wingwatchers climbing out of the underground city. She thought she recognized them — all from Foxglove's year.

"We have a system," Foxglove said, noticing Ivy's puzzled expression. "If anyone else comes out, there will be a signal passed along in time for us to hide. You don't have to worry."

A whole system, Ivy thought as they trekked through the woods. Sparrows flitted through the trees overhead, clinging to the branches when they thrashed in the wind. *With many Wingwatchers in on it. Violet was right about one thing — they have secrets. Foxglove has been sneaking off to the old village, and she never told me.*

Because she couldn't really trust me, after all? Was she afraid I'd tell my father?

Would I have, before I knew about Rose and everything Stone told us?

She doesn't seem worried about it now. Ivy glanced at Foxglove's face, but it was her unreadable expression, the one Ivy still couldn't imitate even after all these years as her friend. She didn't see any signs that Foxglove was angry, though. Ivy hoped Violet hadn't really blackmailed her . . . she didn't think she could handle it if Foxglove was mad at them.

Behind them, she noticed two of the Wingwatchers following at a distance, and then after a while, just one. She guessed they were spread out along the route so they could pass their signals quickly. She hoped they'd be safe — from dragons, from her dad, from everything.

"West," Violet noted, assessing the sky. "We're heading toward the desert."

"The village isn't far from the edge of the forest," Foxglove said. "I see you taking notes in your head, Violet. Remember you promised you would never go to the village by yourself."

"I did promise that," Violet said. "Yes. That I did."

Foxglove narrowed her eyes at her. "Going with Ivy and Daffodil still counts as going by yourself. Stop trying to find a loophole."

"I didn't say anything!" Violet objected. "I wasn't even planning anything! I'm *absorbing knowledge*, that's all. Like a *diligent* Wingwatcher apprentice. That's me. Well-behaved and learning things."

"Ha," Foxglove snorted. "Daffodil!" she called. "Get back here!"

Daffodil obediently wheeled around and charged back toward them. Foxglove signaled for silence and they all crouched in a huddle.

"This might be a little upsetting," Foxglove said softly. "Are you sure you're ready for it?"

"Very ready," Daffodil said.

"Of course," said Violet.

Ivy nodded. She wasn't sure . . . she didn't know what to expect. But she couldn't say no now.

Foxglove gave a low whistle, listened for another moment, and then beckoned them forward. Squirrel stayed behind, climbing a tree.

Up ahead, Ivy could see a break in the trees — a spot where there seemed to be more light, even on such a gray day. As they approached, she began to notice a smell, too, like charred wood.

They stepped out of the forest into a charcoal painting of devastation.

The black, twisted shapes slowly resolved into tree stumps, crooked walls, fallen towers. Ivy could see where paths used to run between houses; she could imagine the gardens that once grew here, before the dragon fire consumed it all.

Foxglove led the way between stone foundations to something that seemed to be an open plaza where all the roads met — like the central cave in Valor. A toppled bell tower marked the center of the square. An old iron bell, large, rusted, and cracked, poked out of the rubble. Ivy couldn't pull her eyes away from it. Was her father the last person to ring it? Had he been so proud of himself? And then what had he felt when the dragons descended?

"Right," Foxglove said, standing next to the bell with her hands on her hips. "What next, clever boots?" She looked at Violet.

"We spread out and start searching?" Violet suggested.

"It's a big town," Foxglove pointed out. "And we can't stay too long. Got any more specific plans?"

Violet pivoted slowly, studying the space. Ivy had to admit it didn't look promising. Where would she hide treasure in a ruin like this?

And didn't it make her father sad? Every time he came back here, wasn't he reminded of everything the town had lost — everything that was destroyed, because of him? Didn't he look around and feel crushed by guilt?

She did, and she hadn't even been alive when it happened. She'd never seen it bustling with people and full of life. If something like this had been her fault, she would never have been able to look at it again.

But she couldn't think like herself. She had to think like the Dragonslayer. He didn't see a ruin — he saw a clever hiding spot. A safe hiding spot, one that he trusted, apparently. Where would he feel like his treasure was safe?

"Dad's old house," she said. "Wherever he used to live. We should start there."

"Sounds great," Foxglove said. "Which one is that?"

Ivy had no idea. She frowned at the ruins, trying to think

of anything that might give her a clue. Her father liked big houses, lots of space, fancy things . . . but his family wouldn't have been able to afford any of that when he was a kid. That was the whole reason he'd gone to steal the dragon treasure, wasn't it? Because he wanted to be rich, and he wasn't.

So, probably not one of these bigger houses around the square, then.

"Guess what?" Daffodil announced suddenly. "Guess WHAT?!"

"What?" Violet asked in her most deliberately bored voice.

"There are FOOTPRINTS over here!" Daffodil cried. She pointed at a muddier area on the other side of the bell. "Leading into town that way! WHAT IF THEY'RE THE DRAGONSLAYER'S FOOTPRINTS? We could follow them straight to his hiding place!"

Violet crouched beside the footprints and studied them skeptically. "These are two different sets of footprints," she said. "They can't be the Dragonslayer's. He only comes here alone."

"Let's follow them anyway!" Daffodil suggested. "I mean, what if someone is here! Maybe they already found the treasure and can save us oodles of time, did you think about that?"

"There is someone here," Foxglove said slowly. "But they have not found the treasure. They have looked, with no success so far. Of course, they were supposed to do a better job of *covering their tracks*," she said loudly. She fixed her gaze on the three girls. "Can you keep a secret? A real one? You can't breathe a word of this to anybody."

"Yes," Daffodil breathed. "I promise!"

"So do I," said Violet. "I would never betray your trust, Foxglove. I believe in keeping secrets as a matter of honor."

"Ivy?" Foxglove asked before Ivy could chime in. "You're the one whose promise I really need. This could be asking a lot of you."

"I really, really promise," Ivy said, a little hurt. "It's not asking too much. You know I'm good at keeping secrets."

"She is," Daffodil agreed, taking Ivy's hand and squeezing it.

Foxglove climbed onto the highest stone step still standing and waved both her arms. A shadow detached itself from a leaning stone doorway and came toward them. Another rose from behind a low wall and followed.

As they approached, Ivy was startled to see that they were both wearing Wingwatcher uniforms — torn and threadbare, but still recognizable. One had a scar along his neck and the other kept glancing at the sky nervously.

"Oh. WOW," said Daffodil. She grabbed Ivy's hand again and squeezed even harder. "IVY," she said, in her famously loud "whisper" voice. "That's PINE!"

"And Azalea," said Violet. "They were both banished from Valor."

Daffodil clasped her hands under her chin. "I can't believe you're still alive!" she said to Pine. "Do you remember me? Pigtails with yellow ribbons?"

He looked at her like he actually did remember. "At the school," he said with a grin. "You were always so excited about the peaches."

"Ye-es," Daffodil said. "Peaches. It was definitely about the peaches. That's what I was excited about. Definitely. I'm Daffodil, by the way."

"Foxglove, what are you doing?" said the other banished Wingwatcher. Azalea's hair was short and wild, as though it had been chopped with a knife and no mirror. Ivy vaguely remembered her kicking a bunch of guards at her banishment. "We've talked a hundred times about whether it would be safe to bring *her* here." She nodded at Ivy. "We said no. A hundred times. Remember?"

"This was different," Foxglove said. "She asked to come. She wants to help."

Azalea's eyebrows shot up and she looked at Ivy with disbelief.

"To find the treasure," Foxglove added quickly. "As we've been trying to do for years. These three think it must be here, too."

"And what do you need with treasure, princess?" Azalea demanded.

There was a pause, and Ivy realized she was waiting for Violet or Daffodil to answer for her. But Azalea was staring only at Ivy.

"We want to give it back to the dragons," Ivy said. "To stop them from burning any more villages."

Azalea tilted her head and took a step back. She looked at

Pine, who had a small smile on his face. He shrugged at her. "Not the worst idea," he said.

"Disagree, but never mind that," said Violet. "Have you been living here this whole time? Since you were banished?"

"Our friends helped keep us alive," Pine said, nodding at Foxglove. "Aster went to take her chances in the Indestructible City and hasn't returned. The dragons got Root a couple of years ago."

"What about the other people who were banished?" Ivy asked. "The ones who weren't Wingwatchers?"

"We know where most of them are," Pine said.

"But we're not going to tell you," Azalea cut in, looking at Ivy. "No offense. But just in case."

"That's fascinating," Violet said, studying Pine. "You were banished because you came here, but then you ended up living here. And now you can search for the Dragonslayer's treasure all day, which is probably why he banished you in the first place."

"No one ever said the Dragonslayer was smart," Azalea said with a shrug. "No offense," she added to Ivy again.

Ivy was quite sure offense was intended; it was pretty clear that Azalea was angry at her and meant to stay that way no matter what Ivy said. But Ivy didn't feel angry back. She felt worried for them, living out here in a burned-down village, with only a few Wingwatchers to help them.

"But you haven't found anything?" Violet asked. "Have you figured out where the Dragonslayer used to live, at least?"

Pine spread his hands. "No luck. I don't think the treasure is here after all."

"But then why banish you, just for *seeing* this place?" Foxglove asked.

"Maybe I offended him some other way," he said.

"Do you remember where you went when you came here the first time?" Violet asked. "Did he catch you here?"

"Yes," he said. "We've searched all over that area, but I'll show you where I was."

The six of them made their way through the ruins, with Foxglove at the back scuffing up the prints they left behind. Pine stopped in a corner of the village that looked pretty much like everything they'd passed, but with smaller foundations, chimneys, and hearths than some of the big houses near the center.

"I was just poking around here, searching in the old fireplaces for iron. He came out of the woods and asked what I was doing, and I told him, and he looked very serious and said we'd better get back to Valor. I didn't realize I was in trouble until we got there and he had two of his guards arrest me."

Ivy walked along the path, studying each of the houses. *There were five people in the family — the parents and three teenagers — so it couldn't be either of these one-room houses,* she thought. *They'd have built on another room or more . . . like these did.*

She stopped in front of a house near the end. The building

next to it was almost entirely gone, but buried in the ash she could see the corner of a blacksmith's anvil. And behind it, the outline of a building that might have been a stable.

"They had horses," she said to Violet, who had followed her. "They rode horses to the desert palace, right? Could they really afford three horses? Or maybe their father was a blacksmith, and they took whatever horses were here for new shoes. Maybe?"

"It's a good theory," Violet said. She pointed at the house that adjoined the blacksmith's shop. "Let's start in there."

Foxglove stayed outside to watch for warning signals while the rest of them searched. With five people it didn't take very long to sweep from one end of the house to the other. There weren't many places to look unless they started digging, but Ivy didn't think her father would have buried the treasure. He didn't like to get dirty, and he hadn't been carrying a shovel when she saw him leave the underground city.

Ivy couldn't imagine her father as a teenager, or Uncle Stone. But she could kind of picture Rose here, skipping in and out, bothering her father while he made horseshoes next door, avoiding her mother whenever chores needed doing.

"Hmmm," said Daffodil, tapping her nose. "You said he caught you looking in fireplaces. Did anyone check this fireplace?"

"I reached up the chimney as high as I could and felt around," Violet said. "It's pretty unstable. I was afraid the whole thing would fall down on me."

"Maybe this is the wrong house," Ivy said.

"Think like Heath," Violet suggested. "Why would he come back here?"

"Because . . . he already had a hiding place?" Ivy said. "Somewhere he hid things even when he was a kid. Like the crack in the wall behind Daffodil's hammock where she puts her love po — not love poems!" she said quickly at the look on Daffodil's face. "Anything but that! Other secrets!"

"Ivy, SERIOUSLY," Daffodil said in outrage.

"Let's see if there are any cracks in the wall in the side room," Violet suggested. "Pine, you're the tallest, you check the fireplace again."

Ivy ran her hands along what was left of the stone walls. She pictured herself as Rose, sneaking in here while her brothers were out so she could play with their things. Ivy had never had siblings, but she'd certainly heard enough about Daffodil's.

Daffodil was an expert at finding every new place where Daisy hid her diary, and also an expert at ranting about how boring it always turned out to be. "She writes down EVERYTHING SHE EATS!" Daffodil had complained more than once. "There's not a SINGLE WORD ABOUT BOYS. Or ANY INTERESTING GOSSIP. How can she be THAT EVIL and THAT BORING at the same time? Unless this is a DECOY BORING DIARY specially designed to throw me off the scent. I bet that's it! One day I'll find her REAL EVIL DIARY and show everyone the truth about her!"

"Daffodil," Ivy said. "Where would Daisy hide her diary in this room?"

Daffodil stood in the center of the room, staring around with a narrowed gaze.

"She wouldn't," she said at last. "Because this is a room we'd have to share. So she'd hide it somewhere I'd never go. Was Rose allergic to horses? Or banned from the smithy for setting things on fire?"

"Where did you get that idea?" Violet demanded.

Daffodil shrugged. "I don't know. She looked like someone I would like, that's all."

"Let's check the smithy," Violet said. They clambered over what was left of the wall and Ivy went over to the anvil. It was so heavy, she could see why no one had managed to bring it down to Valor yet. Anyone trying to transport it would be easy prey for dragons.

Daffodil stuck her head up the chimney and quickly emerged again, coughing. "Blech," she said. "Pine! Come be tall over here!"

Pine and Azalea came over the walls as well, but as they crossed the smithy, suddenly all of them heard a piercing shriek in the sky.

Azalea didn't hesitate. She dove under a pile of leaves and ashes in the corner and vanished in the first heartbeat. Foxglove came running in, grabbed Ivy and Daffodil, and dragged them into the smithy fireplace. Violet and Pine were already over the wall and hiding in the tumbledown house.

"It'll see us," Daffodil gasped, trying to squish farther into the fireplace. Foxglove crouched and lifted Ivy onto her shoulders; a moment later, Ivy's head was up the chimney, and Daffodil was pressed to Foxglove's side below her.

They were all as still as rabbits caught in the garden when the torches were lit. Ivy rested her hands lightly on the chimney walls and prayed that nothing collapsed on them. She could see a small triangle of gray sky at the top of the chimney. She couldn't see the dragon — maybe it was up too high, hidden by clouds, or didn't cross that section of sky. She wondered which kind it was. Was it one of the sand dragons, come back to marvel at what they had done to the village? She heard it shriek one more time, and then again a minute later, a little farther away.

No one moved for a long time after silence fell. Ivy wasn't sure any of them would ever have moved, except that it started to rain, big fat drops plopping down the chimney onto her face. She leaned down to avoid them and felt a loose stone in the side of the chimney wall, near where her knees were.

"Oh!" she whispered. "Foxglove, can you feel this?"

Foxglove reached up and wobbled it with her hand. "Yes," she said. "Let me put you down and I'll check it out."

Ivy and Daffodil waited by the anvil, shivering in the rain, as Foxglove levered out the loose stone and carefully placed it beside the fireplace. "There's a big gap behind it," she said. "This could be his hiding place!"

She climbed up into the chimney. Ivy held her breath — had they really found it? How quickly would her father notice that the treasure was missing? Could they get it to the dragons before he realized he'd been robbed — before he banished anyone he decided to blame?

Foxglove was hidden from view for a long time. Azalea, Pine, and Violet joined them, but nobody spoke. The rain was coming down harder, plastering their hair to their heads and soaking through their green tunics. The feeling in the air was almost unbearable. Ivy wondered what Azalea would do when Foxglove emerged with the treasure. The tension radiating off the banished Wingwatcher was making her very nervous.

Finally Foxglove ducked out of the chimney and faced them. Ivy felt her excitement dim. The look in Foxglove's eyes was hollow.

"I think it was here," she said. "But he must have emptied it sometime after he found you in the ruins, Pine."

"*Emptied* it?" Azalea cried, rushing over to the fireplace. She climbed inside and crab-walked up the chimney wall to see for herself.

"It's all gone?" Pine asked bleakly.

"Almost," said Foxglove. She held out something that flashed in the dim light. "The only thing left in the hole was this."

Glowing in the palm of her hand was a shimmering blue sapphire shaped like a star.

— CHAPTER 19 —

WREN

In the city, some dragons were still awake and wandering the moonlit streets, but Wren had waited as long as she could, and she thought — she *hoped* that most of them were asleep.

She crept out of the trees and down the hill in the dark, through the farmstead, following the same path she'd watched Sky walk earlier that day. A goat bleated huffily at her as she snuck past, nearly giving her a heart attack. But no dragons stirred; the ones who lived on the outskirts seemed to be the early-to-bed types.

The bridge was deserted, but there were two dragons in the market square, sitting on the steps of a statue and arguing about something. Wren stayed low as she crossed the river, in the shadow of the bridge railing. She had to dart from the bridge to the first stall, now covered for the night, but neither of the arguing dragons noticed her in the torchlight.

"Don't be an idiot," one of them growled. "Stick with Burn. She's going to win! We all know it."

"I dunno," said the other. "It sounds all right in the" —

something about scorpions? — "right now, with the" — something about claws — "in charge."

The first dragon muttered a bunch of insults Wren didn't completely understand, although she would have liked to learn them so she could use them on Undauntable one day. She worked her way around the square, staying behind the stalls, and finally she turned the same corner that Sky had turned.

More streets. Another square up ahead. Balconies overlooking the alleys, giant windows for the dragons to fly into.

Wren had no idea where Sky had gone from here. She was a very small human in a very big dragon city.

But I am going to find him.

She followed the streets, trying to think like Sky. Would he have wandered down this road because it was lined with flowering garden boxes? Would he have stopped to climb around on the dragonet playground, even though he was probably too big for it?

It was a little hard to concentrate when every so often a dragon would suddenly swoop out of the sky and she'd have to fling herself into a doorway or under a cart of vegetables to hide. More than once, she had to take a quick, unexpected turn because she heard a whole party of laughing dragons coming around a corner.

But close to midnight, she came upon something that she knew would have caught Sky's attention: a courtyard lined with cages. Most of them were covered for the night, but

Wren could hear twittering and rustling and a few soft growls. This was some kind of shop for dragon pets, just as Sky had hoped for, she guessed. She peeked under a few of the covers and saw mostly weird, lovely birds. The one closest to the torchlight had bright green, blue, and yellow feathers and a large hooked beak, and it tilted its head at her curiously. Another cage held a kind of desert mouse with giant ears and a long tail.

Near the edge of the courtyard were three uncovered, empty cages. Wren nearly went right past them, but something caught her eye about the latches on the doors. She stopped to look at the latches on the doors and realized these cages had been broken open.

Uh-oh.

Oh no. Did Sky decide to free some of the animals? All by himself?

I bet the shop owner didn't like that very much.

She glanced around, wondering what had happened and looking for clues. Had Sky felt sorry for something adorable? Had he just started opening cages?

And then . . . did the shop owner attack him? Or were there guards who might have arrested him?

In Talisman, the dragonmancers had a few goons with sharp sticks who did all the hands-on arresting, and then the dragonmancers decided on the punishment to follow. In Undauntable's city, there was a lord and the porcupine soldiers. Was that how this dragon city worked, too? Was someone in charge?

Wren spotted something on the cobblestones and crouched for a closer look.

The torchlight turned it black, but she was pretty sure it was a drop of blood.

That better not be Sky's blood, she thought, *or I'll be the new dragonslayer in town*.

She searched down each nearby street until she found another drop, and another, a faint trail to follow. The drops of blood led her around a few corners, but she lost the trail, or it ran out, not far from the animal cage courtyard, on a quiet street of what appeared to be family homes. Firelight glimmered behind a few of the curtains, and she could hear dragon voices murmuring, while others were dark and quiet.

Wren paced up and down past the last drop of blood, studying the houses around it. Was Sky inside one of them? Did he want to be? Was he hurt? None of them looked like a jail, at least.

She'd been there a while, trying to peek in some of the windows, when she heard footsteps approaching. Quickly she scrambled up the side of one of the dark houses and hid herself in the greenery decorating the top of the door.

A dragon came along the street, yawning widely. She stopped at the house next to the one where Wren was hiding, sniffed a few times, and swung her head around with a puzzled expression.

You don't smell human, Wren prayed to the three moons above. *Please don't smell me*.

"Hrmph," the dragon grunted. She shoved open the door beside her and went in.

"You're so late!" a voice said from inside. "What took so long?"

"Paperwork," the dragon grumbled. "Very annoying. At least we get to eat the —" She said a word Wren didn't know. "You should have sent someone to clean up out there. I can smell its blood on the street." She waved one wing out at the dark road, then shut the door behind her.

"It was too dark," the other dragon argued, his voice muffled now.

Wren wanted to break something. All that trouble to follow the trail, and it wasn't Sky's blood; it wasn't even a dragon's. It belonged to whatever these two were about to eat. Which meant it had nothing to do with Sky at all.

She was about to jump off the house when the second voice asked, "What happened to that dragon? Did he pay for the lost animals?"

Wren froze. It was harder to hear them with the door closed, and she wasn't entirely sure she was translating right, given how wobbly Sky's Dragon could be sometimes.

"No." The first dragon grumbled something for a while, and then her voice rose again. "— very strange, though. Someone offered to buy *him* from me."

Wren dug her fingers into the side of the house and edged closer, resting her feet on the tops of the windows until she was as close to the conversation as she could possibly be.

"— to cover it?" the second dragon was saying.

"More than enough. Don't know what they want with him, though. Weird, scrawny, and obviously a troublemaker."

The second dragon said something that Wren didn't understand, except that it echoed the word *weird*.

"Ohhhhh, maybe," said the first. There was silence for a while, and some clattering that might have been pots or plates. "Kind of feel sorry for him if that's it," the dragon added eventually.

What? Wren thought desperately. *Where is he? What is happening to Sky?*

"Maybe the (something) will let him go," said the other one.

"We'll know when we see them fly back to the palace tomorrow," said the first. She used a word that wasn't quite *palace*, but sounded close. "He'll be with them, or not."

"I'll be glad when they're gone!" the second replied, sounding a bit louder and more animated. "Marching around the city, knocking things over with their weapons, ordering dragons about. Someone should tell them they can boss around sand dragons all they want, but they're not in charge of the rest of us."

"Ha!" said the first dragon. "It's not going to be me!"

They started joking about which of their friends might be brave enough to do it, but Wren didn't need to hear any more. She was pretty sure she'd figured it out. Marching, weapons — that meant Sky was being held by sand dragon soldiers, wherever they were camped in the city. And if she didn't rescue him, tomorrow he'd be flown to the sand queen's palace, for some mysterious terrible reason.

She slithered back down to the ground and set off running through the city. Her guess was that an army would be camped in the desert outside. But the best way to find out would be to get up high.

Wren followed her instincts, taking turns that led higher and higher, until she came to one of the towers she'd seen that overlooked the city. It seemed to be a landing station for new arrivals, where traveling dragons could get their bearings before entering the city.

Of course, there were no stairs, no door inside, nothing helpful for a small human with no wings. But the walls were made of rough sandstone bricks, and she'd been climbing trees her whole life. Wren saw a pair of tiny lizards chase each other up and around the towers. All right, if lizards could do it, she could do this.

It was quite a bit harder than climbing a tree with lovely useful branches, and it took a lot longer than Wren would have liked, but finally she hauled herself, gasping, onto the top of the tower. There was a little roof here, perched on columns and decorated with carvings of dragon wings. There was also, somewhat hilariously, a large map of the city carved on a smooth block of wood. When Wren stood in front of it, she could see how the shapes of the buildings lined up with the map.

The map was covered in labels, but they were all in Dragon — odd symbols that looked like claws and moons and flames. *It really would be useful to read Dragon*, Wren thought. Otherwise, the map was useless to her. She went to the edge of the tower, held on to a column, and peered out into the night.

It was clear, with all three moons overhead, and she could see pretty far in all directions. It didn't take her long to spot a collection of tents and large sleeping shapes organized in a pattern around a small oasis on the western side of the river, where the buildings began to shift into farmland.

It took a lot longer, though, for her to climb down from the tower and run to the encampment. She didn't like the light gray color the sky was turning, and she kind of felt like murdering the birds who were starting to chirp overhead.

But finally she came within sight of the tents and saw, with a sinking heart, that many of the sand dragon soldiers were awake. They were hurrying around, rolling up the tents and securing supplies and doing other busy-looking army things. It would be pretty dangerous for a human to stroll in between their talons right now.

Was Sky really here? How could she find him?

She crept as close as she could and found a large stack of firewood to hide behind. As the tents were folded down, she watched each one to see if it might have a prisoner inside.

And then, finally, she spotted him.

Sky was sitting by the embers of a campfire, his wings drooping dejectedly. A chain locked his talons to a brawny sand dragon sitting next to him. She wore armor and was grinning with a lot of very sharp teeth.

Oh, Sky, Wren thought, her heart breaking. *I'm here. Don't be sad. I'm here to set you free.*

But she had no idea how.

A voice started roaring from one of the tents and all the soldiers snapped to attention.

"HOW ARE WE ALL THIS FINE, FINE MORNING?" the dragon bellowed. He swept out of his tent and spread his wings wide in the morning light. "HA HA HA! AN EXCELLENT DAY TO FIGHT SOME ICE DRAGONS BEFORE WE GO HOME, DON'T YOU THINK?"

"YES, SIR!" all the soldiers roared in unison.

Oh NO, Wren thought, staring at the leader of the dragons. She recognized him.

He was the one who'd attacked the Indestructible City. This must be the army he was planning to destroy them with.

After fighting some ice dragons, apparently, and taking Sky to the sand queen, maybe.

"THEN OFF WE GO!" the leader shouted. He leaped into the sky.

Wait, now? Wren thought in a panic. *Already?*

A storm of sand surrounded her as the soldiers began vaulting into the air after their captain. Through the stinging wind, Wren saw the dragon guarding Sky give a yank on the chain and drag him up with her.

Wingbeats and hollering and wind drowned out everything for several long moments, and Wren had to crouch down with her cloak over her face and her hands over her ears.

Finally the clamor and the hurricane died down. Wren was able to stand up again, shaking sand off her cloak. She blinked around at the deserted camp.

The general and his army were gone, and they'd taken Sky with them.

CHAPTER 20

LEAF

Rowan lunged for Leaf, wrapping her arms around his legs and dragging him back down. The dark red dragon made an annoyed clicking noise and shook Leaf as though Rowan were a troublesome ant. When she clung tighter, it hissed, grabbed her in its other claws, and yanked her away from him.

"Rowan!" Leaf called, struggling to yell over the edge of the dragon's fist. "Rowan, when you get to the arena, kill a dragon for me!"

"Don't you die, Leaf," she screamed back. "Don't you dare get eaten, too!"

And then the grate was getting dizzily closer and closer, and that was all Leaf could see for a moment, until the dragon soared out of the trapdoor and Leaf caught fractured glimpses of a huge bustling kitchen full of frantic dragons. Dragons chopping fruit; dragons stirring cauldrons of soup; dragons stacking elaborate-looking appetizers on plates.

It looked a lot like Talisman preparing for a feast, except the vibe in this kitchen was a lot more "someone's going to kill us if we get this wrong." Leaf wasn't sure how he sensed that — something in the way the dragons held their wings in tightly, pushed one another aside to grab things, and scurried from station to station with tense expressions.

It was all weirdly human, actually. He was probably imagining most of it — thinking the dragons had feelings like humans did, the way his sister Bluebell used to think every butterfly was her friend and truly loved her.

The world tilted sideways and Leaf was swung upside down as the dragon veered through a doorway and up into the heart of the palace. Leaf remembered copying this from the map, more than once because it was hard and he kept getting it wrong. There was a giant hall in the center, with several levels of balconies all around it, a huge hole in the roof above, and windows open to the night sky everywhere. Fires burned in many of the rooms off the balconies, giving the whole palace an ominous smoky glow and a charred smell.

The wind rushed past Leaf's ears, but he could still hear the flapping of dragon wings all around him. Dragons were rushing from level to level. The one carrying him snapped at a dragon carrying a pile of firewood who nearly crashed into them.

Suddenly the dragon banked left, sending blood rushing into Leaf's ears, and whooshed through a tunnel, then right through an enormous doorway that led outside.

After five days in a box, Leaf would have thought going

outside would be a huge relief. But it was hard to appreciate the fresh air when there were approximately eight hundred zillion dragons out there waiting to eat him.

He was on a plateau surrounded by sheer cliffs going up on one side and even more sheer cliffs going down on the other. The plateau was *full* of dragons milling around, looking exactly as awkward as all the villagers did during Dragonmancer Appreciation Day celebrations.

Globes of fire hung over the party, lighting up the scales below: red and orange, but also many pale yellowish dragons with differently shaped snouts. Rowan was right. There was another kind of dragon here. Where had they all come from? Why were they all here now?

And then the dragon dumped him unceremoniously in the middle of the party and flew away again.

Almost immediately, a massive dragon talon slammed down beside Leaf. He rolled quickly to his feet and darted away, dodging through a sea of tails and claws and other prey. He nearly ran straight into the bobcat, who had its back against a statue and was hissing with all its fur standing on end.

As Leaf stumbled back, he saw that the statue was a smooth white marble dragon wearing a crown and raising one claw as though she was making a speech. Just a few steps away was a black statue of another dragon — or the same dragon? it looked like a similar crown — with rubies glittering in the eyeholes and wings spread behind its glare.

There was treasure everywhere. At least half the dragons wore jewels and gold; more jewels were embedded in the decorations. This dragon queen clearly wanted everyone to know how wealthy she was.

Leaf guessed that thieves could get away with a few jewels without the dragons even noticing. Perhaps the dragonmancers really had been successful dragon-treasure smugglers once upon a time.

The strangest decoration, though, was a contraption like a birdcage that hung suspended on wires over the party. Inside it was a small dragon who was yet another different color from the ones on the ground — more golden yellow than sand pale — but who had a similar snout to the pale yellow ones. He'd thought for a moment that she was another statue, but then a dragon on the ground threw something at the cage and she flinched away from the bars.

A prisoner of war? Leaf wondered. *Do dragons take prisoners?* She looked too small to be a threat to any of these dragons, and as sad as the humans in the kitchen pit.

There you go again, Wren observed, *seeing human feelings in the droop of a dragon's wing.*

At the foot of the tall cliff that backed the plateau, a ginormous golden throne towered over the entire party. Atop it sat the orange queen who had chased Mushroom into the ravine. Leaf wondered whether she'd caught him.

Thyme is here somewhere, he remembered. *Maybe we can figure out a way to kill one of these dragons together.*

Another set of huge talons smashed down beside him, scaly and hot and rippling with muscles, and he took off running again.

I have a suggestion, Wren offered. *Maybe focus on staying alive first.*

Leaf darted between the animals and talons, searching the crowd for Thyme. The tunnel that led back into the palace was blocked by a tall barrier of rock and a pair of grouchy-looking guards.

As he crouched behind yet another statue — this one made of gold with a diamond-studded crown — he saw the guards both look up sharply, then turn their heads in the same direction.

Did they hear something?

A few of the dragons standing near them paused their growling conversation and turned to listen as well. Their expressions caught the attention of a few others, and the listening silence began to spread quickly through the party.

Finally it was quiet enough for Leaf to hear what they heard as well.

It sounded like . . . music?

It was coming from somewhere in the mountains nearby, probably another part of the palace. The moonlight cast silver shadows on the peaks around them as all the dragons lifted their faces to the sky.

It *was* music. It was the sound of many voices singing together, but it couldn't be, because the "voices" sang in the dragon language, rumbling well above and below human registers.

How can dragons SING? Leaf thought, shaken. *How can*

they have music? Isn't music a human thing? Don't you need a — a soul to make music?

Especially music that was weirdly beautiful. Leaf wasn't sure why, but it made him think of Wren, and how she would always fight for things she cared about. He rubbed his arms, trying to scrape the goose bumps away.

Over by the cliff, the dragon queen let out a hiss and leaped off her throne. She stalked through the party, flicking her tail at the large sand dragon who'd been sitting beside her. The dragon stood with a displeased expression and followed her into the palace, as did several of the red and orange armored guards.

In the stillness she'd left behind, Leaf finally spotted Thyme lying near the edge of the cliff, peering over at the rocks below. Leaf waited until the distant music cut off and the dragons started moving and talking again. Then he sprinted over to Thyme's side.

"Don't lie down like that," he whispered. "You'll be easy to grab and you won't even have a chance to run."

Thyme sat back on his heels and put his hand on Leaf's shoulder. "Oh, Leaf. I'm so sorry you're here, too."

"Maybe we can both get out of this," Leaf said. "Maybe now, while the queen is gone." He glanced over his shoulder at the cliff that rose behind the party, then leaned over to peer down the one in front of him. Not far away, he could see the glitter of moonlight reflecting off a waterfall. "I think climbing up will be easier than going down. It looks shorter."

"They both look impossible," Thyme said. "There's no *way* I can climb either one."

Leaf had to admit to himself that Thyme was probably right. Leaf's skill could maybe get him through the sheer spots and over that ledge near the top . . . but Thyme had never trained quite as intensely as any of the rest of them.

Thyme sighed and gave him a rueful smile. "You should go, though," he said. "If you stay to keep me company and get eaten, Rowan will never forgive me."

"I wonder what happens to the animals that aren't eaten during the feast," Leaf said. "Maybe all you have to do is hide until it's over, and they'll put you back in the pit with the others."

"Yay?" Thyme said.

It was the only hope Leaf could think of. He glanced around the plateau again, looking for a hiding spot. "I know — under the tables," he said. There were several tables laden with food and, more important, covered with long gold brocade tablecloths. "You can hide under there until the feast is over."

"Hmmm," Thyme said. "That's a little closer to the hors d'oeuvres than I was planning to get, but it's not a bad idea."

Leaf studied the cliff behind the throne, which probably led to the top of the palace. Maybe there was a way to get from up there down into the central hall and then back to the kitchens. He wasn't about to leave the palace without Rowan and Cranberry, even if he could.

"Are you really going up?" Thyme asked. "Won't the dragons notice you?"

"Hopefully not," Leaf said. "They seem preoccupied. And I think it's the best way back to the others."

Thyme grasped his arm for a moment, then nodded. "Good luck."

"You too."

Leaf wasn't sure how long he had before the queen returned. He ducked behind one of the tables and ran along it all the way to the cliff, then rolled behind the throne. The cliff loomed above him, looking a fearsome amount taller than it had even from the other side of the party.

I can do this. It can't be any harder than killing a dragon. And it might be the only way to rescue Rowan and everybody else.

He took a deep breath, reached for the first cracks he could fit his hands into, and started to climb.

The first half of the night went pretty well, he thought. Leaf climbed and climbed, resting whenever he found a secure spot, freezing whenever he heard dragons lifting off from the party below. He climbed as fast as he could at first, to get himself above the fire globes. Once he reached the darker part of the cliff, he felt a lot safer. This also made climbing slower and harder, though, as it was difficult to see exactly what he was reaching for.

Race you to the top of the cliff! Wren said cheerfully. *Just kidding, I would clearly win. Hey, which of these dragons do you think ate me? I hope it was the queen. Watch out, that part*

*of the cliff looks a bit crumbly. Come on, Leaf, you can do it.
Just imagine me at the top, laughing at how slow you are. And
then cheering when you FIIIIINALLY get there. And then
throwing you a sword and waving my own in the air and charging off to fight the dragons! We'd have been a good team,
wouldn't we? I could have helped you protect the village. First
I would have tied up all the dragonmancers and stuffed them in
a cellar full of rotten potatoes.*

Leaf tried again to imagine the dragonmancers when they
were younger, sneaking around this palace and stealing treasure and hightailing it back into the mountains. Maybe it
had been easier back then — maybe there had been a different, less ferocious queen, or something like that. He certainly
couldn't imagine haughty, sinister Master Trout climbing a
cliff like this.

Inside his head, Wren giggled.

Somewhere around the middle of the night, Leaf's arms
began to shake with exhaustion. He heard the feast breaking
up and felt the rush of wind as guests flew away. When he
glanced down, he saw dragons cleaning up the mess that was
left behind. A few of them gathered the last surviving animals and flew back into the palace with them, but Leaf
couldn't see whether Thyme was among them.

The air was cold against the back of his neck, and his fingertips were going numb. He kept reaching for new handholds
and missing.

I have to stop and rest, Leaf realized.

He glanced up and saw that he'd almost reached a narrow shelf of rock that jutted out from the cliff. He'd seen it from below and thought it would be hard to climb over . . . but if he could get onto it, maybe he could lie down and sleep for a moment.

Leaf gritted his teeth and forced himself onward. That tiny handhold over there . . . toes barely clinging to the cracks in the rock . . . another inch higher . . . fingertips aching, hand muscles cramping . . . one more shove upward on his left leg . . . he reached and caught the edge of the shelf, then hauled himself onto it with the last fragment of his strength.

The shelf was barely wide enough for two people to lie down side by side, parallel to the cliff. A scraggly little bush jutted out from a crack in the rock, glaring at Leaf in a very Wren-like, "this is MY safe spot, go get your own!" kind of way.

Leaf collapsed flat on the stone. His whole body was in pain, especially his shoulders. No, his fingers hurt more. Maybe his knees, which kept scraping against the jagged surface of the cliff.

Sleep will fix it all, he thought as his eyes closed.

Leaf's sleep was deep and dreamless, but it was cut short abruptly by the sound of hundreds of dragons screaming in terror.

He shot up and nearly knocked himself off the ledge. For a moment he crouched against the cliff, clutching the thorny bush branches, his heart pounding.

The sky was full of screaming dragons. Shrieking dragons, roaring dragons, dragons shoving one another aside in a mad panic to fly as high and far as they could.

What is going on? What scared them?

He craned his neck toward the arena-prison, where dragons were fountaining into the sky like an erupting volcano of scales and smoke.

Did the sand dragons attack the mountain dragons? Or was it all a trap for the sand dragons? Did one of them betray the others?

Do dragons do traps *and* betrayal?

He had no idea what could have set them off, but suddenly there were dragons everywhere, and it was midmorning, and he had to get to Rowan before any of these dragons did.

He turned to the cliff and started climbing again.

"I can do this, Wren," he whispered. "I can get to the top of this cliff, and I can find my way into the palace, and I can find Rowan and the others and get them out of that pit, and this is a totally rational plan that is going to happen, no problem."

Several minutes later, he had gotten almost nowhere, his shoulders were screaming with pain, and he was realizing that climbing in the daytime, exhausted, was a whole lot more terrifying than climbing at night. There were so many dragons everywhere, and even though most of them were flapping around panicking, it still seemed highly likely that one would eventually go: "AAAAAACK UNSPECIFIED

CATASTROPHE EVERYTHING IS TERR — ooh, I *do* need a snack right now," and pop him right into its mouth.

He'd barely had that thought when a dragon whooshed past, so close that he felt a wave of fiery warmth from its copper-colored scales. A moment later, there was another rush of wingbeats, and Leaf flattened himself against the cliff. The second dragon flashed past, and he blinked, then blinked again as both dragons disappeared over the top of the cliff.

The second dragon was *blue*.

Blue! Did you see that? he thought to imaginary Wren. *A sea dragon, maybe? Did the sea dragons attack? Is that why they're all freaking out?*

Would a sea dragon be any easier to stab?

A gust of wind made him close his eyes as another dragon whisked by.

Keep going, Wren whispered. *Only four thousand more tiny toeholds to go.*

He reached for the next bump in the rocks, and as he did, he saw the last dragon do a slow, lazy turn in the air and come speeding back toward Leaf.

It was looking right at him.

It was reaching for him.

Its talons closed around him, and Leaf was lifted off the cliff, in the claws of a dragon once again.

CHAPTER 21

IVY

"Yeah, I remember this." Stone turned the sapphire over in his hands. It was so big, Ivy almost couldn't believe it was real.

Violet and Daffodil sat on the bench behind her, wrapped in rough gray blankets, still shivering from the long walk back to Valor in the rain. Azalea had not wanted to let them take the sapphire, but Foxglove and Pine both thought they should show it to Stone, make sure it was part of the dragon's treasure, and then decide what to do with it.

Foxglove stood by the door, her arms crossed, shifting uncomfortably from foot to foot.

"Heath never liked this gem," Stone said. He passed it to Ivy, who was startled by the weight of it in her hands. "He said that holding it sometimes gave him strange waking nightmares of the dragons who torched our village. He said sometimes they would look at him as though they could see him. If it's the one thing that makes him feel anything about the dragon attack, that's probably why he left it behind."

There was something odd about the sapphire, but it didn't feel menacing to Ivy. It had a kind of quiet vibration to it, as if it was reaching for something on another level of the universe. She cupped it between her hands and stared into its facets.

"So if he moved the treasure, where else can we look?" Violet asked.

Stone shrugged. "I have no idea. Sorry."

"Well," Foxglove said as Violet and Daffodil got to their feet, "if you think of anything, let us know." Violet rolled up the blankets and turned to hand them to Stone.

With a brisk knock, the Dragonslayer strolled through the front door.

Violet threw the blankets at Ivy so fast that Ivy almost didn't catch them. They tumbled around her hands and she scrambled to bury the sapphire inside the folds of wool. Her heart was pounding. *I hope he didn't see it.*

"What's this?" her father said with a pleasant smile. "A Wingwatcher party? At my brother's house? Why wasn't I invited?"

"Hi, Dad," she said, clutching the blankets to her chest. "We were just stopping by to say hi to Uncle Stone."

Heath's gaze traveled over Violet's innocent face, Daffodil's wide eyes, Foxglove's blank expression. "Oh?" he said. "Why are you all . . . wet?"

"It's raining," Violet answered.

"We were surprised by a storm while we were out sky-gazing," Foxglove reported. "We came in the closest entrance.

Ivy suggested that her uncle lived nearby and we could dry off here."

Heath raised his eyebrows at her. "You haven't dried off much," he observed.

"I was more concerned for the young recruits," Foxglove said. "I've been caught in the rain before. I'll be fine."

"Holly, right?" he said, pointing at her.

"Foxglove, sir," she said, as politely as always.

"Hmmm," he said. "Ivy, use one of those blankets on your hair. You are dripping all over your uncle's cave. And then get on home — I need to speak with my brother."

Ivy took a nervous step toward the door. Stone was standing with his hands in his pockets, looking resigned to a conversation with Heath. He looked too morose to say anything helpful.

"We'll wash these and bring them back to you, mister Ivy's uncle sir," Daffodil said, patting the pile of blankets in Ivy's arms. "Thanks very much!"

"Yes, thanks, Uncle Stone," Ivy said, relieved. She hurried to the door.

"Foxglove," the Dragonslayer said, and a chill went through Ivy. She could hear the thread of anger under his pleasant tone, even though it was well buried. "Perhaps it would be wise to confine the younger recruits — and yourself — to the tunnels for the foreseeable future. If you can't recognize when a storm is on its way while you're literally staring at the sky, it seems you might all need a little more training." He stepped up behind Ivy and lifted a strand of her wet hair.

"We can't have the daughter of the Dragonslayer getting sick, after all."

"Yes, sir," Foxglove said. She held the door as the three girls went through, nodded to the Dragonslayer, and followed them out.

"Yikes," Daffodil said when they reached a safe distance. "I thought that was the end of everything! I was starting to wonder if I'd have time to pack before we got thrown out of Valor!"

"I'm sorry," Ivy said. She didn't know how to shield her friends if her father's anger turned on them.

"Don't be," Foxglove said, looping one arm around Ivy's shoulder and squeezing her. "You have nothing to be sorry about. We know more than we did at the beginning of the day. And we have something." She took the pile of blankets with the sapphire hidden inside. "I'll find a place for this. And I guess I'll . . . wash these. Daffodil, since you volunteered, if you'd like to come help me do that tomorrow, I would appreciate it."

"I will!" Daffodil said. They split off from Foxglove at the next tunnel and headed back toward Ivy's cave. Violet still hadn't said a word since leaving Stone's cave.

"Violet, are you all right?" Ivy asked.

"Just thinking," Violet said. "Was he really mad about you getting a little wet? Or why did he order us confined to the caves?"

So Violet had noticed Heath's anger, too. "Do you think he suspects?" Ivy whispered. "If he saw the sapphire — he would have taken it from us, wouldn't he?"

"I don't think it was about the treasure," Violet said thoughtfully. "I think he didn't like seeing Wingwatchers with Stone. Maybe he's worried his brother will try to steal his position as lord of Valor."

"No way. Uncle Stone isn't at *all* interested in that," Ivy said.

"But the Dragonslayer is clearly feeling threatened by *something*," said Violet. "I think I'd better tell the Wingwatchers to be extra careful for a while. Even if they just roll their eyes at me and say, 'Nobody is UP TO anything, Violet, buzz off,' like they normally do."

"Do we have to be extra careful, too?" Daffodil asked with a dramatic sigh. "I *hate* being extra careful."

"Have you literally ever tried, even once in your life?" Violet asked.

"What about our plan?" Ivy interjected. "To fix everything? What do we do about it now?" She didn't want to give up. Especially now that she'd seen the village — if dragons were still doing that to other villages, she would do anything to get the treasure back and stop them.

"Well," Violet said, "if seeing Pine in the old village spooked him into moving the treasure, it stands to reason he'd have moved it closer to him. Somewhere he could keep an eye on it all the time." She gestured at the tunnels around them. "Somewhere down here."

"So we keep looking," Daffodil said. "Don't worry, Ivy. We'll find it."

* * *

It was several days before Ivy found herself alone at home again. Her father seemed to be lurking around more than usual, eyeing her with either suspicion or concern. He was short-tempered with her mother and grumbled about everything — the fish stew, the temperature of the cave, all the *whining* people kept doing about tunnels collapsing and vegetable shortages, like it was his fault the architects and gardeners were so lazy.

Ivy noticed that he'd also added several men to his private guard, all of them brawny and surly and devoted to the Dragonslayer. She saw a few Wingwatchers be summoned individually to his office, and she wondered whether that meant they were loyal to him, or whether they were the ones he most suspected of fomenting rebellion.

One day at breakfast, Ivy's father announced that he had to go on an inspection tour of the orchards. "Something about pests eating all the fruit," he muttered. "Don't know what they think *I'm* going to do about it!" He snorted and looked at Ivy's mother. "Wingwatcher training is suspended for today so a patrol can accompany us. So you should stay home with Ivy, Lark."

Mother gave him a puzzled, dismayed look. "But I have that meeting with the gardeners," she protested. "We're working on a new solution to the sunlight problem."

"You'll have to miss it," he said, standing up.

"Ivy can stay home by herself, dear," she said. "She's fourteen! She's almost a full Wingwatcher."

"Yes, I know," he said, frowning. "Still, stay together for today. I'd feel safer if you did."

"I could go to Daffodil's while Mother has her meeting," Ivy suggested.

"No, no," he said. "You spend quite enough time with those girls. Both of you, here. And don't leave until I return."

"Heath —" Mother protested, but he was already striding out the door. She stared after him for a moment with a bewildered expression. Watching her, Ivy realized that there was something different about her mother's face . . . something missing.

The dreamy look, she thought. *The hero-worship eyes she used to give Dad all the time, same as most everyone in Valor. I haven't seen her look at him like that in a while.*

When did that change?

She tried to think back to when the bedtime story stopped, or to some of the fights her parents had had in the last few years. Was it possible her mom had started noticing Dad's lies, too? Had she realized, somewhere along the way, that he was not as much of a hero as she'd first believed?

Ivy knew her mother loved working on projects to improve Valor. Now that she thought about it, those projects had been taking up a lot more of her time in the last few years . . . as though Lark was happy to stay busy and away from Heath.

It's probably good for Mom to see him more clearly, she thought. *But . . . they're my parents. I still want them to love each other.*

No. What I really want, she admitted to herself, *is for Dad to be the person that Mom and I thought he was.*

Her mother was still staring at the door, frowning in a puzzled way.

"Mom? Why is Dad acting so weird?" Ivy asked.

"He's . . . got a lot on his mind," her mother said, looking down at the table. She started to clear the breakfast things and Ivy stood up to help her.

"So do you," Ivy said gently. "Your work on the gardens is really important, too."

"I do think it is!" Her mother stopped and took a deep breath. "Right now your father is worried that something might happen to us. There's a man — a very powerful man — who's been trying for years to get your father to come work for him."

"Really?" Ivy said. "Who? What does he want Dad to do?"

"Slay dragons, of course," her mother said ruefully. "He's the lord of the Indestructible City."

Oh, wow, Ivy thought. She'd heard of the Indestructible City, but she didn't know anything about its lord. What would it be like if they all moved there and Heath became a professional dragonslayer? Would he lead the lord's armies against the dragons?

Dad would never work for anyone else; he likes being lord himself too much. And he doesn't want to fight any more dragons. He'd rather hide from them.

"Anyway, the last couple of messengers have been more . . . persistent than the ones before. Your father is worried about what they might do. I think he's afraid they might even kidnap one of us."

Ivy wondered if that was exactly true, or whether that was her mother's own interpretation of Heath's concerns. *I think he'd be more worried a kidnapper would ask for the treasure as ransom. Would he give it to them? In exchange for either of us?*

"Not to mention all the unrest in Valor," Lark sighed. "So many angry people, all wanting your father to fix everything."

Well, it would certainly help if he tried to fix SOMETHING, at least, Ivy thought.

She glanced sideways at her mother as they washed the dishes. "I think you should go to that meeting, Mom. If you're not there, the gardeners will only get more angry with Dad — but if you are, maybe *you* can help fix things. I promise I'll stay here with the door locked."

Her mother pushed her hair out of her face, leaving a damp streak on her forehead. She gazed at the door, looking worried. "I wouldn't be gone long," she said. "It is pretty important . . . if I go, do you think we could keep it between ourselves?"

"Of course, Mom," Ivy said, giving her a hug. "Go save the vegetables."

"All right. Yes. I will! Thank you, Ivy." Her mother smiled and hurried off to change.

Ivy finished cleaning up, wondering if this was the first time she'd ever seen her mother disobey one of her father's orders, or if had happened before without her noticing. She hoped it wasn't a terrible mistake to encourage her mom to go. She hoped Dad wouldn't find out and be furious. But it didn't seem fair that her mother had to miss a meeting she cared about, just because he was feeling paranoid, when Ivy could certainly look after herself.

Almost as soon as her mother was gone, there was a knock on the door. Ivy checked the peephole, but she already knew it was Violet and Daffodil.

"I was just trying to figure out how to send a message to you," Ivy said, opening the door.

"No need," Daffodil said, sweeping in grandly. "We've been watching and waiting for AGES for them both to be gone."

"Everyone focus," Violet said. She had her hair back in a dark purple band of cloth and was wearing gray instead of her Wingwatcher uniform, but she still looked like she was ready to take over Commander Brook's job the moment it was available. "We're going to search every corner of this place, but we have to do it fast."

"I've already searched every corner!" Ivy protested. "I really have!"

"We're doing it again," Violet said, striding purposefully toward the Dragonslayer's office. *Properly this time* was strongly implied.

"I need a snack first," Daffodil said. "We'll catch up to you!"

Violet rolled her eyes and disappeared into the next cave.

"Guess what?" Daffodil whispered to Ivy, pulling her into the kitchen. "Forest asked me to be his date to the Wingwatchers dance!"

"Oh — wow," Ivy said. She'd completely forgotten about the Wingwatchers dance. "Yay? Yay, right? That's exciting, isn't it?"

"It is," Daffodil said, "except that Violet will be a huge pain in the butt about it." She took an apple from the barrel in the corner and started cutting it into slices.

"You haven't told her?"

"Obviously I will," Daffodil said, "but I was thinking I'd wait until the very last minute, just to minimize the amount of time I have to spend hearing about how all boys are gross and he's the worst and couldn't I do better and so on forever and so forth."

She took the plate of apple slices into Ivy's living room, but stopped short in the entranceway. "Speaking of gross!" she said, flourishing one hand at the tail barb on its pedestal. "How do you *live* with that thing?"

"I avoid it," Ivy admitted. "I'll walk all the way around the tables to get past it."

Daffodil's eyes suddenly went wide. "So," she said slowly, "hypothetically, when you were searching the whole place . . . did you avoid it then, too?"

Ivy gasped. Of *course* she had. She hadn't even thought about it. She avoided it instinctively. She'd never once lifted the tapestry draped over the pedestal to see what was underneath.

"Violet!" Daffodil shouted.

A few moments later, they had folded the tapestry over the glass box and the tail barb, revealing the huge wooden cabinet that formed the pedestal. It was definitely a cabinet, because it had a door, but there was no keyhole. Instead there was a series of tumblers embedded in the wood, with letters inscribed on them.

"It's a combination lock," Violet said. "We have to line up the letters to spell the right word in order to get it to open."

"Wait," Ivy said as Daffodil reached for the first tumbler. "Let me memorize what it is right now, so we can put it back the way it was before Dad comes home." She studied the letters, her heart beating wildly.

"What could it be?" Violet mused. "Four letters . . . maybe a word that means something to him?"

"Try *Lark*," Ivy suggested. "My mom's name."

Daffodil lined up LARK, but that didn't work.

"SLAY?" Violet suggested. "TAIL? BARB?"

They tried all three. No luck.

"What about something no one would expect?" Daffodil said. "Like . . . BOOK? Or LOVE?"

Violet snorted, but she tried both of them. "Shockingly terrible guesses," she said when neither worked.

"I am *thinking outside the box*, VIOLET," Daffodil said.

"Claw?" Ivy said. "Wing? Fire?"

They tried every dragon-related word they could think of, and then all the treasure-related ones, like GOLD and GEMS and RICH.

"Anyone might guess one of those," Violet said. "It has to be something more specific to him, doesn't it?"

"Oh," Ivy said softly. "I know. Try Rose."

She held her breath as Daffodil clicked the letters around. R-O-S-E. The lost sister who he must think about every time he saw his treasure. He must wonder if it had been worth it, losing her in exchange for this.

Daffodil tugged on the door. It did not open.

"Whoa," she said, blinking up at Ivy and Violet. "I really thought that would be it! That would be the *perfect* password. Like a sign that your dad does have a soul after all."

"Hey now," Ivy said. "He has a soul. Sometimes he's really funny or does something thoughtful for Mom. He's not completely evil."

"Try EVIL," Violet suggested.

"Violet," Ivy said, rolling her eyes, but she was secretly relieved when that word didn't work either.

"Maybe IVY . . . S?" Violet said. "Like, all this will be Ivy's one day?"

That didn't work either. Ivy would have been enormously surprised if it had. She didn't think she was that present in her father's thoughts.

Besides, he wouldn't think of the treasure as something that would belong to anyone else, ever. The way he talked about it, the way he loved it — it was his, and he wouldn't ever give it up.

"Maybe . . . try MINE," she said. *As in, this treasure is all mine.*

The letters clicked into place, and the cabinet door swung open.

"Yeesh. Not to be judgy," Violet said, "but that's an upsetting choice of password."

"Oh my stars," Daffodil whispered, staring into the cabinet. Ivy crouched beside her and saw that it was packed, top to bottom, with piles of gold coins, gemstones, and a dragon carved from blue stone with emeralds for eyes.

"We found it," she said. "Now quick, lock it up again."

"Can't I touch it?" Daffodil said wistfully.

"No, Ivy's right," Violet agreed. "Leave everything the way it was."

"Before we take the treasure, we need to work out the rest of the plan," Ivy said. "How to give it back to the dragons . . ."

"And survive," Violet finished.

CHAPTER 22

LEAF

Leaf yelled and fought and pounded on the dragon's claws, but the dragon only glanced down at him and made a low chuckling kind of noise.

Whoa. This one's face was *totally* different, kind of square and flat on top. And it was *brown* — the warm tree-bark brown of Wren's eyes. Its eyes were brown, too, and more human than any other dragon's he'd seen before.

If it wasn't the silliest thought Leaf had ever had, he might say the dragon's eyes were *twinkling* at him.

Also, the last two dragons had held Leaf tight and carelessly, like a squirmy, annoying carrot; this one carried him cupped in both hands, the way Wren used to carry baby rabbits out of the garden so no one would catch them and kill them.

"What the heck kind of dragon are you?" Leaf shouted. "I'm not scared of you! If you eat me, I will kick out your teeth and poke your guts and make you generally miserable! I'm going to be a dragonslayer, you hear me?! It's my destiny, so you can't eat me, because that's *not* my destiny, so —"

The brown dragon reached the top of the cliff and landed

awkwardly on its back talons. Using its wings for balance, it crouched and opened its claws, setting Leaf down behind a boulder with astonishing gentleness.

Leaf's legs almost gave out underneath him. He stared up at the dragon, blinking in confusion.

It . . . it looked like it was *smiling*.

Dragons don't smile, do they, Wren?

"Rrrrrr rrrrrmble rrrrrgle rrrrrbpity rrrrrflte," the dragon said.

It's TALKING TO ME.

The dragon pointed off into the mountains, nudged Leaf gently with one claw, and then turned and flew back into the palace through the hole in the roof of the central hall.

Leaf had to sit down.

He covered his face with his hands and tried to think.

Did that dragon just . . . help me?

Why didn't it eat me?

What was it trying to say? It looked like it knew I was escaping . . . like that's what it wanted me to do.

WHY WOULD A DRAGON HELP ME ESCAPE?

He couldn't figure it out. There was no reason for that dragon to catch him and then let him go. Did it really see him climbing, figure out that he needed help, and decide to lift him to the top of the cliff?

It could have eaten him in a heartbeat. It *should* have eaten him.

Surely any other dragon would have eaten him, or left him to fall and die.

Was that dragon . . . weird? Or are there actually lots of friendly, helpful dragons in the world? Just . . . living side by side with the murderous, person-eating ones?

He'd been sitting there for a little while, trying to wrap his head around this idea and recover from the climb and the shock, when four dragons burst out of the roof hole nearby. They looked like the ones he'd seen before — one coppery and wreathed in smoke, one blue and scowling, and the kind brown one — plus one more, this one much bigger and red, with a burn scar on its face.

Leaf hid in the shadow of the boulder as they soared into the sunlight and then away, back down over the cliff he'd been climbing.

"Kind brown one" indeed. It probably just has indigestion today. That would explain the expression that looked like a smile. It was full and its stomach hurt, so it let me go.

Dragons can't be kind.

They can't be sympathetic, or helpful, and they can't possibly see us as anything but prey.

Right?

Wren?

She was uncharacteristically silent, as though even the imaginary voice in his head was confused by the situation.

Maybe the *brown* dragons were different from the others? Maybe they were vegetarians or only ate crocodiles or something.

"I'll ask Rowan," he whispered to Wren. "That's a good

idea, right?" That was a decision that would stop him from thinking in circles anymore, and one that would make him get up and go find his big sister.

He was worried that his shoulders couldn't take any more climbing, but it turned out to be a lot easier to climb down into the palace than to climb out. There were columns along the top balcony that rose up to the roof, so once he shimmied onto one of those, he could slide down to the floor of the balcony fairly smoothly.

The top level seemed to be deserted. He could hear dragons roaring in the distance and muttering from the levels below, but up here each room was empty, looking as though the inhabitants had left in a hurry.

It was very unsettling to stand on a balcony with no railing, looking out over a long drop to the distant ground. Leaf glanced over the edge and thought he saw a dead dragon lying at the bottom, but there were other dragons milling around down there, so he wasn't sure.

He began the long walk through the tunnels, spiraling down and down through the palace.

"This is weird, Wren," he whispered. "I drew these hallways so many times! I remember marking this throne room up here."

He hesitated a few steps from the doorway. Something was in there, stumbling around, knocking into things. It was kind of growl-groaning, a noise of pain and rage combined.

Leaf crept forward until he was close enough to peek inside.

The dragon queen was in there alone, leaning over her throne, breathing heavily. Something was wrong with her face, from what he could see of it. Even in silhouette, it wasn't quite the right *shape* anymore.

The blueprint hadn't noted how much gold there was in the throne room. It was all over the walls and floor and throne like someone had painted it on in thick wild strokes. Leaf thought it looked terrible, but he knew Rowan and Grove and Thyme would have loved it.

The queen groaned again and collapsed in a heap on the floor before her throne.

Someone attacked her, he guessed. *Well. That's good. With what, I wonder?*

He could probably manage to stab her now, while she was unconscious and injured.

Yes! Stab her in the face! Wren suggested with gruesome enthusiasm.

Oh, now you have something to say? Well, I don't have a sword, he reminded her. *And I think it would be pretty dishonorable to kill an unconscious dragon.*

The Wren in his head rolled her eyes. *Dragons don't care about honor. You are such a moosebreath.*

Some dragons might care about honor, he thought, remembering the brown dragon. *Shush. I'm trying to be stealthy here.*

Leaf was about to race across the open space of the doorway when something moved in the sky outside. He crouched and froze as five sand dragons soared into the throne room, including the massively gigantic one who'd been with the queen the night before.

That one pointed at the unconscious queen and growled an order. The other four went to pick her up, their wings and tails tangling as they figured out how to share her weight. And then the five sand dragons flew out again, carrying the queen of the mountain dragons with them.

I was right, Leaf thought. *The sand dragons must have attacked the mountain dragons.*

Well, at least someone *is probably going to stab her in the face, then*, Wren said cheerfully. *This might be a good time for a daring rescue, while everyone is going, "Ack! Betrayal! Where is our queen?!"*

Yes, yes. Leaf darted across, ran down another curve of the balcony, and turned into a tunnel that, if he remembered right, led to the kitchens.

He did remember right. The kitchens, unfortunately, were not deserted, but all the hustle and bustle of the previous night had been swallowed by a weird aura of disaster. Half-prepared food was scattered across the tables and countertops. A pig was burning on a spit over a fire, charred almost entirely black on one side. Dragons stood in small clusters around the huge room, talking to one another in hushed growls.

Leaf edged along the wall, behind barrels and piles of animal skins. At one point he nearly ran into a mouse as tall as his knee; it looked up at him, squeaked something indignant

(*"This is MY thieving ground, you scoundrel!"* the Wren voice suggested), and stalked away with a cross expression.

Soon he found the pit, which appeared to be unguarded. He couldn't see any rope nearby, but there was a nearly empty sack of potatoes half his size. If he pulled on one of the loose threads . . . Yes, it spooled out into a long winding puddle, nearly as thick as a regular human rope. He dragged it over to the grate, tied one end to the metal, and dropped the other down into the hole. He couldn't see the bottom very clearly, and he didn't dare call out to Rowan in case it caught the attention of the kitchen dragons. He just had to hope they'd see the rope and start climbing it.

But they wouldn't fit through the holes in the grate, so he'd have to get the trapdoor open — and it was locked with a padlock. He shook it hopelessly for a moment. Was there anything he could use to pick it?

"Grrrble?"

Leaf dropped the padlock and leaped back. A tiny, tiny dark red dragon with a long neck and sparkling eyes was staring at him from under the nearest table. It was the first dragon Leaf had ever seen who was smaller than him.

Maybe I could fight that one, he thought ruefully.

You promised to kill a dragon, Wren scolded him. *THAT is barely a gecko.*

A gecko with very sharp teeth! Leaf pointed out.

"Blrrrrb!" the dragon chirped. It dropped its front half in an about-to-pounce position, looking like the wild dogs around Talisman as they tried to play with one another.

"Shhh," Leaf whispered. "Go away."

"Lorp lorp lorp!" the baby dragon yodeled. It cavorted around the grate, as if it was nervous to step on the holes. "Lorp! Groble frrrrorble blrrb!"

Well, Leaf thought. *If one dragon can be helpful, maybe this one could be, too.*

Leaf pointed to the padlock. "Key?" he whispered, miming a turning action. "Any idea where it is, if you're so determined to make friends?"

The little dragon sat down, tilted his head back, and began to sing at the top of his lungs. At least, that was what Leaf guessed he was trying to do; there was a *hint* of melody in it, but mostly enthusiasm.

Very *loud* enthusiasm. Leaf sprinted back to the wall and dove behind the potato sack as a new dragon came bustling into the room, clearly harrumphing at the baby.

The baby yelped in protest. The two of them argued for a little while, and then the small dragon came stomping right over to the potato sack.

Oh no, Leaf thought. *Baby dragon! Don't betray me!*

The tiny dragon whisked the potato sack away and pointed triumphantly at Leaf.

Aaaaaaaaaaaaaaaaaaand now you get eaten, said Wren.

But the bigger dragon did not seize Leaf and bite his head off. It didn't even throw him back in the pit. It sighed impatiently, just like any parent or teacher in Talisman might do, and reached up to take a key off a hook on the wall.

"Yormorbleflorp!" the baby dragon said with enormous

glee. It bounced over, took the key, and bounced back to Leaf — with a little difficulty, as the key was as big as one of its wings.

"Oh," Leaf said, in shock, as the baby placed the key in his hands. "Th-thank you."

The older dragon growled something, the little dragon warbled and waved at Leaf, and the two of them went out the way the last one had come in.

What was THAT all about? Wren asked in his head. *Did you roll in something awful-smelling? Why doesn't anyone want to eat you today?*

Do you think that baby dragon actually understood me? Leaf asked her. *It must have, right?*

Yeah, Wren agreed. *Although I'm not sure that was helpfulness so much as a toddler having a temper tantrum until he got his way, which, in this case, worked out for you.*

Leaf noticed that the rope was tight and swinging — someone was climbing it! He ran over and unlocked the padlock, dragging it aside. The trapdoor was too heavy to open all the way, but he was able to lever it up enough to brace with a few potatoes, and that left a crack just wide enough for Rowan, then Cranberry, to crawl through.

And then, right behind them: Thyme.

"You survived!" Leaf whispered in awe.

"I can't believe *you* survived!" Thyme whispered back.

"Nor us!" Cranberry chimed in. "They sent us to the arena this morning, Leaf! We had to fight a blue dragon and a black dragon, and I came *this close* to stabbing the black one in the eye! Rowan was amazing; you should have seen her."

Rowan enveloped Leaf in a fierce bear hug that went on remarkably long. Rowan was *not* a hugger; he couldn't remember any other time when she'd ever hugged him. On the other hand, he'd just saved her life, so it made sense that she'd be a little pleased about that.

"Cardinal?" he asked over her shoulder. "Arbutus? Are they coming?"

Cranberry shook her head, twisting one of her braids around her fingers. "They were in the arena, too," she said. "They didn't make it."

"It was the worst thing I've ever seen," Rowan said, finally releasing Leaf. She did look shaken, even more so than she had after the dragonmancers threatened Grove.

"But we're alive," he said. "We're all right, Rowan; we can still escape. Come on, I think I remember where one of the entrances to the trash chute is from here."

"Leaf," Rowan said, gripping his shoulders. "I have to tell you something." Her eyes were as serious as the day she'd told him about the Dragonslayer.

"Now?" Leaf asked. "Couldn't we escape the palace full of hungry dragons first?"

"Give us a moment," Rowan said to her friends. She tugged Leaf behind the potato sack and turned to face him, but in a weird way, like she couldn't quite hold eye contact with him. Her hands kept twitching like she'd forgotten where to put them.

"Rowan?" Leaf prompted her when she didn't say anything for a moment.

"Last night," Rowan said in a rush, "I realized that I might never see you again. I realized that you might die, or I might die, and you would never know the truth."

"The truth?" Goose bumps trailed along Leaf's arms. "What — what truth?"

"About Wren." Rowan glanced into his eyes and then back down at the flagstones. The kitchen felt much colder than a dragon kitchen should be. "She wasn't just accidentally eaten by dragons, Leaf. She was . . . sacrificed."

Oh dear, said the Wren in Leaf's head. *I don't think we're going to like this story.*

"It was the dragonmancers," Rowan went on quickly. "They said they had a vision, and she needed to be given to the dragons in order to protect the town. But it was my fault, Leaf."

"*Your* fault?"

"Do you remember those books she stole from the dragonmancers' private collection?" Leaf nodded — he remembered Wren sneaking off to read them and telling him how smart she would be when she'd finished them and how they had lots of boring parts.

"She was hiding them in my loft," Rowan went on, "and reading them whenever Mother and Father were out. She didn't care if *I* knew she had them. And then Mother found one while you guys were at school, and she was so mad, and she thought *I'd* taken it, so I told her it wasn't me. I . . . I told her it was Wren."

Rowan rubbed her face with both hands. "I thought she'd be normal-punished, you know? The way she usually was. I mean, I knew it was bad, but I had no idea the dragonmancers would . . . that they'd decide she was so much trouble they had to get rid of her."

"For reading their books?" Leaf said numbly. "They fed a seven-year-old to the dragons for that?"

Such upstanding civilized people, Wren said. *Thank goodness we have moral giants like that leading our village.*

"I tried to stop them," Rowan said. "When I found out what they were going to do — I yelled at our parents, I threw a few things — but I should have done more. They locked me in the cellar when they took her. I should have figured out a way to escape and help her. *You* would have."

Leaf was still thinking about the punishment compared to the crime. "Maybe they were trying to shut her up," he said. "She must have read something in the books that they didn't want anyone to know." He racked his brain — had she told him anything? He'd been eight, and not at all interested in the scribblings inside a moldy book. He remembered her saying there was a lot of math in it. That couldn't be right — that didn't sound like a secret at all.

"I'm sorry, Leaf," Rowan said.

He looked up at her, and it suddenly hit him that she'd been lying to him for seven years. Her and Grove, they both had. Every time he talked about Wren, they had stuck to the lie. Rowan had let him blame the dragons — she had let him build his *whole life* around blaming the dragons — even though she knew all along who the real villains were.

The dragonmancers. And Mother and Father, who let this happen.

"Did you ever really care about slaying dragons?" he asked. "Getting justice for Wren? Protecting the village?" He took a deep breath. The kitchen smelled like onions and burnt pig and betrayal. "Or did you only spend all that time training me because you wanted help to steal treasure?"

"I mean . . ." She kind of shrugged. "Both? Two birds with one stone? It was still the dragons who ate her, after all. We can be mad at them *and* at the dragonmancers, can't we?"

"But you were using me and the way I felt about losing Wren," he said. "You let me hate the dragons because it made me more useful to you." His destiny was crumbling like sand around him. He wanted to press it all back together and be himself again, the person he'd imagined he'd be one day, slaying dragons and saving the world. Simple and uncomplicated; bad guys with scales and claws over there, good guys who were human over here.

"No!" Rowan cried. "I thought I was helping you! I saw how upset you were — I wanted to give you a way to fight back!"

"But against the wrong bad guy!" Leaf cried. "I could have spent all this time trying to stop the dragonmancers instead! *They're* the ones endangering the village." He took a step back. The room felt like it was expanding and contracting around him. "That's why you believed they would sacrifice Grove. Because you know they've done it before. Were there others? Before Wren?"

"I think so," Rowan said. "I remember one of their apprentices being sacrificed when I was really little. They didn't say why. Just another vision. The dragons demanded it, all that."

"And you let me go work for them," Leaf said. He crouched, burying his face in his hands. All he could think of was little Wren and how she must have felt. Did she know that Mother and Father had let her be sacrificed? Did she think Leaf had known, too; did she think he didn't care? Did she go to the dragons feeling completely abandoned by everyone?

Poor me, Wren whispered sadly.

Thyme poked his head around the edge of the potato sack. "You know, we could still go steal treasure," he whispered.

"Not a good moment, Thyme," Rowan snapped.

"I'm just saying, now that we're free and inside the palace . . . if we're quiet and avoid the dragons . . . there's treasure everywhere. We have to bring *something* back to save Grove anyway, right?"

Leaf could sense Rowan glancing at him, but he didn't look up. He couldn't even imagine thinking about treasure right now. He didn't know what to do next. He couldn't go back to the village; he couldn't face his parents or the dragonmancers again, knowing what he knew. But what was he supposed to do with this handful of sand that used to be his great destiny?

"You're right, Thyme," Rowan said finally. "We have to steal treasure to save Grove. We'll give the dragonmancers enough to free him, and then we can keep the rest for ourselves."

Leaf snorted and stood up. "That's not going to work," he said. "The dragonmancers are murderers and thieves, and obviously they'll kill to keep their secrets. If you go back to them, they'll still 'sacrifice' Grove and you as well. And no one is going to stop them. Just like no one tried to save Wren."

Rowan wrapped her arms around herself. "You'd stop them," she said.

"I'm not going back to Talisman," Leaf said. "You can steal treasure and walk back into the dragonmancers' trap yourselves, if that's what you really want to do. You don't need me for that."

"Leaf?" Cranberry said from behind him.

"You're not even going to help us steal the treasure?" Thyme asked.

"I never wanted to steal treasure!" Leaf said. "I came to kill a dragon and instead I learned that it's almost impossible."

You also learned that some dragons might be good, and some sisters might be liars, and that maybe your whole destiny plan was wrong all along, Wren pointed out.

"Then where are you going to go?" Cranberry asked, putting one hand on his arm.

Leaf thought for a moment, but the answer had been ricocheting around his brain ever since he tried to stab the dragon and his sword bounced off. There was one person out there who was a real hero. One person who could tell Leaf the truth and help him find a destiny that would be worthy of Wren.

He met Rowan's eyes. "I'm going to find the Dragonslayer."

Here Be Dragons?

Here Be Dragons

Desert Dragon
Palace

Here Be Dragons

Valor

Terrifying
Viper Pit of Dragons

PART THREE

CHAPTER 23

WREN

It was amazing that Wren hadn't been eaten by a dragon yet.

Or bitten by a scorpion. Or that she hadn't just fallen over on the sand and let the sun burn her into bleached white bones.

She had certainly been walking through the big hot horrible desert long enough for any of those things to have happened.

First, she had tried to follow the army and Sky to their fight with the ice dragons. They had gone west from the dragon city, so she went west, even though she lost sight of their flashing wings within minutes. But she remembered the vague maps she'd studied; the ice kingdom was this way and north. If she kept going, she'd reach it eventually. Maybe she could rescue Sky while all the dragons were distracted with their battle.

She didn't know how many days later it was, but she had just reached a stretch of rocky ground that wasn't sand anymore — when she looked up to see the whole battalion flying back south again.

"WHAT?" she shouted as they whipped past without noticing her. "I just GOT HERE!"

She thought she caught a glimpse of Sky flying with them, but she was sure she recognized that arrogant giant who was leading them and his stupid bellowing laugh.

She ran after them as long as she could, but soon they banked east and sailed into the clouds, and no matter how fast she ran, they were quickly out of sight.

"ARRRRRRRRRRRRRRRRRRRRRRRGH!" she screamed, grabbing tufts of the thin spiky grass from between the rocks and tearing it up.

But she didn't have time to be furious. She guessed they were angling back toward the dragon city, so that was where she had to go, too.

"It's *good* news," she muttered to herself, stamping through the sand in the middle of the chilly desert night. "Sky will be easier to rescue from the city than from the sand palace." Also, she knew where the city was, and she could get there by following the coast until she reached the river. She had no idea where the palace was. Out in the vast desert somewhere, presumably.

But when she reached the city, there was no sign of the obnoxious general or his army or Sky. Wren spent a couple of nights sneaking around and eavesdropping until she confirmed her worst fear: They'd landed here for a day and then flown off to the palace.

In the dragon city, she felt like one of the mice that used

to invade her parents' kitchen, vanishing into the walls the moment the torches were lit, leaving little tracks through the flour and holes nibbled out of the bread. It was easy to find food and restock her supplies; everything the dragons ate was so big, they wouldn't even notice if she took a fig here, a quarter of a biscuit there.

But what she could not seem to find was a map to the queen's palace, or any kind of map of the whole desert kingdom. She wasn't sure if she was looking in the wrong places, or whether the sand dragons didn't bother to have one, because they figured anyone could just fly over the desert and find it easily.

Should she stay and keep looking for a map? Or should she march out into the desert and hope she ran into the palace eventually? Days were passing and poor Sky needed help, and she felt a kind of agony in her chest when she thought about it. But it wouldn't help him if she got lost in the desert and died out there. Rushing off was what she *wanted* to do, but it wasn't the smartest plan.

If only I had wings. I could fly there in a heartbeat.

Around the fifth time Wren had that thought, it was followed suddenly by another: *What if I got wings?*

What if I kidnapped a dragon?

She was hiding in the attic of a storehouse, where she'd been sleeping during the day on one of the grain sacks. She crawled over to the window and looked down at the dragons hurrying through the streets below.

What if I could get a dragon alone and convince it to take me to the palace?

That would give her speed *and* a map, in a sense, assuming she found someone who knew how to get there.

So how do I convince one? With something sharp and pointy?

Sky would tell her to ask nicely. He'd be quite sure that any dragon would love to help her out. He'd have to be reminded about the part where most of them would rather eat her for lunch.

But there must be others like Sky. Dragons with hearts; dragons who might listen for a moment before munching on me.

I just have to find one.

That night she stole a weapon, just in case. It was probably a practice sword or a dagger for a dragonet; for most dragons, it would be tiny, but for her, it was the size of a real sword, and rather heavy. It took her half the night to figure out a way to tie it to her back so she could pull it out quickly if she needed it, but it would also be mostly out of the way.

And then she started stalking dragons.

She couldn't approach one in the center of the city — even at night, if she found one alone, it would only take one yell for it to summon a whole bunch of friends. She was up for threatening one dragon by itself, not a large group.

So she worked her way to the outskirts, looking for relatively deserted spaces and hapless solitary dragons.

Two days later, she found her mark.

The best part about him was that he was clearly trying to avoid attention. The second-best thing was that he was reading a scroll when she spotted him, which seemed like a good sign. A dragon who was a reader was probably smart and thoughtful and not the sort of fellow who would gobble a person before hearing what they had to say.

Wren had been exploring an alley that led out of the city, past some abandoned houses with sad little black-and-yellow flags fluttering out front. Her theory was that the dragons who had lived here had gone off to war and not come back.

The alley opened into a courtyard shaded by fruit trees and smelling of lemons. Under one of the trees, a black dragon was curled up, reading a scroll.

Wren crouched behind a planter and watched him for a while. She hadn't seen any other black dragons in the city; in fact, she'd hardly seen any at all in her travels with Sky. She guessed there was a group of them living somewhere secret, but she'd studied her map and wasn't sure where.

This one had a pouch around his neck and a scattering of silver scales that twinkled under his wings like stars. Occasionally he'd look up from the scroll and check the sky, then sigh and go back to reading.

Wren wondered if she was just imagining that he looked lonely. Maybe he'd also lost his best friend somewhere.

She heard a dragon approaching along the alley, so she swung herself into the planter and then up the tree, to hide among the bright yellow lemons and glossy dark green leaves. The black dragon heard the footsteps, too. He rolled up his scroll and did an interesting fade back into the shadows where he closed his wings, hiding the silver scales, and stood so still in a dark spot that even Wren could barely see him, despite having her eyes fixed on him.

He's being careful. Whoever he's waiting for, he wants to make sure this is the right dragon before showing himself.

A sand dragon hurried into the courtyard. She kept looking left and right and up, as though someone might pounce on her from anywhere. She had a sly, furtive way of moving and a few frostbite scars along her tail.

The black dragon emerged from the shadows and bowed his head slightly to acknowledge her.

"Here," she said, thrusting a small scroll into the black dragon's talons. "New assignment."

"Hello to you, too," he said. He broke the seal on the scroll and unrolled it.

"We're not here for chitchat," she hissed. "If you have any questions, send them the usual way. But you shouldn't. They said it's pretty straightforward."

The black dragon was staring at the scroll as though it had personally disappointed him. "This is . . . quite a serious assignment," he said. "Are they sure that's what they want?"

"It must be!" she snapped. "I'm just the messenger. And you're just the —" She said a word that Wren had never heard before. "Let's both do our jobs and not be annoying about it!"

"Wait," he said as she turned to go. "Have you heard anything about where the dragonets might be heading next?"

"Ice Kingdom is the rumor," she said. "Two (somethings) down, one left to meet, I guess. Maybe they'll freeze to death and save you some trouble." She chuckled and slithered away before the black dragon could ask anything else.

He sat down slowly, studying the message. Wren was pretty sure she recognized his expression. That was the face Sky made when he'd been told to do something, and he was trying to figure out a clever way around it. Like if she said, "Sky, stop giving our best nuts to the chipmunks! *I* need them to survive the winter, too!" And then he'd make that face, and she'd have to clarify that he could also not give them to any squirrels, and in fact to please not give away *any* of the food she'd gathered to animals with adorable pathetic eyes.

Poor Sky. She wondered what he was doing right that moment, and whether there were any chipmunks or snails wherever he was.

I have to act now. This is the dragon I want, and he's completely alone here. Just be brave, Wren. He probably won't eat you immediately. *Talk fast, be convincing, and if that doesn't work, be scary!*

Here goes nothing.

She slid down from the tree and marched across the courtyard, up to the dragon's feet. The black dragon glanced up from the scroll and leaped back at the sight of her, but he didn't immediately bite her head off, so this was already going very well.

"Listen up," she growled in Dragon. "I need your help."

The black dragon's eyes went very, very wide. He slowly pivoted his head around to check behind him for another dragon.

"Stop that!" she barked. "Look at me! It's me! I'm the one speaking Dragon!"

He swiveled his head all the way back to stare at her.

"I'm in a hurry," she said. "Take me to the desert palace. Please," she added, thinking of how Sky would have asked. He'd made a special point of teaching her that particular word in Dragon.

"This is impossible. Scavengers don't speak Dragon," the dragon said in his rather elegant voice. His accent was different from Sky's, and a little harder to follow.

"Obviously I do!" she snapped.

"Scavengers," he explained, as though she might be a misinformed hallucination, "generally go squeak squeak squeak and then fall over and die. In my experience."

"Well, of the two of us here, who do you think knows more about scavengers?" she asked, using the dragon word for *humans*. "Listen, I don't have time to fall over and die. My friend is in trouble and I need you to take me to him."

"If your friend was taken to the desert palace," the black dragon said, actually looking sympathetic, "he has already been eaten by now."

"My friend is a dragon!" Wren shouted, making him jump. "So unless there are cannibals there, he's still alive, but trapped, and wondering where I am!" She didn't know the word for *cannibals* in Dragon, so some of that probably got lost in translation.

"See, that doesn't make sense either," he said. "A dragon who's friends with a scavenger? Doubtful." He picked up the date cake he'd been eating and studied it suspiciously. "What was *in* this?"

"You can pretend you're imagining me if it'll make you feel better," Wren said. "As long as you still take me to the palace."

"But then *you'll* get eaten," he pointed out. "Which would be quite a shame if you're the only scavenger in the world smart enough to speak Dragon."

Wren wasn't sure whether to agree that she was, or argue that she might not be. She didn't remember any other humans from her village who would have even bothered to try, and Undauntable would have laughed at the suggestion. Maybe Leaf . . . She'd managed to stop thinking about her brother quite so often after the first year away from him, but sometimes he still popped up in her head.

"Do you have a name?" the black dragon asked curiously. "I once knew a dragon with a scavenger pet named Rover, but it didn't last very long. Not his fault; his friends were bad at remembering the difference between snacks and pets. Has your dragon named you?"

"No! I'm not a pet, and I already had a name," Wren said crossly. "It's Wren. What's yours?"

He said something that she couldn't quite figure out. She tilted her head at him.

"What?"

He said it again, a string of growls that sounded like two words strung together, but with the meanings a little muddled.

"Provider . . . of . . . Corpses?" Wren guessed in her own language. "That can't be right. Plague . . . Carrier? Who would name their child that, even a dragon child?" She thought for a moment, running the sounds around in her head. "Murder Basket!" she blurted. "Wait, Murder Basket? Is your name really Murder Basket?" She tried to repeat the sounds back to him and he looked mildly offended.

"No," he said. "Grumble growl roargle grawrf."

"Murder . . . basket," Wren said. "Yeah, that's definitely what you said. OK." She switched to Dragon again. "Mr. Murderbasket, could you *please* take me to the desert palace right now? I promise not to blame you if I get eaten."

"Oh . . . no, no," he said warily. "I really can't. I'm actually rather busy at the moment." He held up the message scroll. "Looking for some dragons. On a bit of a mission. I'd be in quite some trouble if I took a detour to assist a hallucination. So sorry." He tried to edge away from her.

"This is important!" Wren yelled, making him jump again. "Come on! It will take you, what, less than half a day to get me there? It will take *me* FOUR HUNDRED YEARS to walk there, apparently, based on the evidence so far and the fact that I have no idea where it is. Murderbasket! Listen! A dragon's life is at stake!"

"Oooooorgh," he grumbled, rubbing his head. "I had no idea scavengers could be so loud."

"Isn't a dragon's LIFE more important than your mission?" she said. "Besides, you don't even want to do your assignment. I can tell."

"That's true," he said with a slightly alarmed look. "But you probably know that because you only exist in my head anyway."

"What's the dragon word for a voice in your head that tells you what to do?" Wren asked.

He said something, and she echoed it back until she got it right.

"There you go," she said. "That's me. Your conscience. And I'm telling you: Don't do your assignment. Whatever you don't like about it, your instinct is right. Instead you should fly me to the desert palace so I can rescue my friend."

Murderbasket broke the date cake in half and inspected the inside of it for a minute.

"Would it help if I pulled this out?" Wren said, brandishing her new sword with a flourish. "It's very sharp." She jabbed at one of his claws and accidentally stabbed the membrane between them.

"OW!" he roared, leaping back. A small drop of blood welled up and he pressed another claw to it, giving her a wounded look.

"Sorry!" she said. "Sorry, it's really heavy, and I still haven't gotten — you know what, no. I'm not sorry! That's what happens when you defy me, Murderbasket!" She pointed the sword at him. "Take me to the desert palace now."

"You know, I've never understood what happened to Queen (something)," he said. "But now I see that scavengers are tiny ferocious mean little monsters, and it all makes sense." He examined his injury. "I'm really not imagining you, am I?"

"Nope," she said. "Extremely real. Also in a hurry."

"Well, put your violence away first," he said, pointing at the sword. She slid it into the sheath on her back. He wrinkled his snout for a moment, and then he said, "All right. I can take you to the desert palace. But I feel like I should warn you that most of the dragons there won't be nearly as charming or patient as I am."

"I don't care," Wren said. "I wasn't planning on having a tea party with them. I'm going to rescue Sky."

Murderbasket held out one leg for her to climb up. It was super strange, climbing scales that were black instead of pale orange. Murderbasket was bigger and more wiry than Sky, and it took Wren a few awkward scrambles to find a spot that felt safe on his shoulder, clinging to his neck spines.

While she scrabbled around, the dragon tucked his scrolls into the pouch around his neck and finished his date cake. He brushed the crumbs off his talons and twisted his neck around to look at her.

"All settled?" he said. "This feels very odd. I had a monkey climb on me once while I was on a mission in the Kingdom of the Sea, but it was lighter and a lot less bossy than you."

"Maybe you just weren't listening to it carefully enough," she suggested.

"You're very sure you want to go to the palace?" he asked. "I can think of some dragons who would love to study you."

"Horrifying," Wren said. "No, thank you. To the palace!"

"To the palace," he agreed. He leaped into the sky and Wren held on tight, watching the dragon city drop away below her.

Hang on, Sky. I'll be there soon.

— CHAPTER 24 —

IVY

"What if we ride out there in the middle of the night," Daffodil suggested, "while all the dragons are definitely sleeping, and we leave the treasure in a pile at the front door of the palace with a note that says, 'WE'RE REALLY SORRY ABOUT THIS! PLEASE STOP EATING US!' And then we ride home *very fast*."

Ivy leaned all the way back until she was flat on her branch and looked up at the sky. Blue and clear beyond the trees, rimmed with gold where the sun was rising over the mountains. The ripples of sunshine through the leaves, the sounds of birds and squirrels, the smell of green things, anything but cold stone and dirt walls. She was so happy to be outside again at last.

It had taken forever for her father to relax his rules. She didn't understand all the reasons why he finally had, but she thought it was partly because her mother had helped fix the gardening problem, and the grounded Wingwatchers had shored up one of the collapsed tunnels, so the citizens of Valor had stopped grumbling quite so much. There hadn't been any more messages from the lord of the Indestructible City. And then four new baby foals were born, and they were adorable, and now that was most of what everyone was talking about instead of complaining, which made the Dragonslayer happy.

And once the Dragonslayer was happy, Ivy and her friends had been allowed back on missions. Back to skygazing at least, but she'd take it.

Foxglove was outside again, too, helping keep watch while a few builders worked on concealing one of the entrances a little better.

"Daffodil," Violet said patiently, although Ivy knew her "patient" voice was actually her "drive Daffodil insane" voice. "First, there will be dragons guarding the palace, even in the middle of the night. Second, we'd have to get ourselves and the treasure and three horses out of Valor without being noticed. And third, DRAGONS CAN'T READ."

"Well, our choices are (a) leave a note or (b) explain it to them ourselves," Daffodil argued. "And I'm not up for talking to dragons! That is a much worse plan than mine!"

"No one is saying we should talk to the dragons," Violet said. "Even Ivy, who loves them the way normal people love treasure or family or cheese, isn't ridiculous enough to want to talk to a dragon."

Imagine if we could, though, Ivy thought dreamily. *What would they say to us? What do dragons think about? What are their stories about? Do they know anything about us?*

"Ivy," Violet said sternly. "Reassure me that you are not thinking right now about talking to a dragon."

"I'm just . . . wondering what they'd say," Ivy admitted.

Daffodil laughed and Violet made a despairing sound.

"A sea dragon could tell us what's at the bottom of the ocean," Ivy said. "An ice dragon could tell us what a polar bear tastes like! And they could all tell us what it feels like to fly."

"Sometimes I feel like you're unclear on the basic reality of dragons," Violet said. "Perhaps I should remind you about the giant teeth. And the fire-breathing. And the claws. But mostly the teeth."

"I know, I know," Ivy said. "I'm going up a bit higher." They were in one of the tallest trees; it poked out above the rest of the forest canopy. If she climbed up there, she'd be able to see the sky all the way to the mountains, and maybe some faraway dragons.

She heard Daffodil and Violet scrambling to follow her up. This was another thing she'd missed about being out-side — there weren't nearly enough interesting things to climb in Valor. According to her uncle Stone, Rose had been a natural climber, too. Ivy liked thinking about that . . . She wasn't as mischievous or brave as Rose, but they still had things in common, like climbing and drawing.

She climbed until she found a high section of branches fairly well hidden by greenery, and then settled in on one side of the trunk. Daffodil beat Violet to the branch on the other side and made a little *ha!* noise. Violet sat down just below them with her nose in the air, acting as though that was where she'd planned to sit all along.

"What if we left it in the desert," Ivy said, thinking aloud, "just outside the forest — near the old village — and we drew big arrows in the sand pointing to it, so they could see it from the sky?"

"Someone might come along and steal it before the dragons found it," Violet pointed out.

"Including the wrong dragons," Daffodil agreed. "I mean, I assume there are dragons who *shouldn't* get the treasure, right? Like, it came from the sand dragons, so it should go back to them? So if the mountain dragons took it, that would be bad?"

"Unless that meant the sand dragons would start attacking the mountain dragons instead of us," Violet said, adjusting the green wrap around her hair.

"They might not realize the mountain dragons stole it, though," Ivy said. "All right, so not that." She parted the leaves in front of her. "Oh, look!" she cried, her voice dropping to a whisper even though the dragons were miles away.

Three glorious dragons soared down from the higher peaks, shimmering crimson and orange like living flames darting across the blue sky. The sun lit up their enormous wings as the three dragons spiraled up to the clouds and then plummeted down toward the forest.

"I'm suddenly feeling a little visible up here," Daffodil whispered.

"We're all right," Ivy whispered back. "Just don't move." Once in her training with Foxglove, they had been up this high and a dragon had flown past close enough for the wind to rip leaves off their tree and throw them in her face. But it hadn't noticed them. If her friends kept still, they should all be fine.

Ivy watched the dragons swing lazily closer and closer. Their gaze was trained on the ground. *Probably hunting*, she thought.

Suddenly one of them whipped around and dove into the trees. A moment later it roared, a sound like all the walls of the village collapsing in at once. It burst out of the trees, lashing its tail, and Ivy saw that its talons were empty. With another roar, it seized one of the trees, ripped it out of the ground, and tossed it across the forest. Then it dove again.

What has it found? Ivy wondered. *A deer? A bear? It wouldn't try that hard for something small like a rabbit, right?*

She peered down through the branches and saw a boy dart between the trees.

A person! she thought, her heart pounding. *Who is that?*

He wasn't coming from the direction of Valor. Had he been out hunting and gotten separated from his group? But he also wasn't wearing the brown of a hunting apprentice, or the green of a Wingwatcher in training.

Is he one of the banished? She leaned farther out, trying to get a better look at him.

"Ivy!" Daffodil whispered.

"Do you see him?" Ivy whispered back.

Daffodil gave a little nod. Her gaze was trained on the shape racing through the forest below them.

The boy vaulted over a fallen log and crouched on the other side, digging himself into the leaves.

That's never going to work, Ivy thought.

She had a clearer view of him now — thin but muscular, and browner than her, like he'd spent a lot more time in the sun than she ever had. His tangled dark hair was snarled with leaves, and there were rips and holes all over his clothes. He looked her age, or perhaps a bit older. She was pretty sure she'd never seen him before.

He's from somewhere else, she thought. *Maybe somewhere far away — maybe* he's *seen a sea dragon!*

And now I'm going to watch him get eaten, she thought with a terrible lurch in her stomach.

The dragon was on the ground and slithering through the trees, twisting its head in an unsettling way as it searched for its prey. Its red-gold scales glittered like dragonfly wings. It was getting closer and closer to the boy's hiding place.

Don't move, said Foxglove's voice in her head. *Do NOT leave this tree for ANYTHING. Stay in place until we return. Just watch. That's all you're allowed to do.*

But she couldn't let someone die right in front of her.

She slowly, carefully slid her hand into her pack. She had an apple in there that was supposed to be lunch for all three of them.

Violet looked up at her and shook her head slightly. *Don't do anything stupid*, her face said loud and clear.

Ivy tried to make a face back that said, *Saving someone*

ISN'T stupid, Violet, but she wasn't sure her eyebrows were communicating that very precisely.

She waited until the dragon was facing away from her, and then she threw the apple as hard as she could into the forest, away from the boy and the entrance to Valor.

The dragon's head snapped up, and it bolted after the sound.

Ivy swung around and slithered down the tree, burning her hands on the bark and scraping her knees. Daffodil was already in motion, too, dropping from branch to branch. She heard Violet make a sound like "AARGH" and follow them.

The boy was on his feet when Ivy hit the ground. He spun and stared at her with wary brown eyes. The dragon was crashing through the bracken somewhere off in the forest to their right. Hopefully all the noise it was making would mask the sound of their escape.

"Come on," Ivy whispered, beckoning.

The four of them ran through the trees, keeping low. The sound of wingbeats overhead had faded away, so the other two dragons must have moved on to hunt elsewhere.

The closest entrance to Valor was the one Foxglove was guarding, a dark hole in the side of a hill. It was risky to go that way — she didn't want the dragon to see them going in. But Ivy knew that Foxglove would want them to go straight to · her, and it was the fastest way to get everyone underground.

The dragon let out a frustrated roar behind them. Ivy grabbed the boy's hand and put on a burst of speed. To her surprise, he kept up easily, even though he must have been running for a while before she saw him. He was fast, and he didn't even seem tired yet.

Daffodil ran ahead to shove the workers inside, but they had heard the dragon and were already gone. The entrance was now well hidden by a net structure woven with branches and leaves. When they reached it, Foxglove was waiting to drag them inside.

Safe, shadowy darkness closed around them. Foxglove lit one of the lanterns and raised her eyebrows disapprovingly.

"Mountain dragon in the woods," Ivy gasped to Foxglove. "Tried to eat him." She pointed at the boy, then rested her hands on her knees, catching her breath.

Daffodil lay down on the floor with a thump and Violet collapsed beside her, leaning against the cave wall.

"Has anyone ever told you three that you are *very bad* at following directions?" Foxglove demanded. "Such as 'stay in this tree'! Or 'never run from a dragon'! Remember that? Lesson number one?"

"I *tried* to stop them," Violet said.

"Dragon!" Ivy cried again, wounded. "Him! Nearly eaten! We were — It was —"

"Very heroic," Daffodil supplied from her prone position. "You should have seen Ivy. She was brave as anything! I mean, if you had to guess which one of us would leap out of a tree to save a stranger from a dragon, wouldn't you have guessed me? But it wasn't me! I was too scared! It was totally Ivy!"

"*I* wasn't scared," Violet interjected. "I was being *sensible*. And *following orders*, unlike these two."

"Well, I thought Ivy was amazing," Daffodil said loyally.

"They did save my life," the boy said. "I'm so sorry to have endangered yours," he said to Ivy. "I'm supposed to be the one saving people."

"You can have the next turn," she joked, and he smiled at her. He had a smile that looked rarely used, as if it only slipped out when he really meant it.

"I am grateful to them, really," he said to Foxglove. "I was recently very nearly eaten by dragons, and it's terrifying."

Ivy really wanted to hear more about that, but Daffodil sat up and said, "What's your name? Why were you out in the woods by yourself?"

"I'm Leaf," he said, blowing his hair out of his eyes. "I come from a village in the mountains called Talisman. Travelers told me I might find the Dragonslayer near here."

"The Dragonslayer?" Ivy said. Her heart sank. *Is he hoping my father can save his village?* They'd had a few visitors like this before, who had traveled across the continent to plead desperately for the help of a man who could slay dragons. *A dragon is terrorizing my family, my people, my home. Please, Dragonslayer, come kill it for us.*

Her father's usual response was to send them away with a promise that he would follow in a few weeks. Sometimes he left Valor with a lot of fuss and pomp, then returned triumphantly to claim that he'd chased off the dragon — but Ivy was sure he never really went to the beleaguered villages.

Those poor people, waiting and waiting for a hero who never comes.

"What do you want with the Dragonslayer?" Violet asked Leaf.

Leaf picked a twig out of his hair, looking oddly lost. "It's . . . complicated," he said. "I guess the short version is I've always wanted to kill a dragon. I was hoping the Dragonslayer could teach me how."

Ivy could feel her friends' eyes on her, knowing how she would react.

Always wanted to kill a dragon. What kind of life dream was that?

Maybe he had a reason. Maybe he came from one of those desperate villages, but instead of asking the Dragonslayer to come save them, he wanted to learn to save them himself.

Or maybe he's dreaming of treasure. Maybe he's just another idiot like my dad, willing to set the world on fire to get rich.

She hesitated. He didn't *look* like a selfish treasure-hungry dragon murderer. His eyes were too sad. She wanted to trust him, but maybe that was the aftereffects of saving someone's life.

"I don't think anyone's ever asked him that," she said slowly. "I can't promise what he'll say, but let's go see him and find out."

~ CHAPTER 25 ~

LEAF

Leaf couldn't believe he'd finally found it. Valor, home of the Dragonslayer! It was real, and he was here at last.

Somehow, he'd never pictured it underground. The name Valor made him think of a towering city on a hill, facing down the dragons with no fear. But the citizens of Valor lived like moles. He supposed it was safer that way, but it was still unexpected.

His heart beat nervously as he followed his rescuers through the tunnels. He'd never been to another human village beyond Talisman. A traveling family had given him directions to Valor and a message for the Dragonslayer, and he'd only stayed with them for a night. He'd never been surrounded by this many strangers before.

Leaf, you daft blueberry, Wren scolded him in his head. *You survived a giant palace full of dragons. I think you can handle a bunch of strange humans. I mean, at least they* probably *won't try to eat you.*

Well, if any of them did, it would most likely be Violet — she was the tall one with the short hair and the assessing look.

She kept studying him from head to toe like she was taking notes for a test, except he'd be the one who had to take it.

Next to her was Daffodil, who kept jumping up to touch the ceiling tunnel, making her ponytail bounce. She stayed close to the other two, especially Violet, and her hands were constantly moving as she talked, which she did a lot.

And then there was Ivy, the one who'd distracted the dragon and brought him into Valor. She had a friendly smile and long dark hair, which had been tied up when he first saw her but had fallen loose while they were running. She also had an interesting way of keeping an eye on her friends all the time, as if she was waiting for them to bump off course so she could steer them straight.

She fell back to walk beside him and started pointing out the sights and geography of Valor. They went through a giant central hall where "announcements and banishments happen," Ivy said, but he didn't register the word *banishment* until much later. He was too distracted by all the people who strolled the tunnels as though this were any ordinary village. In fact, the biggest difference between here and Talisman was the fact that the villagers didn't keep glancing up at the sky, shivering with fear at every sound that might be a wingbeat or a dragon roar or a warning bell. Everyone here seemed so *calm*.

See, there is an advantage to living underground, he thought, and the Wren in his head made a scoffing noise.

"Why isn't anyone else wearing green like you guys?" Leaf asked Ivy.

"We're Wingwatchers," Ivy said happily. "This is our uniform. But we're not the only ones — see, there's Moth, he's another." She waved to a boy walking by with a basket of yarn.

"What do Wingwatchers do?" Leaf noticed a beam of sunlight coming into one of the caves through a small hole near the ceiling. Another Wingwatcher was crouched on a ledge, looking out at the sky.

"We study dragons," she said, "and we watch for them when people are outside, and we guard the entrances to make sure no one leads them to us."

His stomach plummeted. "Are you like dragonmancers?" he asked nervously.

"I don't know what that is," she said, tilting her head at him.

"They have visions about what the dragons want and how to appease them," he said. "At least, they *say* they do. But they're liars."

She raised her eyebrows. "Um, no, that's not what Wingwatchers are like at all."

"Sorry," he said. "I'm sure you're not."

"Why do you want to kill a dragon so much?" she asked.

He looked down at his feet and kicked a rock out of their path. "My sister was eaten by dragons seven years ago," he said. "I tried to avenge her, but it turns out slaying dragons is actually really hard."

"Oh," she said. "I'm so sorry. That sounds awful."

"Yeah," he said. "You know, it's weird. I always say it that way, but I know more about it now and I still haven't said the worst part out loud." He took a deep breath. "She wasn't accidentally eaten. The dragonmancers sacrificed her."

"What?" Ivy cried. "Leaf, that's terrible!"

He nodded. "And now I don't know what to do. I feel like, all I've wanted for so long is justice for Wren, but am I even doing it the right way anymore? Would she want me to go after the dragonmancers instead?"

Yes, the Wren in his head said snippily. *Obviously.*

"But how would I even do that?" he asked. "They run Talisman. Everyone listens to them. And I'm not going to stab *them* with a sword."

Maybe you should, Wren muttered.

I could never do that, he told her again. *I'm not a murderer, even if they deserve it.*

"So, I guess for now I'm trying to stick with my original plan," he said to Ivy. "Go after the dragons and protect future kids like Wren. If I can learn how."

"Hmmm," she said, winding a lock of hair around her finger. "Have you ever thought . . . maybe going after the dragons would make things *more* dangerous for future kids?"

He tilted his head at her. "What? How? Surely fewer dragons equals less danger."

"Unless the survivors get really mad and vengeful," Ivy pointed out. "They don't particularly like their family members getting killed either. Right?"

Leaf tried to imagine angrier, more vengeful dragons. A dragon like him, who was heartbroken over losing someone to the humans. Could dragons be heartbroken? Did they love their families? Not like humans did, surely.

But maybe some did . . . like the brown dragon who'd helped him . . . or the baby and its caretaker in the kitchen. What if he accidentally killed a dragon like that? How would he know?

Maybe the Dragonslayer would know. He'd be able to tell Leaf how to slay the right dragons the right way.

"Well, here we are," Ivy said. "Where the famous Dragonslayer lives." Violet and Daffodil were waiting by a door in the tunnel; Ivy unlocked it, and they all went inside.

Leaf was startled by how enormous the Dragonslayer's caves were. They were almost as big as a room in the dragon palace, and furnished with beautiful things. *Of course*, Leaf remembered. *He's probably the richest man in the world*. That was something else he'd never thought about — the treasure the Dragonslayer had stolen from the queen.

But he wasn't like Rowan and Thyme and Cranberry, Leaf told himself. *He was fighting to save his people.*

Wasn't he?

Or . . . is that just how Rowan told me the story, so I'd want to be like him?

He felt uneasy for the first time since entering Valor.

"Dad!" Ivy called. "There's someone here to see you!"

Leaf blinked at her. "Dad?"

"Oh, yeah," Daffodil said. "The Dragonslayer is Ivy's father." She threw herself down on one of the large green-and-gold pillows along the walls of the living room. Leaf saw something in a glass box on a pedestal in the center of the room, but it was misshapen and ugly, out of place among the rest of the beautiful décor. He wanted to take a closer look, but he didn't want the Dragonslayer to find him poking around in his things. He decided to stay where he was, standing with his hands behind him, ready for inspection.

"Is it my new hat?" a voice called from the next cave. "Tell him to leave it on the table!"

"No, Dad, it's not a new hat!" Ivy called back.

There was a pause, and then some grumbling and shuffling noises. After a moment, a man appeared in the doorway and squinted across the room at Leaf.

That's him. The Dragonslayer! The only living man to ever kill a dragon! The mighty hero of the stories!

Bit shorter than I expected, imaginary Wren commented.

The Dragonslayer was barefoot and looked as though he'd been asleep. He had a tangled black beard and sleepy eyes and a gold earring shaped like a sword dangling from each ear. He looked like he ate more than Master Trout and moved as rarely as possible; he wasn't big, but all his limbs looked like bread dough.

"Who's this?" the Dragonslayer asked, scratching one of his feet.

"Dad, this is Leaf," Ivy said. "We found him in the woods. He's come a really long way to see you."

"It's a great honor to meet you, sir," Leaf said.

The Dragonslayer cleared his throat and shot a look at Ivy's friends. "Official Dragonslayer audiences are held in the main hall once a month," he said. "You just missed one, I'm afraid. Ivy, you know better than to bring him here."

Violet and Daffodil exchanged significant glances.

"Sorry, Dad," Ivy said carefully. "He has a kind of unusual request, so I thought it might be all right."

"Well, it isn't," he said. "Find a place to put him, and I'll hear him at the next audience."

"Wait, sir!" Leaf said, grasping at one straw that might catch his attention. "I have a message for you from the Indestructible City!"

He sensed immediately that this was the wrong thing to say. Ivy blanched, and the Dragonslayer's eyebrows drew together like a lowering storm front.

"You're from the Indestructible City?" the Dragonslayer growled. "Another one? Is your lord deaf?"

"N-no," Leaf stammered. "I've never been there. I just met someone who said — they said to tell you the Invincible Lord is expecting you before the next crescent moons."

The Dragonslayer crossed the room in three large steps, seized Leaf by his shirt, and lifted him into the air. "Are you *threatening* me now?" he snarled.

"I'm not! I'm not!" Leaf instinctively did one of Rowan's twist moves to slip free and jumped away from the Dragonslayer. "That's what they told me! I don't know what it means — I thought it was just a friendly greeting between lords!"

The Dragonslayer glared at his hands, then at Leaf, as if

considering whether to grab him again, but not wanting to look foolish if Leaf escaped once more. "The presumptuous, pompous, self-styled 'invincible' Lord Jackanapes is not my friend. You can get out of my city now."

"But that's not why he's here!" Ivy said. "I swear, Dad, he just wants to learn from you —"

The Dragonslayer had turned to eye Daffodil and Violet with suspicion. "You brought him into the city?" he demanded.

"We found him," Ivy said, trying to draw his attention to her. "Dad, really, he's just another guy looking for a hero. He's not working for the lord. I promise."

"We'll see," the Dragonslayer muttered, tugging on his beard. "Everyone get out." He stalked off into the other cave as Daffodil and Violet leaped to their feet.

"I'm so sorry, Leaf," Ivy said. She pushed up her sleeves and rubbed her face. "I did that all wrong."

He couldn't see anything that she'd done wrong; it was the Dragonslayer who'd acted strange and unfriendly (*and a little bit like a dragonmancer*, Wren whispered ominously). And it was Leaf's own fault, for being such an idiot. "I'm the one who's sorry," he said. "I had no idea the Invincible Lord was his enemy. I should — I should go apologize —"

"No, don't," she said, jumping in his way. "That's not a good idea. Not right now."

"But he's a man of honor and courage," Leaf said. Out of the corner of his eye, he caught Violet making a face at

Daffodil, but he wasn't sure what it meant — maybe she was mocking his sincerity, but he didn't care. "He'll understand if I —"

"Trust me," Ivy said, putting her hands on his arms and walking him backward to the front door. "We need to get out now and wait for a better time." She looked truly sorry, as though she'd failed him. And so worried. He didn't want to make anyone feel as unhappy as she looked.

He put his own hands over hers and stopped her momentum. "I do trust you," he said. "Don't be sad. I'm sure everything will be all right after I talk to him. In a month, I mean," he clarified quickly. "At the next audience."

She gave him a relieved smile. "I think I know somewhere you can stay."

He wanted to say, *Can't I stay with you?* but it was pretty clear he wasn't welcome in the Dragonslayer's cave. So he followed her without arguing to the cave of a man she called "Uncle Stone," who looked like a taller, sadder, slightly less hairy version of the Dragonslayer.

"Yes, fine," Stone said glumly. "I have room, if he's not too loud."

"I imagine he sings in his sleep," Ivy said, "but apart from that, the strong, silent type."

"Thank you, sir," Leaf said.

"I have to go give Foxglove my notes on the dragons and what happened out there," Ivy said. "But I'll come check on you after that." Her smile almost made up for her leaving, except then Leaf was alone with her morose uncle. Stone looked him up and down, pointed at an extra straw pallet, and went into a corner of the cave to mash some vegetables.

Leaf set down his pack and unbuckled his sword, wondering what he'd gotten himself into.

"Nice sword," Stone commented.

"Useless sword," Leaf said. "Against dragons anyway."

Stone gave him a wry smile. "Yeah, I wouldn't recommend trying that."

"I already did," Leaf admitted. "It *really* didn't work. That's why I'm here — I'm hoping the Dragonslayer will tell me how he did it."

Stone let out a snort. "Heath? Got lucky, that's what he did. Unlike some of us."

"Have you tried to kill a dragon?" Leaf asked. He was slightly unnerved by the way Stone talked about the Dragonslayer.

"I was there when it happened. Don't they tell that part of the story in faraway villages?" Stone asked.

Leaf suddenly, for the first time in years, remembered what his father had said when Rowan first told the Dragonslayer story. Something about a partner who'd been left behind. But that couldn't be Stone — he was right here.

"You *were*?" he said. "What was it like? What did he do? I want to know everything!"

Stone's face hardened. "Well, if you want worshipful stories of the great Dragonslayer, you've come to the right place," he said. "This place is full of zealots who'd love to tell you the great saga. But I'm not one of them." He dropped his masher, smacked his hands together, and moved toward the exit.

"Wait, no. That's not why I'm here," Leaf said. "I promise, I want to know the truth. What *really* happened."

Stone paused with his hand on the door and looked at Leaf for a long moment.

"No, you don't," he said, and disappeared into the tunnels.

CHAPTER 26

WREN

Wren and her ride arrived at the palace after dark, which was Murderbasket's idea. He might be a bit of an idiot about human intelligence, but he was clearly an expert at skulking around. He approached on a quiet glide down from the clouds, avoided all the guards, and landed in a deserted courtyard.

"All right," Wren said, sliding off his neck. "I'm impressed."

"You're welcome," he said, looking pleased.

"With myself," she said, "for picking exactly the right dragon for this job."

He looked down his nose at her. "Hmmm. You're still welcome."

"You are also welcome," she said. "For my excellent advice and for the part where I did not stab you with my dangerous weapon."

"You DID stab me with your dangerous weapon," he objected.

"Oh, barely," she said. "Imagine if I'd been doing it on purpose."

He shuddered. "I'd rather not." A distant roar cut through the silent night, and he turned his head toward it, then looked back down at her. "Are you sure you want to be here?"

"I definitely do not," she said, "but I have to find Sky. And probably stab all the dragons who took him. In the EYEBALLS! They'll be sorry they stole my friend and made me walk all over the desert! Mostly the first thing." She pulled out her sword and brandished it at the shadows. "Watch out, evil dragon eyeballs!"

"Three moons," he said. "I think you're the most violent dream I've ever had, and considering what I do for work, that's saying something."

"*Your* eyeballs are totally safe with me," she said, patting his claws reassuringly. The sword overbalanced in her hand and jabbed his talon membrane again, in a different spot this time.

He jumped away from her with a hiss, shaking a new drop of blood off.

"OK, I'll admit that was terrible," Wren said. She put the sword away. "This time I'm really sorry."

He let out a small disbelieving laugh. "No one has managed to draw my blood in years," he said. "And now a tiny scavenger has done it twice. I have this great idea: Let's both never, ever tell anyone about this."

That is a good idea, Wren realized. She didn't exactly want gossip spreading about the sweet fireless dragon she was going to steal back from the desert queen.

"Agreed," she said. "Don't you ever tell anyone about me."

"No one would believe me anyway," he observed. "I hope you find your friend, that you both survive this place, and that you never corner me in a dark alley again."

"Thank you," she said. "I hope you decide not to kill whoever it is you're supposed to go kill."

"How did you — no, never mind, I don't want to know," he said. He spread his wings to go and she stepped toward him, suddenly wishing he could stay, although she would never say so out loud. He was her new second-favorite person, easily outpacing stupid Undauntable.

"I mean it," she said awkwardly. "Thank you, Murderbasket."

"Murderbasket," he muttered, shaking his head. He gave her an exasperated smile and then lifted off into the clouds, as silently as they'd come.

Now I just have to find Sky, Wren thought. *In a gigantic dragon palace. How hard could that be?*

She started as she did in every new place, by getting a sense of the geography. For one thing, there was a giant wall around the outside of the palace, specially designed to be impossible for humans to climb, as far as she could tell. Which meant probably the only way she was getting out of here was on Sky. Also, she discovered in the morning, it had several dragon heads on spikes at the top of it.

That was a little unsettling. Despite everything she'd read about dragons, she still believed they weren't as awful as humans, and she didn't like seeing evidence that they might be. She forced herself to check each of them for pale orange scales, but none of them were Sky.

Most of the palace was a labyrinth of winding hallways, lined with tapestries, which opened onto courtyards and enormous ballrooms and feasting halls. Here, again, it was very easy to find food and survive on the dragons' crumbs and leftovers. The hardest part was actually moving faster than the mice and oversized ants who wanted to get to them first.

Twice she found herself caught in an unfamiliar room with not enough hiding places when a dragon walked in. Strangely, though, each time the dragon barely glanced at her, muttered something about overwatered plants (Wren thought), grabbed whatever it was looking for, and left, even though she was *sure* it had seen her.

Am I just a giant mouse to them? Not even worth eating or squashing?

As she crept through the palace, she could hear a particular dragon roaring with fury, and she finally followed the sound to a tall tower that radiated creepiness. Someone was trapped in there, and they weren't afraid to let everyone know how displeased they were. Sometimes the prisoner roared words — "I'LL MURDER YOU ALL! YOU'LL BE SORRY! I'M GOING TO START WITH YOUR TONGUE AND EAT YOU ALIVE!" — and sometimes she just roared pure fury.

Wren had initially been inclined to feel sorry for whoever it was, but the more violent her threats became, the more

Wren felt like perhaps the world was better off with this dragon inside that tower. But it did make her wonder — was this where they kept prisoners? Could Sky be in there, too? Trapped with the angry dragon? Probably with his talons clasped over his ears and his wings over his head, wishing he were a snail and had somewhere to hide.

There were no windows, so there was no way for Wren to get inside. But she found a safe spot to spy on the tower for a couple of days and she studied the food that went in and out. It was almost all meat, and it was mostly all picked clean when the plates were removed. It didn't seem like enough for more than one dragon either — there would be only one bowl, for example, or a single tray of charred grasshoppers, or something like that.

So if he wasn't in there, where else could he be?

She scouted the palace until she found where most of the soldiers slept: in the low buildings nestled against the inner walls of the main entrance courtyard. Armored sand dragons went in and out of their barracks all day long, doing drills in the hot sun.

Wren needed a spot where she could watch the soldiers, and she found it in a closet full of dusty linens that had a small hole in the back wall looking directly out over the courtyard. There was a strange monument out there, a tall black obelisk with carved words painted in gold on it. A large circle of sand surrounded the obelisk, but the rest of the courtyard was lined with white stones that reflected the glare of the sun.

The closet was a good place to sleep and hide during the busiest parts of the day, while Wren waited for some sign of what the soldiers had done with Sky.

Two days later, the loud giant appeared, whooshing in the front gate like a sudden thunderstorm in the mountains. Wren thought of him as the general, although she didn't know whether dragon armies had titles like that. He shook a vast quantity of sand off his wings and bellowed a name. Soldiers clattered in behind him and he waved them off to the barracks, then shouted the name again. The name was something like what fires do when they're burning low — Smolder? Wren thought. *I'll go with Smolder.*

Finally a dragon came out of the central palace and slowly paced across the courtyard. He had black diamond patterns along his spine, like a snake, and a lot of keys and pouches on a ring around his neck. Wren noticed that he skirted around the circle of sand to reach the dragon who'd stolen Sky.

"Prince Smolder," the general said, inclining his head in a way that was somehow perfectly respectful but also conveyed an ocean of contempt at the same time.

"Sandstorm," said the new dragon in a similar tone, eyeing the mess the soldiers had made coming in the gate. "Anything to report?"

"Nope," said the general. He puffed up his chest and lashed his tail. "Any word from Queen Burn?"

"No," Smolder said with a sigh. "But don't worry, I'm sure she'll be back soon and you can give her your gift the moment she arrives."

"YESSSS," Sandstorm said with a smug grin. "Still alive, is he? I think she'd like him better that way. For now. HA HA!"

Smolder winced. "Yes, he's fine. Why don't you have your dragons clean this up, and I'll go make sure food is ready for them."

"I want that cinnamon drink!" Sandstorm bellowed after him. "The new one from the kitchens, like last week! Tell them to make me another!"

Wren wasn't sure who was the boss of who here — she would have thought the prince would be in charge, but the general seemed very comfortable ordering him about. Prince Smolder turned back to the palace with an expression that suggested he had several thoughts about that question, too. Unconcerned, or perhaps unaware, Sandstorm strutted over to the barracks to shout orders at some soldiers.

Wren was sure they'd been talking about Sky, although she didn't know why he'd be considered a "gift" for the queen. But that meant he was alive, and he was here. And he belonged to Sandstorm, it sounded like, until this Burn character returned. So surely Sandstorm would want to check on him as soon as he could . . .

She thought for a moment, then slipped out of the closet and hurried down to the courtyard. By the time she got there, the general was done ordering the soldiers about and was striding toward a low door that led to some of the kitchens.

Wren followed him, carefully but as fast as she could. It

was lucky that most of the doors in the palace were always open, covered by long billowing white curtains to let the breeze through. She'd also found a few where she could crawl right under the door, but there were others that were too thick or too close to the floor, and a few that seemed to have special, spiky anti-human flaps added on at the bottom for some mysterious reason.

Sandstorm marched through the kitchens, laughing his annoying hearty laugh and shouting jokes at various dragons as he went by. Wren didn't think she was just imagining it; she was pretty sure from their eye rolls that they all found him annoying, too. He yelled at someone to bring his drink to his room, and then he clattered on through and up a flight of stairs.

Dragon-sized stairs were a pain, but better than the parts of the palace where dragons just flew from ledge to ledge and left no way for a human to follow. Each step was about as tall as Wren's shoulders, so she just had to pull herself up and then run to the next and do it again, one after the other.

At the top, Sandstorm had disappeared, but she could hear his obnoxious voice chatting away in one of the rooms off the corridor. She tiptoed along the passage until she found the right one. The door was ajar. Wren peeked inside.

Sky was sitting in a corner of the room, chained to the floor, with his wings puddling dejectedly around his talons, watching Sandstorm talk. He had on one of his hopelessly sweet expressions, the one that said he was sure he could befriend that angry grizzly bear if he smiled at it enough.

"Not much longer!" Sandstorm was saying. The general dropped some of his armor with a clank that reverberated through the stones under Wren's feet. "This will be so great! I've never brought her anything for her —" something Wren didn't understand. "Bet this will get me a new command."

"But aren't we on the same side?" Sky said. "My tribe and your queen?"

"For now, more or less," Sandstorm said with a snort. "You weren't with any army, though; I'd wager you've never fought a day in your life. So I'm guessing your queen — or whoever is queen over there now — won't miss you too much."

A sound on the stairs warned Wren that someone was coming. She slipped through the door, staying low so the bed would hide her from the general, and crawled under one of the loose blankets on the floor.

One of the kitchen dragons came in, set a cup down on the table, bowed to the general, and went out again. Sandstorm drank it with a lot of loud smacking noises, and then sauntered out the door.

Wren waited until it was quiet in the corridor outside and Sandstorm's booming laugh had faded away. Then she threw off the blanket and ran over to Sky.

"Wren?" he yelped, his eyes as wide as they'd been the day he found the turtle.

She jumped over his chains, climbed up his leg, and threw her arms around his neck. He wrapped his wings around her and they stayed like that for a long moment, together, the way they always should be.

"I'm sorry, Wren," he said. His voice trembled with tears. "You were right about the dragon city."

"No, don't be sorry," she said. "It's these awful dragons who kidnapped you who should be sorry. Who *will* be sorry, when I'm done with them." She let go of him and hopped down to examine the chains.

"How did you find me?" he asked.

"I'm extremely clever," she said. "And you're my best friend, so I was definitely going to find you eventually, no matter how long it took. How do I get these chains off you?"

He lifted one arm to display a wrist cuff and dropped it again. "There's a key, but General Sandstorm always has it with him."

"What does that blowfish want with you anyway?" Wren asked, kicking one of the chain links. It did not promptly collapse under the weight of her wrath, as she'd been hoping it would.

"The queen here collects weird things," Sky said mournfully. "And apparently I'm a weird thing, because no one else is this color, and SkyWings are supposed to have fire."

"You're not weird!" Wren objected. "I mean, you are, but you're perfect weird. Like me." She grinned at him, and he smiled back. "Can I get the key while Sandstorm is sleeping?"

"I don't think so," Sky said. "It's around his neck. I'm afraid he'd wake up and kill you."

Wren folded her arms and frowned at the chains. That windowless tower with the furious dragon — that was probably where the queen kept her weird-things collection, or at least any live parts of it. Which meant she might put Sky in there, and then it would be even harder to rescue him. It would be better if she could get the key and free him now, as soon as possible, before the queen returned.

And she could think of only one way to do that.

"Well," she said to Sky, "then I guess I'm going to have to kill him first."

CHAPTER 27

IVY

The arrests began while Ivy was asleep.

It was Daffodil who woke her up, startling her out of a dream about dragons setting each other on fire.

"Ivy," Daffodil whispered. "Ivy, help, Ivy, please wake up." She shook Ivy harder, sitting down on the bed next to her. "I know I say this all the time but it's a real real emergency, I mean it now."

"Daffodil?" Ivy sat up and rubbed her eyes. "What's happening?"

"Your dad is arresting Wingwatchers," Daffodil said. "He has Foxglove and Squirrel and — and Ivy, he has Violet." She started to cry. "I was with her, I was in the other room, I was supposed to sleep over — but I guess they didn't know I was there — they burst in the front door and grabbed her, and Ivy, I didn't do anything! I didn't run out and fight them or anything!"

"You did the right thing," Ivy said, taking her hands. Her own hands were shaking, but she tried to keep her voice calm. "You didn't get arrested, and you came to tell me. So we can do something about it together." She climbed out of bed and started to get dressed. Her first instinct was to reach for her Wingwatcher uniform — but that might be exactly what her father's guards were looking for. She grabbed her charcoal-gray tunic instead.

"What are we going to do?" Daffodil twisted her hands together. Her hair was out of its ponytail, a tangled mess around her shoulders, and she was still wearing her pajamas, which were the last item of clothing she owned that her mother had managed to cover in bright yellow spots. Ivy grabbed a long brown cloak and threw it to her. "Ivy, why is he doing this? Do you have any idea?"

"I think he's afraid of someone taking his power away," Ivy said. "Maybe he heard the same rumors about the Wingwatchers that Violet heard, or maybe he thinks they're — we're — working with the lord of the Indestructible City."

She'd felt the tension closing in around her home since Leaf arrived and delivered his ill-fated message. All her father's paranoia had been reactivated. He'd gathered his brutes to follow him everywhere, and more than once Ivy had caught him staring at the pedestal where his treasure was hidden, as though he was considering grabbing it all and running away.

Ivy had been waiting for him to calm down so she could talk to him about Leaf and try to explain. But he hadn't calmed down. He'd gotten worse; more and more short-tempered and snapping at everyone, especially her mom. Last night he'd broken a few plates in a rage in the kitchen while Ivy and her mother stayed in Ivy's room and pretended not to hear.

"It might be something else," Daffodil said. "I heard one of the guards say they'd start searching once they'd arrested everyone."

Ivy stared at her, rubbing the goose bumps on her arms. "Do you think he discovered that the sapphire was missing?" she whispered. She hadn't thought that he might go back to check on it. He'd moved the rest of his treasure here — she'd assumed he didn't take the sapphire because he didn't even want to see it.

Daffodil's eyes widened. "No matter what they're looking for, they'll find the sapphire in Foxglove's cave!" she whispered.

Ivy wasn't sure what the punishment would be for actually stealing the Dragonslayer's treasure, but given what he did to Pine for just being near it, she had a bad feeling that it would be worse than banishment.

"We have to get it first," she said, heading for the door.

She was startled to find her mother awake and pacing around the living room. She hadn't realized her mom must have let Daffodil in.

"Mom?" Ivy said. "Are you all right?"

"I'm just worried," her mother said. She had one of Heath's scarves in her hands, which she kept winding through her fingers as she walked. "I've never seen him like this. I don't know what to do to get him back to normal."

"He always calms down eventually," Ivy said, hoping she sounded more convinced than she was.

"Yes, usually, but —" Ivy's mom stopped and pressed the scarf to her face. "I just don't know whether he —" She stopped again.

Whether he might arrest you, too. Ivy had had the same thought herself. If he was willing to arrest her best friend . . . and he knew how much time she spent with Foxglove . . . and he didn't trust any of the Wingwatchers . . .

"We need to check on our friends," Ivy said, taking Daffodil's hand.

"Stay out of your father's way," her mother said suddenly. She put the scarf around Ivy's neck and arranged Ivy's hair around it with fluttering hands. "If you need to — go somewhere — just for a little while — I understand."

Ivy hugged her fiercely, then tugged Daffodil out the door. They ran through the tunnels toward Foxglove's. A cluster of guards were gathered at one of the turns, arguing with one another; Ivy whipped around and dragged Daffodil a different way to avoid them. They'd almost reached Foxglove's cave when another trio of the Dragonslayer's goons came marching around the corner. Ivy shoved Daffodil through the nearest door, and they waited in a storeroom half-full of dried fruit until the soldiers were gone.

How many men does Dad have working for him? Ivy wondered. She knew he always had guards with him, and she knew there'd been more and more men she didn't know added on over the last few years. She'd even seen him handing out silver coins to the ones in charge, the only time she'd ever seen him pay real money for something. But she hadn't realized that he was essentially building his own army, loyal only to him.

"I don't think it's quite fair," Daffodil whispered, "that you're the nicest one of the three of us *and* the most competent in a crisis. I feel like I should get to be at least one of those."

"You're the funniest," Ivy whispered back. "And the best dancer. And the one everyone has a crush on."

"Ha, no," Daffodil said, looking a little more cheerful. "Not everyone. Leaf can't take his eyes off you."

I hope Leaf's all right, Ivy thought. *If this is about the sapphire, Dad has no reason to suspect him. And he's not a Wingwatcher. And he's with Uncle Stone . . . They'll take care of each other.*

They reached Foxglove's door and discovered two of Heath's men posted outside, scowling. Which was bad, but hopefully meant they hadn't searched the rooms yet, Ivy told herself.

"You stay hidden," she said to Daffodil. "I'll be right back."

"But —" Daffodil started to protest.

"Shhh," Ivy said. "If they didn't start with me, I'm probably not on their list. But you might be, so stay here."

Daffodil nodded, drawing back into the shadows. "Be careful," she whispered.

Ivy took a deep breath, aimed for the taller guard, and

strode up to him, pretending she had all of Foxglove's confidence.

"Evening," she said to the guards. "We need to do a sweep of these rooms." She pointed to Foxglove's door.

"No one's allowed in until it's time for the search," the tall guard grunted. "Not even the Dragonslayer's daughter, little miss."

"Very good," Ivy said, "but that's the thing. We think there's someone already in there. A fugitive she was hiding or someone helping her. If we leave them in there, they could destroy the, ah, the evidence we're supposed to be looking for."

The guards exchanged a troubled glance. "I don't know," said the shorter one. "We don't want to get in trouble."

"I'll take the blame," Ivy said. "I know you're just following orders. You can stay out here or come in and help look, either way."

"I'll go in," said the tall one, tucking his sword away. "You keep an eye on things out here," he said to his partner.

She followed him into Foxglove's tiny cave, which she shared with another Wingwatcher. Ivy could see signs of a struggle in the small living space; there were chairs overturned and a pot of bean stew spilled on the table, still dripping onto the stone floor. The guards must have taken both Foxglove and her roommate. From the shoes scattered by the door, she guessed they hadn't even let them put anything on their feet. She felt sick to her stomach.

The guard looked around, frowning. "I don't see how anyone could be hiding in here," he said.

"I'll check this room," Ivy said, pointing to the roommate's cave. "You look in there." She pointed to Foxglove's cave, and the guard's eyes narrowed.

"No," he said. "I think *you* should look in there." He pointed at Foxglove's cave. "And I'll check the other one."

Ivy shrugged and went where she was told. As soon as she heard him stomp out of sight into the other room, she dove under Foxglove's mattress, poked through the straw, found the hole she knew was there, and wiggled the sapphire free. She tucked it into her sleeve and rolled out again, so she was standing upright a moment later when the guard came storming back in.

"There's nobody here," he snarled.

"Great!" Ivy said. "I didn't find anyone in here either. What a relief. I told Dad I was sure you guys had done an excellent, thorough job, but he was just worried, you know."

"Right," he said. "Time to get out, then."

She nodded and slipped past him, thanking the other guard politely as she went by. The sapphire was clamped in her armpit, which was very uncomfortable. As she walked away, she kept expecting one of them to notice the lump and shout to call her back, but they were busy muttering to each other. Ivy rounded the corner and took her first real breath in a while.

"Now what do we do with it?" Daffodil whispered.

"Get it out of Valor," Ivy said. She wished they had time

to go get Leaf, too, but if they were caught with the sapphire, she and Daffodil would both be in the worst trouble of their lives. And she didn't want to drag Leaf into this. She had to hope he'd be safe for now.

She secured the sapphire in her belt, took Daffodil's hand, and ran toward the nearest escape from the underground city.

— CHAPTER 28 —

LEAF

Something woke Leaf just before the knock on the door.

He wasn't sure what it was — some instinct for danger, perhaps, after his time with the dragonmancers and in the mountain palace. But his eyes popped open and he was lying there with all his muscles tensed when the knock came.

Stone wandered into the room, yawning. Leaf stood up quietly and Stone paused, sensing his alarm. Leaf pointed at the door and tilted his head, trying to signal: *Is this normal? In the middle of the night? Should we be worried?*

A slow frown creased Stone's forehead. He pointed to a large cabinet in the kitchen. Leaf slipped over to it, took out the bag of grains inside, and squeezed himself into the space as quickly as he could. Stone waited until he was well hidden, and then he opened his front door.

"What?" he grunted.

Leaf couldn't see anything, but he could hear the shuffling of feet in the corridor and shouts echoing from some distance away.

"We're looking for the stranger," growled the voice at the door.

"What for?" Stone asked, equally surly.

"To arrest him," said another voice. "For conspiracy to murder the Dragonslayer."

Leaf managed not to gasp, but his heart felt as if it was flipping inside out. *Murder the Dragonslayer! Why would I DO that? I came here for his help! I've worshipped him my whole life!*

There was a muffled *oof*, as though the first man had elbowed the second. "We know he's here," said the original voice. "Hand him over, and we'll go peacefully."

"He is here," Stone said, and Leaf's heart stopped again. "I just sent him for water. He'll be back any minute."

"Water? At this hour?" said the second voice.

"Yeah, he used up my whole supply," Stone grumbled. "Pain in my neck. Glad you're taking him off my hands."

"Should we go look for him at the lake?" asked another guard.

"Nah, just wait out here," Stone said. "He'll be along soon and you can grab him."

"You three go to the lake," ordered the first voice. "The rest of us will wait."

"Wonderful," Stone said flatly. "I'm going to bed."

"If he doesn't show up soon," said the second voice threateningly, "we'll be arresting you instead, old man."

"Sounds fun, can't wait," Stone said, and shut the door in their faces.

A moment later he yanked open the cabinet and beckoned to Leaf. Leaf crawled out, quietly lifted his pack and his sword, and tiptoed after Stone into the back bedroom.

He hadn't been in here, even though he'd been staying at Stone's for days now. He hadn't wanted to be nosy or aggravate his host. It was spartanly furnished, like the outer room, but there were large tapestries covering each wall, all of them dark green and woven with patterns of roses in pink, white, and red. Stone crossed to one of these and pulled it aside to reveal a narrow tunnel leading into the wall.

Leaf raised his eyebrows, but Stone gestured impatiently for him to climb in, so he did. He heard Stone grab something that clinked softly and then follow him.

Leaf crawled along the tunnel as fast as he could. It curved upward through the earth for a long time, and it wasn't very wide; Leaf felt as though the dirt was pressing in on him, dark and smothering. He'd always thought he would die in a dragon's jaws. He'd never imagined he might die buried alive, suffocated by dirt.

He reached the end well before Stone. In the dark, all he could feel was dirt all around him, crumbling and soft.

"Here," Stone panted, tapping his foot with something. Leaf reached back and felt him press a large spoon into his hand. "Dig up, and dig fast."

Leaf did as he was told. He tried to remind himself that climbing the cliff over the dragon feast was worse than this; being held in dragon's talons was worse than this. Sitting in a pit with his friends waiting to be eaten was worse than this. Earth rained down into his hair and he felt worms squirming around his hands as he dug the spoon in, again and again.

For a moment he thought they'd drown in the dirt before he broke through, but then he felt the spoon dislodge a chunk that came with a gust of cold air. He dug faster, widening the hole, until there was enough of a space for him to wiggle out into the open.

He was on the side of a hill, just above the tree line. He could see the forest stretching out below him, toward the mountains, lit by the silvery moons.

Stone grunted behind him, and Leaf turned back to make the hole bigger. After a few minutes of digging, he was able to reach down and pull the older man through into the air.

"Thank you," Leaf said, clasping Stone's hands.

"Bah," Stone said, shaking him off. "I was saving my own skin, too. First they come for the strangers, next they come for anyone else Heath feels threatened by. I've been digging that tunnel since I got back to Valor a year ago." He jerked his thumb at the hole behind them. "Figured I might need it eventually, although I hoped I wouldn't." He kicked as much loose dirt into the tunnel as he could, blocking it up again, and then started down the hill toward the trees.

"You made that in case you needed to escape the Dragonslayer?" Leaf asked, confused. He jumped from boulder to boulder, keeping up. "Your own brother?"

"He's been paranoid ever since we stole the treasure," Stone said. "Always thinking someone would try to steal it from him. Looking for enemies in every corner. He built his power on the story of how great and brave and special he is. It stands to reason he'd eventually have to take out the one person who might tell everyone he's a fraud."

"You?" Leaf said. "Why, what would you tell everyone?"

Stone sighed and paused for a long moment. Finally he said, "I could admit that I'm the one who really killed that dragon. I realized it years later. It was my spear in her eye." He rubbed the back of his neck as Leaf stared at him, disbelieving. "And I'd tell them all about Rose. Some of them already know, but many of them don't. Heath just wrote her out of the story, over and over again."

"Rose," Leaf said, remembering his father's voice again. "Is she . . . the one who got left behind?"

"You do know something," Stone said in surprise. "Yes, our sister. Long dead. Braver and better than either of us." He fell silent, and Leaf got the distinct feeling that he shouldn't ask any more questions for a little while.

They traveled quickly through the forest, keeping one eye on the sky and one ear out for any sounds from Valor.

"Where are we going?" Leaf asked finally. There was an odd smell in the air, like woodfires and burned applesauce.

"The old village," Stone answered. "Rumor has it that's the place to go if you need help after the Dragonslayer banishes you."

Leaf remembered Ivy saying something about banishment, too. He thought about that, the idea of the Dragonslayer sending villagers who disobeyed him out into the world, unprotected. It was the opposite of everything Leaf had always thought the Dragonslayer would be. The whole point of slaying dragons was to help people — to save them — to be the one standing in front of the fire and the teeth, making sure nobody else got hurt.

That was how he'd always thought of it, at least.

"Why did you all go fight the dragons?" Leaf asked slowly. "You, Heath, and Rose?"

"Heath's idea," Stone said. "For the treasure, of course. The plan was to get in and out without seeing any dragons."

The Dragonslayer is not a hero after all. Leaf's whole understanding of the world shuffled around like a deck of trick cards in Cranberry's hands. *He wasn't protecting anyone. He's just like the dragonmancers and everyone else — a lying, treasure-grubbing thief.*

Who, let's not forget, arrests random strangers on made-up charges, Wren piped up cheerfully in his head. *And scared his own brother into building an escape tunnel. Hey, I think he might be terrible! Have you thought about that? That he might be terrible?*

Yes, Wren, Leaf argued. *I'm thinking about it NOW.*

"Shh!" Stone said suddenly, grabbing Leaf's arm. Leaf froze, hit with a sudden memory of Rowan doing the same thing during training, as they both tilted their heads to listen for dragons.

She may have lied to me, but she always took care of me, he thought.

"Someone's coming." Stone pulled Leaf down to the ground and they lay in the leaf mulch, small insects crawling past their noses. Soft footsteps were hurrying through the trees nearby. Someone in a hurry and trying not to be heard. Could it be more guards, coming after them?

A shape moved through one of the slivers of moonlight, and Leaf recognized the way she moved.

"It's Ivy," he whispered to Stone, standing up.

"Wait," Stone said, trying to pull him back. "She's Heath's daughter — we don't know if —"

But Ivy had already seen them. She skidded to a stop and came running over. Daffodil was right behind her. To Leaf's surprise, Ivy threw her arms around him. He thought of Rowan again, and the one hug she'd ever given him.

Wait, there was another, he remembered. *The night we found out about Wren. She found me outside when I couldn't sleep, looking up at the stars, and she gave me a hug then.*

Nobody else had, even that awful day; hugs were rare in his family. He put his arms around Ivy and breathed the peach-scented smell of her hair brushing over his arms. He felt safe, for once, and peaceful, like he could exist in this moment for a long time.

"What are you doing out here?" Ivy asked.

"Heath sent men to arrest him," Stone said.

"You?" Ivy pulled back, looking into his eyes. "Why? I thought they were only arresting Wingwatchers."

"Wingwatchers?" Stone said sharply. "What's that about?"

"Some kind of conspiracy," Daffodil offered. "I guess the

one Violet's been trying to find out about, because they took her, too."

"I thought it was about the treasure," Ivy said. "I thought maybe Dad realized the sapphire was missing. But he can't possibly think *you* have it," she said to Leaf. She was still holding his hands.

"Sapphire?" Leaf echoed.

"If he's worried about a conspiracy, anyone could be under suspicion," Stone said. "Even you, Ivy. And me."

She glanced back toward Valor. "I'll find out more when I go back," she said. "First we have to hide the sapphire and you guys."

"You can't go *back*," Leaf protested as they started to hurry through the woods again. "Stone just said you could be arrested, too."

"Agreed, agreed, very much agreed," Daffodil said. "You absolutely definitely cannot go back to Valor."

"But how can we rescue Foxglove and Violet and the others without more information?" Ivy asked.

"Some way that doesn't end up with *us* having to also rescue *you*," Daffodil suggested.

They stepped suddenly onto a path that was clearly a path, between shapes that were not trees. Leaf had been thinking about the danger back in Valor; he was startled to discover that they were out of the woods, surrounded by the husks of burned-out buildings.

"Whoa," he said, looking around. "What happened here? I mean, dragons, obviously. Sorry, stupid question."

"No, it's not," Ivy said. She told him the whole story of what the dragons did after Heath and Stone rode back with the treasure. They walked through the ruins, and he imagined something like this happening to Talisman — the entire village in flames.

Would the dragons have done this to Talisman if he'd succeeded in killing one of them?

He felt cold all over. Why hadn't anyone told him this part of the story? He'd always thought the dragon was the threat, and the slayer had gone after it to protect his village.

It changed the story quite a bit if you mentioned that the slayer went after the dragon first, and *then* the dragon's relatives came for his village.

"I had no idea," he said, stopping near the bell at the center of town. Daffodil and Stone had gone to find someone called Pine, who Daffodil said would help them hide.

"I could tell," Ivy said. "When I heard the way you talked about my dad — I had a feeling you'd only gotten part of the story. Especially once you told me about your sister."

"She'd be so mad," he said. He looked down with a smile. "Wren hated incomplete stories. Sometimes I'd start telling her a story, and then stop before the end, just to drive her crazy. She didn't like liars or smug people or grown-ups who acted like they knew everything either."

Ivy laughed. "She sounds awesome. And a little intimidating." She sat down on the tumbled pile of rocks around the burned-out bell and he sat next to her. It was almost morning; the sun was rising over the mountains.

"She was." Leaf shoved his hands in his pockets. "I wonder what she'd want me to do next." There was no answer from the Wren inside his head. He felt like his Destiny Plan B had been shredded into tiny pieces and scattered to the wind. The Dragonslayer was just a liar, a con man, and a thief. Nothing Leaf had believed in had turned out to be true.

"Maybe you could help us," Ivy said. "We have a kind of sort of plan that we think will make the world a better place."

"Really?"

"We were thinking there might be a way to get the dragons to stop attacking villages," she said. "I mean. Maybe it's impossible. But Violet and Daffodil and I thought, what if we gave the treasure back? Maybe the dragons need it for some reason. Maybe they'll forgive us."

Forgiveness, Leaf thought. *From giant flying sharks. Really?*

An image flashed in his mind of the brown dragon who had helped him.

"I know," Ivy said. "It's silly. They'll eat us before we can even shout 'HELLO PLEASE DON'T EAT US!'"

"Maybe not," he said. "If we find the right dragon." He told her about what had happened to him inside the mountain palace. By the time he was done, there was sunlight all around them.

"Wow," Ivy breathed. She hadn't said a word the whole time he talked. She closed her eyes and took a breath. "I can't believe you've been there. *Inside* the dragon palace. I wonder if we could find that brown dragon again. He must live in the swamps, right? Maybe he could help us. Or at least, we could try to communicate with him. Can you imagine, communicating with dragons?"

"I don't know if I'm quite ready for that yet," Leaf said wryly. He hesitated. "Um. Do you know that your dad isn't really a dragonslayer?"

Ivy tipped her head at him. "What do you mean?"

"He's not the one who killed the dragon," Leaf said. "It was Stone. He just told me."

"My uncle?" Ivy blinked several times. "*Stone* killed the sand dragon queen?"

"Not on purpose," Leaf said. "They were there for treasure, not to fight any dragons."

"But then why does he let my dad tell everyone *he's* the Dragonslayer?" Ivy demanded.

"I think he doesn't want the attention . . . and Heath definitely does want it," Leaf pointed out. "But you might want to ask him yourself."

"I will," Ivy said. "Moons above, that fits so much better with everything I know about my dad. I always wondered how he managed to do one brave, dangerous thing and then spend the rest of his life being the exact opposite of that person. If he didn't even do that . . . it kind of all makes sense." She rested her chin on her hands and her elbows on her knees. "So even the founding story of Valor is a lie. I guess that makes sense, too."

Leaf saw Daffodil waving from one of the ruined buildings. "Daffodil's summoning us."

"Let's go tell her your story," Ivy said. "I have

approximately a million questions. For you and also for Uncle Stone."

As they climbed down the rocks, Leaf saw movement in the trees. He pulled Ivy behind a wall and they both crouched, peeking through the gaps.

A dragon stepped out of the forest.

Leaf felt Ivy shiver beside him, but when he reached to put his cloak around her, he realized that she wasn't scared; she was suddenly radiating excitement.

"Oh, *wow*. I've never seen a dragon that color before," she whispered to him. "This could be a whole new kind that isn't even in the guide!" Her fingers twitched. "I wish I had something to draw with."

He looked back at the dragon. It was small — smaller than the brown one who'd rescued him, but much bigger than the baby in the kitchen. It had golden-yellow scales and greenish eyes, and it was looking around with an open, curious expression.

"I think I saw one that color," he said. "In a cage over the dragon feast in the palace."

"Oh," Ivy said. "In a cage? So they must be enemies with the mountain dragons."

The golden dragon took a few steps into the village, then lifted into the air and flew in a circle overhead, as though it was studying the ruins from the sky. Leaf pulled his cloak over both himself and Ivy and they flattened themselves against the wall, trying to look like an uninteresting pile of dirt.

After a while they heard the dragon land again, near the

old bell. Ivy pushed down the cloak and leaned over to study the dragon some more. It was wandering around the village square, poking through the ashes and making little *hmmm* noises.

"It's really cute," she whispered to Leaf. "I've seen lots of amazing dragons, but none I'd call cute before this one."

"Um, no. Chipmunks are cute," he answered. "*You* are amazing, and a little bananas. Dragons are neither cute nor amazing; dragons are terrifying."

She smiled, but she kept her eyes on the dragon until it finally flew away.

"A whole new species of dragon and a story about the inside of the mountain palace," she said when it was gone. "Leaf, isn't everything incredible?"

"Except the part about your dad arresting your friends," he reminded her, and then felt terrible as her face fell. "Sorry."

"Right," she said. "But . . . that's probably a misunderstanding. I can fix it. I'll talk to him and fix it once he calms down, I'm sure."

As they headed toward Daffodil in the bright morning sunlight, Leaf wondered if she was right. Was there any chance the Dragonslayer could be talked out of his paranoia? Could Ivy convince him to let everyone go?

Leaf was afraid the answer was no . . . and that they'd never see Violet or Foxglove or the inside of Valor ever again.

— CHAPTER 29 —

WREN

There were a few possible ways to kill a dragon. The classic approach, with all the stabbing and shouting and blood and gore, seemed a little too obvious and a lot too messy and complicated to Wren.

"I'd have to find a longer, better sword, I think," she said. "Then wait till he's sleeping and stab him in the eye. But he'd have time to wake up roaring, maybe kill both of us, and definitely alert the whole palace. There's no way I'll get to steal the key and sneak away with you if there are eighty dragons in here sliding around in his blood and shrieking about a human attack."

"Especially after the last one," Sky added helpfully. "A human killed the last SandWing queen, so they're EXTRA super paranoid about you here."

"Really?" Wren said. "How did she do that?"

"I'm not sure," Sky admitted. "The stabby way, I think."

"Huh." Wren thought about that for a moment. That didn't mesh with her experience wandering around the palace. The two dragons who had caught a glimpse of her hadn't reacted like she might be dangerous. They'd carried on as though it wasn't weird at all to run into a human in their cupboards.

She also wondered why a human would go to the trouble of killing a dragon queen. Maybe the dragon had threatened her village. Wren didn't think she would kill a dragon to save Talisman or any of the mean, horrible people who lived there. But there was a small part of her that hoped killing General Sandstorm would mean stopping the attack he was planning on the Indestructible City.

Not for Undauntable. Undauntable was stupid. But there were lots of other people in the Indestructible City or trying to get into it, and possibly one or two of them were not awful. The kids she'd stuffed into the hidey-hole with Undauntable during the last attack had seemed worth saving, she figured.

"If I want to do it quietly," she said, "what are my options?"

"Drop the ceiling on his head?" Sky suggested.

Wren gave him a look. "How is that the QUIET option, Sky?"

"I don't know," he said. "One brick at a time?"

Wren laughed. "I wish you really had a snail army," she said. "This would be an excellent time for an army of belligerent snails to help us out."

She looked out the window to the desert beyond the wall, where Sandstorm was leading a squadron of soldiers in some aerial maneuvers.

"Maybe you could get some other dragons to help you!" Sky said. "Like the black dragon who flew you here. You could go say hello to some dragons around the palace and see if anyone would like to help you murder Sandstorm. Ooh, maybe the prince. He seemed less hostile than everyone else."

"As fun as that plan sounds," Wren said, "and although I'm quite sure there are many dragons who'd love to see Sandstorm dead, I think I'm unlikely to find another dragon as helpful as Murderbasket."

"I don't think you're saying that right," Sky said, not for the first time. "Maybe it's Death-something? Deathwarrior? Deathconqueror?"

"No, it wasn't either of those," Wren said. "Anyway, he was fine with Murderbasket. I wonder how *he* assassinates other dragons. He was incredibly stealthy."

"I can be incredibly stealthy," Sky said jealously, and quite incorrectly.

"Of course, sweetness," Wren said, patting his talons. "Well, the stealthiest way I can think of to kill someone is poison. So I'll go work on that, and I'll be back soon."

"Poison!" Sky said. "Wait, where are you going? Don't leave me."

"I can't stay here," Wren said regretfully. "He's finishing up out there, so he'll probably be back before long. But I'll come see you again as soon as he's gone, and hopefully by then I'll be all ready to slay a dragon."

"Be careful," Sky said, nudging her with his snout. His wings drooped as she patted his nose and started across the floor. "I don't like it here, Wren."

"I don't either, Sky. We'll fly right back to the mountains as soon as those chains are off. All right?"

He nodded, and she waved good-bye before ducking out the door.

She'd seen about a hundred mice scurrying about the palace, and she guessed that meant someone must be trying to get rid of them. In the absence of cats, surely that meant rat poison somewhere . . . most likely the kitchens.

"Don't eat that."

Wren nearly fell off the counter. *Was that a human voice?* She whirled around, and in fact, there was a real, actual person standing behind her. A woman, hands on her hips, standing out on the kitchen counter as bold as a salt shaker.

Wren stared at her. *Now* I'm *having hallucinations.*

The woman was only a little taller than Wren, with long, messy dark brown hair and a defiant expression on her face. Her outfit looked like it had been hacked off the end of the curtains and then tied together with bits of leftover string. Wren could tell she was a grown-up, but she couldn't guess her age.

"Holy dragon scales," Wren said. "Who are you?"

"I'm Rose," the woman answered. "Are you here to steal treasure? Because, speaking from experience, I can't say I'd recommend it. Also, that's not treasure, that's mouse poison." Her gaze traveled to the net bag Wren had borrowed from a pile of oranges, which contained the first two poison pellets Wren had found. A slow frown of puzzlement crossed Rose's face.

"I'm not here for treasure," Wren said. "What are *you* here for?"

"I live here," Rose said, as though that were obvious, as though it were her palace and of course a human lived here among the dragons.

"Really?" Wren said. This human was suddenly a lot more interesting than most. "And nobody eats you?"

"Not so far." Rose grinned suddenly, like a flash of lightning in a rainstorm. "OK, I'm playing it cool, but I'm actually dying of curiosity. What *are* you doing?"

"You can't tell anyone," Wren said.

Rose threw back her head and laughed and laughed. "I literally haven't spoken to another human being in decades," she said when she could finally breathe again. "There's no one I could possibly tell, don't worry."

"You could tell one of the dragons," Wren said, "and I need you to not do that."

"These dragons do *not* pay attention to me," Rose said. "Apart from my dragon, the others all reluctantly refrain from eating me, and they studiously ignore me. That's it."

"Ohhhhhhhh," Wren said. "That's why the two who saw me didn't freak out or kill me. They must have seen a human and thought I was you." Overwatered plants — maybe they thought of Rose as a spoiled pet who had the run of the palace.

Rose looked her up and down. "See, and you don't look anything like me. That just goes to show you how little they pay attention to me. So please tell me what you're doing, tell me tell me!"

"All right," Wren said. "There's this dragon I have to kill — the general, Sandstorm. So I thought maybe I'd poison him with these." She shook the bag of pellets, picked up the new one, and stuffed it inside.

"That's a decent idea," Rose said. "But you'll need a lot more than that," she added skeptically.

"That's true," Wren said. "So I'd better keep looking. Nice to meet you, good-bye."

"Hang on," Rose said, following her behind the fruit bowl and down the stack of crates beside the counter. "Maybe I can help. I've seen a lot of those around the stronghold."

Wren reached the floor and turned to look at her. Asking a dragon for help was bad enough; asking a human for help was more risky than she was up for. A dragon would be straightforward about eating her, at least, if it wanted to do that. A human might pretend to help and then betray her by pushing her into a dragon's jaws, or something like that.

"That's all right," Wren said. "I can handle it myself." She set off toward the fireplace.

"Oh, I'm helping you anyway," Rose said. "Sorry, I shouldn't have made it sound optional. Did I mention the part where I haven't talked to a human in years? I'm kind of overexcited about the idea of a real conversation. Plus, check it out, there's one over here." She darted behind a basket of yams and emerged triumphantly with another poison pellet. "See? Helping!"

Wren accepted the pellet warily. Rose might be all right. She seemed to prefer the company of dragons to humans, like Wren did. It was probably pretty interesting, living in a dragon palace.

And Wren could stay on high alert and make a run for it if Rose did try to feed her to anyone.

They made a circuit of the kitchens and surrounding feast halls and wound up finding nine poison pellets in all. The net bag was almost too heavy for Wren to carry by herself now, although she didn't let Rose see that.

Rose chatted cheerfully as they went, asking questions about the world beyond the palace but never getting too nosy, which Wren appreciated.

"Are you a prisoner here?" Wren asked. *Should I be offering to rescue you?* she wondered.

"Not really." Rose shrugged. "I mean, it's all a matter of perspective, right? They might think they're holding me prisoner, but I kind of like it here. I like my dragon. He's pretty adorable."

Wren nearly admitted that she had her own dragon friend, too, but she wasn't *quite* ready to trust Rose all the way. It was sort of thrilling to find a human so much like her, though. *Someone who understands that dragons are like us — but better.*

"I hope this is enough," Wren said to herself, hefting the bag of pellets.

"I think it should be," Rose said. "Wait, why do you have to kill this dragon? Tell me it's not for treasure."

"No way," Wren said. "I would never kill a dragon for something as pointless as treasure."

Rose laughed. "I wish I'd been as smart as you when I was your age," she said. "Although I guess it worked out for me. But back then, I was totally excited about treasure . . . or maybe I was just excited to help my brother, who was REALLY excited about treasure."

Wren thought of Leaf and the adventures she used to drag him on. She wondered how quickly he forgot her — within a week? A month? A year? Did he ever think of her now?

Probably not. Which is fine. They don't need me, I don't need them.

"Anyway, I made it into the treasure room and out of the palace — twice!" Rose said, with all the excitement of someone who'd done something amazing but didn't have anyone to tell about it for twenty years. "Buuuut then the dragon queen caught us. So, that was bad."

"The dragon queen — wait, the one who got killed by a human?" Wren asked. "Was that you?"

"No, that was my other brother," Rose said. "Kind of an accident, though. Anyway, they rode off into the desert, but I'd hurt my leg, so I hid in a sand dune. That's where my dragon found me. I knew he wouldn't eat me. He has kind eyes." She thought for a moment. "OK, that's not *entirely* true. I spent the first couple of years expecting him to change his mind or, like, eat me in his sleep or something!"

Wren laughed. "Well, Sandstorm does *not* have kind eyes," she said. "He's been threatening the Indestructible

City — I figure if I get rid of him, it'll keep the city safe."
This was true, and seemed like a safer explanation than telling Rose about Sky.

"Which one is Sandstorm?" Rose asked. "And how do you know his name? Or did you just make that up?"

"I heard the prince say it," Wren said. "Sandstorm is the big, loud soldier commander with the annoying laugh. He's been booming around the palace for days bragging about the prize he brought back for the queen."

Now Rose looked *extremely* confused. She studied Wren for a long, thoughtful moment. "Wren," she said slowly, "you said all that as though you understand what dragons are saying."

Wren had sort of assumed that if Rose lived here, she must also speak and understand Dragon. But all the next few questions led straight back to Sky.

"Oh, um," Wren said. "I was just guessing. Anyway, I have to go. You know. Dragons to slay. Thanks for your help." She tossed the net bag up onto the first step and heaved herself after it.

"I'll come keep watch for you," Rose said cheerfully. "And then you can tell me how you understand Dragon." She hauled herself after Wren and flung the pellets up another step.

"I don't!" Wren said. "That would be so weird! Humans can't understand Dragon. No, no. Look, I'm sure you have other things to do."

"I guess I could steal some more cheese," Rose said. "Or

draw on my dragon's wall some more, but hmmm, I can do that anytime, and how often do I get to interrogate a girl who understands dragons?"

"I do NOT," Wren said, putting her hands on her hips.

"Oh, admit I can be helpful," Rose said. "Don't you need a lookout while you poison this loudmouth dragon?"

"He's out on patrol," Wren said. "I can't poison him until he comes back tomorrow morning, so you can't help me right now."

Rose blinked at her again. "I suppose you're going to tell me you're guessing that, too?" she asked. "About patrols and when they'll be back?"

"Sure," Wren said.

A bell rang somewhere nearby, soft and silver and twinkling.

"Oh — never mind, I'm being summoned," Rose said. "Probably means I'm going back in the tower for a bit."

"The tower?" Wren asked. "Where the queen keeps her weird things? Are you one of her weird things?"

"Oh, no, not at all," Rose said. "I stay far away from the queen. My dragon watches out for me, and sometimes the tower is the safest place to put me, like if the palace has a lot of visitors who might eat me, or the queen is on a rampage, or anything like that." The bell rang again, closer now. Rose took a reluctant step away from Wren. "So . . . good luck with your dragonslaying."

"Thanks," Wren said. "Good luck with the tower." Rose jumped lightly down the steps and pattered away into one of the feasting halls. Wren was surprised to feel a little pang in her chest, like she kind of wanted Rose to stay and keep talking to her. A human who made her laugh, who understood that dragons were complicated just like people, whose life story was as interesting as Wren's? Wren hadn't thought anyone like that existed.

She knew Sandstorm's patrol would be gone for a full day, probably returning early in the morning, which meant she had that long to find a good hiding spot in his room. Then she just had to wait for one of the servants to bring in his cinnamon milk and hope there was time to poison it before the general burst in.

The hiding place wasn't too hard — Sandstorm had an end table beside his bed with a single drawer, but it was poorly made, so there was a gap at the top of the drawer. Wren climbed down into it and found the drawer half-empty, with enough room for her to squeeze herself and the pellet bag into. It was highly uncomfortable, and she did not want to know what all the odd random things were that were poking her in the dark, but she could handle it for a little while.

She left the bag there and spent the day keeping Sky's spirits up. He was worried about everything about this plan, and he was especially worried about something bad happening to Wren. They took turns dozing during the night, each of them listening for the sound of the general approaching.

Wren was the one awake and watching out the window when the patrol came flying in from the north. She darted over to the table, shimmied up the leg, and squished herself into the drawer before Sky was even fully awake.

A short while later, a server dragon from the kitchens came in and left a cup on the table where Wren was hidden. As soon as he was gone, Wren scrambled out and hauled her net of pellets up after her. The cup of cinnamon milk was nearly as tall as she was, but standing on tiptoes, she could drop the poison into it.

Splash went the first one.

Dissolve, dissolve, Wren prayed, shaking the glass. She could see white powder swirling around inside. In a moment it disappeared into the milk.

She hefted another pellet into the glass. *Splash*, shake, shake. Seven more, one after the other. Would it make the drink too chalky or change the taste? She had to pray that he wouldn't notice before he drank it all.

"I think he's coming," Sky whispered in a panic.

Wren scooped up the net, gave the glass one last shake, and dove through the crack into the drawer. She wedged herself in the back of it, behind all the knickknacks and sand and odd little things Sandstorm had collected.

Footsteps thumped into the room.

"HEY THERE, PRISONER," Sandstorm boomed. "GOOD NEWS! Burn should be back today sometime! HA HA! Isn't that great? I can't WAIT until she sees you. And then it's off to the weirdling tower with you, and I can finally have my room to myself again!"

"I'm not that weird," Sky said plaintively. "I'm just an

ordinary dragon, like you or any of your soldiers. Couldn't you please let me go?"

"Ridiculous," Sandstorm scoffed. "You're nothing like us. You're less than a dragon! You're a fascinating beetle. Burn will love prodding you to figure out what's wrong with you, and then she'll probably kill you, stuff you, and put you on display."

Wren could imagine the crestfallen look on poor Sky's face. Wren felt even less bad than she ever had about killing General Sandstorm, and she'd been at zero bad before. This dragon was the worst.

"Ah, good!" Sandstorm thudded over to the table and picked up his drink. "Just what I need." He chuckled, and then there were some very loud gurgling-slurping noises.

Yes, Wren thought triumphantly. *Now lie down for a nap. And never wake up.*

Sandstorm yawned loud enough to shake the table. "What a day, lizard. You have no idea how important I am to Queen Burn. Wait until I find her treasure in that spiky human city! She'll probably give me a palace of my own. HA HA! I'll burn all those humans to ashes. It'll be GREAT!"

Wren heard creaking and rustling as he settled onto his cot. The general let out a sleepy grunt and a weird gurgling noise, probably from his stomach. "Hm," he grumbled to himself. "Too sweet today."

"General Sandstorm!" A dragon burst into the room. "Help! Help! We're under attack! It's the end of the world!"

"Arrgh, calm down, Camel." The general struggled back

up again. His stomach made another ominous gurgling noise. "Who's attacking?"

"I don't know, sir! SandWings, but no one I recognize — they just appeared out of the sand!"

"Any SeaWings with them?" Sandstorm demanded. "IceWings?"

"No, sir! I don't think so, sir! But there are a lot of them and they're very angry and scary, sir!"

Sandstorm snorted. "Let's go kill them, then! HA-HAaaa." He staggered into the table.

Die now, Wren thought frantically. *Do ONE THING RIGHT and die NOW and HERE.*

But the general shoved himself up and stumbled out of the room with Camel. Wren rolled to the front of the drawer, wriggled out through the crack, and raced over to the window. From there, she could see Sandstorm leap into the sky from the nearest courtyard, wings spread wide, with a bunch of soldiers behind him. He roared and dipped sideways, then shot toward the desert outside the palace walls.

Wren scrambled out the window.

"Wren!" Sky protested. "Where are you going? That's not safe!"

"I'll be right back," she called. "Don't worry, everything's fine!"

That was decidedly untrue: Everything was far from fine. She wedged her toes into the cracks in the stone and clambered all the way up to the roof. From there, she had a view of the dragon battle down below.

An awfully clear view of General Sandstorm plummeting into the midst of the fighting. He roared and swung his venomous tail in a dangerous arc. Dragons scattered out of his way. He spun and seized a small SandWing, wrapping his talons around the dragon's neck. With a grin, he started to lift the dragon up to choke him . . . and then General Sandstorm clutched his stomach and collapsed to the sand.

The dragon he'd dropped stumbled back for a moment, then recovered and edged forward. He poked the general's body once, twice with his claws. Looking confused but very pleased with himself, he finally swaggered off to fight someone else.

With a shriek of terror, the dragon named Camel came pelting back toward the palace, probably to find backup.

Wren dropped to her knees on the roof.

She'd done it. She'd slain a dragon. And yet she'd still failed.

General Sandstorm lay dead in the middle of the battle, out in the desert.

Outside the giant human-proof walls. With the key that Wren needed around his neck.

CHAPTER 30

IVY

Heath's guards came through the old village the day after the arrests. They poked long spears through every leaf pile, peered up every chimney, and knocked over a few unstable walls.

If Ivy's father had been with them, she might have tried talking to him. He was still her dad — even if he was mad at her, or suspicious of her, he'd still listen, wouldn't he?

But he wasn't with the guards, and they all looked very angry. Daffodil said it wouldn't do any good for Ivy to get arrested for no reason, and that it would only make them search harder for the others who were hiding nearby, which was a good point.

They weren't in the village, exactly. Pine had taken them to the spot where most of the banished hid at first, a kind of ancient temple farther off into the woods. Two of the walls were missing, with only weathered marble columns left to hold up the roof on those sides. But at least there *was* a roof, and a mostly covered corner to tuck into, and a window to leap out of if anyone approached, though no one did.

Ivy wished she could find out more about the temple. It was

carved all over with dragons — flying, roaring, lounging on clouds, prowling through trees, snarling at each other. She would have liked to draw them.

By the time the guards left, it was past midday, and Ivy's notion about going home was wavering. She'd been gone long enough now that her father could be sure she was with the fugitives, especially after the lie she'd told the guards in front of Foxglove's door. She wondered what her mother had said to him, too. She wondered whether he was also looking for Daffodil.

She wondered whether she'd even be able to look at him now without giving away that she knew his whole Dragonslayer story was based on a lie.

Maybe she should give him a couple of days to calm down . . . but she couldn't stop worrying about Violet and Foxglove and the others. Would he punish them right away? What would he do to them?

Then, the next day, an unexpected visitor appeared in the village ruins. Ivy and Daffodil were in a tree, watching for more guards or the little gold dragon Ivy had seen, when they saw someone in a green uniform slowly picking his way through the rubble.

"That's Forest!" Daffodil said, surprised.

It was, in fact, the goofy class clown and fellow Wingwatcher who had a crush on Daffodil. He looked a lot more serious than Ivy had ever seen him. He stopped in the center of the town square, shoved his hands in his pockets, and looked around mournfully.

"Maybe he can tell us what's happening," Daffodil said.

"Unless he's working for my dad," Ivy said, although she didn't want to.

Daffodil stared at him for a moment. "I don't think Forest would betray us," she said. "Do you? Really?"

Maybe now was the time to become a suspicious person; to watch everyone for signs of treachery and keep her secrets well hidden. Violet would certainly tell them not to trust anyone.

But wasn't that exactly how her father had ended up like this? Ivy didn't want to become paranoid and distrustful. Her instinct was to trust Forest. That was the person she wanted to be.

"Let's go talk to him," she said, shimmying down the tree.

Forest's face lit up when he saw them waving from one of the fallen buildings. He hurried over and crouched behind the wall with them.

"Oh, man," he said. "I'm so glad you're all right."

"You too," Daffodil said, hugging him. "I thought maybe they arrested all the Wingwatchers!"

"No, but most of them," he said. "Including my mom."

Ivy gasped. "Commander Brook? Why?"

"There was a big mandatory meeting today," Forest said. "The Dragonslayer told everyone that there's a price on his head, and the Wingwatchers have been plotting against him for years."

"Whaaat?" said Daffodil.

"What does he mean by 'a price on his head'?" Ivy asked.

"He said the lord of the Indestructible City wants him dead."

"But he doesn't," Ivy said, puzzled. "The lord wants Dad to come work for him — he wants his own dragonslayer. He's sent so many messages about it. If he wanted Dad dead, there have to be easier ways than trying to lure him to the Indestructible City."

Forest spread his hands. "I have no idea, but that's what he said. He said people have been trying to kill him for years, but never succeeded, so the lord started scheming with the Wingwatchers, and finally he sent an assassin to help take him out. After that, the Wingwatchers were going to take over."

"But that's not true!" Daffodil said indignantly. "The Wingwatchers aren't sneaks and murderers! Their conspiracy isn't an assassination plot!" She caught Ivy's startled expression and added, "I mean . . . um . . . if there *were* a conspiracy, and if *I* knew anything about it, which I certainly don't . . ."

"Daffodil!" Ivy said, smacking her shoulder. "What do you know?"

"Well, I . . . might have tricked Violet into telling me a *few* things," Daffodil reluctantly admitted. "Things I really really promised not to tell you. Because you wouldn't want to know! You don't need the stress! was my position on the situation."

"Such as?" Ivy demanded.

Daffodil squirmed for a moment, then covered her face and blurted, "OK, fine! The Wingwatchers wanted to organize a vote. They wanted to see whether the people of Valor might be interested in having a different leader — someone who actually fixed things, paid his or her debts, and never banished people. That's all, though! There was no assassination plot and definitely no conspiracy with some random, faraway lord."

"You could have told me that," Ivy said. "I would have helped you guys. I don't think my dad is a great lord either. Getting him to retire peacefully would be perfect. I mean, speaking of people who don't need the stress. He'd be so much happier without all that responsibility, I think."

"I'm not sure I should be hearing this," Forest interjected. "My mom has been trying to keep me conspiracy-free my whole life."

"Where are Violet and the others?" Ivy asked. "Are they all right?"

"For now," he said. "The Dragonslayer wants to capture the assassin so he can execute them all together."

Daffodil gave a yelp and overbalanced.

"Execute?" Ivy said faintly. *He can't mean that. He wouldn't really* execute *my friends . . . and the other citizens of Valor wouldn't let him . . . would they?*

"What assassin?" Daffodil asked. "Who is he talking about?"

"That new guy," Forest said. "The one who's been wandering around Valor asking lots of questions about the Dragonslayer."

"Oh *no*," Ivy cried. "Leaf isn't an assassin! He's never even been to the Indestructible City!"

Forest raised both of his hands palms up. "He could come back and try to explain that, if you know where he is. But he might be executed on sight."

"Dad's never executed anyone before!" Ivy protested. "What is going on? Isn't anybody trying to stop him?"

"How?" Forest said hopelessly. "He's got the guys with the weapons, and he sounds very logical when he talks about it. You know: He has to stop his enemies! It's part of keeping Valor safe! And so on and so on. I think half the people agree with him and half of them are afraid if they say anything, they'll be accused of being part of the conspiracy." He glanced around. "I mean . . . that's one of the things I'm worried about anyway. I don't see what I can do by myself." He ran his hands down his tunic, as if he was wishing it would change into a less dangerous color.

"We'll think of something," Ivy said. "I should talk to him."

Daffodil shook her head. "Ivy, no. He's not in a listening mood."

"I have to go," Forest said. "I'll try to come back if there's any news."

"Thanks, Forest," Daffodil said, squeezing his hand. "You are doing something, you know. Coming to tell us all this, that was something."

He gave her a wan smile and left.

Ivy considered sneaking into Valor that night, but it began to rain, and she didn't want to leave a trail that could be traced back to Daffodil and Leaf. It rained all that night, while she thought about what she could say to her father, and all the next day. By evening, the rain had invited along some hurricane-style winds, and the roof of the old temple was doing a particularly pathetic job of protecting them.

Leaf and Ivy and Daffodil sat huddled together with their cloaks over their heads, trying to brainstorm, since it was impossible to sleep — although apparently not for Stone, who snored on a blanket nearby. Ivy's feet were cold, even in her boots, and raindrops kept sneaking under the cloaks and smacking her in the face or dripping down her back. This was really not helping with her general feelings of hopelessness. Maybe Forest was right, and there wasn't anything one person could do, or three people, or anybody.

"What if we go to the Indestructible City," Daffodil suggested, "and get the lord to write a letter that says he doesn't know Leaf and isn't plotting with anyone?"

"That would take a long time, getting there and back," Leaf pointed out. "And I'm not sure the Invincible Lord can be trusted either. If we go to him for help, he might use the situation to take over Valor himself, or something worse we haven't even thought of."

"Can we bargain with my dad?" Ivy offered. She took the sapphire out of her cloak pocket and watched it glimmer wetly in the dark. "We could tell him we'd give the sapphire back if he lets everyone go. I'm not sure he likes it enough to agree to that, though."

"And *I* still think you're right and we should give all the treasure back to the dragons," Leaf said.

"I don't even think he likes being lord of Valor," Ivy said. "I think he'd be so much happier if he could just drink and hang out with his friends and tell tall dragon tales all day." She sighed. "I wish the Wingwatchers had pulled off their *actual* conspiracy. Now even if he lets them go, he'll never trust them enough to make a deal with them."

Later that night, the rain finally stopped, and Leaf and Daffodil both fell asleep propped against the wall. Ivy still felt restless, so she got up and walked through the forest to the ruins.

Why does Dad keep hurting people? she wondered, running her hand along one of the blackened walls. *The same thing changed both Dad and Stone — killing the dragon and losing Rose. So why did Stone become all sad and shut down, while Dad took more and more power and started using it to be terrible?*

She sat down on someone's old front step and took out the sapphire. It caught the moonlight like a trapped cobalt spirit, shimmering deep in the gem. She cupped it in both hands, closed her eyes, and rested her forehead on its cold surface.

What do I do? Ivy asked it silently. *How do I save my friends from my dad? How can I stop the dragons? How do I get everyone to stop fighting?*

She wondered if the little gold dragon was as kind as the brown one who'd helped Leaf. *I wish I could get up closer and study it, and find out what it was really like.* She pictured the gold dragon in her head, each sunlit scale and perfect claw.

And then suddenly the dragon was in front of her, and she was standing in a desert.

"Whoa," Ivy yelped, jumping back. Her feet stumbled in the sand as the dragon let out a cry and took a step back, too. They stared at each other for a long moment.

Am I dreaming? Just like that? Ivy wondered. *When did I fall asleep?*

Something moved on the gold dragon's shoulder, peering around her neck.

A person. There was a *person* on the dragon's shoulder, looking back at Ivy. She was about the same age as Ivy's mom, with long tangled dark hair, but there was something familiar about her face. She leaned forward to study Ivy and smiled.

Ivy gasped. *It's Aunt Rose!*

But not the Aunt Rose in the drawing — this Rose was twenty years older.

The dragon took a step toward Ivy and Ivy stepped forward, too. She pointed at her aunt. "Are you real?" she asked. "Are you Rose? Are . . . are you still alive?"

But Rose didn't answer. She patted the dragon's neck and the dragon growled something, flicking its tail at the sapphire in Ivy's hand.

The sapphire . . . What if it was magic? What if it was showing her the little gold dragon wherever she was right now?

Wait — then it might be showing the dragon where *Ivy* was, too — and that she was holding a piece of dragon treasure.

Ivy clutched the sapphire to her chest with a yelp of alarm and her eyes popped open.

She was still in the ruins, alone. A cold, wet gray morning was slowly coalescing around her. There was no desert, no little gold dragon, no Aunt Rose.

And yet, Ivy was sure it had all been real, somehow. She looked down at the sapphire, turning it over in her hands to see if it had any magic words inscribed on it. Nothing that she could see. She tucked it into her belt and ran back to the temple.

"Uncle Stone!" she cried, pelting up the steps and between the columns. She crashed to her knees beside him. "Uncle Stone, wake up. I think Aunt Rose is alive."

CHAPTER 31

LEAF

"Here's what we do," said Ivy. "Steal horses, ride to the desert palace, rescue Aunt Rose. Ride back, bring her into the city of Valor, show everyone that she's still alive. Everyone celebrates! Everyone is thrilled! Dad is *so so* happy that his sister isn't really dead after all, it fixes his whole brain. I say to him, hey, Dad, you don't really want to be lord anymore, do you? And he's in such a good mood, he says, yeah, you're right, let's free the Wingwatchers and let them elect a new lord instead. And then we all live happily ever after! It's such a great plan!"

"That sounds like one of *my* plans," Daffodil objected. "The kind Violet would *heartily* make fun of."

Leaf didn't want to burst Ivy's bubble — her face was all lit up for the first time since seeing the golden dragon, and she was so full of hope. But he couldn't imagine any single part of this plan actually working out.

"Ivy," Stone said, pouring cold tea into a cup. "I know this feeling. Believe me. I had a dream about her, too, remember? I sent myself on a pointless yearlong quest as a result. But it's not possible. She's really dead."

"This wasn't a dream!" Ivy said. "This was magic! Look, in your dream, was she still the teenager you remember?"

"Yes," he said slowly.

"In mine, which wasn't a dream, it was totally a vision, she was twenty years older. The age she really is now! And she was with the golden dragon! In the desert! I think the dragons have her out there!"

Stone handed her the tea and took the sapphire, examining it like a vegetable that might turn out to be poisonous.

"If she's with dragons," he said, "why haven't they eaten her?"

"I don't know," Ivy said. "She was on the dragon's shoulder, as though she rode around on it all the time. Maybe they're keeping her there like, like, like that parakeet Violet's dads had for a while, remember? Or Daffodil's pet rabbit! Maybe the dragons think she's cute."

"Dragons don't keep pets," Stone argued. "Humans are the only species who do that."

Leaf tried to remember whether he'd seen any pets in the mountain palace. He could kind of imagine the little red dragon having a pet, but certainly none of the big scary ones who smashed goats with their talons.

"We have to go find out," Ivy pleaded. "If there's a chance she's in that palace, still alive, don't we have to go see?"

"Rrrrrrrrrrrrrrrrrrrrrrgh," Stone said, burying his head in his hands. "Yes."

"What?" Daffodil cried. "I thought you were talking her out of this madness! I would have said more things if I knew she was convincing *you*. Ivy, what if the dragons don't think *you're* cute and they end up eating you? I mean, obviously *I* think you're too cute to eat, but dragons might not be smart enough to realize that!"

"Also the flaws in every other part of the plan," Leaf said. "(a) Going back into Valor to steal horses, (b) trying to get into the dragon palace, (c) coming *back* to Valor and hoping the Dragonslayer is happy to see you . . . all of these things sound kind of impossible, Ivy."

"I'll go get the horses," Stone said, standing up. He pointed at Ivy as she started to get to her feet. *"Alone."*

"But you can't go to the palace without me," she said. "I'm coming, too. You have to promise you won't go without me."

"Or me," Leaf said. "I'm the only one here who's escaped from a dragon palace before. I can be useful."

"Also me!" Daffodil said. "I'm not at all useful, but I don't want to sit here wondering if you're all dead!"

Stone waved his hand at all of them. "I will get what I can get," he growled, and stomped off into the forest.

"What about the treasure?" Ivy said. "Should we take it with us? Maybe we can exchange it for Rose!"

"I don't think there's any safe way to get it, Ivy," Daffodil pointed out.

That was probably true. They debated it for a while longer, but even Ivy had to agree it was too risky.

"We can take them the sapphire, at least," she said. "Maybe that'll be enough."

By nightfall, Stone still hadn't returned, and Ivy had practically paced a groove around the temple. "We could walk to the palace!" she cried. "Who needs horses? I shouldn't have let him go. It would only take a few days to walk to the palace, right?"

"Through the blistering hot desert," Daffodil pointed out. She was lying on a blanket with her arm over her eyes. "With no water. That would be a very efficient way to die."

"Let's go back to the ruins," Leaf suggested. "Maybe your friend Forest has come back, or maybe we'll see Stone on his way."

"Yes, please!" Daffodil said. "You guys go. When Ivy's the one wearing *me* out, something is seriously wrong with the universe."

Leaf lit a small lantern that Pine had left for them, and he and Ivy set off toward the ruins.

"What do you think about walking to the desert palace?" Ivy asked.

"Let's give Stone a chance to come back with those horses," he suggested. "I think it's pretty hot out there."

"I just feel useless," Ivy said, waving her hands as though she was drawing a picture of all the nothing she was doing. "I don't know how to stop my dad, I don't know how to get the treasure to the dragons, I don't know how to make everyone stop being angry. I feel like the only thing I *can* maybe do is go rescue Aunt Rose. Don't you think that would make everyone feel better?"

I like her, imaginary Wren suddenly chimed in, after days of silence. *She's sort of ridiculous and I am enjoying it. You have my permission to like her, too.*

I wasn't ASKING for your permission, he pointed out.

Ivy led the way through the village to a set of stone stairs that had mostly collapsed. She sat down on one of the steps and he sat on the one below it, setting the lantern down beside them.

"If Aunt Rose were still here, I bet Dad wouldn't be like this," Ivy said. "She seems like someone who wouldn't let him be terrible. I mean, maybe she'd be better at it than I am. Don't you think?"

I wonder if you can stop people from being terrible, if that's who they choose to be, Leaf thought. *Maybe all you can do is be the opposite of terrible, as hard as you can, to balance them out.*

"I've wondered the same thing about Wren," he said. "Would Talisman be different if she had lived? Would she have told everyone the dragonmancers' secrets? Maybe she would have stood up to them, and they wouldn't be in charge anymore."

"Roar roar roargle," said the dragon that stepped out of the shadows right in front of them.

Leaf and Ivy both screamed and jumped off the stairs. All of Leaf's instincts kicked in and he started to run — but when he looked over his shoulder, he saw that the dragon had moved to corner Ivy.

"ROAR roar ROAR!" the dragon shouted. "ROAR!

GROARF!" Ivy tried to dart away and the dragon threw its tail in front of Ivy, tripping her. "ROARITY ROAR ROAR ROAWR!" The dragon leaped over and trapped Ivy between its claws, like a cat with a mouse.

Leaf pelted back toward them, grabbed the lantern, and flung it at the dragon as hard as he could. "Get away from her!" he shouted.

The lamp bounced off the dragon and it roared again, sounding distinctly angrier this time. Leaf's legs were suddenly knocked out from under him, and he landed hard on his back. The dragon picked up Ivy and hopped back a step. It growled at Leaf and then at Ivy, who was struggling violently in its claws.

I'm not going to let this happen. I can fight this dragon. I have to stop her from eating Ivy! Leaf shoved himself back to his feet, trying to catch his breath.

The dragon made a very grumpy noise, stomped over to a tall stone wall nearby, and stuck Ivy up on top of it. Leaf was just picking up a rock to throw when the dragon snatched him up as well. He felt air whoosh by his face dizzily, and then he was suddenly on top of the wall next to Ivy.

It was very tall, too high to jump off without breaking an ankle, and then they'd be easy prey for the dragon to eat. Leaf clambered over to Ivy and put his arms around her.

"That was so much scarier than I expected!" Ivy said, clutching him. "Like, my whole body just went DEATH FROM THE SKY and made me scream and run, even while a little tiny part of my brain went, *oh, amazing, a dragon!* But the scared part won. It's still winning. Why do you think it put us up here?"

"Orgle roargle roarfy growl," the dragon said in a strangely pleasant voice, for a dragon. "Roarble groarf?"

Ivy looked at Leaf, then back at the dragon. "That sounded like a question, didn't it?" she whispered to him.

"Maybe it just wants to talk to us," he said, feeling like that was a HIGHLY optimistic view of the situation.

The dragon picked up a tree branch, set it on fire with a single breath, and stuck it in the ground like a giant torch.

"Oh!" Ivy said, seeing the color of its scales in the firelight. "Leaf, look! It's the golden dragon! The one we saw! The one in my sapphire vision!"

The dragon cupped its front talons together in a bowl shape and rumbled something that also ended in an upward inflection — another question, or the same one.

"She knows I have the sapphire!" Ivy said. "I think she's asking for it, don't you?"

"How would she know that?" he argued.

"Because she saw me holding it! In my magic vision that I totally really had!" Ivy said. "I told you guys it was magic!"

"Isn't it possible she's just been hanging around the village waiting for a human to come along with treasure?" Leaf asked. "Or maybe she's hungry. That could be a sign for food."

"I hardly think a dragon needs *our* help to find food," Ivy said skeptically.

"I'm just saying, if that's not what she's asking for, how is she going to react when you give it to her? What if she gets really mad and sets us on fire for being treasure thieves?"

"Or *maybe* she can help us find Rose and stop the dragons from burning villages," Ivy said.

"It's not her treasure, though, right?" he said. "If we give it to her, we can't give it to the sand dragons."

Ivy hesitated. "She was in the desert when I saw her, though . . . maybe she's working with them."

"ROARBLE roargrr argh roarf," the dragon interjected. She reared up and put her open talons between them, palm up as if waiting for something. "Groar? Owrl? Roar?"

Ivy looked at Leaf for a moment, then reached into her belt and pulled out the sapphire. She dropped it into the dragon's talons, where it suddenly looked a lot smaller.

The dragon made a delighted approving noise and held it up to inspect it in the firelight.

"See, she liked that," Ivy said to Leaf.

"Boarf," the dragon said. "Roarble roarble?"

They both stared at her. "What is she asking now?" Leaf whispered. "Isn't that what she wanted?"

The dragon hummed a little impatiently. She put the sapphire on the ground, picked up another stick, and drew a big circle around it. She walked around the circle, adding stones to it and pretending to pluck things out of the air to put in the circle, too. Then she sat down and waved her wings at it. "Roarble roarble!" she insisted. "ROAR!" She picked up the sapphire and brandished it at them.

"See, I knew she'd be mad," Leaf said. "Now she thinks we have lots of jewels and she wants all of them."

Ivy pointed at the dragon's shoulder. "We gave you the sapphire," she said. "Now where is Aunt Rose? We want her back!"

The dragon tapped her chin thoughtfully, looking them over. Leaf didn't know what to think of that look; it could have been an "ah, well, one jewel is enough, might as well let them go" kind of look. Or it could have been an "I'm going to need some salt and seasoning for these two" kind of look.

Maybe I can save Ivy, he thought. *If I do something just a little bit insane. That's my purpose, isn't it? To save people? That's what I've always wanted, even if I was doing it wrong before.*

"I can get you the treasure," he said to the dragon.

Ivy grabbed his shoulder. "Leaf, what are you doing?"

"I'll go get it!" he said. He pointed at the circle the dragon had drawn on the ground, then at himself and the dragon, who looked extremely curious about all this miming. "Let us go, and I'll come back to give it to you."

Ivy stamped her foot. "Leaf, you can't! We already agreed there's no way to get back into my house!"

"I can try, can't I?" he said. "And if she agrees, then at least you'll be safe."

The dragon growled something in what Leaf was starting to think of as her "friendly" voice. She reached out and gently scooped Leaf off the wall.

"YAAAAH!" he yelped, startled. "Wait! What about Ivy? Get her down, too!"

The dragon set him down and rumbled something, looking very pleased, then patted Ivy on the head.

But she didn't lift her down.

"You have to let Ivy go!" Leaf shouted. He pointed at her and then the forest. "Let Ivy go first, and then I'll go get you the treasure!"

"Roarble roarble roarble," the dragon argued back. She pointed at the forest, too, then waved the sapphire, then pointed at Ivy.

"Oh, come on!" Leaf cried. "I can't leave her here with you!"

"Roar roar roar growl roar," said the dragon, pointing at all the things again, as though he might just be thick.

"I KNOW what you're asking," he said. "I'm just saying no! You have to let her go first!"

"I don't think that's going to work!" Ivy called, cupping her hands around her mouth. "You'll have to go get the treasure. Unless you can convince her to switch me for you."

"No — I'll go," he said. "I just don't really love leaving you alone with a dragon."

"It'll be fine!" she said. "I'll be safer here with her than you will be sneaking back into Valor. We'll make friends. I'll negotiate for Aunt Rose. Listen, the treasure is in the cabinet under the pedestal with the dragon tail on top. The combination is M-I-N-E, mine. Be SUPER CAREFUL, Leaf! Please don't get caught and executed!"

"All right," he said, taking a step back toward the woods. "You be careful, too!"

She waved, and then, hilariously, so did the dragon. Leaf turned and ran into the trees.

Find the treasure, find the treasure, his heart pounded. *Don't get caught. Come back to save Ivy*. He wondered what the dragon would do to her if Leaf did get caught and couldn't come back. Would she get angry and eat Ivy?

He ran faster.

It took him a little while to get his bearings and find Valor, but finally he recognized the hill he'd been on with Stone just a few nights ago. He scrambled back up it, climbing from boulder to boulder, until he reached the hole to Stone's secret escape tunnel.

It looked untouched, half-filled-in just the way they'd left it. Had the guards not found the tunnel? Had they even checked Stone's cave, or had they assumed Leaf escaped some other way?

There was no way for Leaf to know. He dug through the dirt with his hands until the hole was big enough to squeeze into again, and then he crawled back through the tunnel. It was slightly less terrifying this time, now that he'd done it once without suffocating to death.

He reached the tapestry and listened carefully, but there was no sound from the other side. He lifted it and peeked out to be sure — no one in Stone's bedroom. No one in the next cave either, he discovered. And no one guarding the door, when he chanced a glance outside.

Leaf threw one of Stone's cloaks around his shoulders and pulled up the hood so he could hurry through the corridors unnoticed. No one spoke to him; everyone seemed to be moving quickly with their heads down, as though they were all afraid to catch the wrong kind of attention.

He reached the tunnel outside Ivy's caves and hesitated. What if the Dragonslayer was home? He certainly couldn't knock, and there was no back way to sneak in, or Ivy would have told him about it. Leaf hovered in the hallway for a minute, then ducked back around the corner and searched until he found a discarded basket nearby. He crouched beside it, just within sight of Ivy's door, pretending to arrange things inside the basket — a few rocks from the ground and nuts from his pockets, anything to make him look busy if someone came by.

It felt like a painfully long time passed. Leaf kept thinking of Ivy shivering on that wall, waiting for him. *The Dragonslayer's probably asleep*, he thought. *He's probably not coming out until morning. I can't lurk around here all night. But I can't just barge in there either.*

Yes. There were definitely some holes in this plan.

In desperation, he finally walked past the door, knocked quickly, and then flew around the corner to hide.

He heard the door open. "Hello?" said Ivy's mother's voice. "Hello?"

"WHO IS IT?" the Dragonslayer bellowed from inside the cave.

"Nobody, as far as I can tell," she answered. "Strange." She went back inside and closed the door.

So he is there. And not asleep, Leaf thought, pressing his shaking hands together. *What do I do, what do I do?*

Could he draw the Dragonslayer out somehow? With a message?

He wondered whether Ivy's mother would recognize him. They'd only met once, briefly, in the market on Leaf's third day in Valor. She'd been walking with Ivy, and Ivy had introduced them, but her mother had seemed distracted by the choices of vegetables, and their conversation had been short. And lit only by torches. Maybe she wouldn't recognize him.

He didn't have anything to write on, he was running out of time, and he didn't have a choice.

Leaf took a deep breath, pulled up his hood, went back to the door, and tapped on it lightly again. This time he held his ground as footsteps approached.

"WHO IS IT NOW?" the Dragonslayer's voice shouted from a back room as the door swung open.

Ivy's mother was standing there, looking at Leaf in surprise.

Oh no. Maybe she does recognize me. He braced himself to run, ducked his head, and said, in as old a voice as he could muster, "Trouble down by the lake, ma'am. They're asking for the Dragonslayer to come as quick as he can. Maybe, um — maybe both of you better come, actually."

Her eyebrows slowly lifted, and she looked at him for a moment in silence.

She's going to grab me. She's going to call him and hand me over and I'll have failed Ivy completely.

"Of course," she said instead. "I will make *sure* he comes.

Right away." She looked into Leaf's eyes again, then closed the door.

He let out a breath and went back to his hiding spot, around the corner in the opposite direction from the lake, bending over his basket. He heard shouting coming from inside Ivy's cave ("Why ME?" *crash crash crash* "You didn't ASK?") and felt guilty for putting her mother in the path of the Dragonslayer's anger.

After a few moments, the door slammed open and shut, and Leaf heard the Dragonslayer storming away, muttering curses to himself.

Had Ivy's mother gone with him? Or was she still inside? Maybe she'd gone to bed . . .

"Come on," said a quiet voice above him, making him jump. Ivy's mother was standing there, beckoning.

"Um — I —" he stammered.

"It must be important, for you to risk coming back here," she said.

He nodded and followed her into the cave. She shut the door and turned to watch him. "You don't have long," she said. "He's fast when he's angry, and he'll be very angry he was lied to. Is Ivy all right?"

"Yes, ma'am," Leaf said, crossing quickly to the pedestal. He folded the cloth over the box and saw the cabinet Ivy had mentioned. "She's safe. But I need to bring this to her for her to stay safe — it would take a long time to explain." He crouched and fiddled the combination to M-I-N-E. The door popped open, and Ivy's mother gasped.

There was *so much treasure* inside. Leaf had no idea how he was going to carry all this. Was this everything they'd stolen from the palace? Surely the Dragonslayer must have spent some of it over the years.

Ivy's mother appeared behind him, holding a canvas bag. She knelt down and started helping him transfer the treasure into it.

"It's so beautiful," she said. "I asked him so many times if I could see it, but he always said it was hidden far away, somewhere safe. I had no idea it was right here all this time." She lifted out a blue stone statue of a dragon. "I just wanted to see it, just once. I guess he didn't trust me, same as every-one else."

Leaf didn't know what to say to that, and she didn't say anything else as they finished filling the bag. She closed the door on the empty cabinet and reset the combination lock, then folded the cloth back over it.

"Hurry back to Ivy," she said. "Tell her I love her, and that it's not safe to come back yet."

He wanted to ask her what was happening with the Wingwatchers and what she thought they should do about the Dragonslayer, but there wasn't time. The bag was heavy on his shoulder as he checked out the door and found the corridor empty.

"Thank you," he said to Ivy's mother.

"Stay safe," she said, and closed the door behind him.

He hid the bag under his cloak as he hurried through the

halls, but he made it back to Stone's cave without running into anyone. He ducked inside, ran to the tapestry, and dragged the bag into the tunnel with him.

I'm coming, golden dragon. Please don't eat Ivy before I get there.

CHAPTER 32

IVY

Ivy and the golden dragon regarded each other. After a long moment, the dragon said something that sounded very polite to Ivy, at least as far as a bunch of roars and growls could sound polite.

"I, too, find you very interesting," Ivy said. "I wish I knew what you were saying. And I wish *you* could tell me where Aunt Rose is."

"Roar roar growl roar roar," the dragon said, in the same conversational tone.

"Aunt ROSE!" Ivy tried shouting. Maybe the key was to be loud and dragonlike. "Where is the PERSON who was on your SHOULDER in my VISION?" She pointed at the spot where Rose had been sitting. "ROOOOOOOOOOOOOOSE! Where is she?"

The dragon tilted her head, as though she suddenly understood. "Roar? Roar roargrr roar?"

"Yes," Ivy said firmly. "I am looking for Rose!"

"Roarble roarble," said the dragon with a shrug, and she suddenly reached out and seized Ivy in her talons. Ivy screamed instinctively and the dragon jumped, nearly dropping her, then gave her a disgruntled look.

To Ivy's utter and complete astonishment forever, the dragon lifted her up and set Ivy on her shoulder. There was a dip between her spine and her wings that was just the right size for a human to kneel in, with her arms around the dragon's neck.

"What is happening right NOOOOOOOOOOOOOW," Ivy shrieked as the dragon leaped into the sky.

They were flying. They were FLYING! Ivy was flying ON A DRAGON!

Ivy hugged the dragon's neck, overcome with awe. They were up so high, surrounded by stars. The mountains went on forever, and there over to the west was the desert, and that went on forever, too. The world was so, so much bigger than she'd realized.

It was freezing up in the night sky, with the wind whipping Ivy's hair all around her face, but the golden dragon's scales were warm, like lying on sunbaked rocks in the summertime.

"I think I love you," Ivy said to the dragon, resting her cheek on the dragon's neck. They soared over the forest, over the hillside that hid all the entrances to Valor. The dragon glided in a wide circle, as if this was the simplest evening stroll for her. As if she was just popping down to Violet's cave and back, when in fact she was taking Ivy three times as far as Ivy had ever been.

Valor is just one city in this enormous world, Ivy thought.

We're just one tiny group of people. All their heavy, insurmountable problems were like dandelion seeds up here; Ivy felt like she could blow them away with one breath.

She didn't know how long they spent flying — later it seemed like a dream. But at some point the dragon tilted its wings and arrowed down toward the blackened hole in the forest; the ruins got closer and closer, and then the dragon landed gracefully, and there was Leaf.

He leaped back with a yelp of fright. "Ivy! I thought she'd taken you and eaten you and — IVY! YOU'RE ON A DRAGON! YOU'RE SITTING ON THE DRAGON IVY I THINK SHE MIGHT NOTICE!"

"She put me there!" Ivy said, sliding down the dragon's wing to the ground. The warm scales moved away from her and her legs felt wobbly. "It was her idea! Leaf, she took me flying! I have no idea why!"

"That sounds very unsafe!" he cried. "I don't know why I'm shouting. But it was alarming to come back and find you gone. I can't believe you rode a dragon!"

"It was everything, Leaf! I want to do it every day for the rest of my life!"

The dragon cleared its throat, reached over Ivy, and seized the bag that Leaf was holding.

"Oh," Ivy said as the dragon carried it over to the torch. "Oh, wow, you got it!"

"Your mom helped me," he said. "She says she loves you and not to come back yet."

Yet, Ivy thought with a thrill of relief. *That means she thinks we can sometime. And she helped Leaf— I wouldn't have guessed she'd do that. Oh, Mom, I love you, too.*

The dragon emptied the treasure into an enormous glittering pile of gold, with gems the size of fists, each one more than enough for an entire family to become rich. Ivy remembered how her father talked about the treasure and how much he loved it. But he didn't *need* all this. It made him powerful, but it also made him paranoid and suspicious and furious all the time.

Ivy watched the dragon sort through the gems, carefully at first, and then faster, with a look on her face that Ivy would have called distress if she'd been a human.

She's looking for something specific, Ivy realized. *Something she really needs.*

Maybe all the dragons are looking for it, and that's why they burn villages — not for vengeance, but because they need it back.

The golden dragon whipped around and roared at them.

"That's all of it!" Leaf cried. "It's all there, I promise!"

She roared again and lashed her tail, smoke rising from her snout. "ROOOOOAAARRR roargrrrrROARGRRROAR! ROAAARGH?"

"We're sorry?" Ivy said. "Maybe . . . someone else has what you're looking for?"

"GRRRRMPH," said the dragon, sitting down and glaring at the treasure.

"She seems less thrilled than I expected," Leaf said to Ivy.

"I can see that," Ivy said.

The dragon started talking to herself in little growls and

grumbles, as though she was listing all the things wrong with stupid treasure-stealing humans. Or possibly she was trying to figure out where else to look. Or she might have been debating whether to eat them, since they'd disappointed her so much; Ivy couldn't really tell.

Ivy edged closer until she was right at the dragon's feet. She reached out and patted one of the warm golden talons. "It'll be all right, big scary dragon. Don't be mad."

The green eyes looked down at her like the dragon actually understood her. *We can communicate with dragons*, Ivy thought. *If we try harder. They're not all mindless hungry monsters. At least some of them are like this. If dragons like this can convince other dragons to stop eating us . . . maybe one day we can all be safe.*

The dragon said something else, possibly to itself.

"I'd still like to know about Aunt Rose," Ivy said. She pointed to the dragon's shoulder again. "What happened to the human? Where is she? Can we have her back?"

"Roarmorgrrroarble," the dragon said. She turned and swept the treasure back into the sack, including the sapphire. Then she made a little bow to Leaf and Ivy, spread her wings, and said something else in her growly way.

"Wait — don't go," Ivy said. "This is an enormous breakthrough for human-dragon relations! And you have to help me find Rose!"

The dragon patted Ivy's head and then Leaf's, and then she leaped into the sky and soared away, carrying the treasure sack in her talons.

"Wait!" Ivy cried, waving her arms. "Come back!"

The dark sky swallowed up the little golden dragon, and in a moment, she was gone.

Ivy looked at Leaf. Leaf looked at Ivy.

"So, wait," he said. "Did . . . that dragon just . . . fly away with all our treasure?"

"Um," said Ivy. "Yes. But! Maybe she's going to give it back to the sand dragons?"

"She went that way," Leaf observed, pointing east. "The desert is in the other direction."

"True," Ivy said. "True. Concerning, I'll admit."

"Do we think she's coming back with your aunt?"

Ivy gazed up at the empty sky. "Maybe?"

But the dragon did not return. Not that night, not the following day. Ivy's new best friend, her best chance at establishing peaceful human-dragon coexistence, had apparently not understood one single word that she'd said, and had flown away forever.

"That's just fine," Ivy said to Daffodil. "Who needs her? I'll find a *different* dragon to change the world with me. No problem."

"At least you got to fly!" Daffodil said indignantly. "SO unfair! I would *obviously* like to go flying, too, all you friendly dragons out there! Come on!"

Stone appeared next to the temple — very literally, suddenly materializing out of thin air about an arm's length away from Leaf.

"YIIIIIIEEEE!" Leaf yelped in alarm. "What — how —"

"Oh, your invisibility necklace!" Ivy said. "I forgot about that! Did you use it inside Valor?"

"Did you see anyone?" Daffodil asked. "Like Violet or Foxglove?"

He shook his head. "Got horses," he said. "Ready to go?"

Ivy scrambled to her feet. "Now? Yes! Now! OK! I'm ready. Oh, wow, we're going to a dragon palace! Uncle Stone, wait until you hear what happened to us last night!"

Stone stopped Daffodil as she jumped up, too. "I could only get three," he said. "Sorry — but a mob of humans showing up at the gate probably wouldn't go well anyway."

"I'm not a MOB," Daffodil objected. "Ivy's my best friend! Wherever she goes, I'm going, too!"

"Violet's your best friend, too, though," Ivy said, taking one of her hands. "She needs someone here in case things go badly in Valor. You and Forest might have to rescue her or something."

"Yes!" Daffodil whispered, her eyes lighting up. "A heroic rescue, and then she'll have to be grateful to me for forever! I am so up for that!"

Ivy hugged her. "We'll be back as soon as we can. Hopefully with Aunt Rose. Stay safe."

"Um, *you* stay safe," Daffodil said. "You're the one charging off into the dragons' jaws."

But as she and Leaf and Stone galloped into the desert, Ivy thought of the golden dragon again, and she felt just a bit less terrified.

They're not all monsters, she reminded herself. *That means we have a chance. A chance to save Rose, a chance to bring her back and save our friends, maybe even a chance to communicate with them.*

Whatever was waiting for them at the palace of the desert queen, they could face it.

After all, Ivy told herself, *now I'm a girl who's ridden a dragon.*

CHAPTER 33

The palace was in an uproar, and Wren, for the first time, really did not know what to do.

The dragons fighting in the desert had ended up inside the palace and there was a lot of hubbub and commotion and then some more fighting, and finally several dragons had flown away, but then a very short time later more dragons had arrived, and one of them was apparently the queen everyone had been waiting for, which made absolutely all the dragons FREAK OUT.

On the plus side, in all the chaos and commotion, everyone seemed to have forgotten about Sky, who was still chained up in General Sandstorm's room. Sandstorm had been saving him to be a special gift from the general alone, so nobody else apparently remembered or cared that there was a weird little dragon waiting to be handed over.

For now . . . but Wren was sure someone would remember him eventually. That prince, perhaps, or one of the kitchen dragons who had been assigned to bring him food. Nobody showed up for the whole day after Queen Burn arrived, but at some point someone would go, "oh, right, wasn't there a gift for the queen around here somewhere?" and maybe also, "hey, *I* can take credit for that present now!" And then they'd come for Sky, and her chance would be gone.

"His body is just lying out there!" Wren said, pacing back and forth on the windowsill.

"They'll bring it inside the walls eventually, won't they?" Sky asked.

"But when?" She picked up one of the general's sparkly pebbles from his collection and threw it as hard as she could at the stupid endless sand. "What if they pick up his body, see the key, remember you, and come straight here? Or what if they decide to burn all the bodies out there and the key melts along with everything else?"

"Yeeeesh," Sky said with a shiver.

"I don't know what this tribe does with its corpses," Wren said. She put her hands on her hips. "I have to get to it. I'll have to climb over the wall or sneak through the gate." But she was worried about leaving Sky alone for however long it would take for her to do that. If someone remembered him while she was gone, he could vanish into the tower, or somewhere else in the palace.

Or worse. Wren remembered what the general had said about killing and stuffing her friend. She wasn't thinking about it; she couldn't think about that.

"I wish I had fire," Sky said disconsolately. "Maybe I could burn up these chains if I did."

Wren climbed down from the window and went to hug him. Sky hadn't said anything about wishing he had fire in years. She wished she could chop off the heads of every dragon who'd made him feel bad about it again.

"They wouldn't have left you in chains that fire could melt if you had fire," she pointed out reasonably. "So don't even think about it."

"Can we break them some other way?" Sky whacked his wrist cuff into the stone wall and winced.

They tried everything. Wren found a large knife in Sandstorm's things and tried to pry one of the links open, but she only succeeded in nearly impaling herself. She jabbed several pointy things into the keyhole to see if she could pick the lock, but none of them worked.

By nightfall, the chain was still on, and the body of General Sandstorm was still out in the desert.

"Maybe that human could help you," Sky said. "The one who lives here."

Wren rubbed her eyes, thinking about that. She didn't like the idea of asking a human for help — but then again, Rose wasn't like other humans. Wren would have to tell her about Sky . . . but if anyone could understand being friends with a dragon, it was Rose.

"I'll see if I can find her," Wren said. "Good idea, Sky." He looked so delighted with himself, she couldn't resist hugging him again.

Of course, it wasn't the easiest thing, finding another small human in a palace this size. Wren searched for part of the night, and then decided to at least try scaling the giant wall from one of the empty courtyards.

"Ow!" She leaped back with a hiss. Sharp spikes and glass were embedded in the wall all the way to the top. Its height wasn't the only thing that was human-proof about it.

"Sorry, I should have warned you," Rose said, appearing from the shadows. "It's pretty awful, isn't it? The new queen here — the one who took over after the one my brother killed — *really* hates humans. *I* can't even climb these walls, and climbing was always my thing."

She ripped a strip of cloth off the bottom of her pants and took one of Wren's hands, wrapping the bandage around it with no particular skill or gentleness. *She hasn't taken care of another human in a long time*, Wren thought. *Something we have in common.*

"I'm fine," Wren said, pulling her hand back and rewrapping the bandage herself. "What were all those dragons fighting about earlier today?"

"Wasn't it exciting?" Rose said. "I mean, I missed a lot of it because my dragon put me in a room and tried to make me stay there. But I eventually found a place to watch some of the action."

"And?" Wren said. "Who was attacking?"

Rose lifted her hands, palms up. "Who knows? Other desert dragons, for some reason. I think they came to get this one prisoner, because they flew off with her."

"The one in the tower?" Wren asked. "Who was always roaring about killing everyone?"

"No," Rose said, squinting at her again. "The one who arrived two days ago, who was little and cute. I mean, for a dragon. She had sunshine-yellow scales, kind of golden, and she looked a little bit like a sand dragon, but with no tail barb. I kept her company in the tower for a night. Poor little thing, she was so scared. I'm glad she got away."

"I don't think I saw her," Wren said. She realized she was walking back toward Sky without even thinking about it. It made her nervous to have left him alone for so long.

"The other prisoner left, too, though," Rose said, falling into step beside her. "They're both gone. Maybe the dragons who attacked wanted both of them? But they went in different directions. I don't know, it was confusing, but the queen was absolutely FURIOUS."

"What did she say?" Wren asked.

Rose looked at her sideways. "Um . . . ROOOOOOOOAR, and by the way ROAR and oh, wait, she also said, ROOOAR ROOAR ROOAR."

Wren couldn't help laughing. She didn't know how Rose had lived with dragons all this time and not picked up *some* of their language, but that was still pretty hilarious.

"So what are you up to?" Rose asked. "Did you slay your dragon? And now it's time to go?"

"Sort of. Yes and no," Wren said. They walked for a moment, and then Wren realized from the expectant look on Rose's face that she was waiting for more of an answer. "Yes, he's dead," she clarified. "But I need the key he's wearing, and his body is out in the desert."

"Oh!" Rose said. "You should have told me that in the first place! I know where there are a lot of keys. My dragon keeps copies of all the keys in the castle around his neck."

Wren stopped and faced her. "He does?" Her mind was racing. Rose must be talking about Prince Smolder — he *did* have a lot of keys clanking around his neck.

"Sure." Rose pushed her hair back. "What does it look like?"

"I can get it, if you tell me where to find him," Wren said.

"But I can get it way more easily!" Rose said. "Come on, I haven't had a quest in years. I can be so helpful!"

Wren was surprised to realize that she believed her. Rose *could* be helpful.

What is this weird feeling? she thought. *Like . . . being able to rely on someone else? Believing they will not betray you? Someone other than Sky?*

First Murderbasket, now Rose. Am I making . . . friends?

She kind of wanted to laugh at herself, and she kind of wanted to go build a snail shell of her own to hide in for a while.

"Sure . . . but maybe you don't have to," Wren said. "Would you say Prince Smolder is a pretty reasonable dragon?" They stepped back into the kitchens, where only a pair of older dragons were still awake, preparing breakfast for tomorrow at the far end of the room. The dragons didn't look up at the small patter of feet scurrying along the walls.

Sky had said the prince was less hostile than the other dragons in the palace. And Wren herself thought Smolder seemed different from Sandstorm — not amused by the loudmouth dragon either. Perhaps she could bargain with him. Or wave her sword at him, if all else failed.

"Who?" Rose asked.

"Prince Smolder, your dragon," Wren said impatiently. "Unless there's some other dragon around here with lots of keys around his neck."

Rose pulled her to a stop and dragged her behind one of the baskets of lemons. "You did not just guess a name like that!" she cried. "Is that real? Is his name really Prince Smolder?"

"How can he be your dragon if you don't even know his name?" Wren demanded.

"I've been calling him Ember all this time!" Rose said. "We sort of traded names at the beginning. He pointed to a picture of coals burning low in a fireplace . . . I guess he could have meant Smolder. I thought it was Ember!"

"It's Smolder," Wren said. She'd confirmed that with Sky, and also learned a few new dragon words like *weirdling* and *general*. Sky had picked up a lot more Dragon while he was with the SandWing soldiers, although some of it was language that Wren did not care for.

"You *do* understand the dragons!" Rose said. "How is that possible? I've lived with them for twenty years and I've only figured out a few words! How old are you, fourteen? Where did you learn it?"

Do I trust her, or don't I? Wren asked herself. She'd always always kept Sky a secret — but if she wanted Rose's help, she had to take a chance.

"I have a dragon of my own, too," Wren confessed. "His name is Sky, and he's chained up in Sandstorm's room. I'm trying to set him free before someone gives him to the queen. Sandstorm said she might kill him and stuff him."

"Oh!" Rose said, her hands flying to her face. "Poor little dragon! She really might, she's so scary. But we'll save him, Wren. Don't worry. You have me now."

"Could you take me to Smolder?" Wren asked. "Do you think he'd give the key to me if I ask nicely?"

"*Ask* him?" Rose said, clutching her head. "You can *speak* it, too?"

"I mean," Wren said, "not *well*. I always mix up my grr-roars and my grrawrs."

"Good heavens," Rose said. "You do sound like them. Smolder would probably have a heart attack if you suddenly appeared speaking his language. He doesn't exactly *love* surprises. Or change. Listen, I'll get you that key right now, I promise. But can you please please stay and teach me Dragon?"

"Oh, no, I can't," Wren said, alarmed. "That would take forever! We need to escape in a hurry as soon as we possibly can. Sky is in danger every moment he's in this palace."

"Teach me anything," Rose pleaded. "I can help you both hide for an extra day — even one day would be so helpful! Just teach me how to say 'Smolder, stop putting me in places I can't get out of.' Or 'Smolder, I want a tangerine today, not another boiled fish.' Ooh, or 'Smolder, it is *unreasonable* that *any creature* should snore *quite as loudly* as you do.'"

"I could try to teach you a little," Wren said, rubbing her forehead. "If I knew that Sky was safe."

"I'll get the key," Rose promised. "Describe it to me and I'll go get it right now, and then we'll hide and you can teach me for however long you can stay."

Wren's instinct was still to try to get the key herself. But if Rose could get the key as easily as she thought she could, it would be the fastest way to save Sky . . . and meanwhile Wren could stay with him to keep him safe.

I could teach her a little bit before we go.

One human. I just have to trust this one.

"All right," Wren said. "Let's do it."

CHAPTER 34

IVY

The palace of the desert dragons was the biggest anything Ivy had ever seen: bigger than the entire area covered by the old village ruins, bigger than all the underground tunnels and rooms of Valor put together.

It LOOMED. That was a word Daffodil had always found hilarious, but it was exactly the right one for what this palace was doing. LOOMING out of the sand in the moonlight like it was planning to squash any approaching humans beneath its giant talons.

"It looks different," Stone said. They'd reined in the horses on top of a dune, far enough away that Stone hoped they'd blend in with the cacti, if any dragons were watching from the towers.

Also, this was as far as the horses would go. Even Ivy could smell the dragon fire and iron scent of blood in the air; it made the horses skitter and stamp their hooves. She slid off and helped her uncle tie them to one of the tall, multi-armed cactus plants.

"Different how?" Leaf asked him.

"From the last time I was here," Stone said. He nodded at the palace. "There's an extra wall now. Bigger, higher. I'm guessing that's exactly why they built it — to keep us out, if we ever tried coming back."

"That seems fair," Ivy said. "We build stronger defenses against them all the time. And you did kill their queen."

You, not my dad. That still felt strange, like her mind couldn't quite fit anyone else into the word *Dragonslayer.*

She wished they had the treasure. The plan was to sneak into the palace, but if they got caught, she would have liked to have something to offer the dragons. Something to distract them from the grand idea of eating them all.

"So how are we going to get inside?" Leaf asked. He was looking at Ivy, but Stone answered him.

"I'll go in alone," he said, pulling the long silvery-black chain out of his pocket. "With this." He looped it over his neck and disappeared from view.

"Oh, no you don't," Ivy said, tackling the spot where he'd been. She collided with something heavy and warm that went "oof!" and toppled over.

"Ivy, GET OFF," Stone growled.

"Take that off first," she said. "So we can make sure you don't run away."

"All right, all right." He reappeared, holding the necklace in his fist. Ivy stood up, but stayed near him.

"You can't go in by yourself," she said.

"Why not?" he demanded.

"Because we want to go with you!" Ivy said. She was not going to get *this close* to a dragon's lair and not go inside!

"And because we can help," Leaf added.

That, too. "Besides, we might find Rose and you might miss something," she added.

"I can hunt through a giant palace just as well as you can," Stone said. "Better, because there is one of me, I am quiet, unlike you, and *I* am invisible."

"If you go in there alone and invisible," Ivy said, "we are just going to follow you. Together and uninvisible."

Stone's jaw worked in silence for a moment. "No," he said, and he leaned forward to drape the glittering chain over Ivy's neck. She looked down, surprised, and saw that she'd vanished. She could see right through her feet to the sand underneath.

"Wait, no," she said. "I didn't mean to take this. You keep it." She started to take it off and he stepped back, waving his hands.

"If you insist on coming," he said, "then you *have* to wear that. For me, Ivy. I'm not losing another family member to this place."

She let go of the chain with a sigh. She recognized this stubbornness. They could stand here arguing all night, or they could each take a half step sideways and move on.

"Well, then, let me scout ahead," she said. She looped the extra length of chain around her shoulders a few more times. "We'll get as close as we can, and then I'll check out the gate."

They ran lightly down the dunes, closer and closer to the strangely silent palace. Ivy got a fright when she looked up and saw dozens of dragons staring down at them — but after a momentary heart attack, she realized they were not alive. Those were dragon heads, defeated enemies mounted on spikes at the top of the walls.

Remember that for Daffodil, she thought. That was the kind of gruesome detail Daffodil would love.

She wished Violet were here, too — Violet would definitely be able to think of a clever way to get them inside the palace.

Stone and Leaf stopped a few lengths away from the wall and lay down behind a wave of sand. Ivy ran on ahead toward the gate, which was as tall and thick as the walls, and flanked by two enormous statues of dragons roaring.

A pair of dragon guards stood outside the gate, twitching and stamping their feet. They kept looking back at the palace as though they were more afraid of what might come from there than they were of anything out in the desert.

Ivy crouched beside one of the statues and watched them carefully. She noticed that they held their wings tense and high, and they weren't speaking to each other. In fact, if she had to guess, she'd say they were in a fight, or at least very close to angry with the other one. They had all the signs she'd seen in her father, or when Violet and Daffodil were about to have a serious argument — the way one narrowed his eyes, the coiled flicker of the other's tail, the way one hunched her shoulders away from the other and quivered with rage when he coughed.

Could she use that? Could she take her peacemaking skills and reverse them?

Silently she reached down and scooped sand and pebbles into the pockets of her cloak. She climbed as high as she could get on the statue, then took out a handful of sand and blew it into the face of the dragon on the opposite side.

"ROARGH!" the dragon snapped, sneezing and shaking its head. It snarled something grumpy at the closer guard, who growled back. They turned away from each other, glaring out at the desert.

Ivy took another handful of sand and did it to the closer dragon this time. As he whipped around to snarl at his partner, she threw a rock at the other dragon's ear as hard as she could.

The guards started snarling furiously at each other. Each time one started to turn away, Ivy threw a rock to keep the fight going. Soon the dragons were face-to-face, hissing and lashing their tails. One of them roared something, turned to unlock the gate, wrenched it open, and stomped inside.

To get a different dragon to guard in his place, Ivy guessed. He'd left the gate ajar behind him, as though he planned to return or send someone back in a moment.

She leaped down from the statue and ran back to Stone and Leaf. "I know what we can do," she whispered, making them both jump with her disembodied voice. "Come, quickly!" She unwound the chain from around her shoulders, then draped one end around Leaf's head and the other around Stone's, with her in the middle. The chain was long enough to encircle all of them — and make them all invisible.

Arm in arm, they raced back to the gate. It was still ajar, but they could hear shuffling and muttering in the courtyard beyond. A new dragon guard would be there soon.

Ivy pushed Leaf ahead of her through the gate and they bundled into the wide-open space on the other side. A soldier was stomping toward them, so they had to scurry out of the way as fast as they could. Ivy thanked the universe that the dragon was too sleepy and grouchy to notice their footprints in the sand.

She wished they could stop for a moment to stare around the courtyard — she wanted a closer look at the obelisk monument in the center. But Stone had moved ahead of them now, making a beeline for the palace doors. With the chain still linking them together, she and Leaf had to hurry to keep up with him.

They stepped onto the marble floor of the old palace, between billowing white curtains, and Ivy looked up, up, up to the dome overhead. A mosaic of jeweled tiles glittered back at her, reflecting the moons and the torches in opal and flame. In the deserted room, Stone paused to resettle the chain around only Ivy. "So you can run if you need to," he whispered.

They crept through halls where dragons slept beside

overturned tables, with half-eaten antelopes and spilled flagons of agave nectar scattered around them. They avoided the small rooms where they could hear pairs or trios of dragons playing games with tiny bones or hissing secrets to one another in the dark of night. They climbed long flights of stairs with dragon eyes glaring down at them from the tapestries, and they tiptoed past a vast throne room where a dragon glowered alone over a giant map.

The palace was so big, Ivy was starting to think they'd have to find a place to hide and stay for several days so they could search every corner of it. She could see the moons slipping across the sky every time they passed a window. It would be morning before long.

They went down a tunnel and found themselves suddenly in a huge kitchen. Copper pots and pans hung from the ceiling, and ominous-looking jars lined the shelves all along one side of the room. Ivy saw something she thought was pears right next to something else that looked like eyeballs. *Yeeergh. I pity the cook who mixes those two up.*

The room seemed empty, so they set out across the floor to the far doorway — but the room was not empty. A dragon was hunched over one of the counters, taking notes on a scroll, so absorbed and quiet that they didn't notice her until they were out in the open and she suddenly looked up with a hiss.

Ivy leaped forward and threw the extra length of chain around Leaf's neck. He vanished as the dragon darted toward them, but before Ivy could reach Stone to make him invisible, too, the dragon swooped him up in her talons.

"Oh no," Ivy whispered, clutching Leaf's arm.

"GRRRROAR!" the dragon shouted. She shook Stone a little bit and waved her wings at the kitchen around her, roaring some more.

Ivy half expected her to throw Stone into one of the jars, or set him on fire on the spot. But instead the dragon tossed him in a net bag, hooked the bag around her shoulders, and stormed out of the kitchen.

"Quick!" Ivy whispered, nudging Leaf. They raced after the dragon, who was muttering and growling to herself as she charged through the halls. Around a few corners, across a courtyard, and up a few steps onto a roofed terrace lined with mirrored mosaics. Here the dragon stopped at a door covered in small jewel-colored tiles and banged on it furiously.

Leaf and Ivy caught up as the dragon waited for a response. They crept close enough to see Stone, upside down in the bag and struggling to wrench one of the holes bigger.

The dragon pounded on the door again, and it suddenly flew open.

"ROARGRAWRARGRROARF!" the dragon holding Stone shouted at the dragon in the doorway. The new one was a sleek, sand-colored dragon with black diamond patterns on his scales and a ring of keys around his neck. He blinked at the other dragon with sleepy bewilderment.

She growled something else and pushed past him into the room beyond. Ivy and Leaf sprinted over the tiles and skidded inside, into a lavishly furnished suite of rooms where everything looked expensive. Silk tapestries hung from the walls, most of them depicting dragon faces or dragons in flight over the desert. Emerald-green pillows were scattered across the woven rugs and low couches. A warm glow lit the room from bejeweled lamps in the wall sconces.

The first dragon brandished the bag with Stone in it and waved it at the key-ring dragon. "GRRR ROAR ROARF!" she shouted, pointing at her hapless human captive.

"Hmmm?" said the sleepy dragon with all the keys. "Roargrawf?" He gave a puzzled shrug and pointed to a large pile of pillows, surrounded by scraps of paper with drawings all over them.

The corner was so cluttered, it took Ivy a moment to see what he was pointing at. But then it moved, standing up on the pillows and tilting its head, and she gasped.

It was Rose, unmistakably Rose from the sketch — Rose, twenty years older, with longer hair, but with the same defiant spark in her eyes. She looked exactly the way she had in Ivy's sapphire vision. Ivy couldn't believe it. It *was* real and she *was* right and somehow Rose was actually, completely alive.

The dragon from the kitchen saw her and nearly jumped out of its skin. It flung the net bag away from itself as though it had just discovered it was holding a poisonous spider. Stone crashed into one of the pillows with an "ooof!"

The two dragons started arguing, but Rose sprang off her pillow and ran over to Stone. She pulled the net bag off of him and turned him over to see his face.

"No way!" she cried, her eyes lighting up.

"Rose!" Stone cried. He tried to sit up and reach for her. "Rose, it — it can't be. *Rose*." He burst into tears and covered his face. She knelt to wrap her arms around him.

The dragons finally noticed what the humans were doing. The one from the kitchen growled something in a warning voice and stalked out of the room again. The other one shut the door and regarded Rose skeptically.

Rose looked up at him and growled something that sounded like the language the dragons had been speaking. The dragon made a low chuckling kind of noise.

Ivy gasped. Could Rose *speak Dragon*?

Rose looked around in surprise, and Ivy remembered that she was invisible. She took a step closer to the reunited siblings. Beside her, she could feel Leaf's warm arm brushing hers, but he was silent, and she couldn't see his face to guess what he was feeling.

"Why isn't that dragon eating us?" Stone asked, lifting his head and grabbing Rose's hands. "Are you in danger?"

"Not at all," Rose said with a little laugh. "This is my dragon, Prince Smolder."

"*Your* dragon?" Stone echoed.

"Well, he thinks I'm his human," Rose said. "It's basically the same thing in the end."

"Why didn't the other one eat me?" Stone asked.

Rose laughed again. "I *think* she thought you were me. She's driven me out of her kitchen more than once, and I think she's also yelled at Smolder about keeping me away from her food. She thinks I'm a mouse, basically, who's going to leave holes in all her cheese. I mean, fair, I do actually do that, sometimes. Anyway, so she saw you, thought you were me, brought you over here to yell at Smolder, and then discovered that I was already here. Which meant she'd picked up a wild human, which apparently gave her quite a fright."

Ivy couldn't contain herself any longer. She dragged Leaf over to crouch beside them. "What did you say to him?" she whispered. "Were you speaking Dragon?"

Rose jumped and twisted around to search the room with her eyes. "Um," she said. "Stone? Did you just hear another human voice?"

"There are two others with me," Stone said. "Can you make that dragon go away?"

Rose stood up, put her hands on her hips, and said something bossy-sounding to the dragon. He laughed again and pointed at Stone. She shook her head, stamped her foot, and repeated herself.

Still laughing and shaking his head, Prince Smolder sauntered out of the room and closed the door behind him.

Ivy whipped off the chain. "Oh my gosh! You do speak Dragon!"

"Not really," Rose said ruefully. "I only know a few phrases, and apparently my pronunciation is 'abominable.' Also, I'm pretty sure Smolder thinks I'm just an adorable mimic. He keeps *laughing* at everything I try to say! So I think I told him to get me some dried apricots, but we'll see what he actually comes back with. Who are you, by the way?"

"I'm your niece," Ivy said. "I'm Ivy."

"Not my daughter," Stone said as she turned to him. He looked a lot more relaxed with the dragon out of the room. "Heath's."

Rose's eyebrows shot up and she laughed. "Seriously? Heath had kids? Who was silly enough to marry him?"

"Do you remember Lark?" Stone said. "Her. And just one kid, just Ivy."

"Aw, Lark," Rose said. "She could have done so much better."

"Heath is the lord of the town now," Stone said with a shrug. "And he's the famous Dragonslayer. It doesn't get much better than that."

Rose snorted. "You know what I mean. So, wow. I have a niece! Nice to meet you, Ivy. And who's this?"

"I'm Leaf." He held out his hand to shake hers.

"This is wild," Rose said, grinning from ear to ear. "I haven't seen another human being in twenty years, and suddenly it's like the palace is full of them."

"We've come to rescue you!" Ivy said.

"That's right," Stone said, taking one of Rose's hands in both of his. "I would have come years ago if I'd known you were still alive, Rose. I thought you died that night. I don't know how you've survived in this palace for so long — but we can take you home now."

Rose looked from Stone to Ivy and back. "But I don't need rescuing," she said. "I don't want to leave."

"That's ridiculous," Stone said slowly. "Of course you want to escape this place. Of *course* you want to come home."

"I don't, actually," Rose said, disentangling her hand from his. "Because of exactly that tone of voice, Stone. Why would I want to go back to the people who spent my whole life telling me what to do and who to be and what *not* to do and what was *wrong* with me? Dad had a husband all picked out for me — someone who could finally 'calm me down,' in his own words. Someone who could trap me in a boring life in a boring little village — everything I didn't want."

"You want *this* instead?" Stone asked, waving his hands at the dragon's room.

"Yes!" Rose said. "Life in a dragon palace, Stone! It's never ever boring here. Who else can say they've lived with dragons?"

Ivy thought wistfully that she could see the appeal — she wished she could stay and explore and meet all of Rose's dragon friends. And maybe even learn Dragon, too!

But we have to get back for Violet. And Foxglove, and Commander Brook, and all the others . . .

"Aunt Rose, you have to come home with us," Ivy said. "You're my big plan for making peace between my dad and the Wingwatchers. I think if he sees you — if he finds out you're alive, he'll stop feeling so guilty and awful all the time. He'll be able to listen to reason, and he won't be so mad, and then we can fix all the things he's done." She rubbed the back of her neck. "Well. Not all the things. But the things he's doing now, at least."

"Heath feels guilty and awful?" Rose said with a skeptical expression. "About me?"

"Um," Ivy said. She thought of the combination code on her dad's treasure, and the fact that he'd never mentioned Rose to her. But he must think of his sister — he *must* feel guilty and awful about losing her. Who wouldn't? "I think so?"

Rose shook her head. "You can tell him I'm alive, but I'm not coming back. Whatever's going on with him, it's not about me, kid. Heath *never* listened to reason and he was *always* losing his temper over little things. Me being there won't change him. I'm not going back into a situation where he's the new boss of me, same as Dad, the old boss of me."

"But, Rose," Stone said helplessly. "It's too dangerous for you to stay here. Dragons can't be trusted."

"What makes you think humans can?" Rose asked. "Dragons are no worse than we are. Smolder has taken care of me for twenty years, and I'm happy here."

"These dragons destroyed our village!" Stone said. "They burned it down, Rose. We live underground now. Dragons are burning down human settlements all across the continent. They hate us. I don't know why they haven't killed you yet, but I'm sure they will at some point."

"They're burning villages?" Rose echoed. She looked at Ivy, who nodded.

"I think they're looking for something," Ivy said. "We met one who was searching for the treasure — but when we took Dad's and gave it to her, she clearly couldn't find what she wanted. She needed something specific that wasn't in the treasure Dad stole."

"Oh," Rose said. She looked toward one of the high windows, where a ray of moonlight was slipping through the glass. "Huh. Maybe it was in one of the bags you left behind, Stone."

"Left behind?" Stone echoed.

"You left two whole bags!" Rose said. "I went to all that trouble, and you only took half of what I stole!" She grinned at him, but he looked too heartsick to be amused.

"What happened to you?" he asked. "After we abandoned you?"

"The queen knocked me into a sand dune," she said. "I landed weird and I must have sprained my ankle. There was so much fire, and smoke, and sand flying everywhere — remember? It was hard to see anything. By the time I struggled back to the queen, she was dead, and you guys were running for the hills. I knew I couldn't carry the rest of the treasure and follow you. I didn't even think I could catch up to you at all, especially since, like, a million dragons were coming out of the palace to see what all the noise was about. So I hid the treasure — in a most excellent place, if I do say so myself — and I buried myself in the sand, hoping they wouldn't find me."

"But they did find you," Stone said in a hollow voice. He dropped his head into his hands.

"Not for a while," Rose pointed out. "And luckily it was Smolder who dug me out. I didn't even realize he was a prince until a few days ago. I thought he just worked for the new queen, but it turns out he's her brother. Isn't that wild? My dragon is royalty!"

"Can you get the treasure you hid?" Ivy asked. "And give it back to the dragons?"

"Yeurgh. It would be *real* tricky," Rose said. She saw Ivy's expression and added quickly, "But I can try. I will try." She gave Ivy a little smile. "I'd have to stay here to do that, though. Which is what I want to do anyway, big brother. Smolder is my friend, and I don't want to leave him. Especially now that I know a little bit of the language, thanks to Wren."

Beside Ivy, Leaf started and gave Rose a sharp look. "Who?" he asked.

"The girl who really speaks Dragon," Rose said. "She was here to save her dragon, and she taught me a little after I basically threw myself at her feet and begged."

"There's another girl with a dragon?" Ivy said. "Who can talk to them?! Why am I living the completely wrong life over here?"

"And her name was —" Leaf prompted Rose.

"Wren," she answered.

He put his hands to his head and gripped his hair for a moment, as though he needed to convince himself that he was still on the planet and everything really existed. "There are probably lots of Wrens," he said to Ivy. "Right? It's not an uncommon name."

Oh, Ivy realized suddenly. "Your sister!" she cried. "Her name was Wren!"

"But it's not — it couldn't be —" he started.

"She did look a bit like you, now that you mention it," Rose said thoughtfully. "She didn't say where she came from. About fourteen years old? Curly hair, extremely fierce?"

Leaf looked as though ghosts had suddenly burst through all the walls and started yelling in his face. He didn't seem able to speak.

"Where is she?" Ivy asked Rose.

"She left earlier tonight," Rose said. "On her dragon. They flew off east, toward the mountains. I'm so sorry, I don't know any more than that."

Leaf grabbed Ivy's hand. "I have to go after her," he said. "Ivy, if that's really my sister, after all this time . . . I have to go after her *right now*."

CHAPTER 35

LEAF

The world around Leaf had suddenly come into bright, sharp focus, as though he'd been underwater up until Rose said Wren's name and shocked him into this new place. As though maybe he'd been underwater since he was eight years old.

It's probably not her, he tried to tell himself. *Don't get your hopes up. How could it possibly be her?*

Because it's ME! Wren shouted in his head. *Of COURSE I would survive being fed to dragons! I probably ate THEM!*

But if it was her and she was really alive, what should he do? What could he do? He felt like he should be running, but which way and how?

This is my actual destiny, he thought. *Finding Wren. This is what I should have been doing my whole entire life. I should have known she survived; I should have left home that same night and tried to find her. That was my true purpose. It is. I just had no idea.*

"You said east?" he said to Rose. "How long ago did she leave?"

"Long enough that you won't catch her on foot," Rose pointed out.

"On horseback?" Ivy suggested. "Our horses are pretty tired but . . ." She trailed off as Rose shook her head.

"No, what you need," Rose said briskly, "is another dragon. One that's faster than Sky, which is most of them, I suspect. I mean, he's cute, but he's much smaller than Smolder."

"*Yes,*" Ivy cried. "You have to follow her on a dragon!"

Leaf's legs decided to stop working for a moment, and he sat down hard on one of the shiny green pillows.

"You two are both living in a fantasy world," Stone said, pointing at Ivy and Rose. "Where dragons can ever be cute or sweet or friendly. In the real world, dragons are monsters who eat people. A dragon will definitely eat this poor boy if you try to make him ride one."

"They are not monsters!" Rose cried in outrage.

"And you did it yourself," Ivy interjected. "Uncle Stone, *you* rode a dragon from the desert back to Valor. Remember? With your invisibility necklace on? Leaf could do the same thing."

He frowned at her, working his jaw so his beard went up and down. "I've also stabbed a dragon queen in the eye," he said. "I wouldn't consider myself a role model."

"But that proves it can be done!" Ivy said. "Leaf, you'll do anything to get to Wren, wouldn't you? Even ride a dragon?"

"Yes," he said, and then he stood up and said it again, this time in a voice they could all hear. "Yes. I'll do it."

"Then I know just the dragon," Rose said, leaping off the pillows. "I call her Sweetface. She's one of the night patrols, and I think she's actually sort of fond of humans, so even if she realizes there's a human on her, with luck she won't eat you."

"Fond of humans," Stone muttered as they followed Rose out of the room through a fascinating little human-sized flap built into the door. "For breakfast, maybe."

"I'd offer you Smolder," Rose said apologetically, ignoring Stone, "but he's VERY stubborn and just a smidgen bit lazy, and there's no way he'll fly out into the desert in the middle of the night." She crossed the tiled terrace and jumped down into the courtyard.

"What makes you think this dragon is fond of humans?" Ivy asked. The three moons were all high overhead as they crossed through more courtyards, winding back through the palace toward the outer wall.

"Well, she loves me anyway!" Rose said with a laugh. "She makes these hilarious cooing noises every time she sees me, like I'm an adorable baby rabbit or something. Sometimes she sneaks me treats, even though I'm pretty sure Smolder has grumbled at her about it."

"So you are a pet," Stone growled.

Rose shrugged. "I don't see it that way. Besides, even if I am, I'm a pet who gets to fly on a dragon. Which is objectively awesome. Leaf will tell you I'm right when he gets back."

"If he gets back," Stone muttered ominously.

Leaf was having a hard time concentrating on the conversation between freaking out about Wren and freaking out about being moments away from trying to ride a dragon. "Do you have any advice?" he asked Stone. "Like, any tips on dragon riding?"

"Number one, don't do it," Stone said, rather predictably. "Number two, if you must be an idiot, hang on tight."

Leaf caught Ivy and Rose doing matching eye rolls.

"I thought twenty-year-old you was curmudgeonly," Rose said, elbowing him in the side. "I had no idea how much worse you could get!"

"Wait, he was like this even back then?" Ivy asked.

"Like what?" Stone demanded.

"Brooding?" Rose offered. "Overprotective? A little judgy? Yeah, definitely."

Ivy giggled, and Stone gave Rose an offended look. "I beg your pardon," he said. "How am I supposed to be an intimidating authority figure to my niece if you keep making fun of me?"

Even through his nervousness, Leaf could see that being around Rose was bringing down some of the walls around Stone. *Ivy thought finding Rose would fix her dad . . . but I think the person it's going to help the most is Stone. The real Dragonslayer.*

They finally reached a tower not far from the outer wall and everyone fell silent as they focused on climbing the spiral staircase inside. Several of the stairs were covered in drifts of sand that had blown in through the narrow windows. Leaf got the feeling the stairs were rarely used; he guessed most dragons would just fly to the top, and he wondered whether there were any who preferred the stairs, or why they'd been built in the first place.

It was an exhausting climb, with each stair nearly as tall as they were, and by the end he and Rose were helping pull Ivy and Stone up the last few steps. At the top, they emerged onto a huge stone circle high above the rest of the palace. There was no railing, nothing to stop a person from walking right off the edge, which gave Leaf a weird lurch of dizziness. He tried looking up instead, into the endless spray of stars that glittered overhead. A comet blazed in the center of them all, bright as one of the moons and nearly as big.

The wind tugged at them, colder and clearer away from the stench of blood in the palace.

"There's nobody up here," Ivy pointed out.

"She'll be here soon," Rose said. "She flies out to scout the desert a few times a night. You and Stone should hide, and I'll distract her so Leaf can climb on." She gestured to the invisibility chain.

Ivy gently draped it over Leaf's head and looped it around his neck a few times. Her hands paused on his shoulders, and she pulled him into a hug.

"It's so weird to hug someone you can't see!" she whispered.

"Thank you for helping me," he whispered back.

"I hope you find Wren." Her breath was warm against his

neck. "And bring her back so I can meet her and her dragon. I mean, I hope you find her so you can see her again, not *just* so I can meet her dragon. I mean, that would be amazing, but that's not the only — you know what I mean."

He laughed. "I shouldn't take this," he said, touching the chain and moving one of her hands to rest on the links. "You'll need it to get out of the palace."

"You need it more," she said. "Besides, apparently we're friends with the prince of the sand dragons, so I think we'll be OK." She hesitated, then slid her hands up his neck to cup his face. "I hope you'll come back, though. I mean, I understand if you need to stay on her trail once you're out there. But if you don't catch her tonight, and Sweetface brings you back here, I promise you, Leaf, I'll help you look for her. We'll find your sister, no matter what."

"I will come back to you," he promised. "And I'll help you free your friends."

She smiled. "Hey, quit that. *I'm* the one making noble declarations about *your* destiny right now."

"But noble declarations are my whole thing!" he said with a grin.

She pulled his face closer and reached up to kiss him, but her lips landed awkwardly on the side of his nose and she broke away with a laugh.

"All right, it is even *weirder* to kiss someone you can't see," she said, or mostly said, before he interrupted by kissing her back.

"Here she comes!" Rose whispered. "Ivy, hide!"

"Good luck," Ivy said against his lips, and then Leaf's arms were empty, and she was vanishing down the stairs after Stone.

He looked through his hands, feeling about a hundred million different things, and then he looked up and saw pale yellow scales and long curved claws descending toward him. He stepped back as the dragon landed in a gust of warm air and cocked her head at Rose.

Just another dragon, he told himself. *You should be an expert on these by now, Leaf. How many other humans have been carried around by four different dragons and still survived? If Rose is right, this one is like the brown one. Not terrifying at all.*

It wasn't an entirely convincing speech, though, with the massive dragon towering only a few steps away from him, her venomous tail coiled up like a scorpion's behind her.

Rose waved up at the dragon and bounced on her toes a little bit. "Hi, Sweetface!" she called. "Who's a big sweet dragon?"

The sand dragon's face cracked into a giant grin and she lowered her head to Rose's eye level. "Oooorble roooargooor," Sweetface warbled affectionately.

This is my chance! Leaf realized. Rose made a little gesture with her hand and he sprinted over to the dragon's front leg, which was bent in a crouch. He made a flying leap onto the smooth scales and scrambled up toward her shoulder.

"ROAWR?" Sweetface made a puzzled noise and shook her leg as if she'd felt an insect on it. Leaf had to throw himself up the last stretch, grabbing her wing and tossing himself onto her back.

At the same time, Rose burst into song and started dancing a busy, foot-stamping dance in front of the dragon. Sweetface swung her head back and stared at her for a moment with a delighted expression, then looked over her shoulder again to see what was on her back.

Leaf lay still, wedged between the frill along her spine and the curve of her wing. Sweetface shook herself all over, then twisted her neck around the other way, clearly confused about why she could *feel* something on top of her, but not see anything.

Rose stopped dancing and patted one of Sweetface's talons. The dragon looked down at her and smiled again, and then lifted her head as a second sand dragon came whooshing in over the outer wall. The two dragons roared something at each other.

And suddenly Sweetface crouched, sprang into the air, and flung out her wings. Leaf was so startled by the jolt that he nearly slid right off her, but he managed to grab her spinal frill at the last moment. He held on for dear life as the dragon soared over the palace wall and out into the desert sky.

I'm flying, he thought in a terrified daze. *I'm flying! Wren! I'M ON A DRAGON!*

So am I, he imagined her saying with a nonchalant shrug. *And mine's cuter.*

The sand rushed past below him in a blur. In the

moonlight, the dragon's scales were as pale and colorless as the desert below, flickering with shadows as her wings beat up and down, up and down.

This is a terrible idea. Which way did Wren go? Even if I knew, I can't steer this dragon. Are we going east? I think we are. Yes, when he risked lifting his head, he saw a ridge of dark mountains on the horizon ahead.

Sweetface shook herself and peered over her shoulder again. Leaf imagined being her; it must feel like having an invisible squirrel on you would feel to a human. Fairly unsettling, he was sure, but he was also in a spot too awkward for her to reach with her talons. He hoped her scales were less sensitive than skin, and maybe she would get used to his weight after a while.

She flew straight toward the mountains for a long while, scanning the desert and the skies with sharp movements of her head. Leaf tried to search the sky, too, for any sign of a dragon up ahead. He couldn't hear anything except the rush of wind, the steady thrum of the dragon's wings, and the faint thump of her heartbeat.

Was that something? A flicker of motion in the distance, flying over the silver ribbon of a river . . .

Sweetface saw it, too. She whipped her head toward it, then tilted her wings to soar closer.

Leaf held his breath as they approached. It was another dragon, as pale as Sweetface in the moonlight, flapping its wings with slow, concentrated effort. Leaf wasn't sure if he was imagining the dark shape curled on its back.

They were close, nearly close enough to fly right over the strange dragon in a few more wingbeats, when Sweetface checked herself in the air, made a noncommittal noise, and veered back toward the palace.

Wait! Leaf thought frantically. *We were so close!*

He pressed his feet into the dragon's wing, trying to turn her around. She yelped and twisted in a circle, reaching for her back. He ducked her claws and threw his arms around her neck and leaned hard to the right. With another, more alarmed yelp, she flung her wings out and shook herself vigorously. She was as determined not to turn around as he was to make her turn, but she was probably a hundred times heavier than he was.

"WREN!" Leaf shouted desperately, at the top of his lungs. "WREN! OVER HERE!"

He did not see Sweetface's tail come swinging out of the sky behind him. Suddenly he felt the side of it smack into his chest, knocking him straight off her back.

With his last coherent thought, he yanked the chain over his head as he fell.

—— CHAPTER 36 ——

WREN

Wren would have ignored the commotion behind them. She was happy to lie on Sky's back, feeling the wind in her face as they left the desert and its creepy dragon queen in their dust.

But Sky's ears were sharper than hers, especially when they were flying, and he paused to look back.

"What?" Wren asked.

"I thought I heard someone shout your name," he said.

Wren laughed. "That seems literally imposs — oh, wait, no! I do have another friend now! Is it Rose?" She sat up and looked in the same direction.

A sand dragon was in the sky behind them having some kind of midair seizure. It twisted and flared its wings and grabbed at its back and whacked itself with its own tail and generally seemed to have lost its mind.

"Yikes," Wren said. "I think let's stay far away from whoever that is."

"Wait," Sky said. He pointed. "Look — she dropped something."

Wren squinted. There *was* something falling from the dragon. Something rather big, actually.

"What if you were right?" she said. "Sky, could that be Rose?"

Sky was already powering toward the shape as fast as his wings could fly.

"But that's not Smolder," Wren called over the rush of the wind. "Why would she be riding a different dragon?" She wasn't expecting an answer. Sky was putting all his energy into his wingstrokes.

I don't think we can make it, Wren thought with alarm. It was too far off, and falling fast. *Oh, I hope we're wrong. I hope that's not Rose.* She'd only really spent one day with the other woman, but Rose had found the key to save Sky, and she'd understood everything Wren had never expected another human to understand.

The strange dragon gave herself one last shake and stopped writhing. She looked down, saw Sky soaring toward her, saw his talons reaching out, saw the shape below her plummeting toward the sand.

She gave a yell of horror and dove after it.

Wren leaned forward with a gasp. They were close enough now that she was sure it was a person, arms and legs flailing in the air.

The other dragon's claws caught him a few heartbeats above the ground. Sky landed beside her a moment later, just as the dragon was gently setting the human on his feet.

Wren slid off Sky's back and floundered through the sand.

"Rose?" she called.

The human turned toward her. It was not Rose.

It was a boy, around Wren's age, with short dark hair and a sword strapped to his back and an oddly familiar dumbfounded expression.

"Wren?" he said.

She stopped short and stared at him.

He said, "Wren," and then he said it again, "Wren — it *is* you. Isn't it?" and it didn't make sense because nobody knew her, nobody said her name like they were looking for her, nobody was out there thinking of her . . . except here was somebody who said "Wren?" like she had actually been missed by someone, all these years, after all.

He came toward her through the sand, wobbly and awkward as though he'd just flown on a dragon for the first time. There were tears in his eyes.

"It's me," he said. "Your brother. It's Leaf."

Wren found herself looking down at the sand just to see if it was still there, and then at the dragons; yes, they were there, too, watching curiously. She was not somehow back in Talisman, and she was not dreaming.

"Well, that's . . . surprising," she said.

He laughed, a kind of bark of relief, and then he was suddenly hugging her, and three moons, human hugs were nothing like dragon hugs. Wren couldn't remember if this had ever happened to her before. Had her parents ever hugged her, before they fed her to dragons? Or any of her sisters?

No. Only Leaf, long ago, when I was small and lost the snail he carved for me.

"Wren," he said. "I just rode on a dragon! And fell off! And nearly died! I have to sit down." He dropped onto the sand, shoved something in his pocket, and rubbed his face.

"Clumsy of you," Wren said. "I ride a dragon, like, all the time and haven't nearly died even once." She sat down next to him. Next to her brother. Her brother, who remembered her name, who'd ridden a dragon to find her.

"I thought you were dead," he said. "All these years . . . Mother and Father said you'd disobeyed the dragonmancers and so the dragons got you."

"I *knew* they would say that!" she cried. "I told you they would, didn't I?" She turned and looked at Sky, who nodded sympathetically. "That's such a total lie. Those lying liars!"

"I can't believe I believed them," Leaf admitted. "Rowan finally told me the truth not too long ago. When I think about all the people who lied to me, who knew exactly what the dragonmancers did to you, but did nothing to help you — it makes me so angry, Wren."

"Welcome to my life," she said. "How funny that it was Rowan. She wasn't even there. I always wondered whether any of our sisters knew the true story."

"She tried to stop them, actually," Leaf said. "They ended up locking her in the cellar while they took you."

"*Rowan* tried to stop them?" Wren tried to wrap her head around that. Rowan had never paid one iota of attention to her littlest sister. On some days, Wren would have guessed that Rowan didn't even know her name; on others, she knew she'd annoyed Rowan enough that she'd have happily fed Wren to the dragons herself. She would never, never have imagined Rowan trying to fight for Wren's life.

Leaf took a deep breath. He lifted a handful of sand and watched it pour through his fingers. "The truth is, she thinks she's the reason you were sacrificed. Mother found one of the books you stole from the dragonmancers, and Rowan told her you took it."

"Oh, she *would*!" Wren cried. "I mean, I guess that's fair, though, since I did."

"Do you remember what was in it?" Leaf asked. "I figure you must have read some awful secret about them, and that's why they decided to get rid of you."

Wren remembered the feel of those books in her small seven-year-old hands, heavy and smooth and crisply important-smelling. She barely remembered anything inside them, though. Lots of columns of numbers, she thought.

"Do you think that's really why?" She pulled her legs into her chest and wrapped her arms around her knees. "I thought they just decided I was annoying and loud and awful and they didn't want me there anymore. I thought maybe . . . maybe everyone agreed with them."

"Oh, Wren." Leaf put his arms around her again. It was different from having wings around her, but still comforting. She rested her head on his shoulder.

"Not me," he said, "I missed you so much. You have no idea. I never stopped thinking about you."

"Really?" she said. "Not really. I mean — you were only eight."

"Yeah, but you were my favorite sister," he said. "And my best friend. I just . . . I didn't know how to *be* without you. I felt like I couldn't figure out who I was or what to do with myself, or who to trust or what was real."

"I could tell you those things," Wren said. "I'm pretty clear on all that."

"I know!" he said. "I missed that. It was awful without you. I decided to be a dragonslayer, can you imagine?"

She couldn't. Leaf as she remembered him had been a quiet, obedient kid who followed the rules and never caused trouble. She would never have pictured him with a sword or chasing after dragons.

"Why a dragonslayer?" she said. "The only one I've heard of sounds like a jerk, I have to say."

"Because of you," he said simply. "I had this whole plan to avenge you. Rowan was training me, and I was going to go kill the dragons who ate you. We got all the way to the mountain palace. But guess what? It turns out it's really hard to stab a dragon!"

"Eh." She shrugged her shoulders under his arm. "Not *that* hard. I've done it a couple of times."

"By all three moons, of course you have," he said with a laugh. "Have you managed to kill one, too?"

"Yes, actually," she said. "But he really had it coming."

"Are you serious?" He pulled back to stare at her.

"Long story," she said. "Go back to yours."

He told her all about his time in the mountain palace, the dragons who nearly ate him and the dragons who saved him, and Rowan and her friends, and how they were looking for treasure, and then his quest to find the Dragonslayer — who really was a jerk, she was right about that — and the city of Valor, and Ivy (Ivy Ivy Ivy), and looking for Rose (and how she didn't want to be rescued, which made perfect sense to Wren), and how he had ended up flying on a strange dragon in the middle of the night.

"Wow," she said when he finished. "It sounds almost as exciting as my life! Not quite, but close."

He grinned at her, and she had a flash of being seven again, back when her primary goal every day was to prove that she was just as smart and brave and tough as her big brother.

"I can't believe you rode a dragon just to find me," she said. She wouldn't have thought there was a human in the world who would do that for her.

"I would have ridden a different wild dragon *every day* to find you, if I'd known you were alive," he said. "I really should have known. My first thought when they told me was, *Wren would never stay still long enough to be eaten by dragons! And what dragon would be dumb enough to try to eat her?*"

Wren laughed.

"So how did you survive?" he asked. "Tell me everything about your life. Everything I missed."

I actually want to tell him, Wren realized. She'd always kept her life with Sky so secret, it was strange to think of sharing it all with someone else. First Rose, and now Leaf; what was happening to her?

"Well," she said, "let me introduce you to the most important part."

Behind them, the two dragons had been chatting quietly. From the snatches of conversation she'd overheard, Wren gathered that the sand dragon was asking Sky about where he'd found his human pet and how often he had to feed her. Wren had decided not to be outraged about this, since the dragon had saved Leaf from falling to his death, after all.

"Sky," she called. "Come meet my brother."

"Brother?" Sky echoed in Human, bounding over to them. "Hello, brother!"

Leaf's eyebrows made a run for his hair and his mouth dropped open. "Did that dragon just talk?" he asked. "He can TALK?"

"They can all talk, goober," Wren said. "But he's the only one who speaks our language, because he's a perfect genius. This is Sky." She put one hand on Sky's snout. He leaned into her palm, his cold scales like river pebbles under her fingertips. One of his wings folded around her back, shielding her from the desert night wind. "He's my very best friend. Sky, this is my brother, Leaf."

"Leaf," Sky said. The name sounded a little odd in his voice, but also quite right. She could see that Sky was trying to make a good impression, perhaps to prove her "perfect genius" description. Using only Human, he said, "It is most beyond wonderful to meet you."

"It is most beyond wonderful to meet you, too," Leaf said. Sky stuck out one talon, and Leaf gravely rested one hand on it for a moment. "Thank you for taking care of my little sister."

"Oh HECK NO," Wren objected. "*I* take care of *him*!"

"It is quite difficult," Sky said seriously to Leaf. "She is always getting into trouble. Really it's very lucky that I —" He dissolved into giggles and fell over on the sand.

"You are an extremely silly turtle-face," Wren told him affectionately in their hybrid language.

"Ivy would love to see this," Leaf said. "She believes that humans and dragons could get along instead of fighting."

"I think that's true of most dragons," Wren said. "And some humans. Maybe."

"Can I take you to her?" he asked. The sky was turning a pale orange the color of Sky's scales as the sun rose beyond the mountains. "I should take this back to her so she can get out of the palace." He took out the invisibility chain and held it so it gleamed in the sun. Sky made an *ooh* sound and touched it with one claw.

"I don't want to take Sky back into the desert palace," Wren said. "I'm worried about that queen — we avoided her before, but we might not be so lucky a second time. But maybe this dragon with the adoring expression can take you back and get you all out of there, and then I can meet you somewhere safe." She turned toward the sand soldier and switched to Dragon. "Hey, friend. Could you do us a favor?"

The dragon looked enormously delighted. "She makes

dragon noises!" she said to Sky. "You've trained her so well! That's the cutest thing I've ever seen!"

"I don't just 'make dragon noises,'" Wren said crossly. "I *speak Dragon*."

"That's so impressive," Sweetface said, still talking to Sky. "Wow! I didn't know they could do that! I don't think Smolder has his trained nearly so well. What else can she say?"

"I can say HEY STOP BEING A DIMWIT AND LISTEN TO ME!" Wren shouted.

"Awwwwwwwmygoodness," Sweetface cooed. "I *love* her! I want to snuggle her and put little hats on her!"

Wren threw her hands in the air. "Sky, would you please ask this ridiculous dragon to fly Leaf back to the palace safely? And then to hop him and Ivy and Stone back over the wall to their horses before anyone catches them?"

Sky relayed those instructions with a wickedly amused expression. Wren had a feeling she'd be hearing about "little hats" for years.

Sweetface — whose real name turned out to be Cereus, but Wren rather thought the name Sweetface suited her better — was delighted to be helpful to the "adorable scavengers" and thrilled to give Leaf another ride. "A safer one this time," she chortled. "What a clever little squirrel he is. Invisible! So cute!"

"We'll meet you back in the forest below the mountains," Leaf said. He described the burned village to Wren, and where it was in relation to the twin-peaked mountain at the southern end of the range, and who she might run into once she got there.

"We traveled down there a couple of years ago," Wren said. "We didn't stay long, but I probably walked right over Valor and didn't realize it was there. Ooh, I can add it to my MAP! Which, incidentally, is much bigger and more detailed than your little mountain palace map."

"I'm sure it is," Leaf said with a laugh. "So — see you in a couple of days? You promise you'll be there?" He was holding one of her hands like he was afraid it might vanish if he let it go.

"If I'm not," Wren said, "just hop on another dragon and fly around until you run into me."

"I WILL, though," he said. "You'd better be there, or I'll tear up the whole continent looking for you."

She punched him lightly in the shoulder. "Deal."

He climbed back onto Sweetface, with a lot of ineffectual help and little boosts and enchanted baby talk from the sand dragon. Wren leaned against Sky and waved as they took off into the sky and arrowed west toward the palace.

"That dragon was GOOFY," she said to Sky once they were gone. "I had no idea there were dragons as silly as my sister Bluebell." She hadn't thought about Bluebell in years, or Rowan, or anyone else in Talisman. Only Leaf, when she couldn't stop herself, and the dragonmancers, when she couldn't keep the nightmares at bay.

"I had no idea there were other humans as marvelous as you," Sky said.

"*Almost* as marvelous," Wren said. "He missed me, did you hear that part? He actually cared that I was gone." She felt like her heart was doing what Sky's wings did when they caught a new air current, rising up and up toward the sun.

"Of course he did," said Sky. "You're Wren. You're extremely lovable." He cast her a sly sideways look. "Of course, you would be *more* lovable in a little hat . . ."

"You're the one who's going to wake up in a little hat one day!" Wren yelped, climbing onto his outstretched talon. "Just you wait; I'll make you one shaped like a snail and then you won't be able to resist it."

"Like a SNAIL!" he breathed, his eyes shining.

Wren settled onto his back and looked up at the comet, still faintly visible as the sunlight spread toward it. Leaf was kind of like that comet, hurtling into her life like a new extra moon out of nowhere.

"Wren," Sky said before he lifted off. "I'm very glad you have found some humans who are *almost* as marvelous as you."

"Me too," Wren answered, surprising herself. "Me too."

CHAPTER 37

IVY

Ivy met Wren and Sky in the ruins of the ancient temple, in a forest glittering with raindrops from the storm the night before, and her first thought was, *This is going to change my life, and everybody's lives, forever.*

Sky was a mountain dragon; she could see that immediately from his bone structure and the size of his wings, even though his scales were much closer to peach than red or orange, and his eyes were a tranquil pale blue. He was lying in the grass at the foot of the temple steps, his wings folded gently behind him, watching a caterpillar as it climbed a dandelion.

On the steps, Daffodil was sitting with a teenage girl with wild dark curls and freckles all across her nose and arms. They were both laughing as Ivy, Leaf, and Stone rode out of the woods.

"IVY!" Daffodil shrieked, making Sky's wings flare up with alarm. She leaped down and pelted over to Ivy's horse, catching Ivy in a hug as Ivy slid off. "Guess what?" she cried before Ivy could say anything. "I rode a dragon! ME!

Remember how Violet said I never ever would? WELL, HA, I TOTALLY DID! This is him, the very best dragon in the world, isn't he handsome?" She flourished her arms at Sky, who rolled onto his back and beamed at them both.

"And this is Wren," Leaf said, smiling at his sister.

"Ah, yes," Stone said. "The other lunatic who befriends dragons. Nice to meet you." He tipped his head, gathered the reins of the thirsty horses, and walked them off to the nearest stream.

Sky watched them go with a delighted expression — half "horses! look at their amazing manes! they're so cool!" and half "I traveled the same distance and *I'm* not tired, you silly animals."

"Hi, Wren," Ivy said. *I hope she likes me!* "Leaf talks about you all the time."

"Hi," Wren said. "You must be the magical Ivy."

"I never said *magical*," Leaf objected, looking embarrassed.

"Well, I thought that would be less embarrassing for everyone than all the things you *did* say about her," Wren offered.

"WREN," he yelped.

"Oh, wow," Daffodil said, giving Wren an awestruck look. "You've missed out on so many years of being a little sister, but you're a natural! Stick with me and I will teach you all my terrorizing ways."

"So, you're doomed," Ivy said to Leaf with a grin. He clutched his head in mock despair.

Ivy's grin faded as she turned back to Daffodil. "Has there

been any news from Valor?" she asked. "Has my father . . . done anything else terrible?" She was scared that they'd been away too long, and she felt horribly guilty that they'd had an amazing dragon-riding adventure without bringing anything back that would help their friends.

Rose was probably right about my dad, she admitted to herself. And she understood why Rose would want to stay where she was, probably more than anyone but Wren would understand.

But now how was Ivy going to save Violet and Foxglove and the rest of Valor?

She had one idea . . . but it involved asking an awful lot of someone she didn't even know.

Daffodil shook her head and crouched beside Sky to scratch his chin. "Forest came by yesterday. He said things are still mostly the same, except more people are getting restless and upset with the Dragonslayer the longer he spends searching for Leaf. The Wingwatchers have been protectors of the village since before Heath was even born, back before we were underground . . . it's hard for everyone to see them as the enemy, Forest said. But he also said that means your dad might not wait much longer. If he thinks he's losing control of Valor, he might start executing people, even if he doesn't have the 'assassin from the Indestructible City' to hold up as proof."

"So we have to do something soon," Ivy said.

"Wren told me Rose said no," Daffodil said.

"Right." Ivy sighed. "It was maybe not the most well-thought-out plan."

"Rather like giving all the treasure to a strange dragon because you thought she was adorable," Leaf suggested.

"I'm going to find her one day," Ivy said, "and it'll turn out that it was really useful and important for us to give her the treasure, I bet you anything. You wait and see."

"So what you need," Wren said suddenly, "is some way to stop the Dragonslayer. Right?"

"Right," Ivy said. "We want him to free everyone he arrested and ideally step down from power, so someone else can run Valor. It's hard to imagine anything that would convince him to do that, though."

"Well, I'm no fan of humans who stab dragons for treasure," Wren said. "And the Dragonslayer has caused problems all over this continent. If there's anything I can do to help take him down, sign me up."

Ivy twisted her hair around her finger and glanced at Daffodil. "I did think of one possibility," she said slowly. "But it's kind of risky."

Wren looked over at Leaf and took his hand. "I trust anyone Leaf trusts," she said. "Tell me your idea."

"WHAT is this plan?" Sky asked as the three of them hiked toward Valor: Ivy, Wren, and the dragon. He nearly ran into another low branch and made a hilarious grumpy face at it.

Ivy couldn't stop watching him. She had this constant impulse to babble at him about how perfect he was, and she was repressing it with great difficulty. "Explain it to me again."

"We're going to terrorize a town!" Wren said. "We're going to strike fear in the hearts of all the puny villagers! Just like every little dragon dreams of doing!"

"Do they?" Sky asked. "We? Dragons? Did you say terrorize? Really? Us?"

"Mostly you," she said, whacking aside a large fern with a stick. "Mwa ha ha! Cower in terror, all you cowards who send your enemies into the jaws of dragons!"

"Mostly *me*?" Sky said. "Have you met me? I don't think I should try to scare anyone."

"No, no, definitely don't try," Wren said. "Just stand there and frown a little bit. Yes, like that, but let's try a bit more angry, a bit less confused. All you have to do is look terrifying."

"I'll do all the talking," Ivy promised.

"I'm confused." Sky spread his wings and tipped them from side to side to catch the sun on his scales.

"The main thing to remember," Wren said, "is don't speak Human in front of them. Only Dragon. I'll translate for Ivy if you need to say anything. And do NOT smile at anyone. No picking up snails or cooing at kittens."

"There will be kittens there?!" Sky cried, his face lighting up.

"No, no, NOT that face!" Wren protested. She batted at his wings as they got in her way. "The opposite of that face!"

Sky mustered a small frown and Wren sighed. "I hope this works," she said to Ivy. "We're working with exactly the worst dragon for the job, I'm afraid."

"I'm RIGHT HERE," Sky said indignantly.

"Yes, but you know this about yourself," Wren pointed out.

"The people of Valor won't know any different," Ivy said. "All dragons are scary to them." She led the way to the biggest entrance to Valor, the one built for horses, hidden by a net of branches.

Ivy noted that no one was guarding it. She'd half expected to find one of her dad's mercenaries, but it didn't surprise her that he'd keep his goons with him instead. With most of the Wingwatchers and Commander Brook locked up, was anyone protecting the town?

"We'll have to make this bigger," Wren said, studying it. It was still not quite big enough for a dragon, even a small one.

"I know. I feel guilty about this," Ivy said. "People worked hard on these tunnels. But we need to get you in there, so . . . whatever you have to do."

Sky stepped forward and clawed at the top of the tunnel opening. Dirt and earthworms and beetles rained down as he made the entrance bigger and bigger, until finally there was a gaping hole in the side of the mountain. Inside, the tunnels widened enough for him to wiggle in if he folded his wings in close.

Ivy led the way, with Wren walking behind Sky's tail.

I'm home, she thought, but after flying on the golden dragon and creeping through the desert palace and living in the forest temple, somehow nothing about Valor felt like home anymore. All the familiar tunnels and caves seemed like uncomfortable tunics that no longer fit her; as she walked deeper and deeper, it felt like climbing back into a box after finally escaping from it.

The first people who saw them screamed, dropped their baskets, and ran. That brought other people out of their caves, setting off a chain reaction of commotion and panic.

"Into the main hall!" Ivy shouted. "This dragon has a message for us! If we listen, he may leave peacefully!"

She nearly crashed into Forest, who was standing frozen in the middle of the tunnel, gaping up at Sky. Sky blinked pleasantly down at him, then seemed to remember his instructions and plastered a weird scowl on his face.

"Ivy, what are you *doing*?" Forest said in a hoarse voice.

"Saving everyone," she said. "I hope. It's complicated. Get everyone to come to the main hall." He turned and ran, and she beckoned Sky forward.

The tunnel ended at the central gathering hall, a huge natural cave studded with rock formations and laced with crystals, white and pomegranate pink and lime green melting into one another. The ceiling was high enough for Sky to stand on his hind legs and stretch his wings. Ivy saw Wren hop onto his tail and balance along his spine until she was standing on his shoulder.

About three-quarters of the people in Valor were packed into the farthest corner of the cave, huddled together in fear, staring up at the dragon.

Sky let out a pleasant growl. All of them screamed and fell over one another trying to get farther away.

"Don't worry," one of the men at the front shouted. "The Dragonslayer is coming! He'll save us!"

"Tell him to hurry," Ivy said, grabbing the man and pushing him out into the tunnels. "Tell him the dragon is holding me hostage and the citizens of Valor need him." She thought for a moment. "If that doesn't work, tell him the dragon is holding an enormous ruby."

"But — there's no —" the man sputtered, looking at Sky's empty talons.

"Just tell him," Ivy said. He bolted away, shouting, "Heath! Heath! Dragonslayer! Help!"

"There's a person on top of that dragon," one of the women murmured, and they all looked up at Wren. Ivy knew Wren must hate the feeling of everyone staring at her, but the other girl just folded her arms and leaned against Sky's neck like she could wait all day.

Finally they heard scuffling in the corridor, and after a long moment, a whole group of the armed mercenaries came in, pushing Ivy's dad in front of them.

Did he get smaller? Ivy thought. She was so mad at him, but she also felt a stab of pity. He looked terrified. Heath was holding the sword he always carried around, but it was shaking like a branch in a hurricane, and his feet didn't seem to be working entirely properly. The guy behind him was nearly propping him up.

Ivy glanced back at Wren and pointed to her dad. Wren nodded and nudged the dragon.

That's your cue, Sky.

"RAAAAAAAAWWWWR!" Sky bellowed. The roar echoed off every corner of the small space and several people clapped their hands to their ears. Even Ivy, who'd been expecting it, and who knew Sky would never hurt any of them, felt a wave of terror along her spine. It was a perfect roar.

The Dragonslayer shrieked, dropped his sword, and crumpled to the ground.

"I'm sorry!" he shouted. "I'm sorry!"

The other men with swords stared at him, then up at Sky's stern face. Or, to be more accurate, his "trying to be stern" face. But this was the closest these men had ever come to a dragon, and they had no practice reading dragon expressions.

"RAAAAARRRWRWR!" Sky hollered again. He gave Wren a "how was that?" look and she patted his neck reassuringly.

Ivy raised her voice so everyone could hear her. "Citizens of Valor! This dragon has come to seek the man who murdered his queen!" She knew only Wingwatchers would notice that Sky wasn't a sand dragon, and all the good ones were locked up.

"But it wasn't me!" Heath wailed. "I'm not the real Dragonslayer! It was Stone! Stone is the one who killed her! He's the one you want!"

A gasp ran through the crowd, followed by ripples of shocked murmurs. The men around Heath drew away from him, some of them with disgusted expressions.

That's it, Ivy thought. *He burned his own throne down. They'll never follow him again.* But she had to make sure.

"His tribe demands justice!" Ivy shouted. "His tribe demands vengeance!"

"Take him!" cried one of the guards, throwing down his sword and pointing at Ivy's father. "He's right there! You can have him, just please spare the rest of us!"

"Yes!" shouted several others, also flinging down their weapons.

Ivy had expected and hoped for this, but she still wasn't impressed with their loyalty. Then again, her father had lied about killing a dragon, stolen treasure, banished subjects to the dangerous wilderness, and locked up anyone he thought might be a threat. He didn't exactly deserve any loyalty.

Don't feel sorry for him, Ivy reminded herself. *Not now. Stay focused.*

"That is not enough," Ivy said. "The dragons who captured me made their demands clear. They will destroy all of Valor unless . . ."

"What?" someone shouted.

"Anything!" called the woman who'd first noticed Wren.

"Unless we return the treasure he stole," Ivy said, pointing at her father. The Dragonslayer groaned with despair. "And choose a new lord for our city."

Everyone started talking at once.

"Where is the treasure, Heath?" the men around him demanded.

"No, no," Heath wailed. "It's mine, it's mine."

"I know where it is." Ivy's mother stepped between Heath and the angry guards. She rested one hand on Heath's shoulder for a moment, then looked up and met Ivy's gaze. "I can get the treasure."

"Lark, no," Heath cried. He started to stand up, but Sky growled lightly, and he curled into a ball again.

"Then run!" the guard said to her. "Go get it!"

"Only if you free the Wingwatchers," Ivy said to him. "Bring them all here."

The guard nodded at two other men, who ran into the tunnels. Ivy cupped her hands around her mouth and called up to Sky, "They're getting the treasure now! Please don't eat anyone!"

Wren nudged Sky and he roared again, although with a bit less gusto; he was clearly feeling sorry for the little worried humans.

Very soon, Lark was back, carrying a large mysterious sack. Ivy took it from her and checked inside. Her mother had filled it with all of the knickknacks Heath had gathered over the years, particularly the ones Lark disliked, including a particularly dreadful set of garishly painted plates. But from the outside, it looked like a believable sack of dragon treasure.

"Here is the treasure," Ivy called up to Sky, dropping the bag carefully at his feet.

Sky made an *ooh* noise, peeked inside, and looked disappointed. Luckily the crowd was distracted by the arrival of the guards with several blinking prisoners in green uniforms behind them.

"I knew you'd do something," Violet said to Ivy as Ivy hugged her fiercely. "Didn't I say Ivy would do something?" she said to Foxglove.

"Yes, but you didn't say she'd *bring a dragon into Valor*," Foxglove whispered. "Ivy, *what is happening*?"

"Tell you later, I promise," Ivy whispered back. She stepped around Violet and took Commander Brook's hand, pulling her out to stand in front of everyone. The commander's shoulders were tense, and her eyes were flicking rapidly between the dragon's claws and teeth. "Trust me, Commander," Ivy said, squeezing her hand. She held it high and turned to face the rest of Valor.

"And here is our new lord!" she called.

"What, me? Shouldn't we have a vote?" Commander Brook said to Ivy, but her voice was drowned out by Violet shouting, "Yes! Commander Brook!" and then the rest of the Wingwatchers, and then what sounded like the entire cavern: "Commander Brook! Commander Brook!"

Sky gave an approving nod, picked up the sack of treasure, and awkwardly twisted himself around to head back into the tunnels with Wren.

The crowd let out a cheer and surged toward the commander. Brook raised her hands with a giant grin, trying to calm them down so she could speak.

Ivy quietly stepped back from the celebrating townspeople. Her dad was huddled near the exit, his face buried in his hands. She edged through the crowd and knelt beside him.

"It's going to be all right," she said. "It's going to be much better, actually."

"I'm nothing now," he said in a broken voice. "I'm nobody."

"You're still my dad," she said. "If you want to be."

He reached out blindly and she took his hand. She felt her mom come up behind her and hug her.

"Thank you for helping," Ivy whispered to her.

"You were extraordinary," Lark whispered back. "Heath, don't overreact. You'll be happier this way. Being the lord of Valor was never right for you."

"But my treasure," he muttered sulkily.

"If losing your treasure is the worst punishment you get for everything you've done," Lark said, "you'll be more lucky than you deserve. Let's go home." She hesitated. "Ivy?"

Ivy shook her head. "I'm sorry to leave you," she said, "but I can't stay here. Not after everything I've seen outside. We're going to change the world, Mom."

Now she *knew* it was possible. Dragons could learn to speak Human; humans could speak Dragon. Wren and Sky proved that, and they were only the beginning. There were kind dragons out there, thoughtful dragons, dragons who liked humans. Dragons who were ready for peace.

Ivy just had to find them. And with Wren, and Leaf, and Sky, and anyone else who wanted to join them, she was going to try.

— CHAPTER 38 —

LEAF

It was just a lovely coincidence that they arrived on Dragonmancer Appreciation Day. The entire town of Talisman was gathered for the festival, awkwardly drinking apple cider and talking in loud voices about how wonderful the dragonmancers were, as they had to do every year.

The sun was shining in a cloudless azure-blue sky when Wren dropped into the town square on her dragon.

"Hello," she sang, sliding down his leg. "I'm baaaaaack!"

There was no screaming or running like there had been in Valor. In Talisman, the villagers stood petrified, their apple doughnuts halfway to their mouths. They stared at the dragonmancers, waiting for them to save them.

Master Trout was caught by the food table with a mouthful of goat cheese. He blinked at the dragon in horror as Wren sauntered toward him.

"Hello, you very terrible person," she said. "This is your last Dragonmancer Appreciation Festival, I'm afraid. Remember me?"

"No," he said in a choked voice.

"Yeah, you do," she said. She beckoned to Crow and Gorge, who were trying to sidle behind some of the bigger townspeople. "Come on over and be appreciated," she called.

In the trees, Leaf and Ivy darted around the outskirts of the village. They'd found Cranberry and Thyme two days earlier, hiding in one of the caves where Leaf used to train with Rowan. They told him that Rowan had gone back into the village on her own to bargain for Grove's life, and the dragonmancers had thrown her in jail. She'd refused to give them the treasure until Grove was free, and they'd refused to let either of them go until they had it.

"Because they won't actually let them go," Wren had said. "They'll sacrifice them to the dragons as soon as they have it." She rubbed her hands together. "But we're going to stop them."

"Are you sure you're up for this?" Leaf asked her.

"I've been up for this for seven years," she pointed out. "I just didn't think it would make any difference to anyone, until you found me. And I didn't know what I knew, until I was standing in Valor, looking down at that treasure, and I realized what I'd read. Now that I do, I can't *not* do something."

Leaf shimmied up to the top of the jail roof. From there, he had a clear view of Wren facing off against Master Trout. The dragonmancer looked old and pale, but every inch of him still radiated evil.

He narrowed his eyes at Wren. "You," he said slowly.

"Should be dead?" she guessed. "My dragon and I disagree. We think the world is better with me in it."

Leaf smiled. He had started making a habit of telling Wren that every day.

"How —" Master Trout started, and once again Wren jumped in to finish his sentence.

"Did I survive?" she said. "I used that temper and that bad attitude you were always complaining about. Listen, this conversation is going to take forever if we have to wait for you to complete a whole sentence. I'll just cut to the exciting part. Hey, town of Talisman, did you know that your dragonmancers used to be treasure smugglers? They stole treasure from the mountain palace, probably more than once. But there weren't three of them back then. There were four." She held up four fingers and pivoted in a circle, making sure everyone's eyes were on her.

"Guess what happened to the fourth?" Wren said. "No, not you, Trout; we know you'll just lie. The *fourth* treasure smuggler, ladies and gentlemen, was the very first person our fine dragonmancers decided to 'sacrifice to the dragons.' Why? Two great reasons. One, it was very dramatic. It established the dragonmancers as mystical visionaries who received messages from the dragons; messages like 'kill your friend for us, we're hungry today!' Which are all lies, in case you're curious.

"But the second reason was more important, of course. The second reason was that with her dead, these three only had to split the treasure three ways. More treasure for them! Plus a town full of gullible idiots who worshipped at their feet. Two excellent upsides, for just a tiny bit of murder."

"Lies," Crow hissed. "You don't know anything, brat."

Sky snarled at her, and Crow staggered back into a table with a squeak of terror.

He's doing a much better job of being scary, suddenly, Leaf thought. This was the most ferocious he'd ever seen the gentle dragon look. *Because he's actually mad at these people. He knows what they did to Wren.*

"And then some time passed," Wren went on, ignoring Crow. "And they missed the treasure, but they were too lazy to go get more themselves. New brilliant idea: Let's get some apprentices, train them up, use them as free servants for a while, and then send them off to the palace in our place. If they die there, no big deal; just get another apprentice. But if they *succeed*, and return with treasure . . . well, that's great, but then we have the dividing-treasure-four-ways problem again. There'd be so much more treasure for the dragonmancers, plus a little useful fear in the hearts of the villagers, if we just had another sacrifice."

"Is that true?" called Leaf's old teacher. "Did you send my nephew to the dragon palace? Is that how he really died?"

"What about my daughter?" cried another. "What happened to her?"

"Now, now." Master Trout raised his hands with a superior, patronizing expression. "Are you all seriously going to listen to the mad ramblings of a bitter teenager? Everyone knows teenagers are melodramatic and hysterical. Especially the girls."

"Sky, eat this gross man," Wren said.

Sky took a menacing step toward him and Trout let out a shriek of fear, throwing his arms over his head. Wren held up her hand and Sky paused.

"Just kidding. For now anyway." Wren glanced around. "I'm happy to show everyone the proof. Let's check the books. You know, the ones I read when I was seven, which made you decide a little girl was too dangerous to be allowed to live. Gorge, the keys to the dragonmancers' meeting house, please."

"Do not give them to her," Trout cried.

But Sky leaned forward with a growl, and Gorge quickly fumbled them out of his robe and tossed them to Wren. She lobbed them to Cranberry, who was already in place by the door of the meeting house. Cranberry unlocked the door, then removed the ring of keys and threw them up to Leaf.

"Hey," Gorge protested as Leaf vaulted off the roof and started sorting through the keys. "You didn't say you'd be unlocking the jail as well."

"Surprise!" Wren said. "Let's think of it as payback for that one time when you didn't mention that you were feeding me to dragons."

Leaf found the right key and let himself into the damp, musty cell. Rowan was kneeling on the only cot, her eye pressed to a crack in the wall so she could see everything happening in the square outside. Her hair was matted and she was thinner than before, but her face lit up like a sky full of lightning when she saw Leaf.

"It *is* you!" she cried. "I thought I was hallucinating — am I hallucinating?"

"I'm really here," Leaf said. He crouched to check on Grove, who was lying on the floor, looking ill. Grove gave him a weak smile.

"But out there — is that — it can't be —"

"It is Wren." Leaf helped Grove to his feet. Rowan slung his other arm around her shoulders, and they all staggered back out into the sunshine.

"I can't believe it," Rowan whispered, staring at Wren. Her eyes drifted to the dragon, then back to her long-lost sister.

Cranberry emerged from the meeting house with three books stacked in her arms and carried them over to Wren. In a calm, ringing voice, Wren held up each one, explained the contents, and read a few passages. Lists of accumulated treasure. Drafts of vision-related speeches and ceremonies. Notes on each apprentice and how they'd died.

The silence in the square was hollow, as though she read to a crowd of empty wax figures.

She closed the last book and looked around. "I don't care what you do with them," she said. "That's up to you. But if I hear that any more kids are going missing in Talisman, we will come back, and we will burn all your houses down, and we will take the children away somewhere safe." Her eyes fell on a small boy. It was Butterfly, Leaf realized, not much taller than he had been when they hid in the cellar together six years ago.

"You be in charge of these," Wren said, placing the books in his arms. "This is about all the glorious homecoming I can stand."

Cranberry and Thyme came forward with horses and helped Rowan and Grove to climb on. They had a horse for Ivy and one for Leaf as well.

Somebody moved, finally, in the frozen crowd. Leaf's father stepped forward, his hand outstretched toward his children.

"Wait," he called. "Wren —"

"No," she said to his face. "No to you, and no to her." She nodded to their mother, close behind him. "No forever." She turned her back on them and climbed onto Sky. The dragon hissed at them, spread his wings, and vaulted into the air.

"Leaf?" his mother called. "Rowan?"

Neither of them answered. They turned their horses and galloped away, following the trail of the dragon overhead.

A long time later, Wren finally spiraled down to land by the river. She grinned at Leaf and Ivy as they rode up.

"Holy dragons, Wren!" Ivy cried. "You are so scary when you want to be!"

"Eh, it was all right," Leaf said. "I would have done a little more tugging on the heartstrings, maybe —"

"Shut *up*," Wren said. "Sky, splash this impertinent loud-mouth for me."

Sky enthusiastically whacked his tail in the river, dousing all of them as thoroughly as if they'd fallen in, including Wren.

"Ack!" she yelped, holding out her drenched sleeves. "Sky! Naughty dragon!"

He chortled with delight and flapped his wings.

Wren looked down and noticed Rowan, standing at Sky's feet and gazing up at Wren as though Wren might be a dragon herself. Leaf saw Wren hesitate before saying, "Hey, Rowan."

"Wren, I'm so sorry," Rowan said. She reached up to touch Wren's foot, and then pulled her hand back. "I am so, so, so sorry I told on you about the books. I had no idea what would happen."

"Oh, that," Wren said. She thought for a moment. "Hmmm . . . no, I don't forgive you. Sky, eat my sister."

Sky swung his head around and said something stern in their mixed-up language; the only word Leaf caught was *teasing*.

"All right, all right!" Wren leaned down and clasped Rowan's hand. "I forgive you. For that anyway. Not for making Leaf such a warrior, though. He's totally insufferable now."

"He forced me to!" Rowan protested. "He was driving me nuts about becoming a dragonslayer! Um, no offense," she added quickly, glancing up at Sky.

"Thank you for not becoming a dragonslayer," Sky said to Leaf in Human. Ivy started giggling at the astonished expressions on the others' faces. "It would be very confusing to be friends with you if that was your job."

"I thought I had to slay dragons to protect people," Leaf

said. "I never thought I could actually work *with* a dragon to protect them instead."

"I'm very grateful," Rowan said, and Grove nodded in agreement.

"What are we all going to do now?" he asked.

"Well," Leaf said, "you could take your stolen treasure and do something good with it. Like build a town where people can actually be safe."

"People like the refugees living in the shadow of the Indestructible City," Wren suggested. "The ones whose villages have been burned, who need somewhere to go that will actually welcome them in and protect them."

"And tell them the truth about dragons," Ivy added. "That we could communicate with them, if we try. That there's hope for peace."

"We could do that," Cranberry said. "Dibs I get to be mayor!"

"But what about you three?" Rowan asked. "Don't you want to help build it with us?"

"Maybe when we come back," Wren said.

"We're trying out kind of a new idea for our destiny," Leaf added. He looked at Ivy, who smiled back at him.

"That's right," she said. "We have a little golden dragon to find."

EPILOGUE

UNDAUNTABLE

From the window of the throne room, Undauntable could see half the world, and he found it all aggravating.

There were the jagged teeth of the mountain range stretching north and south, full of dragons who might eat Wren. There was the blue-green river winding away toward the sea, the one Wren always followed when she left. There was the forest that was supposed to magically produce her again, any moment, but there was no sign of her and she kept not being there, moment after moment, day after day.

It had been fifty-nine days since he'd proposed to her and she'd stormed off. If she stayed away a full year again, that meant hundreds more days like this, long and boring and Wren-less.

But she can't, he thought to himself. *She didn't get the supplies she needed. She doesn't have any books to read. So she has to come back sooner.*

It was not all right with him that she cared more about

books than about seeing Undauntable, but at least she'd have to come back to the Indestructible City.

And maybe next *time she'll stay.*

The spiked helmet was oppressively hot and the spiky jacket was worse, jabbing him in weird places whenever he shifted his weight. He could feel sweat rolling down his back and gathering in his armpits. But he was only allowed to sit by the window if he wore his spikes, and this was where he had to sit if he wanted to see her coming.

Sometimes Undauntable wondered what would happen if he decided to leave with her one day. What if he snuck away from his guards and followed her to wherever she went when she left him? He had no idea where that was. He'd always imagined a small village down the river somewhere, but sometimes she would say things or buy things that made him think she lived alone, traveling around instead of staying in one place.

What would that be like? Seeing a new place every day, instead of the same walls over and over again?

It would be terrifying. Without the walls, the dragons could get you. Without the catapults and spikes and guards and weapons, you'd be the easiest prey they ever ate. Staying in the Indestructible City was the only way to stay safe. Undauntable *knew* that was true. He was terrified for Wren all the time; every time he heard a dragon overhead, he wondered if it had Wren in its claws. It made no logical sense to him that she'd survived all these years out there.

It made even less sense that she would choose that life instead of safety with him.

He heard movement behind him and turned to see his father entering the throne room with his usual entourage of councillors and sycophants. The Invincible Lord spotted Undauntable and beckoned imperiously.

Undauntable sighed and took off his helmet. He knew his hair must be slick and disheveled, and that his father was judging his appearance as he approached. The lord looked perfect, as always, each dark hair combed into a thick royal mane, rings on every long thin finger, ruby-red robes without a wrinkle in sight.

They reached the throne in the center of the room at the same time and Undauntable made a polite bow.

"Father," he said.

"Sit with me, boy," his father said, indicating one of the stools beside the throne. "Apparently we have a visitor with a story worth hearing."

Undauntable unbuckled the spiked jacket with some difficulty and handed it and the helmet to one of the servants, trying not to gasp for air as it came off. His own pale orange robes were crumpled and damp, but he smoothed them out as best he could as he sat down.

Even when I'm not perfect, I have something no one else has, he reminded himself. No one else in the Indestructible City wore dragon scales like the ones embedded in his earring, rings, and necklace. Wren's scales were completely unique.

They made him special, even when he felt alone and awkward and out of place and convinced that everyone hated him.

The lord seated himself on the throne in a swirl of scarlet robes and nodded to the guards by the door.

Undauntable squinted at the man who strode into the room, all big shoulders and crooked teeth and rugged streaks of dirt everywhere. He had the aura of someone who would cheerfully kick anyone in the face for money. A mercenary, Undauntable guessed.

"Your Invincible Lordship," the man said grandly, bowing until his forehead nearly touched the floor.

"Boar," said Undauntable's father, and it took Undauntable a moment to realize he was saying the man's name, not commenting on how dull he was. "Welcome back. How was the city of Valor?"

"Very illuminating, sir, but nothing like as great as your city, of course. It was quite easy to get close to the Dragonslayer. He was willing to hire anyone who'd promise to protect him from you."

Father rubbed his chin and frowned. "And what have you learned? Did you plant the stories I told you to?" he asked. "Is he coming here at last?"

"Much more interesting news than that, sir," said Boar. As the Invincible Lord scowled, he hurried on. "There was an incident in Valor, my lord. The Dragonslayer is no longer in charge. In fact, he admitted in front of the entire town that he never killed that dragon after all."

"What?" Undauntable could sense a new simmering rage

building under his father's skin. "But there was a dead dragon! The last two spies said he has its tail!"

"He does, but it turns out it was his brother who did the slaying," said Boar. "But that one's a lost cause, your great and powerful lordship. And the Dragonslayer has been utterly disgraced. Neither one is the hero you're looking for."

"Have you come to tell me that you are?" Father said with enormous disdain.

"No, no." Boar raised his hands. "That's not the interesting part of the story, milord. The interesting part is that the Dragonslayer confessed his lies because a dragon showed up in Valor and demanded the treasure back."

"Demanded — what?" the lord growled. "How could a dragon say anything?"

"He didn't, exactly. But he had someone with him." Boar paused for dramatic effect. The room was deathly silent, everyone listening with wide-eyed fascination. "The dragon was working with a girl."

"A girl?" The Invincible Lord snorted with disgust. "Impossible."

"This girl was riding the dragon," Boar insisted. "I saw it with my own two eyes. She stood up there on his shoulder, and she didn't say a word, but you could tell: she was the one who understood the dragon. She was the one who really brought the message. She made him roar when she wanted to; she told him when to leave — with the treasure, mind you. There is a girl, sir, who can *control dragons*."

The Invincible Lord stared at him for a long moment.

Undauntable tried to study his father's face without staring too obviously. It looked as though wheels were spinning in his mind, gears clicking into place. Undauntable knew he was already figuring out how to use this to his benefit.

"Where is this girl now?" he said in a smooth, silky voice.

"She left with the dragon," Boar answered. "But she's out there, sir. She's the one you want. And she can't be too hard to find, if she sticks with that dragon. I ain't never seen one that color before. It was a kind of light orange, like the mountain dragons but all washed out."

A shock like lightning ran through Undauntable's veins.

Pale orange scales.

A girl who rides a dragon.

If there was anyone in the world he could imagine riding a dragon, it was Wren. Had she been bringing him scales from her very own dragon all these years? Hadn't she been nine when he met her? Had she had her own dragon *when she was nine years old*?

And could she really control them?

He suddenly realized, with a cold, creeping feeling, that his father was staring at him.

"Everybody out," said the Invincible Lord. "Boar, good work, and don't go far. I want every detail of this story." Undauntable stood, hoping to escape with the rest of the people in the room — but his father caught his arm. "*You*. Stay."

Undauntable could feel his heartbeat like a panicked rabbit in his wrist; he was afraid his father could feel it, too, thrumming through the fingers pressed into his skin.

I can't tell him about her. I don't want him to take Wren away from me.

But . . . wouldn't he be thrilled? Wouldn't he be pleased that I could finally be of some use to him? That after all this time of doing nothing, it turns out I could bring him the one person he wants now?

He looked into his father's cold, predatory eyes. *This would finally make me the son he truly wants.*

And yet, when he tried to imagine what would happen to Wren in his father's power, his heart felt like it was shrinking into a little iron pellet.

Wren would hate being Father's puppet. She'd hate being trapped here, or working for him. She'd hate me for giving her to him.

And he would crush her.

Wren was sunlight and wind and far-off horizons; she was claws and wings and bursts of flame. She was everything the Indestructible City was not. *That's why I love her*, he admitted to himself.

"Undauntable," his father said in his icy voice. The room was empty now except for the two of them. "That man described a dragon whose scales seem to match the ones you wear. I think it's time you told me where you've been getting them."

His fingers tightened mercilessly on Undauntable's arm, cutting off the circulation so Undauntable's hand felt numb.

"An old woman," Undauntable blurted. "I met her once in the market a long time ago. She had a small bag full of the scales, so I bought them all, because I didn't want anyone else to have them. I've just been adding them to my jewels one a time for — for effect because you said st-style was partly about t-timing and —"

"Stop sniveling," his father snapped. Undauntable fell silent. The lord regarded him for a long, hooded moment. "You're lying," he said at last. "You're terrible at it."

Undauntable had thought that was a rather good lie, actually, considering he'd only had a moment to think of it. *I'm sorry, Wren. I'll try to protect you as long as I can.*

"I will find this girl," hissed the Invincible Lord, and Undauntable felt a stab of fear for Wren. "I will find her, and her dragon — or dragons, if Boar's theory is correct. You can be of use to me, or you can be a stupid waste of space, as usual. But either way, one day I will control the girl who controls dragons, and then . . . then the whole world will be mine at last."

WINGS OF FIRE

will continue . . .

DISCOVER THE #1 *NEW YORK TIMES* BESTSELLING SERIES!

THE DRAGONET PROPHECY

THE JADE MOUNTAIN PROPHECY

THE LOST CONTINENT PROPHECY

LEGENDS

WINGLETS QUARTET

GRAPHIC NOVELS

■ SCHOLASTIC
scholastic.com/WingsOfFire